Uncle Sol's Women

Uncle Sol's Women

Simeon J. Maslin

This is a work of fiction. Names, characters, places and events are the products of the author's imagination. Any resemblance to actual persons, events or places is entirely coincidental.

ISBN: 1495325369
ISBN 13: 9781495325366
Library of Congress Control Number: 2014901790
Create Space Independent Publishing Platform
North Charleston, South Carolina

To my *Eshet Hayil*, Judy,
and to
Naomi, Doron, David, Eve and Deanna

Contents

Sol's Father

Yisroel Forshtayn and his comrades in the graduating class of the Vilna Hebrew Gymnasium were not content to wait for their Christian neighbors to turn on them on one pretext or another. Motivated by the horrific pogroms that swept over Russia in the aftermath of the assassination of Tsar Alexander II, they organized a self-defense group and established contact with other cadres of young Jewish militants from Odessa to Riga. They trained with sticks and home-made wooden rifles every day except Friday after classes, but it did not take long for them to realize that they needed someone with some knowledge of firearms and military tactics if they were to successfully defend their families against a bloodthirsty mob.

At that very time, agents of the tsar were recruiting cannon fodder on the possibility of war against the Japanese over Manchuria, and they were quite willing to accept healthy young Jews into the overwhelmingly anti-Semitic ranks of the imperial army. Yisroel's group saw this as an opportunity to become familiar with the use of firearms. They thought that the likelihood of being sent to fight in the far east was remote and that two or three years of training, even among those very savages who were the primary participants in the increasingly murderous pogroms, was a small sacrifice to pay for the sacred honor of saving Jewish lives, if and when the need arose.

On the day after his graduation from the gymnasium, Yisroel married Bryna Rivkes, a great-great-granddaughter of the saintly *Gaon* of Vilna, a marriage presided over by rabbis from three of the great *yeshivas* of Lithuania, and their blessings that the couple be fruitful and multiply were answered when Bryna, after consulting with her mother, shyly informed her husband that she was pregnant just four months after their wedding. It was a memorable day, because earlier that very day Yisroel and his best friend, Koppel Ganzfried, hoping to gain the skills that were so urgently required by their cadre, had volunteered for service in the tsar's army. When his wife and parents heard that he had signed up for the army, they tried every possible way to get him released, but to no avail. He was devastated at the idea of leaving his pregnant wife, but there was no way of wriggling out of his commitment. He took some solace from the likelihood that he would be stationed at some nearby post, as were most Vilna recruits, and that he would be able to see his wife and family if not every week then at least every month. And then ....

The Russo-Japanese War broke out in 1904, following the destruction of the tsar's Pacific fleet in Port Arthur. Two months later, after less than a month of training, Yisroel and Koppel found themselves on the rolling stock of the new Trans-Siberian Railroad on the way to Manchuria. They had less than a day to bid farewell to their families, and during that brief reunion, Yisroel made one vow and exacted another. In the presence of the rabbi, he vowed that if he returned from the war alive and not having had to eat *treif* meat, he would never again sit down during prayers in the synagogue. And he made his sobbing wife agree that if she gave birth to a boy while he was away, she would name him Ephraim. Bryna had intended to name their first son Elijah after her revered great-great-grandfather, and there was no way that Yisroel could object to that, but they agreed that the boy would be named Ephraim Elijah. Why, his parents and the rabbi wanted to know, was it so important that his son be named Ephraim? After all, there were no deceased ancestors by that name. "Because," he explained, "I always loved that verse from Jeremiah that we sing in the shul, '*Ha-ven yakir li Ephraim* – Ephraim is the child in whom I delight.'" When he was a little boy singing in the cantor's choir, that was his solo, and he always thought that if he had a son someday he would name him Ephraim and would love him as God loved Ephraim. As he explained his wishes to Bryna, he broke down in tears, turned away and left.

Yisroel barely survived his three years of wretched service in a virulently anti-Semitic company whose every member delighted in both verbally and physically tormenting their *Zhid.* After he was wounded in the shoulder fighting the Japanese at the Yalu River, he came home to the inexpressible joy of fatherhood. He recuperated well and spent his first month back in Vilna hardly ever leaving his home except for prayers in the shul and drills with the militants who had appointed him their leader. He cherished every moment spent with the cherubic three-year-old Ephraim who didn't recognize him when he first came home. He quite simply couldn't get enough of him. When he awoke from nightmarish dreams of bloody battle scenes, he would stumble over to Ephraim's crib to caress the softness of his cheek. He played games with Ephraim, fed him, cuddled him, and began teaching him to read the Hebrew letters, taking pride in the remarkable precocity of his child of delight. Every game and every lesson ended with some sweet treat and a shower of kisses, and the affection that he could hardly control for his son extended to his adoring wife Bryna who announced her second pregnancy to him three months after he returned from the war. And then ….

Just a few days after Yisroel went back to training with his cadre, Ephraim toddled out of the front door of their house and into the cobbled street. Just then, a troop of drunken tsarist cavalrymen, racing heedlessly at a gallop through the Forshtayn's neighborhood, rounded the corner, came upon the startled child and trampled him. Neighbors saw the troop pause for a moment, look around, and then, when one of them yelled to the others that it was only a *Zhid* bastard, they galloped off. The screams of the neighbors brought Bryna rushing out of the house where she saw the broken body of her son lying amid refuse on the blood-spattered stones. She dropped to her knees and fainted, and the neighbors, fearful that she might miscarry, rushed to her aid. Word reached Yisroel a few minutes later, and he ran home to find his Ephraim wrapped in a blanket on the floor and his wife in a stupor of denial. Yisroel ran out to the street, to the blood-spattered spot where Ephraim's body had lain, and shouted venomous curses at the tsar and his sodden, crapulent cavalrymen. The neighbors were so frightened that some nearby *goy* would hear Yisroel and report him to the authorities that they pleaded with him to go inside to take care of Bryna. The grief of the couple was beyond description.

During the *shiva*, the seven days of intense mourning during which the family does not leave their home, Yisroel's friends attended all the services, morning and evening, standing beside their leader as he tearfully recited the *Kaddish*. Koppel, who had returned from Manchuria a few weeks after Yisroel, took over the leadership of the cadre during Yisroel's absence. Both Yisroel and Koppel had managed to return home with stolen revolvers which they hid beneath a hearthstone in the fireplace of the abandoned schoolhouse where they trained. Word had reached Vilna of more and more pogroms – Yekaterinoslav, Odessa, Zhitomir, Gomel, Rovno and dozens of smaller towns – each more bestial and bloody than the ones before, and the young militants redoubled their hours of training and their resolve to take revenge for the murder of their leader's innocent son.

A plot was hatching in Yisroel's mind, an idea which he shared only with Koppel. They agreed, though, that nothing could be done while Bryna, now conspicuously pregnant and frail from the shock of their loss, was still in Vilna. Yisroel had decided after a particularly bloody day on the banks of the Yalu, followed by frustrated abuse from men who were supposed to be his comrades, that there was no future for Jews in Russia, and he began thinking about the possibility of emigration to the United States.

He discussed the possibility with his father, Reb Avrom Yitzchok who, while acceding to his son's desire to leave Russia, was not willing to uproot his own aging wife and to relinquish his honored status in their community.

Assured of his father's support, both financial and moral, Yisroel approached Bryna with the idea and was not surprised to find her eager to leave. She would never recover from the loss of Ephraim, but she agreed that it would be easier to start a new life in a new land without constant reminders of Ephraim at every turn. What made her not only willing but even eager to leave was her fear that the child whom she was carrying might end up like Ephraim. And so it was agreed. Yisroel would arrange for her passage to America as soon as possible so that their baby would be born in the *Goldene Medinah.* She had Rivkes cousins in a town near Boston, also descendants of the Vilna *Gaon*, and her father, after an exchange of letters, assured Yisroel that they would take care of Bryna until he arrived.

The hardest element of the plot was convincing Bryna that her husband could not leave with her but would follow as soon as possible. He found an excuse when word reached the group that the eminent journalist, Vladimir Jabotinsky, who was the most outspoken exponent of Jewish self-defense in Russia, would be visiting Vilna in the late spring. He was touring many of the cities that had self-defense cadres to offer words of encouragement and information about techniques of armed conflict. Yisroel explained to Bryna that there was no way that he could abandon his friends until after the consultation with Jabotinsky. He would arrange for Bryna to sail from Riga to New York right after Passover, and he himself would embark as soon after Jabotinsky's visit as another ship sailed from Riga.

While in the army, Yisroel looked forward to the day when he could sit around the Passover *seder* table with his son on his knee, surrounded by his wife, their parents and a few other relatives, but the *sedorim* of 1907 in the Forshtayn home were dismal affairs. The death of Ephraim was foremost on the minds of all of the Forshtayns and Rivkeses, especially when the time came for the Four Questions. Yisroel had begun teaching the chant to an eager Ephraim just a few days before his murder. Yisroel, as the youngest surviving male, began the chant but became so choked up that he couldn't get through the first question. There were a few moments of silence, and then Reb Avrom Yitzchok cleared his throat and continued with the narration. As soon as they had closed their *Haggadahs,* the relatives left for their homes without a word.

Yisroel accompanied Bryna on the train to Riga. He had arranged for them to spend the night before Bryna sailed in the home of Dr. Doniel Kurlander, the leader of the Jewish self-defense cadre in Riga. They had often corresponded about recruitment and training techniques, but they had never met in person. His telegram to Dr. Kurlander informing him that he and his pregnant wife would be in Riga for the day before her embarkation was answered the very next day with an invitation to spend the night in the Kurlander home. Their hosts could not have been more gracious, and the next day they drove the Forshtayns to the quay in their landau. As Yisroel and Bryna embraced, he assured her that they would embrace again within two or three months, in time for him to be present for the birth of their child. She trusted his word; he did not. His only thought was that she would be safe in America in case he was caught.

On the second Shabbat after Passover, Yisroel and his friends went to the synagogue services as usual, but that afternoon, after their family dinners, they gathered in the courtyard of their old gymnasium for a long and serious discussion of the action that they all agreed was required of them as Jews, as comrades of Yisroel and as enemies of the tsar. They all understood that the finger of suspicion for their action would point directly at Yisroel because of his repeated intemperate remarks about the tsar and his publically shouted vow of vengeance, but after about two hours of shared grief, confession and pledges of loyalty unto death, they came up with the plan that would result in the disappearance of Yisroel that very night.

Each member of the group went home from the synagogue as night fell and participated in the brief *Havdalah* service marking the end of Shabbat. Each then took one or two articles of clothing, bundles small enough to escape detection by family members, and left to spend the evening "at the home of a friend." Yisroel threw a small carpetbag out the window of his parents' home where he was living after his return from Riga, and he retrieved it when he left for the evening. Before leaving the house, though, he kissed his mother and shook hands with his father. They were somewhat surprised by the intensity of his farewell that evening, but they understood it as a sign of his inconsolable grief at the loss of his son. That was the last that Yisroel Forshtayn's parents ever saw of him.

The group of fourteen young militants reassembled at the suburban schoolhouse where the two pistols were secreted under a hearthstone, and they all deposited their articles of clothing in Yisroel's carpetbag. Yisroel took one of the pistols and Koppel took the other. Then, as determined earlier that day, nine of them, after soulfully embracing Yisroel and shaking hands with the other conspirators, slowly wended their ways home and rejoined their families. One, the son of a *baalagolah,* went to the livery stable in town to hitch one of the horses to a wagon and drive it to the railroad station. The remaining four, Yisroel, Koppel, and the two brawniest of the group, waited in the schoolhouse until a quarter to eleven. Then, each of the four proceeding by a different route, they arrived separately at the four taverns around central Vilna that were most popular among the tsarist cavalrymen stationed there. Each of the four slipped in unobtrusively and scanned the patrons looking for any cavalrymen who might be there.

At eleven-thirty the four reassembled in front of the central train depot to compare notes and to make sure that the wagon was where it was supposed to be. Each of the four had observed soldiers in their taverns, but Koppel's report got their immediate attention. He had found two cavalry officers drinking heavily in the tavern that he had scouted, and they were alone. It couldn't have been better for their purposes. That was what they had been hoping for ... and dreading. There was a moment of silence, and then Yisroel said, "It must be a sign. It's perfect. I thought it would take us weeks to find *one* drunken cavalry officer by himself, and now we have *two, Gott tzu danken,* and they're alone." Yisroel looked into the eyes of his four comrades, his heart pounding. For a moment, no one said a word; they just looked at each other, until Koppel said, "You know the plan; we rehearsed it enough. Remember, Yisroel has to be back at the station by one if he's to catch the night train to Riga. Let's go!"

The tavern that Koppel had scouted was owned by Itzik Rabinowitz, a *Chossid,* and was located just two blocks from the railway station. Rabinowitz didn't know Koppel personally, but he could certainly recognize him as a fellow Jew. Koppel at twenty-two was the only one of the four young men who had a beard, and that beard was a part of their plan. He would shave it off in the wee hours of Sunday morning and put on unneeded eyeglasses, just in case he was seen by anyone other than Rabinovitz. As for the *Chossid* himself? It was extremely unlikely that he would volunteer any information to the hated authorities. And why should he? Who would ever know that these two cavalrymen were drinking in his tavern?

Koppel had practiced his role as if for a performance at the Imperial Theater. Leaving his three comrades in the dark alley to the right of the tavern, he swaggered in, went up to the table where the two officers were imbibing, and yelled out: "You two fancy boys look like Polaks! Come on, you lousy Polaks; let's fight!"

He stood there looking at them long enough for his words to penetrate their alcoholic haze, and as soon as he saw one of them beginning to rise and reach for his sword, he ran out toward the alley, hesitating only long enough to see that the officers were on his heels. When he reached the darkness of the alley, he reached into his pocket and pulled out his pistol. Yisroel, with his pistol already drawn, stood beside him just within the alley, with the two others, armed with clubs, behind them. As soon as the officers entered the alley, Yisroel and Koppel fired. Both shots hit their victims but neither fatally. It was then the task of the other two to club them into insensibility, which they did as practiced. Their fifth comrade had been listening for the pistol shots, and he was at the entrance to the alley with his wagon within a minute. Yisroel and Koppel heaved the first of the officers into the wagon, and the other two assassins took care of the second. Then the four of them piled in and they were off to the old schoolhouse. As soon as the sound of the horses' hooves receded from the area of the tavern, Rabinovitz went to the door, looked around, saw nobody, closed the door, lowered the lights, and went upstairs to join his sleeping wife.

Yisroel was able to control his heaving stomach until the five arrived back at the schoolhouse, but as soon as they pulled up, he vomited miserably. Between heaves, he mumbled, "One would have been enough for Ephraim. One, ... why two? God, forgive us. Maybe they had children ...".

Koppel grabbed Yisroel by the shoulders and shook him. "Vomit if you have to; you're a scholar not a killer, but don't hold things up. We have work to do, and you've got to get away from Vilna before the police start asking questions. If they catch you, we're all finished. Get moving!" With that, he went to the closet where they had stored blankets and heavy weights and distributed them.

Within ten minutes the bodies of the two inert officers were trussed up and weighted. They carried the bodies back to the wagon and headed for a wooded area near a bridge over the Vilejka, threw the two bodies in, watched them disappear, and returned to the wagon. As they approached the center of Vilna again, Koppel and two of the accomplices jumped off the wagon without a word and disappeared into the shadows. Yisroel returned with the driver to the livery stable where he retrieved his bag and, again without a word, walked across the square to the railroad station. It was a quarter to one, and the center of the city was eerily silent. Yisroel had to rap on the station master's window to wake him up. He handed him his papers and the requisite fare, received his ticket without any unnecessary conversation, and took a seat near a family and two other men, all waiting for the night train to Riga.

The train was, as usual, late, and Yisroel could only sit there tensely anticipating the worst. Had anyone heard the shots? The area around the tavern was deserted. If the proprietor had raised an alarm, the square would be flooded with police. Would the weights be sufficient to keep the two bodies at the bottom of the Vilejka? If he were caught, would his family be implicated? That was his most urgent concern, his family. They must never know; there must never be even the slightest possibility that they, because of the death of Ephraim, might feel in part responsible for the revenge killings. Better that they never see or hear from him again than that they learn of his hand in the sin of murder, no matter how justified. Yisroel felt certain that the only way that he could be caught or in any way connected to the disappearance of the cavalry officers would be if someone in his cadre revealed what had happened that night, but he trusted them with his life, as they in turn trusted him.

Getting caught, though, before he left the borders of imperial Russia was not the thing that troubled Yisroel the most. He had participated in the murder of two human beings. The two of them may or may not have been in the troop that recklessly and with a total lack of concern had trampled his innocent little son, but they wore the same uniform and were, by definition, Jew-haters. But to kill...., to kill ...., a conscious and premeditated violation of one of the Ten Commandments. He felt the mark of Cain on his brow and furtively glanced at his neighbors in the waiting room to see if they were looking at him. They were dozing. And then, cutting through the deep darkness of the night and the deeper darkness of his soul, he heard the whistle of the Riga train, arriving from Minsk about an hour late.

Only five people disembarked from the train, but Yisroel, fearing that one of them might be a local Jew returning to Vilna after a Shabbat in Minsk and recognize him, stood behind a column until the station master waved his lantern. When the engineer blew the whistle, Yisroel dashed across the platform and climbed aboard. He would feel safe only when they reached Riga, where the local self-defense cadre had been alerted about the possibility of his arrival. But the train had one intermediate stop in Panevezys, where they would arrive between four and five in the morning. Panevezys was the home of a great yeshiva; Yisroel had visited there while at the gymnasium with the idea, mostly his father's, of studying there and someday becoming a *Rov.* But he found the atmosphere and the curriculum – Talmud, Talmud, more Talmud and pietism – stultifying. He had enjoyed studying a wide variety of subjects at the gymnasium, science and English literature in particular, and he could not see himself immersed totally in a one dimensional discipline.

Why was he thinking about the yeshiva with a hundred other thoughts spinning through his aching head? Because someone from the yeshiva might get on the train and, seeing a fellow Jewish student, sit down with him and start a conversation. Another possibility: someone from Vilna might have telegraphed ahead to the Panevezys police and informed them about the murders. They would come aboard to search the train. But to Yisroel's relief, only a couple of businessmen came aboard there, and as the train pulled out, he allowed himself to close his eyes. But sleep eluded him. His eyelids were screens on which the murders were projected over and over again. The train arrived at the Riga station just before eight in the morning, and as he stepped down from the train, he could smell the sea air.

The train station was in the center of the old town, on the right bank of the Dvina. It would be six months before the harbor waters froze, and there were about half a dozen merchant ships unloading tobacco, sugar, clothing and agricultural machinery while another half dozen or so were loading wood pulp, cellulose, matches, boots and cement. Yisroel remembered the way to Dr. Kurlander's house, and he found him at his home, enjoying a relaxed Sunday morning breakfast with his wife and children and his parents. When he reintroduced himself at the door, Doniel embraced him quickly and whispered into his ear that he should say nothing about why he was there to the family. "Just follow my lead," and he ushered him in to the dining room.

"Papa and Mama, Rivka, children, this is a friend from Minsk, Sender Mishkovsky. He is an emissary from the young *shomrim* in Minsk, and he's here to meet with our group and to teach us a few things. Sender, this is my family, and you are welcome to join us."

Yisroel thanked them profusely, adding: "I'm very tired. The night train was not very comfortable. I'm not really hungry, but if I could just have a piece of that beautiful *babke* and a glass of tea, I'd like to close my eyes for a while."

Turning to his wife, Doniel said: "Rivka, if you would be so kind as to make up a bed for Sender while he's having his tea, we'll give him a few hours to wash up and sleep. And while you're sleeping, Sender, I'll get in touch with a few members of our cadre who live nearby, and we'll have our first meeting with you this evening. Is that all right?"

Yisroel could not have been more grateful. He felt the tension ebbing from his aching head as he nodded his agreement and then made the *mezonos* blessing over the large piece of *babke* that Doniel's mother had sliced for him. Before he could finish it, he said: "I'm sorry to be so unsociable, but if it's all right, I'd like to sleep before I drop this glass of tea. Please ..." And with that, Rivka led him to a day bed in Doniel's study, and he slept until late that Sunday afternoon.

While Yisroel slept, Doniel arranged with his parents to take Rivka and the children home with them for the evening. Before she left, she prepared a cold supper of herring, borscht with *smetene,* diced vegetables and a boiled potato, and what was left of the morning's *babke.* This time Yisroel ate with more appetite and, as they finished eating, the members of the Riga Jewish self-defense cadre began to assemble.

Nobody asked Yisroel why he had left Vilna so precipitously. They would read about the mysterious disappearance of two Russian cavalry officers on page six of the Tuesday newspaper and, if they happened to put two and two together, they said nothing. According to the newspaper the government thought that it might be a German plot. Some Germans, ostensibly businessmen, had been in Vilna the preceding week and had left for Danzig on the Sunday train. Inquiries were being made with the German consulate. Doniel showed the paper to Yisroel, but neither of them commented on the article. What Yisroel told the group that Sunday evening was that he had to leave Riga as soon as possible, preferably on a ship bound for America. His English was good enough for honors in the gymnasium, and he thought that he would be able to make a decent living for his wife and child in America.

Yisroel had sufficient money for his passage, received from his father and a few willing friends, but he was grateful when, about to embark on a German passenger ship ten days after arriving in Riga, Dr. Kurlander handed him a purse from his cadre. They embraced, and Yisroel Forshtayn left the blood-soaked empire of the tsars for Teddy Roosevelt's America.

Rowena

Raizel and Shloime Forshtayn were born in Malden, a working-class suburb of Boston, two years apart, she the elder. Their father, Yisroel, having been renamed Isidore at Ellis Island, had made his way to Boston where Bryna was living with her Rivkes cousins. Although not particularly endowed financially, the Rivkes family *yiches* was more than adequate to guarantee the loans from members of the *Litvishe* shul that enabled Yisroel to set himself up in the poultry business in Malden's Suffolk Square. His piety, his love of learning, and his scrupulous adherence to the laws of kosher slaughter prompted his customers and the members of both the *Litvishe* and the *Rushishe* communities to bestow upon him the honorific, Reb Yisroel.

Raizel, raised by Yiddish-speaking parents, entered the first grade of Malden's elementary school with only a few words of English. After her first year, she skipped a grade, and at the graduation ceremonies at Malden High ten years later, she walked off with the English and poetry prizes and a scholarship to Salem Normal School. To her parents and to Sol – he jettisoned Shloime in third grade – she was and always had been Raizel, but she bridled at that embarrassing connection with an old world that she rejected and disparaged with all of its pieties, superstitions and especially its belittlement of women. She insisted that they call her Rowena, the name that Mr. Putnam, her poetry instructor, had bestowed upon her in homage to Sir Walter Scott's Jewess when she arrived at Salem Normal and took her place alongside the daughters of Boston's Congregationalist aristocracy. While her father immersed himself in the wisdom of Hillel and Akiba whenever he could steal an hour from his poultry business, and while her mother gossiped with the portly matrons of Suffolk Square while expertly flicking chickens in the back room of Reb Yisroel's *schlachthoiz,* Rowena practiced her Yankee aah's, seasoning her conversation with rhapsodic passages from her heroine, Edna St. Vincent Millay (whom she referred to archly as Vincent).

In her second year at Salem Normal, Rowena's patriotism was quickened by Mr. Putnam's dramatic reading of Whittier's epic poem, *Barbara Frietchie.* She imagined herself standing proudly in the attic window of the Forshtayn tenement on Malden's Boylston Street next to the nonagenarian Barbara and waving the Stars and Stripes in the face of Stonewall Jackson. More than once in the middle of the night, Bryna came running into her room, in response to her somnambular cry: "*Shoot, if you must, this old gray head/But spare your country's flag!*" So enamored was she at the epic patriotism of Whittier's heroine that she composed a musical setting for all thirty verses of the poem. And so impressed was Mr. Putnam, newly appointed as dean of the school, by her zeal that he agreed to Rowena's entreaty to be allowed to sing her mawkish composition at the commencement ceremonies. By the twentieth verse, accompanied by the muffled snickers of her classmates, even Mr. Putnam was squirming in his seat. She graduated with a teaching degree, several honors and few friends, but a laudatory recommendation from Mr. Putnam garnered a position for her in the Malden High School English department, where she became the first Jew appointed to that faculty.

Sol, on the other hand, was a miserable student from the first moment that he set foot into first grade, timidly holding Raizel's hand and armed only with childish Yiddish. He plodded through the Faulkner School, finally dropping out from the eighth grade at the age of fifteen. He embarrassed his learned father when he faltered through his minimal bar mitzvah Torah portion. Rabbi Borochov, the revered spiritual leader of the *Litvishe* shul, tried to salvage the ceremony, comparing Sol to Moses who was "*slow of speech and slow of tongue*," but Sol never achieved the respect that he yearned for from his father. Yisroel kept inviolate in a secret corner of his heart an image of the cherished and precocious son whom he had lost; there was no way that Sol, as handsome a young man as he was, could replace that icon. When he dropped out of school and began working in the *schlachthoiz*, he dreamed of the day when he could escape the onerous tasks, the constant carping, and the charnel odors of his revered father's domain.

The only hours that he really enjoyed were those when his father sent him off with Tom, the dray horse, to pick up a load of chickens from one or another of the Melrose farms. He loved to steer the horse and wagon through the country roads to the poultry farms, and he loved especially to trade small talk with the farm girls whom he met there and who, unlike Raizel, did not make him feel like a simpleton. One of those farm girls was the daughter of a Jewish poultry farmer, a rarity in Middlesex County. Louie Dubrovsky, refugee from a Galician *shtetl*, was one of the impoverished Jews whom the Baron De Hirsch Foundation had set up as farmers along the northeastern coast of the United States in the 1890's. His two daughters, Sarah and Essie, were pretty young things, respectively sixteen and fourteen, both students at Melrose High where there may have been at best two or three co-religionists among their classmates. Morris had no hesitation in allowing Sol to take Sarah and Essie for rides around the farm before loading up the wagon on his frequent visits. He had all but despaired of finding proper Jewish suitors for his daughters. Sol, the handsome son of a pious and respected Malden poultry man, was a godsend.

Reb Yisroel wondered why his son, who balked at most of the tasks assigned to him, was always so willing to take the horse and cart out to the farms. Before Sol was big and strong enough to lift the crammed chicken coops onto the wagon, he had always sent one of the *shtarke goyim* who hung around the *schlachthoiz* waiting for odd jobs to come their way. But Sol whose body had filled out nicely was more than willing. The reason became clear to the Forshtayns when, during the celebration of their thirtieth wedding anniversary in the vestry of the *Litvishe* shul, Sol showed up with a pretty girl on his arm. He brought her over to meet his parents and Raizel and, when he explained that she was a nice Jewish girl and that they had just been married by a Justice of the Peace on her seventeenth birthday, he was greeted with expressions of shock and dismay. No Rabbi Boruchov? No *chuppah*? No broken glass? No *mazel tovs*!! For shame! Rowena, after correcting Sol for introducing her to Sarah as Raizel, summed up the feelings of her parents with accustomed hauteur, "A farm girl! A Jewish milk maid! Why, Sol! You've brought undeserved honor to the family." And then, turning to the blushing bride, "You've won yourself a real prize, Sarah. Sol's a *shtarke*r; he should be able to keep you barefoot and pregnant."

It would be two more years before Rowena, at the age of twenty-seven, married. She had brief relationships with several eligible young men from the *Litvishe* congregation in the years immediately following her appointment to the high school faculty, but she was so intent on demonstrating her intellectual superiority to any prospective suitor with obscure quotations from Millay and Dickinson that she frightened them off before a second or third date. And then an ill-fated liaison with the brother of one of her Normal School classmates whom she met at their fifth reunion dealt a crushing blow to her relations with men in general. His Back Bay hauteur, his Douglas Fairbanks moustache, and his Harvard degree conspired to lead her to two nights of wild abandon in a Parker House suite, but when she let it slip that she was Jewish that second night, he abruptly jumped out of bed, zipped up his trousers, and was not heard from again.

Aloof, dismissive, cold, yet austerely handsome, she managed to acquire Isaac Ross, principal of the Hebrew School in nearby Winthrop, who supplemented his meager income as an uncertified accountant for several of the small businessmen on Shirley

Street, as a husband. Reb Yisroel was delighted with the match, because Isaac, while lacking in wealth and business acumen, was not only a scholar but also the possessor of notable *yiches*. When Reb Yisroel first met him in the home of Rabbi Borochov, he was informed that Isaac was the grandson of a distinguished German rabbi, Mordecai Rothenberg, a descendant of Rabbi Meir of Rothenberg, the great Alsatian sage of medieval Jewry. When his grandfather arrived at Ellis Island in 1882, a well-meaning immigration officer, untutored in Jewish *yiches,* circumcised his long but distinguished name to Ross. Based on that information and impressed by the young man's modesty and piety, Reb Yisroel invited him to his home for dinner. There he met Rowena, a week after her Parker House debacle, desperate for a husband on the chance that she was pregnant. She wasn't.

Isaac spent every Sabbath morning in the synagogue where he supervised the junior congregation and then joined the adults upstairs assisting Rabbi Epstein for the final hour of the service, but he was rarely accompanied by Rowena. She kept a strictly kosher home and prepared the traditional *Kiddush,* chicken soup and *cholent* for Isaac when he came home from Sabbath services, but she made only rare appearances in the synagogue, unwilling to sit in the ladies' gallery. Disdainful of the synagogue Sisterhood, Rowena became an active member of the Winthrop Garden Club and the Ladies' Literary Guild.

Though hardly a day passed without Rowena subjecting her meekly submissive husband to an onslaught of verbal vitriol, usually harping on his unwillingness to demand higher fees for his accounting services, they did manage to conceive a son who would become the sole and favored nephew of Uncle Sol and Aunt Sarah. Isaac wanted to name him Jacob, after his father, but Rowena insisted on anglicizing it to Justin, a name that Mr. Putnam would have approved.

One of the very few things that Rowena and Isaac shared was their love for their one and only son, but it was a competitive love. Rowena regarded her Justin with wonder and pride but would no more think of cuddling him or stroking his head than she would the Rembrandt portrait of the austere, black-frocked Mevr. Elison that she so admired in the Museum of Fine Arts. Isaac was the one who changed the diapers, cradled his son in his arms and walked the floor with him when he cried and, beginning when Justin was three, held his hand each Sabbath morning as they walked to the synagogue together. Both Rowena and Isaac spent more time interacting with Justin than with each other. They read to him daily, Bible stories from Isaac and children's classics and poetry from Rowena, and Justin rewarded them with attention, obedience and good grades from his first day in the Highland Elementary School through his graduation from Winthrop High. But through those early years, Justin's one reliable source of tactile and unconditional love was his Aunt Sarah.

Sarah

Sol and Sarah began their married life in an attic room on the Dubrovsky farm. For the first year Sol worked on the farm, alongside his father-in-law, but then he got an idea. What if they didn't have to wait for the poultry slaughterhouses and butcher stores to send their horses and wagons to pick up the chickens. You could buy a small Ford truck for just a few hundred dollars. With a truck, Sol realized, he could transport not only the Dubrovsky fowl to market but he could drive around to several of the other farms in Middlesex County and transport their poultry as well, charging a modest fee per coop. Louie liked the idea and lent Sol the money to buy a truck. Sol made it a point to make his first delivery with the new truck to his father's *schlachthoiz*, expecting to earn a few words of praise for his initiative. Instead, what he got was "A Ford you had to buy?!" A gob of spit splattered on the gravel. "My own son makes rich that *paskunyak* of an *antisemit*, Henry Ford! For shame! A Jew don't drive no Ford." But he accepted his allotment of six coops before sending an abashed Sol on his way.

Within three years Sol had acquired customers not only in the farm communities around Malden but as far afield as Billerica and Concord in Middlesex County and Saugus,

Danvers, Topsfield and Andover in Essex County. His first Ford truck had the Forshtayn name amateurishly hand-lettered on the doors; the second, third and fourth, larger and driven by newly hired employees, had the name Fairstone Farm Transport professionally lettered in blue and gold on the side panels. And along with his growing fleet, he and Sarah produced two children. By then it was time to move out of the cramped Dubrovsky ménage and into a six-room house in the Maplewood neighborhood of Malden, where they lived among dozens of other Jews liberated from the cramped tenements of Suffolk Square.

Sarah was a loving wife and mother and, at least through the early years of their marriage, a contented homemaker. She had quit Melrose High at the end of her tenth year in order to help out on the farm, and she had no appetite for any books other than the ones that she kept for her husband, entering all the receipts and bills in a neat hand each night after the kids were asleep. As sociable and popular as she was with her Maplewood neighbors, in their kitchens for morning coffee, at the grocery or the beauty parlor, she felt inadequate whenever Sol decided to take the family to visit his parents in Suffolk Square. The elder Forshtayns spoke only Yiddish or severely fractured Yinglish. The walls of their cramped apartment were buttressed with bookcases jammed tight with Talmudic tomes, the Yiddish works of Sholem Aleichem, Peretz and Mendele, and pietistic literature, and it reeked of *Litvish*e piety and k-rations – *kishke, kugel, kreplach, knaidlach, knishes* and *kartofel mit schmaltz.* Sarah was ill at ease during those bi-weekly duty visits; she felt inferior in the presence of the elder Forshtayns and could find little common ground for conversation.

And then there were her children, Sumner and Hope. Sumner had a severe stammer and was the ready butt of the prankish bullying of his elementary school classmates. And Hope, though fairly pretty, was overweight, awkward and severely introverted. She had to repeat the third grade because of her many absences; she simply felt uncomfortable away from the security of home and mother. When the Fairstones visited with the Rosses in

Winthrop, Sarah could not help being aware of the painful contrast between her Sumner and Hope and her dismissive sister-in-law's precocious Justin. But her resentment of her sister-in-law did not extend to Justin. From the first day that she saw him in the arms of a nurse through the window of the Winthrop Hospital nursery, she adored him. Even as an infant, he was somehow more animated and responsive than her year-old Sumner. When she became pregnant a second time five years later, she prayed that the microscopic life that was harbored within her womb, the daughter whom she would name Hope, would resuscitate her deteriorating marriage..

As the three children grew up, one might have expected that the contrast between them would discourage Sarah from taking her two to visit their cousin in Winthrop, but quite the contrary was the case. Sarah doted on Justin. When he was an infant, often left lying in his crib in soiled diapers and crying for attention while Rowena was busy discussing Garden Club business on the phone, she would pick him up, soothe him, gently set him down on the bassinette, remove his smelly diaper, oil and powder his neglected bottom, and then give it a giggling kiss before pinning on a fresh diaper.

Sol, too, had a special place in his heart for Justin. He found it a chore to play with his own children; they were listless and unresponsive. But he spent his hours in his sister's home alternately playing klabiash with Isaac and playing checkers or fish with Justin. Following the lead of his brother-in-law, he addressed Justin as Jakie whenever Rowena was not around. As Justin grew up, the games progressed to Monopoly or, in good weather, baseball against the steps. And whenever he ran low on Lucky Strikes, he would send Justin around the corner to Sinky's with enough money for cigarettes for himself and a comic book and an ice cream cone for Jakie.

The pleasures of these frequent visits to the Rosses in Winthrop, rarely reciprocated by visits to Malden because of Rowena's many social commitments, did not, as one might have expected, extend beyond the Winthrop town line. There was usually silence in the speeding Fairstone Cadillac until they reached Revere. Then Sol would direct some question to Sumner. "I saw that Jakie was reading *Black Beauty* when we came in. Have you read *Black Beauty*?" "N…n…no, D… Daddy." "Hope, are you learning to read in kindergarten?" Silence. "Sarah, what's wrong with you? Why can't you see to it that our kids do some reading in their spare time. You grew up on a farm, but our kids are growing up in Maplewood; they have to read if they're going to amount to anything. Do you want them to grow up to be chicken farmers like your family?"

When Sarah got up the gumption to remind Sol that he too had dropped out of high school, he would respond with a stony silence. Usually, though, she just began to weep quietly as they sped through Revere and into Malden. When they arrived home, Sarah would busy herself with the kids and with supper. And then, more often than not, Sol would say: "Sorry, Sweetums, no supper for me tonight. I've got to drive up to Manchester to meet with some growers tomorrow morning." He kept a small bag with a couple of changes of laundry in the trunk of the Cadillac. As he reached the door, "Can't you at least stay for supper and help put Sumner and Hope to bed?" A shrug, and he was gone.

When the news came over the radio, interrupting *The Shadow*, that the Japanese had bombed Pearl Harbor, Sol was off visiting clients in New Hampshire and Maine. Sarah thought he might call or acknowledge in some way that something was amiss in the world, but when he did finally get home, three days later, it was to tell her that she had nothing to worry about. "I won't be drafted. I'm thirty-two, probably too old, and I have a sore back from all those years of lifting coops. Anyway, I'm doing vital work hauling poultry; I'll probably even get some army contracts with all the forts around Boston." Her immediate response was to ask whether he would be spending more time at home. "Probably not. If I play my cards right, this war could make us rich." As it turned out, he played them very right.

As busy as Sol was during those war years, he was not too busy for the two joyous family bar mitzvahs that took place while tens of thousands of Jewish thirteen year olds were being annihilated in European death camps. Sarah drove Sumner to his private lessons with old Rabbi Boruchov three days a week after school. He actually began his bar mitzvah instruction with his grandfather, but Reb Yisroel, who delighted in every moment that he could spend over books with his Winthrop grandson, simply did not have the patience that Sumner required, nor would he consider transliterating the sacred Hebrew text into Roman characters – *a shandeh!* – to accommodate Sumner's inability to master the Hebrew alphabet.

Rabbi Boruchov had the requisite patience and enough years of teaching experience to be able to wangle a passable performance out of Sumner. There was no way to get by his stutter, but he knew that the congregation would be sympathetic and overlook it. It was unfortunate that all of the prayers that bar mitzvah boys have to chant begin with the word *Baruch* with its dreaded *b* stumbling block, but Sumner, his new suit and shirt soaked with sweat, got through it. Sarah, sitting in the ladies' gallery, wept through his performance, while her sister-in-law sat smugly by her side offering such helpful comments as "Don't be upset; Justin will make us all proud at his bar mitzvah next year."

Sol had intended to invite the entire Malden congregation to a banquet at a posh Boston hotel following the Shabbat afternoon service, but Rabbi Boruchov told him in no uncertain terms that a lavish display was not proper while Jews were being shipped off to concentration camps. He advised Sol to make a significant contribution to the Jewish Rescue Committee and to enclose with the invitations a note to the effect that Sumner wanted people to give him gifts of war bonds. Sol and Sarah thought that that was a fine idea, and they presided over a modest but *fraylich* luncheon for the congregation in the synagogue vestry.

It was a good thing that Justin's bar mitzvah took place thirteen months after Sumner's, long enough to allay the inevitable invidious comparisons. Whereas Sumner had chanted only the blessings and five brief verses from the Torah portion in a sing-song that never quite managed to settle on a key, Justin chanted the entire Torah portion as well as the prophetic *haftarah* and, of course, the accompanying blessings. After that was all over, he delivered an embarrassingly pompous speech written by his mother. Reb Yisroel, who proudly oversaw his grandson's progress, had discussed an idea for a *d'var Torah* based on the weekly portion with Justin, and Justin was in the process of writing it out when his mother stepped in.

"Nobody wants to hear that kind of rabbinic pilpul nowadays," she informed her son. "I'll help you write a speech about coming of age in a world where young Americans are storming the ramparts of Europe with the flag that represents freedom and democracy! I want my friends to hear a message for today not for a thousand years ago." After a few feeble efforts at composing a message that would satisfy his mother's patriotic ardor, Justin agreed to be her mouthpiece. Isaac thought that the speech that Justin was forced to commit to memory was pretentious, chauvinistic and inappropriate for a bar mitzvah, but there was nothing that he could do once Rowena convinced Justin that he would really impress the congregation with phrases like "valorous youth" and "our nation's pride and glory."

The congregation was, in fact, duly impressed. Justin's voice had not yet succumbed to adolescence, and he chanted the sacred texts in the pure and unwavering alto voice that had made him the boy soloist at the cantor's side on the High Holy Days. Isaac had the honor of inviting the entire congregation to the *Kiddush* collation following the service in the Hebrew School auditorium, without mentioning that a select group, mostly Rowena's friends, were invited to their home following the *Kiddush* for an elaborate luncheon. The *Kiddush* offered the expected *knishes* and *kichel* with herring, but the luncheon in the Ross home, which exhausted Isaac's savings, featured a variety of fruit molds, deviled eggs, smoked salmon, tomato aspic, baked stuffed potatoes, rolled toast with mushrooms, and other delicacies favored by the ladies of the Garden Club.

Rowena had worked for several nights over the seating arrangement for the thirty guests who sat around the Ross dining room table, augmented for the occasion by a long rented table placed at a perpendicular. The guests were a "Who's Who" of Winthrop's Jewish society, the Bromans, the Youngs, the Corwins, the Sandlers, the Landers, the Krafts, and, of course, the doctors and their wives. There were red-white-and-blue place cards and napkins at every seat, and it took the assembled guests only a few minutes to find their designated places. At the main table, facing the guests were Rowena and Isaac, Reb Yisroel and Bryna, Rabbi and Mrs. Epstein, and Sol and Sarah. Sarah's place was empty through most of the luncheon, because she had volunteered to supervise the two hired women in the kitchen and to see to it that empty serving platters were quickly refilled.

It was while Sarah was putting garnishes on the platters of smoked salmon that she looked up and saw Justin standing at the kitchen door looking at her forlornly. "What's the matter, Justin? You look sad. You should be so happy today. Everybody says that you did beautifully. Your uncle and I are very proud of you. What's the matter?"

Justin seemed on the verge of tears. "Aunt Sarah, I don't know where to sit. There's no place for me at the table."

"What do you mean, Justin? Of course, there's a place for you. Your mother set out all the place cards very carefully just before we left for the shul. Your card must be at the head table, probably next to your mother or dad or maybe Zeyde. Go out and look again."

"I did look, Aunt Sarah. I looked twice, but there was no place and everybody was talking. I didn't want to interrupt. Mummy would be angry if I interrupted."

Sarah told Justin to wait in the kitchen, and she went out to the dining room with a platter of salmon. She then sat down at her place and looked around. Indeed, there was no place reserved for the bar mitzvah boy. Rowena had somehow overlooked him while focusing on whether the Bromans should be sitting next to the Corwins or the Sandlers next to the Krafts. Sarah nudged Sol and asked him for his pen. He gave her a puzzled look but handed it to her as unobtrusively as possible. One did not write on the Sabbath in the presence of Rabbi Epstein or Reb Yisroel. Sarah lowered her place card to her lap and, under the cover of the table cloth, turned it over, refolded it, and wrote "Justin Ross" on it. She then placed the revised card on the table and went back to the kitchen, unaware that Reb Yisroel had been carefully watching her. She found Justin there looking greedily at the food being set out by the two helpers.

"Justin, I think that you didn't look carefully enough. I saw your card at the seat next to Uncle Sol. It says "Justin Ross" on it, clear as day. You go back in and sit down at your place and eat. You must be plenty hungry after all you did this morning."

"I am. Thanks, Aunt Sarah. I thought I had looked at all the cards. Good, I'll sit next to Uncle Sol. That's great." And he went into the dining room, slipped into his seat, got a hug from Sol, and dug into the stuffed potatoes. A few minutes later, Reb Yisroel excused himself from the table and went into the kitchen where he found Sarah sitting alone in a corner munching on some jellied fruit. He went over to her, kissed her on the head, and said: "Sora, you're a good woman. You got a heart. God bless you." And he went back to the dining room without another word.

Among the other things that Justin kept among his treasures was a small collection of memorabilia from his bar mitzvah – a copy of his mother's speech, the booklet with his Torah portion, the invitation, the embroidered *yarmulke* that Zeyde Yisroel had ordered from Jerusalem, and a few laudatory notes from friends of his parents. It wasn't until he was sixteen and cleaning out some old things from his closet that he came across his bar mitzvah trove and, looking it over, unfolded his place card. There inside he saw inscribed in his mother's hand: "Sarah Fairstone." He thought back to that afternoon and recalled how abandoned he had felt when he thought that his mother had overlooked him on his day of days. He recalled his conversation with his Aunt Sarah in the kitchen, and he understood. He vowed then and there that he would never forget what she had done for him. He refolded the card and put it into his wallet where it served as a constant reminder of an act of grace,... and he tearfully slipped it under the lid of her coffin just ten years later.

By V-J Day, Fairstone Farm Transport had grown into a million-dollar business, Sol Fairstone was one of the richest Jews in Malden, and Sarah was used to spending her nights alone. It took Sarah a couple of years of mental anguish to come to grips with the fact that her husband was a philanderer. It was a rare week when he spent more than three nights at home, always claiming to be visiting with poultry men in Maine or New Hampshire. And it was not that he disdained his marital bed or the familiarity of its occupant. He believed that he loved Sarah, and she certainly loved him. They both enjoyed their increasingly rare instances of intimacy as much as they had before the advent of Sumner and Hope. Sarah was very careful about her appearance; she exercised regularly and with determination succeeded in erasing the tell-tale signs of motherhood. And it wasn't that Sol wasn't appreciative of her love, her wholesome good looks, her home-making skills and her devotion to his family. He just loved to wander, to escape from the disappointment that he felt every time he looked at his progeny, to respond to the primal urge for new conquests, both entrepreneurial and sexual. When Sol was at home, Sarah was content; when he was away, more often than not, she wept.

One of the rare pleasures of Sarah's life was her relationship with Justin. She was a devoted mother to Sumner and Hope, schlepping them to speech therapists, elocution lessons, games and doctors' appointments, overseeing homework and tucking them into bed with stories, but they didn't provide any of the *nachas* that she derived from Justin. From his earliest childhood, Justin knew whose arms to run to if he needed some comfort after skinning a knee or receiving a scolding from his mother. During his elementary school years, he could only enjoy the loving embraces of his aunt when the Fairstones came to Winthrop, but one of his bar mitzvah gifts, a two-wheeler, made it possible for him to negotiate the eight miles between Winthrop and

Malden in less than an hour. Rowena did not like to hear that Justin wasted his spare hours visiting her sister-in-law, and so one of the secrets that Justin and Sarah shared was the fact that she would maneuver Justin's bike into the back seat of her car and drive him back to within a few blocks of the Ross home so that he could peddle home as if from a ride through Winthrop or Revere.

When Justin was fifteen, he and Sarah shared a second secret. She began giving him driving lessons, and two days after his sixteenth birthday, she drove him to the Bureau of Motor Vehicles in Malden where she paid for his first driving license. And there was a third secret, one that she did not share with Justin but kept buried deep deep within her heart. On those occasions when Justin, now several inches taller than his aunt, dropped in to spend a few hours of refuge from his mother with her, occasions when Sol was somewhere on the road, Sarah could hardly keep herself from suggesting that Justin stay overnight with her. She loved her handsome nephew with all her heart; she was just thirty-seven and achingly lonely. Why not? Why not?! The most heartwarming words that she had ever heard were her father-in-law's "Sora, you're a good woman." A good woman does not seduce her nephew. So she would force herself to say, "Justin, I guess it's time for you to go home now." And after he left, she cried and later found inadequate relief in whatever pleasure she could provide for herself in an empty bed. She had no inkling that her virgin nephew, when he climbed into his own bed after lying to his mother about where he had spent his after-school hours, would fantasize about the secret places beneath his lovely aunt's housedress. Secrets.

Claudette

Sol Fairstone moved his center of operations to Brunswick, Maine, in 1948, the year after the Maine Turnpike opened and the year that his nephew, Justin, graduated from Winthrop High School. He chose Brunswick because it was a quiet, attractive college town, less than an hour's drive from the hundreds of poultry farms in Cumberland, Sagadahoc, and York counties and southern New Hampshire. He bought a twelve-room house on a Bailey Island promontory overlooking Merriconeag Sound and Casco Bay and explained to Sarah that he had done it for her and the kids. He explained that it would be a great place for you the family to spend their summers. "There's a tennis court and a dock and a big lawn for croquet and a magnificent stand of white birch. You'll love it. You can sit on the front porch and see the lobster boats going by, and there's even a lighthouse in the distance."

"You only want us there for the summers? Where are we supposed to live during the winters?"

"Sarah, you'd be miserable up there in the winter. There's a lot of snow, and it's cold, and driving is dangerous. And the kids.... Don't forget the kids. You don't want to take them out of their school....".

"What difference would that make? They both hate school, and they don't have many friends here. The only advantage to being in Malden is that I can spend time with my parents and with your sister and Isaac and Justin."

"But that's it! Exactly! Your mother and dad are in their upper sixties. How much longer do they have, especially your father with his heart and his diabetes? And where are you going to find anyone who'll look after the kids like your mother does when you go shopping or to Hadassah meetings?"

"So you want to be on your own up there in Maine?"

"That's not it at all. You know I'd much rather be here with you. I'll be driving down regularly to take care of business in Boston and to see you and the folks and Rowena's family, and you and the kids can come up during school vacations...... Sarah, let's not argue about this. I've worked it all out and it's for the best. This is the way it's got to be. I have to spend more time in Maine in order to stay on top of my business." And that was that.

The annual Forshtayn family Thanksgiving feast took place in Winthrop that year. Zeyde and Bobbe Forshtayn were there, along with the Dubrovskys (except for Sarah's sister, Essie, who was working for Bonwit Teller in New York) and Sol, Sarah, Sumner and Hope. It was a joyful reunion, celebrating not only the harvest – Americanized Isidore (ne Yisroel) Forshtayn allowed his family to celebrate just this one *goyische* holiday, because it was modeled, he explained, on the Jewish festival of Sukkot – but also the first time that the entire family was gathered together since Justin began his freshman year at Harvard. Sumner had lasted at Malden High only a year longer than his father and was working as an apprentice mechanic at the Fairstone Farm Transport depot in Melrose. Hope was muddling through junior high, miserable, heavier and without friends.

Yisroel liked to spice up Thanksgiving gatherings with questions from the Bible and rabbinic literature. It was his way of deriving some *nachas* from his *einekl* Yaakov (he refused to call him Justin) and, at the same time, diminishing his disappointing son who knew only how to make money. Rowena enjoyed these impromptu quizzes as much as her father did, and for the same reasons. As usual, Justin was ready with all the answers that he had learned from his grandfather during their weekly Torah study sessions through his elementary school years and then in the high school department of Hebrew College. Isaac was sensitive enough to realize how painful this display was to everyone present except for Yisroel and his own tactless wife, and so, after an uncomfortable few minutes while Sumner and Hope sat silently, eyes downcast, he said: "Papa, that's enough questions for today. We know how smart our Justin is. You're embarrassing him. Good work, Justin.... Rowena, I think that it's time to bring out the turkey."

Sol left for his new home in Maine the day after Thanksgiving, and he met Claudette Potvin a week later while enjoying his daily breakfast at Bascomb's on Maine Street. Sol loved the home-baked blueberry or cranberry muffins that accompanied the two 'over easy' eggs that he ordered each morning while reading the *Times Record*. When he asked the waitress where they bought those delicious muffins, she replied that they didn't have to buy them; they were baked fresh each morning in their own kitchen by Mrs. Potvin. "Well, my compliments to Mrs. Potvin," Sol said. "Tell her that I'll keep coming to Bascomb's for my breakfast as long as she keeps baking these great muffins."

As Sol was finishing his second cup of coffee, an attractive, red-headed woman in her upper thirties came out of the kitchen and walked over to his table. "Maggie told me that you like my muffins. Glad to hear it. I've been baking here ever since my husband died two years ago. I've got no plans to go anywhere else, so you can keep coming in. The Bascomb's are nice folk."

"Well, thanks for coming out and telling me that. Sorry to hear about your husband." She nodded. "Your muffins are the high point of my mornings here in Brunswick. My only problem is deciding whether to order the blueberry or the cranberry."

She thanked him and turned to go back to the kitchen when Sol said impulsively, "Can you join me for another cup of coffee for a few minutes? I'm sort of new here in town, and I don't know many people."

Claudette paused for an indecisive moment, regarded the good looking fellow sitting by himself, and then shrugged and sat. "I guess I can spare a couple of minutes. Mr. Bascomb won't mind. Do you know Stu?"

"No; who's Stu?"

"Oh, you've got to meet Stu Bascomb. He's the one sitting behind the cash register. He knows everybody in town. Surprised you haven't met yet."

"Well, I've only been here a week. I'll introduce myself when I pay. So where do you live?'

"Here in town, off Pleasant Street behind the post office, just a couple of blocks from the Catholic church."

"Did you grow up here in Brunswick?"

"Ayup. Been here all my life. My folks came down from Quebec about a hundred years ago. That recipe for my muffins is from my Granmaman Claudette, same name as me."

"Claudette. Nice name. Like Claudette Colbert … and just as pretty. Can I call you Claudette?"

"I guess so.… I've got to get back to the kitchen in a minute. But tell me; what brings you to Brunswick and to Bascomb's every morning?"

"I'm in business here. Have you seen any of those Fairstone Farm Transport trucks around town?"

"Sure; they come out of that depot on the Bath Road near Cook's Corner."

"Right, that's me, Sol Fairstone."

"Wow! All those trucks are yours? There must be thirty or forty of them!"

"And about a hundred more around Nashua and Boston."

"Wow again! Well, I'm glad to have met you." She got up and extended a hand to him. Sol held her hand for a moment without shaking it and then hesitantly ventured "Are you free for dinner tonight? We could take a little drive and then you can show me a nice place for dinner. I need someone to show me around, especially the nice restaurants."

"Well, I don't know. We just met….."

"Don't worry. It's just dinner. I'm alone here in Brunswick and I guess you're alone more than you'd like. What time are you done here?"

"I usually leave after the lunch crowd and clean-up. Around three-thirty."

"Great. That'll give us enough time for a little sightseeing, with you as my guide, and then dinner. Okay?"

"Well, tomorrow's Sunday so I don't have to get in early. Most days I'm in by 6:30 to get started on the muffins. So" – still a bit hesitant – "I guess so."

Sol got up, shook the hand that he had been holding, and said, "I'll pick you up here at three-thirty."

When Sol drove up to Bascomb's from his office, he saw that Claudette had changed her clothes. She was wearing a pretty flowered frock that showed off a trim waste and an ample bosom. When she was comfortably seated in his Cadillac, Sol bowed his head and said: "Where to, Madame Claudette?"

She chuckled at his mock gallantry and answered: "Would you like to see lakes and countryside or ocean"

"Always ocean. That's why I settled on Bailey Island. I love the ocean. I'll probably buy a boat in the spring."

"Umm, that sounds nice. I love the ocean too. Let me think for a minute.... Someplace nice on the ocean and not too far.... I know! Let's drive up to Boothbay. Have you ever been there?"

"No, but I've heard of it. How do we get there?"

"Just take Route 1 north through Bath and Wiscasset, and we should be there in time for some nice views and the sunset at Ocean Point."

As they drove northeastward, Claudette pointed out the sites – the Bath Iron Works, the Kennebec and Sheepscot Rivers and the turnoff to the long Boothbay peninsula. They discovered that they were both rabid Red Sox fans, and when Sol revealed that he had been in Fenway Park on that September day in 1940 when Ted Williams, Jimmie Foxx, Jim Tabor and Joe Cronin had all hit home runs in the same inning, she screamed with delight.

"You were there? Really? I was listening to that game with Charlie. I remember Jim Britt screaming over WNAC: 'I can't believe it! I can't believe it!' You were actually there?"

"Yeah. I just had one truck back then, and I decided to drive out to Fenway after my morning deliveries. I didn't have time for many games back then, but I sure chose the right day to take off an afternoon. I'll never forget it."

The Red Sox made them pals; sitting on the rocks at Ocean Point and looking out at the sea, the soaring gulls and the islands brought them closer; dinner at a seaside window in the dining room of the historic inn nourished familiarity; and yes, there was a room available upstairs for the inevitable progression to intimacy. Sol would have used one of the condoms that he always kept in his wallet, but Claudette said no. "When I was married to Charlie we had lots of sex, but I never got pregnant. I guess I'm just not fertile. Anyway, I'll have enough to confess this week. I don't need to add using birth control."

Sol didn't need convincing and lost himself in the repeated pleasures of the night. There was one awkward moment just after their first ecstatic joining. Claudette took Sol's member in her hand and looked at it curiously. "Don't take this the wrong way but...." She wasn't sure how to pose the question. "No offense, but yours is different from Charlie's. It's rounder."

"I was circumcised when I was a baby."

"Circumcised? Uh...are you Jewish?!"

"Yes; I would have told you but we sort of got carried away. My family's Jewish, but I don't go much to synagogue or anything."

"Wow! I wonder if I have to mention that in my confession. Wow! You're *Jewish.....*".

"Does that really matter to you?"

"I don't know. It just surprises me. We got along so well today, and I haven't had as great a night as this since Charlie...... even *before* Charlie. When I lay in your arms after that second time, really, for the first time I just forgot about Charlie. I don't know......".

Over breakfast, Claudette was pensive and unresponsive to Sol's attempts at humor. She reminded him several times that she had to get back to Brunswick in time for mass. "I usually attend the nine o'clock mass; I guess it'll have to be the eleven o'clock today. We'd better get going."

When Sol dropped her at the church, he asked if he could see her later that day, but she demurred. "Please don't rush me, Sol. I'm confused. I don't know. I'm late. See ya...".

Sol did a lot of thinking that Sunday, and then on Monday morning at seven-thirty he walked into Bascomb's for his breakfast as usual. He looked around for Claudette, but if she was there, she was in the kitchen. He drank a second and a third cup of coffee, hoping that she would come out front for something, but she didn't. Finally he went up to Stu Bascomb at the cash register with his check and asked in an undertone, "Is Mrs. Potvin here today?"

"Sure, didn't you have your usual muffin? She's out back."

"I'd like to ask her about something. Could you ask her to call me at my office? Here, I'll leave you the number." He jotted it down on a napkin and gave it to Bascomb who assured him that he would deliver it to Claudette personally.

Claudette didn't call that day or on Tuesday, nor did she emerge from the Bascomb's kitchen while Sol was there. But she did call on Wednesday afternoon, admitting that she missed him but didn't know what to do. Sol asked her to wait a minute while he closed his office door. He thought for a long moment and then blurted: "Listen, Claudette. I've never had feelings for anyone the way I feel about you. I want to see you; I want to make love to you. But I don't want to hurt you; you're too nice. So I'm going to tell you something else about me. You already know that I'm Jewish. Well, I'm also married, and I have two kids back in Boston, a problem wife and two problem kids, which is why I spend most of my time here in Maine. I'm a rich man, but mostly I feel like a poor bum because I can't stand being with my family. Tell me ... admit it.... You had a good time last Saturday, right?"

Silence, and then a hesitant "Yes."

"Claudette, let me pick you up at about six-thirty and we'll go up to a new place that I found for dinner, Ingrid's in Bath. We'll talk, just talk."

She agreed, and after dinner she let him drive her to his place on Bailey Island. They never made it to the upstairs bedroom that was supposed to be his and Sarah's but that Sarah had not yet seen. They sat down innocently enough to watch the end of the Celtics game on the family room television, but during the final minutes, with the Celtics leading by a lop-sided score, their interest shifted away from the screen as they initiated the new futon. If anything, their second coupling was even more rapturous than the first. And so the third and fourth and .... through a winter of unparalleled delight for both of them. And then came May and the realization that Sarah and the kids would be arriving in just a few weeks.

Sol made it a point to call Sarah and the kids every week from his office, usually telling them how cold and miserable it was "up here in the north woods." Often, after he had managed to eke a few monosyllabic words out of Sumner, he would call his nephew, Justin, for the antidote. Justin was having "an awesome time" at Harvard, taking classes with Pulitzer Prize winners and Nobel Prize winners and meeting girls at the Hillel House. At least once a month, during business trips to Boston, Sol would pick Justin up in Harvard Square after dinner and drive him to the Statler's Café Rouge for his favorite dessert – baked Alaska with fresh strawberry topping. And at each of those meetings, kept secret from the family, he would remind Jakie that there was a place for him in the Fairstone organization.

It was on the first of June 1949 when both Sol and Claudette, sitting over dinner at Ingrid's, made announcements. Sol informed Claudette that his wife and kids would be coming up to join him in less than three weeks and that they had to find some way to continue seeing each other through what he was sure would be a long summer. Claudette didn't respond immediately. She just nodded and offered that she knew that day would be coming.

But then a few moments later, she began to cry softly. Sol looked around to see if the other diners had noticed anything, and then he reached across the table and took her hands, reassuring her. "Don't worry, Detty. We'll find a way to see each other."

Claudette shook her head and dabbed at her eyes with her napkin. "That's not what I'm crying about. I've had something to tell you for the past couple of days, something … well, I don't know how you'll take it…"

"What is it? What couldn't you tell me?"

"Well, I don't know how you'll take it. It's really good news, but bad also…".

"So what is it?"

"You remember how I told you that I must not be fertile because Charlie and I never had kids?"

Silence. Sol sat rigid staring at her. "You… you mean …"

"Sol, I'm pregnant. According to Dr. McFadden, I'm in my third month. I'm going to have a baby, Sol. Can you believe it? A baby! I'll be forty in less than three years, and I'm going to have a *baby*. Dr. McFadden said that I'm healthy and he didn't see any problem…… Sol, say something."

"I don't know what to say, Detty. I'm just so surprised." He thought for a moment, and then added: "You want this baby?"

"Yes, of course. I've wanted a child all my life. But don't worry; I've thought about this every minute for the past two days. I know you're married, and I don't expect you to get a divorce because I'm having a child. I'll be able to raise a child with a little help."

"A little help?! Detty, I love you. You're the best thing that ever happened to me. Let me think about this for a minute. I'm still in shock……"

"Sol, I won't make any demands on you. I know that you're a decent man and that you'll help where you can. But this baby is my responsibility, and I'm happy, very happy about it. I feel …. I feel like a real woman now, like my mother and my granmaman."

Sol sat staring at Claudette for a few moments, and then, "Claudette Potvin, I swear to you on this first day of June, 1949, that I will take care of you and *our* child for the rest of my life. I can't marry you; it's just impossible. I can't. But I can buy you a house and maybe a little business, wherever you want.... I can't live with you, but I want whatever is percolating inside of you to be mine too. Maybe I'll do better this time than Sarah's Sumner and Hope."

It was indeed a long summer. Sarah was more or less content. She enjoyed sharing a bed with Sol even though he usually fell asleep within a few minutes of hitting the pillow. There were more than a few nights when he had to go, as he put it, "on the road to meet with clients." But Sarah managed to find diversions for herself and for the kids. She enjoyed sunning and lolling with a book in an Adirondack chair on the lawn overlooking the sea. Sol did, in fact, buy a 30-foot Chris-Craft and taught Sumner how to operate it. Hope made no attempt at finding friends, but she did enjoy swimming on their private beach and collecting shells and other sea detritus. On Sundays or on those rare occasions when he left work early, he would take Sarah and the kids for a spin in the yacht out to Eagle Island or to the seaside restaurants at Cundy's Harbor or Ash Cove. If the weather wasn't nice enough for the boat, they would take drives along the coast, sometimes up to Rockland, usually stopping at Moody's Diner for lunch and berry pie. But there was rarely any meaningful conversation except....

... except for the ten-day period in late August when Jakie came up. Both Sol and Sarah had urged him to find some time during the summer to enjoy Maine, and he promised them that he would when he finished his eight-week stint as a counselor at Camp Herzl in New Hampshire. As soon as he set foot on the Bailey Island estate, he fell in love with the place. He had learned from his father back in Winthrop how to handle a small boat, not that Isaac had a boat of his own, but he loved fishing, and there were always boats to rent off Winthrop beach, not 30-footers like Sol's, but a boat is a boat. Finally there was something that Jakie and Sumner could share, their delight at pulling up a few flounder or cod from the icy waters of Casco Bay and bringing them back to Sarah for that evening's dinner.

Sol was home every night of Justin's visit with them, and both he and Sarah engaged him in lively conversation at the ordinarily silent dinner table. Justin enjoyed telling them about his courses, about the girls he dated, about the Glee Club rehearsals, about his Hillel activities, and about his weekly visits with Zeyde and Bobbe Forshtayn in Malden. He jokingly referred to his Talmud study sessions with Sol's father as his "Seminar in Post-Biblical Aramaic Legal Texts." "That's what they would call it in the Harvard course catalogue, and you better believe that it's a lot tougher than most of my classes – except that Zeyde teaches with love." Justin reminded his uncle and aunt of how Zeyde would always slip eighteen cents under the cover of whatever Torah portion they were studying when he was a kid, so that he would find it when he closed the book. "Well now I find eighteen dollars under the cover of the tractate, and he tells me to go have a good time with a nice Jewish girl." Justin went on to say that he was worried about Zeyde's health, and Sol promised that he would spend some time with his parents the next time that he was near Malden.

By mid-August Claudette was visibly pregnant, and the Bascombs and all their regulars had no doubt who the father might be. They talked among themselves, but not maliciously. Most everybody who knew Mrs. Potvin liked her and her baked goods, and Sol was Brunswick's leading employer and he treated his drivers and mechanics well. Not much point in making him feel uncomfortable. There were occasional curious glances in Sol's direction when he walked into the restaurant, but no one said anything untoward.

One morning during his visit, Uncle Sol invited his nephew to join him for breakfast at Bascomb's. He explained that he rarely ate breakfast at home because he got to meet the town's folk there, read the copy of the *Times Record* that was always waiting for him, and … "Wait 'til you taste the muffins at Bascomb's.

They go with coffee even better that the baked Alaska that you love at the Café Rouge. I guarantee it."

When Jakie did in fact ooh and aah at his mixed berry muffin, Sol insisted that he had to meet its creator in order to tell her how much he enjoyed it. He asked Stu if he could call Claudette out to meet his nephew. A minute later Claudette came out and walked over to Sol's usual booth. She was surprised to see the young man sitting with her lover and for a moment didn't know what to say. Then tentatively: "Good morning, Mr. Fairstone. Is … is this your son?"

"No, no, Mrs. Potvin, This is my favorite nephew, actually my only nephew, but he'd be my favorite anyway. He's a Harvard man. Jak… Justin, this is Mrs. Potvin who makes the muffins." Jakie stood up to shake Claudette's hand and told her that she should teach a course at Harvard in muffin baking. "This sure beats breakfast at Dunster House." The three of them shared a chuckle, and Claudette returned to the kitchen.

"Uncle Sol, Mrs. Potvin looked pregnant. I guess you'll have to go somewhere else for your morning muffin in a few months."

Sol didn't reply immediately. He took a few sips from his coffee cup and then set it down carefully while looking at Jakie. "Jakie, I want you to know that I love you very much, and I respect you. You've got a good head on your shoulders, and I need someone to talk to, someone I trust. You're not a kid any more. Next year you'll be twenty. Jakie," – he looked straight into Jakie's eyes – "Jakie, can I trust you with a secret?"

"Sure, Uncle Sol. Don't tell me that you're an ax murderer…".

"Jakie, I'm serious. You were right. Mrs. Potvin – Claudette – is pregnant. She's carrying *my* child. I love her very much. That's my secret. Jakie. Can you keep it?"

For a moment, Jakie couldn't respond. He looked at his uncle as if he were seeing him for the first time. "Uncle Sol, I don't know what to say. Why did you tell me this? How am I supposed to act with Aunt Sarah? I love Aunt Sarah. She's always been so good to me. Why did you have to tell me about you and Mrs. Potvin?"

"Why? I'll tell you why, Jakie. First, because I need to talk to someone, and there is no one else. I didn't do this to hurt Sarah. We've been married for twenty-two years, and I don't want to divorce her. But I don't get anything from her. I was first attracted to her because she was pretty and modest and sweet, not like her sister, Essie, who loved to fool around. We've had two kids together, two kids who sometimes make me sick when I look at them. But Sarah always took good care of them. Sumner's all grown up now, and he's working for me. Hope... Hope, she's a real problem. She has no sense. She either sits around looking depressed and eating fudge or she's talking nonsense about movie stars a mile a minute. I can't leave Sarah to take care of her alone. But.... but I love Claudette. I love to be with her, but always it's sneaking around. Sure, most of the people around Brunswick know that we see a lot of each other, but Sarah doesn't mix; all her friends are in Malden. No reason she should know."

Sol paused for a moment while Justin sat there staring at him. He shrugged and asked, "So what do you think of your old uncle now? What do you think your zeyde would say if he knew? My father, oy! I often think about him when I'm with Detty. I think of him because I really respect him, even though he always treated me like nothing because I wasn't a scholar. But he was a good father anyway. He taught me how to be a *mensch* and a good Jew. I wish that he understood me better, but he's my father, and I love him...". His voice trailed off, and Jakie saw a tear running down his cheek.

"Uncle Sol, I can assure you that I'm not going to tell anyone about Mrs. Potvin. But... but what do you want me to say? That I approve? I can't say that. I'm sorry."

"What I want you to say is that you will help me to take care of Detty. She's about five or six years younger than I am. Who knows how long I'm going to live? I have a will, and I'm leaving everything to the family, including you, and a few charities. I can't put Detty in my will, because then everyone would know about us. I'm going to take care of her while I'm alive; I'm going to buy her a house and a little business. I've thought this all out. I'm going to make you the executor of my will, and I'm going to set up a trust. The lawyers will work that out, but I want you to promise me that you will use that trust to take care of Detty and our child. The first reason that I told you about this was, as I said, because I need to talk to someone, but the second reason I just told you. You're the only person I could trust with this."

Justin returned for his second year at Harvard with this burden. Uncle Sol called him every few weeks to keep in touch, and he still took his nephew to the Café Rouge for baked Alaska whenever he could spare an evening in Boston. It was just after Justin returned to campus after the winter holiday break that he got a call from Sol. "Jakie, give me a *Mazel tov.* I'm the father of a healthy eight-pound boy. I'm calling from the hospital. Detty is feeling fine; she's thrilled that it's a boy. And do you know what we're going to call him?"

"I can't guess."

"After my father. You know everybody calls him Reb Yisroel, but you can't have a boy called Israel in Maine. So we're calling him by papa's English name, Isidore. I only hope that he'll be smart and respected like my father and a *mensch,* not like Sumner and Hope. Jakie, you're the only one I can tell this. I need to get a *mazel tov* from someone I love."

"Wow! *Mazel tov!* Mrs. Potvin agreed to name him Isidore? Hmmm. I wonder what Zeyde would think about having a Catholic grandson named after him."

"God forbid he should ever know, Jakie. God forbid! But we made a deal, Detty and me. He's going to be circumcised by a doctor here in the hospital, but then she's taking him to be baptized in her church. She said I don't have to be there, and it's probably best that I stay away because she has some relatives who will be there who've probably never seen a Jew. Oh, and another thing. I bought her a small house in Bath, and there's a bakery there, a nice little place overlooking the Kennebec River. She'll take over as soon as she can leave the baby alone. Nu, that's the news from Maine. How are you doing? You have enough money to go out on dates?"

"Thanks, Uncle Sol; I'm doing fine. My father gives me a small allowance, and I make whatever I need teaching bar mitzvah kids in Cambridge. And, oh, I decided to major in history, modern European history, and so far this year I've got all A's and one B."

"That's my boy. So goodbye. I'll see you next time I'm in Boston. Jakie, I love you."

"I love you too, Uncle Sol."

Essie

Essie, the beautiful younger daughter of Louie and Rochel Dubrovsky, didn't accompany her sister and Sol when they eloped. Innocently, Sarah urged her to come along with them to the Justice of the Peace whom they found in the Melrose phone book. "Essie, you're the only one who knows, and I want you to be my maid of honor."

"Don't do it, Sarah. Don't marry Sol. He's no good. He'll make you miserable. He likes to fool around. You're making a mistake."

"Essie, how can you say that. You've always liked Sol, and he likes you. How can you say those things about him?"

Essie didn't answer. She just looked at Sarah, opened her mouth to speak, and then just tossed her head, snarled and walked away. When Sarah looked for her to say goodbye before getting into Sol's truck for the ride to the J.P. and then to his parents' anniversary party, she was nowhere to be found. She had run off to the woods and sat sobbing under a tree. When she got back to the Dubrovsky house, her parents were angry. "Where have you been? We've been searching for you for almost an hour. Quick, get dressed; we've got to get to the Forshtayn anniversary party. It was so nice of them to invite us. Their boy, Sol, picked up Sarah, and they'll meet us there."

"I don't want to go!"

"Do you think we could leave you here alone, just sixteen years old? You're coming with us. Hurry upstairs and get dressed."

Reluctantly, Essie agreed to go upstairs, having decided to cut her wrists with one of her father's razors. She actually went into the bathroom, found a razor, brought it to the room that she shared with Sarah, set it down on Sarah's bed, and then took out a sheet of paper from her high school assignment book and wrote:

> *I'm sorry I had to do this, but you can blame your new son-in-law, Sol Forshtayn. They're getting married right now. Sarah asked me to be her maid of honor, but I'm not a "maid" anymore. You know why? Sol Forshtayn. He made love to me three times when he took me for rides in his truck. Each time he drove out to the pond behind Payson's farm, and we made love under that big willow tree there. Sol told me that he loved me and that we'd get married when I was old enough. If he hadn't promised me, I wouldn't have let him do it to me. But he couldn't wait. So now he has Sarah for sex. I'm not a virgin anymore, and now no one will marry me. I'm sorry, Mama and Papa. Goodbye.*
>
> *Essie*

Essie folded the paper in half and carefully placed it on Sarah's pillow. Then she picked up her father's razor and looked at it. As she was about to slice into her wrist, her father called impatiently from below: "Essie, hurry up. We've got to get going."

Essie hesitated, began crying again, and dropped the razor. She tore up the paper into little shreds and flushed it down the toilet. And then she got into one of Sarah's nicer party dresses, brushed her hair, and came downstairs. Her father growled: "It's about time, Let's go." Her mother asked: "Isn't that one of Sarah's dresses? Won't she be angry?' A surly, "I don't care! Let's go!" And they were off to the party in the Malden shul where Sol and Sarah would arrive a few minutes later to make their startling announcement. While Rowena made her snide comment to the newlyweds, Essie sat alone in a corner of the room silently vowing revenge.

The day after Essie graduated from Melrose High, she set off for New York. She was addicted to fashion magazines, and in one of them she spotted an ad for cosmetics salesladies at Bonwit Teller. Using the $180 – ten times c*hai* for good luck – that her parents had given her as a graduation present with the hope that she would put it toward tuition at Simmons, she packed a small bag and set off for South Station and New York. She had the address of their one relative in New York, a cousin of her mother who had once visited the Dubrovskys and had impressed Essie with her sophistication and her command of unYiddishized English, and she arrived unannounced at her apartment in the West 70s off Broadway. Fortunately, Cousin Debra was between husbands that year, and, after recovering from her surprise at finding a suitcase toting eighteen year old on her doorstep, she welcomed her warmly.

When Essie told Debra that she was not planning to go back to Melrose and that she intended to find a job at Bonwit Teller, Debra told her that she would help. "But first you have to get some decent clothes. They're not going to hire a farm girl in a dirndl and socks. Do you have any money?'

"Yes, I've got enough for some clothes and a room somewhere … at least until I get my first pay check."

"Fine. Tomorrow we'll go shopping. And then we'll find you a room in some boarding house for ladies around Fourteenth Street. I wish I could let you stay here, but you know how it is. I occasionally have friends in, and well, I need my privacy."

That evening Cousin Debra took Essie out to an Italian restaurant on 71st Street, and for the first time in her life, under the tutelage of her mother's Ethical Culture cousin, she ate *treif.* There was no thunderbolt launched from above, and, to put her previous life away for good, following her veal scaloppini, she brazenly added cream to her coffee. Their dinner conversation consisted of a tutorial on cosmetics in order to prepare Essie for her interview. The next day was devoted to finding an outfit suitable for a position at Bonwit Teller. Debra told her that most of the sales ladies were considerably older and that they usually dressed modestly and fashionably. They found a gray suit with a skirt that hung just below the knee, a pair of white gloves and a small hat with a veil. Debra assured her that she looked lovely and that she could pass for twenty-five. "And that's what you've got to write on your application. You can give my address for the time being; that will be more impressive than someplace downtown. And your name, Dubrovsky? Forget it. With a name like that, you won't even get an interview at Bonwit Teller. A new name… a new name… Dubrovsky…" She thought for a minute, and then: "I've got it! Dubarry! That's it; Dubarry. What a great name for cosmetics! And oh, if the conversation gets around to it, tell them that you voted for Herbert Hoover."

"But I'm not old enough to vote, and I know that my parents voted for Mr. Smith."

"I might have known that they wouldn't have the guts to vote for Norman Thomas. Anyway, just remember: you *did* vote, Miss Dubarry, and you voted for Hoover."

Thus armed, Essie did indeed get her job at Bonwit's, and she worked there for the next twenty-one years, rising to chief buyer in the cosmetics department and then one of fourteen vice-presidents. During the summer of 1950, she acceded to her sister's invitation to join them for a late-August week at the estate on Bailey Island. She had celebrated her thirty-eighth birthday the previous winter by expelling her second husband from their Riverside Drive apartment, and enough years had passed so that she could bear to be in the same room with her brother-in-law without an eruption of bile. She still loathed him and considered her sister to be a simpleton for living with him, but she had a strong attachment to Sarah and felt that she could use some sisterly support. They kept in regular telephone contact over the years, and Essie had hosted her on two occasions when Sarah traveled to New York to attend Hadassah conventions. But this visit to Maine marked the first time that Essie slept anywhere near Sol in almost a quarter of a century.

Justin arrived unannounced at the Fairstone estate the day after Essie's arrival. His was an open invitation, and he knew that there were always rooms available in his uncle and aunt's spacious home. He had just completed his second summer as a counselor at Camp Herzl where he had been promoted to assistant educational director. When the regular camp season ended, Justin and three other counselors stayed on for three days with the camp director to close up the place for the winter. He looked forward to those three days, not only because of the absence of two hundred raucous pre-teens but more so because of the presence of Tova Adar, the luscious Israeli song leader. Tova was completing her national service by working at a Zionist summer camp. Her job: to encourage impressionable pre-teens to think of Israel as their potential homeland. Although she was a few years older than he, Justin had lusted after her all summer. Completing the quartet of camp closers were his friend and Harvard classmate, Sherm Notkin, and a pleasantly buxom girl from Georgia, Gloria Stone.

Tova had had more suitors than she could handle during the eight weeks of the regular camp season. First, there were the two male Israeli *shelichim,* both of whom were veterans of the War of Independence and who thrilled the campers with stories of heroic victories and brave comrades lost in defense of the Holy Land. And then there were the older male counselors, most of them graduate students, who seemed to know how to interact with a nubile young woman. Justin was, to his dismay, still a virgin. He dated a lot of Radcliffe girls and had even managed to unhook a fair number of bras. (He knew exactly how many.) His hands had reached those hidden regions that he yearned to explore more fully, but he had yet to score. When he found out from the camp director that Tova Adar would be staying on as part of the closing crew, he volunteered himself and Sherm to complete the required quartet.

Cleaning up, retrieving lost articles, filing educational materials, storing sports equipment and a dozen other tasks kept the four of them busy all day, but the nights were free. Sherm had a car, and all four of the volunteers were sick of camp food, especially after the departure of the chef. The choice was between cold cuts from the mess hall freezer and the Friendly's on the road to Nashua. The three Americans were all semi-kosher and confined themselves to fried scrod or tuna fish, but Tova's tastes ran to scallops and lobster rolls, delicacies that were not readily available in Jerusalem. She could not understand the discipline that kept her three comrades from the delights of shellfish or at least hamburgers, but she had no compunctions about sitting in a crowded booth, her left thigh cushioned by either Justin's or Sherm's right. She seemed not to be aware of the affect that she had on them, and when she and Georgia said goodnight back at Camp Herzl those first two nights, she certainly would not have claimed responsibility for the manipulations, throes and gasps that preceded the erotic dreams of the two young men.

But that third and last night….. It was beastly hot, and because of the sweat that oozed from every pore of their bodies, the thigh contact that had aroused Justin and Sherm previously was actually unpleasant. When they got back to camp, Tova said, "I can't stand this heat. Come on, let's take a swim. It will cool us off before we go to sleep."

"Great idea," Justin responded," but there's only one problem. I'm all packed up; we're leaving tomorrow morning, and my bathing suits are somewhere at the bottom of my trunk."

Sherm and Gloria agreed that theirs too were already packed, but Tova was not to be deterred. "So, we don't have bathing suits. So what. So we'll go…. eh, what do you call it here?... eh, skinny dipping. Yes?"

Justin looked at Sherm in disbelief. "Skinny dipping sounds great if it's all right with you girls. Anyone know where Mr. Bloom is? If he caught us, we'd be in big trouble."

They all looked toward the small house that he occupied with his wife, the camp nurse, on the far side of the lake. There was a light on in a second floor room, but it was otherwise dark, as was the deserted lake front. "I… I guess it's safe," Justin said. "Are you sure you want to do this?"

"*Lama lo*? Why not," Tova laughed. "We're not children; we can control ourselves, no?"

"Yes, of course," Justin and Sherm blurted simultaneously, and before another word was spoken, the two girls began to strip down. There wasn't much moonlight, but Justin had no trouble seeing the white bra and panties that were revealed when Tova stepped out of her shorts and shrugged off her blouse. His eyes were so riveted on Tova, that he hardly noticed Gloria as she kicked her clothes into a pile next to Tova's. They both ran toward the water, throwing aside their bras before diving in. "What's keeping you boys?" Tova taunted when she came up for air. "Are you so modest? The water's fine."

Sherm and Justin both had their shorts and t-shirts off when Sherm asked nervously, "Do you think we should we take off our jockeys?

"I think that they kept on their panties. It was too dark to see. I don't know. What do you think."

"If we get completely naked, they might misunderstand …."

"Misunderstand? What could they misunderstand? That we want to get laid? That wouldn't be a misunderstanding!"

"So? On or off?"

As they stood there, paralyzed, a shout from the lake: "Are you guys ever coming in? What's keeping you?"

"Come on!" Justin yelled and dashed into the lake to join the two cavorting nymphs.

The next ten minutes in the water went far beyond Justin's fantasies. The girls were not shy; they were having a wonderful time, an illicit midnight swim the night before leaving camp and the summer behind. Tova didn't object when Justin dove under water, between her legs, and hoisted her onto his shoulders. Sherm did the same with Gloria, and they had a mock fight with Justin finally losing his balance and falling beneath the surface with Tova. They came up spouting water and demanded a rematch.

Tova and Justin won the second round, and the rubber match went to Sherm and Gloria. By then they had had enough, and the night air was a lot cooler than it had been driving back from Friendly's. As they emerged from the lake, Gloria asked, "Do any of you know where we can find some towels?"

Silence. And then Tova said tauntingly, "In the Israeli army we keep each other warm." She knew enough not to lie down on the gritty sand, and so she took Justin's hand and led him to the grass fringe above the beach. "Here. Lie down and we'll keep each other warm." Sherm and Gloria followed and lay down a few feet away."

As Justin wrapped his arms around Tova, he had an uncontrollable erection and was afraid that he would spoil this unbelievable moment by prematurely ejaculating. His problem was solved when Tova, rubbing his back, whispered, "Justin, you're a nice boy and I like you, but I have a boyfriend in Israel. We're almost engaged. I know what you want, but I can't let you. I have to keep my panties on. You can look at me, and you can touch my breasts if you want to – *want to!!!* – but that's all. I'm sorry. *Chaval.*"

Justin could barely keep from crying. So close… finally… this gorgeous naked woman in his arms…. She stroking his back…. He did, in fact, ejaculate, to which Tova said chuckling, "S*hovav* – naughty boy, naughty boy! Don't be sad. Soon you'll find someone." And she kissed him on the lips, stood up and got dressed.

As for Sherm and Gloria, they remained at the lakefront long after Justin and Tova had gone to sleep in their respective cabins.

When Justin arrived at the house on Bailey Island, he was warmly welcomed by his uncle and aunt. He found that the cast of characters had been altered slightly; Sumner, now twenty, was living in a small apartment that his father had found for him on the upper floor of an old Victorian on Longfellow Street. They saw enough of each other when Sol had business at the truck depot or when Sumner ran an errand to the main office for his boss. Sarah insisted that he join them for Friday night dinners, but his presence invariably depressed Sol.

The surprise was a visit by Aunt Sarah's New York sister, Essie. Justin had heard about her over the years. His mother usually referred to her as "Sarah's sultry strumpet of a sister" whenever, as was often the case, she was bashing Sarah. He met her for the first time at the Fairstone dinner table that night, introduced by his proud uncle. "Essie, you never met our Jakie. He's like my own son. Sarah and me, we helped to raise him, and now he's going to be a junior at Harvard. So we're not doing too bad. Get to know him a little. Maybe you could learn something to take back with you to New York."

"Oh, I'm sure I could learn a lot from your Jakie. And I could probably teach him a lot too, things that they don't teach at Haavud." She directed her attention toward Jakie. "Do they call you Jakie at Haavud? That doesn't sound very Ivy."

"Well, officially my name is Justin. But the only people who call me that are my mother and my professors. My friends call me Jake. But I guess I'll always be Jakie to Uncle Sol and Aunt Sarah. Anyway, we'll have a chance to get to know each other if you're staying for a few days. Aunt Sarah told me that you're a top executive in a fancy New York store. Sounds interesting."

"And your life at Haavud sounds interesting too. What are you majoring in … aside from girls?"

"I'm majoring in European history, and," a chuckle, "I wish that I were doing as well with the girls as I am with my history courses."

"Don't tell me you're having girl trouble! You're a good looking young man; I've heard that you're intelligent; and you've got Mr. Tycoon here behind you. You've got to be kidding."

Justin blushed. "Oh I guess I've got all the dates I need, but … well, I guess I'm feeling a little disappointed about a girl at camp. I thought I was falling in love, but then … well, nothing happened, and I'll probably never see her again. Let's forget it."

"Sore topic, huh?" Essie pursued. "You should come down to New York someday. I'm sure I could fix you up with one of our young ladies at Bonwit's. '

Sol cut her off. "Our Jakie doesn't need some *shikse* saleslady. When the time comes, he'll find a nice Jewish girl from Radcliffe or Wellesley. Jakie, how about that girl you told us about from Wellesley, the one who was on the rowing team and you liked so much?"

"Oh, you mean Phyllis. She was actually a grad student. The last I heard, she got engaged to one of her professors. Story of my life. The good ones all get away."

"Maybe you're not aggressive enough, Justin," Essie suggested. "You seem a bit shy. Do you know how to romance a girl?"

"Don't go teaching him any of your tricks, Essie," Sol cut in. "Jakie is a nice boy and he'll find a nice girl, someone like him, not some fast New York *shikse*. Anyway, Jakie is here to relax and have some fun before he goes back to Cambridge. Jakie, I figured you'd be showing up one of these days, so I had one of my mechanics go over the boat. It's in tip-top shape, all ready for you. And I got a couple of new rods at Johnson's. And they sold me a few lures that they guaranteed would catch some stripers. It's at the dock waiting for you tomorrow morning if you want."

"Will you come along?"

"No, I wish I could, Jakie, but I've got important business tomorrow. I might have to go down to Boston overnight. But I'll be back in a couple of days, and we'll go out together."

There was a room on the attic floor that Sol and Sarah always referred to as Jakie's room. It had two gable windows looking out to sea, three-foot knee walls supporting slanted upper walls, on one of which Jake often hit his head when he woke up in the morning. There was also a wash stand in the room and a small bathroom just outside the door, between Justin's room and an identical one that was usually empty. Justin referred to the third floor as his suite, relishing his own private bathroom and the privacy he enjoyed, one floor and a hallway removed from his uncle, aunt and cousins on the second floor. Back in Winthrop he had a small back room, and he and his parents shared the sole bathroom. At Harvard he had to share a bathroom with two sloppy suite-mates. Aunt Sarah saw to it that he was supplied with an assortment of fresh towels and boutique soaps, and he could sleep as late as he liked, undisturbed by anything more audible than the gentle lapping of the surf, the screeches of the seagulls, and an occasional fog horn.

On his first morning on Bailey Island, Justin woke up at nine and didn't get downstairs for breakfast until almost ten. He found Aunt Sarah and Essie in the kitchen enjoying a cup of coffee together. "So you're finally awake," Aunt Sarah laughed. "I wasn't going to wake you up until noon. I could see that you were tired from camp. What can I make for you, Jakie?"

"You know what I was thinking, Aunt Sarah? I've been dreaming about those great muffins at Bascomb's that I always had with Uncle Sol. So if it's all right with you, I'll just have some orange juice and a little dry cereal, and then I'll take the car, if you don't need it, to Bascomb's. I need a fix."

"Well, I'm sorry I didn't make something special for you," feigning petulance.

"I love you, Aunt Sarah, and I love your cooking. But there's nothing like a Bascomb's muffin."

Essie chimed in. "Now you've got me interested. What is there about those muffins that could lure you away from two beautiful women who want to coddle you?"

"Come along and you'll see."

"I think I will. Sarah, we'll continue our talk about you-know-who later."

Sol had taken the Cadillac, but Sarah's Impala convertible was in the driveway with the keys in the ignition. Jake opened the door for Essie and waited until she was comfortably seated before he sat down in the driver's seat. "Well, Justin, this is exciting. You're my first date in at least two months, and we're going to have a romantic muffin. How thrilling."

"I think you're making fun of me."

"I wouldn't think of making fun of you; you're a Haavud man!"

"We don't all talk like that. I know I have a Boston accent, but I don't say Haavud. And by the way, what should I call you? Aunt Essie?"

"No! Certainly not! I'm not old enough to be your aunt, and I'm not your aunt anyway. I'm Sarah's *younger* sister. She's almost forty, but I'm still in my mid-thirties. Please just call me Essie."

"Okay, Essie it is. How did you get the name Dubarry? I know that Aunt Sarah's parents are the Dubrovskys."

"I got Dubarry the same place that your dear uncle got Fairstone – from a judge. Dubrovsky wouldn't have worked at Bonwit Teller when I started working there in 1930; no way!"

"I guess I'm lucky having a name like Ross. It's sort of neutral; it could be anything."

"Well, I don't know how it is at Haa… *Harvard,* but I think it's best not to have a name that announces your religion or ethnicity right off the bat. It's sort of like wearing a crucifix or a *chai.* Why let people judge you before they get to know you?"

They had arrived at Bascomb's, and Justin opened the car door for Essie. She took his arm as she emerged from the car. "I want you to be a proper escort."

Once inside, Justin made his way to the booth where he usually sat with Sol. When the waitress came over with menus, he said: "We don't need menus; we're just here for coffee and a couple of Mrs. Potvin's muffins."

"We haven't had any of Mrs. Potvin's muffins for almost a year. She left. She has her own place now in Bath."

"Oh, I knew she left, but I thought you might still be getting her muffins. Where's her new place?'

"It's about fifteen minutes from here, on Commercial Street, overlooking the Kennebec."

"Thanks. Sorry about that, but I wanted to introduce my friend here to one of Maine's delicacies." To Essie: "Are you willing to drive a little more?"

"Sure, why not. We're getting to know each other without the old folks around."

"I don't really think of Aunt Sarah and Uncle Sol as old folks. My zeyde is old, and my parents are pretty old. Not so much my dad, but my mother sometimes acts as if she's living in the nineteenth century."

Essie laughed. "I remember your mother. Pardon my language, but the few times I met her, I thought that she had a steel rod up her *toches*. A real prig, as I remember her. Sorry if I've offended you."

"Well, I wouldn't go that far."

"Sorry. But she's not my cup of tea."

Justin pointed out the Borden campus and the Borden Pines as they drove toward Bath with the top down. It occurred to him that it might be a mistake to take Essie to Mrs. Potvin's place. If she was there, she would probably greet him and he would have to explain how he knew her. But she probably wouldn't be there, he thought. She's probably at home taking care of her baby with someone else minding the store. Anyway, there was no reason why Essie would connect Sol with Mrs. Potvin's baby. And he had promised Essie a delicious muffin.

When they arrived at "Claudette's Kennebec Kitchen," they were greeted with the seductive odor of freshly baked goodies and Claudette behind the counter. Before they could sit down at one of the six tables, Claudette said: "I recognize you; you're Sol Fairstone's nephew, aren't you? Jake, isn't it? You go to Harvard?"

Justin colored visibly and stammered, "Y… yes; I'm Jake. Yes, I remember, we met in Bascomb's." Thinking fast and speaking very distinctly: "This is Miss Dubarry; she's the sister of Mr. Fairstone's *wife*. This is her first visit to Maine, and I told her about your great muffins. I haven't had one since last summer."

"Oh. Very pleased to meet you, Miss Dubarry. What a nice name. Are you French?"

"No, no. I'm just an ordinary American from New York. So you know Sol Fairstone?"

"Oh, yes. Everybody around here knows Mr. Fairstone. He's not as big as Bath Iron Works but pretty close. He helped me start this business."

"Oh really! How did you meet?"

Claudette paused for a minute and looked at Justin. "Well, he was a regular customer at Bascomb's when I worked there. He enjoyed my muffins along with his morning coffee. Right, Jake?"

"Right. And that's what we're here for, a couple of your muffins and coffee."

"Coming right up. How about one blueberry and one cranberry with walnuts?"

"That would be great." And they sat down.

Essie watched Claudette as her assistant poured the coffee and took two muffins out of the display case. "She's quite an attractive woman. And she can bake. Nice combination." She said nothing as the assistant came out from behind the counter with the coffee and muffins and set them down. Jake suggested that they split the muffins so that Essie could taste each of them. They sat munching and sipping silently as Claudette and her assistant served other customers.

"So your Uncle Sol is a philanthropist. I didn't know that about him."

"What do you mean?"

"Didn't you hear Claudette say that he helped her start this business? I wonder why."

Justin reddened and searched for a reply. "Uncle Sol *is* a philanthropist. He contributes to a lot of charities. A couple of years ago he was the Man of the Year for the UJA in Boston. I went to the banquet. He helps out with my tuition at Harvard too."

"You think a lot of your Uncle Jake, don't you?"

"Well, he and Aunt Sarah have been very kind to me. I can talk to them a lot more than I can to my parents."

"Mmm. You were right about these muffins. Claudette is a talented baker." And then, after a few minutes of silence, "Justin... Jake... I want to tell you something about your Aunt Sarah. She's not a happy woman."

"What do you mean?"

"She's not a happy woman because of that uncle of yours who you think is so great. You probably know that he doesn't spend much time at home, especially not in the winter when Sarah is in Malden and Sol stays up here. She'd be happy to move up here now that the kids are out of school, but Sol doesn't want her here. She's pretty sure that he has other women and that he sees them when he's supposedly on the road for business. And *I'm* sure that he doesn't spend all those cold winter nights up here alone. He's a pretty vigorous man, and I know for a fact that… how should I put it…. Well, he's pretty loose about sex." A pause, and then with a chuckle: "I'd say that sexually he's about the opposite of his sister."

Justin was embarrassed. "I don't know about that. I'm sorry to hear that Aunt Sarah isn't happy. She's so nice. Some nights I drive over to Malden from Cambridge and we sit in the kitchen just talking. I've even brought a couple of girls with me to meet her. I'd never take a girl home to meet my mother. She'd scare them away. Aunt Sarah is always so sweet. She listens, and she cares."

Just then, they heard a baby's cry from the kitchen, and they saw Claudette heading that way. She disappeared for a moment and then reappeared carrying an infant and patting it on the back. To the customers: "He's hungry; I'm going back into the kitchen for a few minutes to feed him and change his diaper. Lizette will take care of you."

Essie's eyes followed her as she retreated to the kitchen. "So, she can make more than muffins. I guess she must have a husband somewhere around."

Jake immediately picked up on that suggestion. "I guess so; I haven't met him."

Essie and Justin got up to leave and went to the counter to pay the check. As Justin reached for his wallet, Essie slapped his hand lightly. "No, no; this is on me. I really enjoyed those muffins. Consider this my thank-you gift for introducing me to a new taste treat." As she accepted the change for a five-dollar bill from Lizette, she passed back a dollar. "Please tell Claudette that we not only enjoyed her muffins but we also enjoyed catching a glimpse of her baby. What's his name?"

"She calls him Izzy, but I think it's Isidore."

"Isidore! That's an interesting name, probably not too common here in Maine."

As they went out to the car, Justin's mind was racing. Why did she have to ask the baby's name? Why did the baby have to cry just then? If only he had waited a few minutes….. and then it came.

"Jake, your zeyde Yisroel, isn't his English name Isidore?"

"I think so," weakly.

"You *think* so? I remember from twenty years ago, the sign over the door to the *schlachthoiz* – 'Isidore Forshtayn, Kosher Fowl.' I'm sure I remember. My dad did business with Reb Yisroel, and sometimes I went along. Hmmm, that's quite a coincidence. A little Isidore up here in Bath, Maine. And Sol helped her with her shop. Curiouser and curiouser….".

Justin didn't know what to say and, after helping Essie into the car, he sat silently for a minute or so. Then he brightened and asked: "Would you like to see any more of Bath? It's a nice little town. The big general store is Povich's; they're pretty big here. And there's a nice little shul and the Iron….".

"No thanks, Justin. I'd like to get back to Sarah. I think she needs me more than I thought. Let's go."

When they got back to the Fairstone estate, they found Sarah sitting on the veranda reading. Essie took Justin by the hand and said: "Why don't you go down to the beach or out on the boat or something. I want to sit here with Sarah … alone."

Justin was more than willing to get away. He asked Sarah: "Are the keys to the boat on the dock in the usual place?"

"He keeps them in the cabinet beneath the sink down there. And if you want to do some fishing, you'll find a couple of rods on the dock where Sumner left them. And don't forget a life preserver, and be careful. You hear, Jakie? Be careful."

"I will. And don't make any lunch for me. I'll pull up at one of the shore places and have a fish sandwich. And if I have any luck, we'll all have fresh fish for dinner."

Justin headed the boat out past Ram Island, past Mark Island and toward Seguin Light. His mind wasn't on fishing. He was cursing his stupidity in taking Essie to Claudette's. Was Essie right? Was Sarah really unhappy? He would never have guessed it from the way that she always welcomed him and listened to him those nights in Malden. Did he tend to excuse his uncle because he was so generous to him? Here I am, he thought, on this great boat with the kind of fishing gear that my father could never afford.... His mind was awhirl with questions and self-doubts. And what about Essie? He wasn't sure whether he liked her or not. She was really quite pretty and sophisticated too. She seemed so much younger than Sarah or his mother. So much to think about, and he still hadn't gotten over his frustration over that last night with Tova. Almost twenty years old and still a virgin....

Justin shook his head and then leaned over the side of the boat and splashed some sea water on his face. "I didn't come up here to think; I do enough of that at Harvard. I'm here to relax and have fun. I'll talk to Uncle Sol. But now......"

As soon as he spotted Seguin Light on the far horizon, he idled the engine, picked a promising lure out of the fishing box, set it on the leader and put the rod in the starboard holder near the helm. He shifted to forward, trolling speed, about six knots, nudged the clicker button on the reel and turned the boat around to the southwest. He decided to troll on a straight course from Small Point to Jaquish Island. By the time he reached the gut between Jaquish and Lands End, it was after one, and he was hungry. No luck, and so he headed the boat down the bay toward Mackerel Cove and tied up for lunch.

There was no point looking at the menu. He knew what he would have – his usual fish sandwich with sides of fries and slaw. Funny; people came to Maine from all over America for lobster and other fresh-caught seafood, but Justin still couldn't bring himself to indulge. Every time that he was tempted, he thought of his zeyde. He knew the family lore by heart. Zeyde Yisroel had made a *neder* – a vow – when he was conscripted into the tsar's army. If he could get through his years of service without eating real *treif,* shellfish or pork products, he would never sit down in shul. He was reminded of his zeyde's vow every time that he accompanied him to the *Litvisher* shul in Malden. Zeyde would stand in his place from the moment that they entered until the final *Adon Olam.* The worshippers in Malden were used to seeing Reb Yisroel standing, but on those rare occasions when he spent a Sabbath in Winthrop with his daughter, people asked why the elderly gentleman with the Edwardian beard never sat down. And Justin's father, and later Justin himself, would tell the story of Reb Yisroel's vow.

Even at Harvard, Justin ate in his house dining hall only when there was no real *treif* on the menu. When there was forbidden food and no alternate, he would go to Clark's Sea Grille and order broiled halibut. Whenever he went out to dinner with his uncle and aunt, Sol would tempt him to at least take a taste of his lobster. "I know about my father's *neder,* and I respect him for it, but we're living in America and it's the middle of the twentieth century, for God's sake! You're in Maine, Jakie. Let me order you a lobster." But there was something that kept Justin from going "high *treif,*" as he thought of it. His grandparents wouldn't eat in restaurants at all; his parents would order only vegetables or broiled fish when out, although his mother thought of it as her one superstition. But Sol was a real *treifniak.* He prided himself on his love of shellfish and bacon, often invoking the old Yiddish saying, *"Az men est shain treif, zol rinnen fun moil* – If you're determined to eat *treif,* then let it ooze from your mouth." But Justin knew that for all his talk, Uncle Sol never ate ham or pork and that Aunt Sarah kept a mostly kosher house.

After lunch, Justin decided to troll down the east sides of Bailey Island, and just as he sailed opposite the "Giant Steps," he heard a sharp *zzzzz* to his right. He cut the engine, grabbed the rod and gave it a quick yank. Ah, a good one! Must be five pounds, at least. Reel in, give some slack, reel again, some slack, and reel, reel. A gorgeous striper! Ten minutes later, same spot, and he caught his second striper, more than enough for a delicious supper for the five of them. Satisfied, he headed back to the Fairstone dock and the plaudits of the two sisters. He had tried to put the family situation out of his head, but he couldn't help but notice that Sarah's eyes were red and that her enthusiasm over his catch was forced. By the time that Sol arrived a couple of hours later, Sarah had repaired her face and greeted him with the news of Jakie's catch. Sol was delighted. He clapped Justin on the shoulder and said: "I'm proud of you, and I've got just the bottle, a nice light Rhine wine, to go with it. Tonight we feast!"

To Justin's great relief, there was not a word spoken at the table about Claudette and baby Isidore. Sarah was a bit less animated than usual, and Hope was her usual sullen self, but both Sol and Essie kept the conversation flowing. They didn't engage each other, but both of them directed their conversation toward Justin. From Sol, it was mostly talk about Justin's shining future and his hope that Justin would one day be living in Maine and be able to go boating and fishing whenever he wanted. There were a couple of barbs directed to Essie, about her citified ways and her brief second marriage, and Essie responded in kind, making fun of Sol's conservative politics and especially his voting for Tom Dewey. But otherwise, Justin was the focus of attention. Essie seemed to be particularly curious about his love life.

"You mentioned that girl at camp, the one from Israel? Did you make out with her?"

From Sarah: "What a question to ask, Essie, especially in front of Hope! You're embarrassing the boy. Jakie, you don't have to answer her."

"Oh, I guess it's all right. You're always a good listener, Aunt Sarah. Maybe it runs in your family. Short answer: No, I didn't make out with her. I found out at the last minute that she was engaged to a soldier back in Israel."

"And that stopped you?"

"No," with a forced laugh, "*she* stopped me. I'll admit it; I haven't been too successful with the ladies. Maybe you can give me a few pointers, Essie. I need all the help I can get."

"Hmmm, maybe I can," eliciting a sharp look from Sol.

The next morning when Justin came down for breakfast a bit after nine, he found Essie alone in the kitchen. "Where's everyone?"

"Well, Hope was down here a few minutes ago and took a stale doughnut up to her room with one of her paperback bodice rippers; Sol left in a foul mood when he saw me coming down; and Sarah is in her bedroom. I found her there crying, so I sat with her for a while until she stopped, but she's really depressed."

"What happened? Did you tell her about seeing Claudette and her baby?"

"No, of course not. She has enough suspicions about her dear husband without my confirming them. Justin, I know you love your aunt, but don't you realize how depressed she is?

"I know that she has it rough with Hope and Sumner, but she always seems happy when I see her."

"You're just about the only person she cares for who doesn't depress her. I won't ever tell her about Claudette, and I'm sure that you won't, but Claudette is just *one* of Sol's women. Sarah has known for years that Sol fools around, to put it nicely. When the kids were growing up, he couldn't stand being around the house. He would get fed up and simply walk out. He always had 'business.' And so Sarah was left to deal with the kids alone, knowing that her husband was off somewhere enjoying himself."

She took a sip of coffee and went on. "Your mother was no help; she has about as much empathy and warmth as a slug. She used to despise your uncle when they were younger, because he was no match for her intellectually, but when he began making real money, her attitude changed. She blames Sarah for the dullness of her kids, as if Sol had nothing to do with their genes. You probably don't know it, but last winter Sarah spent six weeks in a private hospital in Manhattan because of her depression. I made the arrangements for her to get admitted to the Life Institute, and I visited whenever they allowed it. I don't know whether Sol ever tried to visit, but the doctors there wouldn't allow it if he did try. I'll say this for Sol, though; when I told him what it would cost for the Institute, he said he didn't care about the cost."

Justin listened to Essie's long recital in disbelief. "But how come I didn't know about any of this? I didn't have a clue, and I used to see Aunt Sarah at least every few weeks. Did my parents know? If they did, they never said a word to me."

Essie snickered. "Of course your mother knew. There's no way that Sol didn't tell her. But I can see why she didn't tell you. Do you know that your mother blasted Sarah on more than one occasion, accusing her of trying to take you away from her?"

"What!"

"You heard me. Since you were a little baby, your mother was jealous of Sarah because you seemed to like her so much. How do you think your mother felt when Sol would tell her that you visited them in Malden and that you would sometimes bring girls to meet them. Your mother actually used the words "alienation of affection" and threatened Sarah with a law suit."

"My God! How stupid could I be? I never had a clue about any of this." He sat for a few moments letting it all sink in. "But how could I not have known that she was away, for six weeks you said, in a New York hospital?"

"Didn't you used to call her or visit pretty regularly during the school semester? So how come you didn't know that she wasn't in Malden?"

"Come to think of it, I think I know why I didn't realize that she was away. She must have been in that Institute place while I was in France. I was taking a tutorial in post-revolutionary French history, and I got permission to do research for a paper in Paris, in the French national archives. My mother didn't want me to go, but Uncle Sol gave me the money for my air fare and hotel. I was there from January 3 to February 22. Was that when Aunt Sarah was in New York?"

"I checked her in right after New Year's Day, and when she got out, she stayed with me in my apartment, and we spent a few days shopping until she felt strong enough to go back to Malden. That was around the end of February."

"She never said a word! I remember when I drove over to Malden about a week after I got back to the States, she wanted to hear all about my time in Paris. She kept asking me if I had fallen in love with any mamselles, and I just kept talking and talking. I had no idea. God, I feel lousy."

"Justin, don't beat yourself up. She didn't want you to know, and, please, don't let her know now that you know. She would be mortified. Sol has her convinced that she's weak and incompetent and that that's why she had to go to a mental hospital. You're the last person that she'd want to know about her stay at the Institute. I'm surprised that your mother didn't tell you, just to rub it in."

"You said that Aunt Sarah was crying up in her room. Is there anything I can do?"

"I can't think of anything. If she doesn't snap out of it, I'll probably take her back to New York with me. We'll see. For now, I think that we should just act normal. You're here for some vacation between camp and your senior year. I know that it would make her feel worse if she thought that she was ruining your vacation, so just enjoy yourself, and I'll try to also."

They sat chit-chatting for a few more minutes, and then Sarah came down and joined them. She looked fine, and she immediately asked: "I'm sorry I overslept. Essie, did you see to it that Jakie had a good breakfast?"

"Not yet, Sarah. He was telling me about all the girls that he impresses with his Harvard education. He can hardly beat them off with a stick."

"Oh sure. Essie, Aunt Sarah knows about my troubles with girls. She knows the truth. I don't try to kid Aunt Sarah. She knows all about me."

"So, Essie, you didn't feed this young man? How is he supposed to keep up his strength to go out and catch fish for our dinner? Never mind. I'll make him a nice omelet, and I'll toast you a bagel, and there's the coffee."

"Sarah, you sit; I'll take care of your Jakie."

"No, no; it's my pleasure." And Sarah got to work. After the three of them finished eating, Sarah said, "You know, Essie, I feel a lot better than I did before. I think I'll do a little reading out on the lawn, and then I'll drive into Brunswick to the market and get us some nice fresh vegetables and maybe some steaks for dinner. I think Sol will be home tonight, and he likes a good steak. But if you catch some more fish, Jakie, I'll save the steaks for tomorrow."

"Sarah, you'll be okay?"

"Yes, Essie; I'm fine now. I was just a little tired when I woke up. It's a beautiful day, and I'm looking forward to going into town. Hey, I just got a thought. Maybe you'd like to go out on the boat with Jakie? Jakie, would you mind taking Essie for a spin? Maybe you could take her to one of those nice restaurants where you can sail up to the dock. I know you loved doing that with Uncle Sol."

"Sounds like a great idea. Essie, would you like to come along?"

"I don't want to spoil your fun, Justin. You probably prefer to go out alone, don't you? And Sarah, wouldn't you like me to come along with you to Brunswick?"

"No, not at all. You are my two favorite people, and I want you to have fun here. Maybe when I'm in town. I'll call Sumner. If he's free, we could have lunch together. He hardly ever comes here. And Essie, if you're going out with Jakie, don't forget the suntan lotion. There's plenty of it in the upstairs bathroom cabinet. You've got such fair skin."

"Sarah, you're a dear." And she gave her sister a kiss. "Justin, are you sure you don't mind? I don't want to be a shlepalong."

"Mind! This will be my first chance to take a beautiful woman out on a boat. Until now, it's either been my father or Sumner or Uncle Sol, and you've got them both beat for looks."

"Oh, thanks a lot! That's the best compliment I've had so far this morning.. Give me a few minutes to get on some boat shoes and shorts, and I'll meet you down on the dock."

"Better idea! Would you like to take a swim at a nice sandy beach?"

"I love to swim, but I didn't think there were any sandy beaches nearby. I guess that we could swim at the beach right here, but I checked it out yesterday, and there are so many rocks and clam shells and …".

Justin interrupted her. "If you want, we can take the boat to one of the nicest sand beaches in Maine. It'll take us pretty close to an hour to get there, but it's worth it. Uncle Sol took me to see it last summer. And there's a little restaurant just off the beach, Spinney's, where we can have lunch. How does that sound?"

"It sounds great, but …. Sarah, do you feel well enough for us to be gone until the afternoon?"

"Don't worry about me. I'm fine. You kids go off and have a nice time. It's so beautiful out today…."

Essie began laughing. "Kids?! Sarah, you've got to be kidding. I'm a New York executive, and Justin here is a Harvard *man*. But thanks."

"Essie, you're still a kid to me, my kid sister, and you could pass for a twenty-five year old. Jakie, wait 'til you see her in a bathing suit. Betty Grable's got nothing on our Essie."

"All right, enough already. Justin, give me a couple of minutes to get into my bathing suit, and I'll meet you on the dock."

Ten minutes later Essie appeared on the dock with shorts and a man-style shirt over her bathing suit. Justin handed her into the boat with a "Welcome aboard, M'lady. You'll find your life jacket and a cap in the cuddy below. And we're off."

When they got out beyond Ragged Island, Justin deployed a rod in the starboard rod holder and set the clicker. But then he changed his mind. He decided to take a chance. Maybe … And so he called to Essie who was sitting on the cushioned seat at the bow: "Essie, how would you like to fish?"

"I don't really know how except from pictures."

"Come here and I'll show you."

He eased back the throttle until they were doing about three knots, and he put the rod into her hands. "How do I hold it?"

"Here, let me show you." He got behind her and put his arms around her, putting his hands over hers as she grasped to rod. As he maneuvered the line over the side, he leaned his body against her back, and they both felt the tug as the lure hit the water. "Now we release about thirty feet of line.... Easy... easy.... And now we just flick this lever and we wait."

"Uh, Justin, I think I've got it now. You can let go." He hesitated, just slightly rubbing his crotch against Essie's buttocks. "Justin, that's enough. That's not what we came out here for, is it?"

Justin was flustered. "No, no! I just wanted to make sure that you were holding the rod steady. Really. I wouldn't think ...".

"I think you *would*, but... but... well, Justin, ... Look, let's just fish, okay?'

"Sure; I didn't mean to ... to ...".

"It's all right, Justin. I won't report you to Sarah. I know how horny young men can be. Let's forget it, okay?"

Justin returned to the helm and increased their speed to about six knots, as they continued in silence approaching Seguin Island. Essie's arms were getting stiff, and so she asked Justin to relieve her of the rod. He avoided looking at her as he took the rod, reeled in, and set it in the rod holder. It was clear to Essie that he was embarrassed and uncomfortable. Wanting to ease the tension, she said, "What a beautiful lighthouse! Justin, I'm so glad you took me out with you this morning. It's lovely out here. Tell me where we're going?"

Justin felt relieved that she seemed to be taking his crude gesture so lightly. "Well, I thought that we'd pull into Popham Beach and go for a swim. Then there's that little restaurant, Spinney's, that I mentioned where we can have lunch. They specialize in lobsters and other *treif* seafood, but I'll be able to get some fish."

"That sounds lovely. And we can talk over lunch. I think that you can use some counseling from an older woman."

Popham Beach wasn't crowded, and they found a nice spot to spread out the blanket that Sol had thoughtfully stowed in the cuddy. There were a couple of anglers casting for stripers from the beach, but no one seemed to be having much luck. The water was pretty cold, as Bay of Maine waters tend to be in June, and so after a few minutes in the water, they both lied down on the blanket and let the sun dry them off. A little after noon Justin said that he was getting hungry, and Essie agreed that it was time for lunch. They climbed up the dunes, crossed the road and found Spinney's where they were seated at a table on the screened porch and began to peruse the menu. After a moment Justin said: "I guess I'll have my usual, a haddock sandwich, but you go ahead, Essie. Order whatever you want. It won't bother me if you have a lobster. I'm liberal."

"Are you really, Justin? How liberal can you be if you don't allow yourself to try some delicious Maine seafood? Isn't that a bit old fashioned? If you're so liberal, why can't you be your own man? Are you afraid that your parents or your zeyde will find out?"

"No, that's not it. I respect my zeyde, and I respect his beliefs. He would be very disappointed if I ate *treif*."

"Justin, Justin. You're going to be a senior in one of the world's greatest universities; you're a man, at least technically. I'm sure you weren't thinking about what your zeyde taught you when you rubbed up against me on the ...".

Justin broke in. "I didn't mean to do that. It was an accident...".

"Justin, please be honest with me. I'm not your mother or even your aunt. I may be older than you, but I'm not that much older, and I'm not going to judge you. I'm not angry at you for what you did. In fact, I'm a bit flattered, if you want to know the truth. Anyway, let's get back to the menu. I'm going to start with some clam chowder. They probably have the real thing here, not the kind of tomato soup with clam flavoring that they serve in Manhattan. You want to join me?"

"I'd better not. I'll have the fish sandwich with fries."

Essie shrugged. "Your choice. I won't try to tell you what to eat. I just want you to be man enough to know your own mind. If you think that it's really wrong to eat shellfish... well, that's your choice. But make sure that it's really *your* choice and not your zeyde's."

Justin didn't answer for the few moments before the waitress came over and asked for their orders. Essie went first. "I'll have some of your clam chowder, and I'll follow it with a lobster roll and some coffee."

When the waitress looked at Justin, he blurted, "Make that two!"

"Two chowders, two lobster rolls and two coffees; right?"

"Right," Justin replied, almost shouting. And the waitress left.

"I hope that you're not doing this for my sake, to impress me. You can call her back. This is a big decision that you're making. I hope that you're doing it for the right reasons."

"I hope so too. I've been pretty sure for a year or so that I wasn't going to graduate from college still kosher. One of my friends, Danny Sheiner, promised me that he would pay for my first *treif* meal. Sorry he isn't here." Then with a nervous laugh: "I was pretty sure that by the time I graduated, I would divest myself of both *kashrut* and virginity. One down and one to go!"

Essie laughed. "You haven't eaten yet. Are you sure you'll be able to hold it down? We still have to sail back, and I don't want you hanging over the side and feeding the fishes."

"If I'm not hit by a thunderbolt from heaven when I take the first spoonful, I think I'll be okay. But I'm glad you're here, just in case."

And so it was on a hot summer day on Popham Beach that Justin Ross, beloved grandson of Reb Yisroel Forshtayn, ate his first *treif*. There was no earthquake, no thunderbolt, not even a slight queasiness. Justin, first tentatively and then enthusiastically, enjoyed his first bowl of clam chowder and his first taste of lobster, albeit heavily mayonnaised, and nothing happened, nothing, that is, except for an intriguing bit of dialogue after Justin had finished his chowder, smacked his lips and declared it delicious.

"I'm so glad that you enjoyed that, Justin. Not feeling guilty?"

"No; really, not at all. I'm surprised."

"So, as you said, 'One down and one to go.'" Essie thought for a moment and then asked, "Justin, I wonder; how much do you know about Benjamin Franklin?"

"About Benjamin Franklin? Not too much, just the usual grade school stuff – the kite and key, the diplomacy in Europe, *Poor Richard*; that's about it. I'm into French history, not American. Why do you ask?"

"Have you ever heard about his letter to a young friend who reminds me of you?"

Justin was puzzled. Where had this suddenly come from? "How does this friend remind you of me?"

"Well, it seems that this young friend was having a hard time with the ladies who attracted him. He wrote to Ben Franklin who, by the way, had quite a reputation with women, asking him whether he had to get married in order to have sexual relations. He didn't feel ready to get married; he was afraid to go to a brothel because of the stories that he had heard about diseases; and he was frustrated. He desperately wanted a woman. From the things that you've told me and the things that I've heard from Sarah, I think that you and that young man have a lot in common."

"Sounds familiar. So what did Franklin advise him to do?"

Essie was thoughtfully silent for a moment and then said, "I'll tell you back on the boat. Consider it your dessert."

This time Essie allowed Justin to pay the check, and they walked slowly back down to the beach. Essie suggested that they sit a while digesting lunch before a second quick swim, and then they climbed aboard the Chris-Craft and headed back out to sea. As they passed Popham Point, Essie said, "You know what I'd like to do? Let's sail out past Seguin Light and anchor there for a while instead of fishing. I'd like to lie in the sun for a while with no one around. Okay?"

"Fine," Justin answered flippantly; "your wish is my command."

When they were about a quarter of a mile west of Seguin, Justin cut the motor and dropped anchor in about fifty feet of water. He then asked Essie if she would like him to spread out the blanket on the deck aft and bring out one of the cushions from the cuddy. "That would be nice, Justin, and when you've made me nice and comfy, I'll tell you how Ben Franklin answered his young friend."

Once she was settled, she said: "You sit there on the bench." He did as she said and then looked at her quizzically. Then she said, "Old Ben Franklin was a wise man. He told his young friend that if he was not ready to get married, he should find himself an older woman for his 'amours,' as Franklin put it. Why an older woman? Because, he wrote in that famous letter, an older woman is more experienced and more ... discreet. Do you get what I am saying, Justin?"

Justin wasn't sure that he understood. If she was saying what he thought she was saying.... But no, that was impossible. He remembered how she had reacted to his clumsy move before they arrived at Popham. But why was she telling him about Ben Franklin's advice? Was it possible? He turned red and looking slightly past her, "I... I'm not sure what you mean."

"Oh Justin; no wonder you've had such a hard time with your girlfriends. You're not very good at picking up signals. Remember when you ordered your first *treif* meal, you said 'One down and one to go'?"

Justin nodded dumbly. "Well, Justin, it's time for dessert." And with that she reached behind her back and released the hooks to her halter. As Justin stared, she shrugged off the halter and looked at him. He sat transfixed. "I would appreciate some reaction. I think that I've kept my figure. Cat got your tongue?"

Justin gulped and said, "You're gorgeous. I... I know I'm staring, but I can't help it. But... but...Essie, please don't tease me. I've never seen a woman's breasts in daylight and without having to beg. Please don't tease me."

"Justin, I'm not a tease. I like you very much. I think that you're a lovely young man, and I know that like most healthy young men, you're hungry for sex. Think of me as Ben Franklin's older woman – experienced and discreet. This afternoon I just want to make you happy."

Justin wanted to get up and join Essie on the blanket, but he was embarrassed by the conspicuous protuberance in his trunks. Essie laughed. "Justin, Justin, come here, baby. Don't be embarrassed." Hunching over, he joined her on the blanket. "Now why don't you just remove those trunks and let your throbbing friend out." He did as she said.

"Nice! Oh, you're going to make the girls very happy once you get some confidence. That's what I'm going to give you today, self-confidence." And with that, she peeled off the bottom half of her bathing suit and, as Justin sat gawking, she took his sex in her hand. But before she could say or do anything else, Justin shuddered and ejaculated.

"Oh God! Essie, I'm sorry. You got me so excited. I couldn't help it. I'm such a jerk. It's my fault. I want so much to… to have… intercourse…. No! I want to *fuck*! That's what I want to do. I want to *fuck*! Finally! And now I've ruined it." Justin was so ashamed of himself that he thought he might start crying. He looked away.

Essie put her arm around him and said: "Justin, Justin; it's all right. I probably came on too strong. I got you over excited. Please don't be embarrassed. It's my fault. This isn't going to happen to you every time. With experience, you'll learn how to control yourself…." She sat quietly for a minute, contemplating the rapidly drying pool of semen beside her on the blanket, and then said, "Justin, do you trust me? Do you really trust me?"

His head down, still looking away, he whispered, "Yes."

"Good. Now I want you to do as I say. Exactly. Trust me?"

"Yes;" still looking away.

"Now don't ask any questions. Just do as I say. Okay?"

"Yes."

"I want you to get up…" He stood slowly. "Now I want you to climb over onto the swim platform and into the water."

"Out here? Naked?"

"Justin, there's nobody within a mile of us. Do you trust me?"

"Yes. Whatever you say." And he got up, his back to her, and climbed over the transom. "It's cold!" he yelled, "much colder than at the beach. What now?"

"I want you to just kick around in the water for a couple of minutes. If you feel like it, you can swim around the boat."

"What…."

"You said you trusted me. Just do as I say."

After a few minutes, Essie called out, "Time to climb back in." Relieved, Justin grabbed the swim platform and heaved himself in.

"Now, my dear young friend, look at your .... What do *you* call it? Not your peepee, I hope."

"Don't make fun of me. I know what you mean. It's all shriveled up because of the cold water."

"Right; now lie down here next to me, cuddle up under the blanket, and let's start again."

With that, Essie launched into an illustrated tutorial on sexual relations, not the usual fifty-minute academic tutorial, but a full hour and more in the course of which Justin ejaculated ecstatically twice .... in the proper place. He learned how to use his fingers and his tongue to give pleasure and how much pleasure he felt in giving pleasure. And when they both collapsed under the blanket, Justin did indeed cry. "Essie, I'm so happy. I can't help it. I love you! I love you! Oh, I've never felt like this."

"Justin, listen to me. You don't *love* me. You *like* me, and I like you. And right now you feel grateful. I like you very much, otherwise this wouldn't have happened. Now let's just lie quietly for a while. There's something I want to tell you. It's something intimate that I've never told anybody – well, nobody except my psychiatrist. But let's just lie here for a while. It must be after three. We should get back before five." And with that, Essie closed her eyes and seemed to fall asleep. Justin was exhausted, but he couldn't sleep. He kept replaying the momentous events of the day. He grinned as he said to himself: "*Treif* ain't shit compared to sex!"

After about twenty minutes, Essie got up and slipped back into her bathing suit with Justin focused on her every move. "Justin, I think it's time for you to get your trunks back on and to take us home."

Again, Justin followed orders. He hauled anchor, started the motor, and headed toward Bailey Island. As they passed Small Point, Essie sat down in the seat next to the helm and said:

"What I have to tell you is pretty intimate, and I don't feel comfortable shouting over the noise of the motor, but I want you to hear this before we get back."

Justin couldn't imagine what she had in mind, but there had been something nagging at him since they made love. "Essie, is it about birth control? I'm sorry I didn't have a safe, but I …".

"Justin, don't be silly. I told you that you could trust me. I had my tubes tied after I was promoted to the executive track at Bonwit's and after I saw the results of Sarah's two pregnancies. Those two things together made me decide not to have kids. But that's not what I wanted to talk to you about." She paused for a moment, gathering her thoughts, and continued, "Justin, you admire your Uncle Sol, don't you?"

"I guess you could say that. He doesn't have much education and he's very opinionated, but he's always been very kind to me, and he built up a terrific business from scratch. He helps with my tuition, and he took care of my expenses to Paris last winter, and he likes to take me out when he's in Boston." A little chuckle: "And he has the guts to call me Jakie in front of my mother. My dad only calls me Jakie when my mother isn't around. Yuh, I guess that you could say that I admire Uncle Sol. I disagree with him completely politically, but he's basically a good guy, I think."

"You've probably noticed that I don't get along very well with Sol. It all goes back to a couple of years before you were born – ancient history. But there's some history that you can never shake off. I can never shake off the fact that your beloved uncle …. he … he took advantage of me when I was a starry-eyed, stupid sixteen year old."

Justin looked at Essie. There were tears running down her cheeks. He throttled back to lessen the noise of the engine and asked, "What do you mean, 'he took advantage?' Did he force… did he *rape* you? I don't understand."

"No, Justin, he didn't rape me, well, not exactly." She dabbed at her eyes with the corner of her blouse. "I don't know why I'm crying about this now, twenty years later. But this has been an emotional day, and I've finally found someone who I want to share this horrible secret with. Anyway, getting back to the subject of rape, I guess that they would call it statutory rape today because I was only sixteen and he was twenty-three. I was a kid, and I thought that he loved me. He *said* he did and that we would get married someday. He was just about the only Jewish young man that I knew, and he was always driving out to our farm to pick up loads of chickens, and he would take Sarah and me out for rides. It was fun to drive around with the two of them. But there were a few occasions when Sarah wasn't home; she sometimes went on errands for Pa. On three occasions Sol took me for rides alone, and each time he drove to a farm in Melrose, and he began sweet-talking me and putting his hands where he shouldn't have. What did I know? I was thrilled that he cared for me and not for Sarah."

Essie was no longer crying; there was a hard edge to her voice. "The first time he lay down under the tree and invited me to lie down next to him. Then he said that it was too hot to be wearing his heavy work pants, and he took them off. When he lay back down again, I could see that tell-tale bulge in his shorts, but I was so innocent that I wasn't sure what it was. He told me that he was excited and that if I didn't help him, he would be in pain. To this day, I remember his words: 'If you love me the way that I love you, you'll help me out.' Great line, and I believed him. Anyway he got me to take care of his problem, and after a while, I actually enjoyed it. About a week later, he found me alone again, and he took me out to that farm again for a replay. That second time, I couldn't have enough. Why not? We were going to get married. And then there was the third time, and I loved him. Hah! A few weeks later he eloped with Sarah. I was so devastated that I almost committed suicide. Anyway, I guess I was lucky; at least I didn't get pregnant."

Justin didn't know how to respond. He looked at Essie for a minute, and then he took her hand and kissed it. "I'm so sorry. I had no idea. So that's why you're so snippy with Uncle Sol. I wondered. And you've never told anybody about this? Not Sarah?"

"Certainly not Sarah!! Just my shrink and now you. Sarah's having a tough enough time with her suspicions about Sol's current affairs. He's really not at all discreet. It's almost as if he doesn't care if she finds out. She's bound to hear about Claudette one of these days. We found out just by going into Bascomb's. Brunswick's a small town, and Sarah's not dumb."

As they approached the Fairstone dock, Essie said: "I feel relieved that I could finally tell someone about that sordid business with Sol so many years ago. It's been a tremendous burden, and I couldn't share it with anyone for fear that Sarah would find out. I love her, and I know that you do too, but I think that it's important for you to know more about your Uncle Sol. Anyway, let's see what we can do to brighten up the next few days for Sarah."

Justin voiced his enthusiastic agreement as they tied up the boat. He wanted to say something to Essie about their relationship during those next few days together, but he didn't know how to put it without sounding horny or, worse, puerile. He glanced toward the house and, seeing no one, he took Essie's hand and looked into her eyes. She returned his look for a moment and then dropped his hand. "Justin, let's be careful. All right?" He nodded, and they went up to the house.

Hope was sitting on the front porch reading. She didn't look up to greet them, but when Essie asked where her parents were, she informed them, without looking up, that her mother was in her room with a headache and that her father was still not home.

Essie went to her room to get out of her bathing suit, dressed quickly and then went to Sarah's room. Sarah was lying on her bed with the shades drawn. As Essie approached her, Sarah sat up and asked, "Where's Jakie?" Essie told her that he was up in his room. Sarah looked around and said: "I don't want him to hear this."

"It's all right, Sarah. He's probably showering and getting dressed for the evening. What is it?"

Sarah looked around again and then said in a low voice, "I wish I had never left the house today. It's terrible. I don't know what to do, what I can say to him. I may go back to Malden." And she began to cry.

Essie put her arms around her sister and whispered, "Sarah, tell me what happened in town."

Between sobs, Sarah recounted the events of her day. It had started out nicely enough. She had called Sumner at the truck depot before leaving the house and invited him to join her in town for lunch. He suggested that they meet at Bascomb's, and she spent the rest of the morning driving down to L.L. Bean in Freeport for some sneakers and shorts and then back to Brunswick for groceries. This was her first visit to Bascomb's and she was looking forward to a relaxed lunch alone with Sumner. He was usually tense and defensive when Sol was around, and she thought that this might be a good opportunity to find out about his bachelor life in Brunswick. Their lunch was uneventful until she asked about "those famous muffins" that she heard about from Sol and Jakie. She ordered one for dessert with her tea, and Sumner began to laugh.

"M…mom, they d….don't have those m…muffins here anymore. D…dad saw to that!"

"What do you mean?"

"You m…mean you don't know about Claudette P…Potvin, the m…muffin lady, and Dad?"

"Sumner, I don't know what you're talking about. What about this Claudette whatever?"

"I'm sorry, M..mom; I thought you knew. Everyone in B…Brunswick knows. I d…didn't mean to let the cat out of …"

"What cat? What are you talking about? Tell me!"

"M…mom, take it easy. I should have kept m. ..my trap shut."

"Well, you opened it. Now tell me what you're talking about."

Sumner thought for a minute. Then, recalling the scorn that his father had so often heaped on him, he told his mother all about Sol and Claudette Potvin, concluding with the item that bothered him the most. "The b…baby's n…name is Isidore, like Zeyde Yisroel. So I'm n…not his only s…son. He n…never loved m…me, and n…now he's g…got another s…s…son!"

As Sarah recounted the afternoon's revelations to Essie, she was wracked with sobs. "What can I do, Essie? I feel like I'm falling apart. I know that Sol likes the ladies, but to hear that he has a secret son and that he set his latest *nafkeh* up in business just fifteen minutes away. That's probably where he is now, with her. I was wondering what could keep him from being here while Jakie is with us. He loves Jakie, but he must love that no good *nafkeh* even more." More sobs. "Essie, Essie, I can't take any more of this. I need help."

Essie hugged her older sister and tried to sooth her, but she couldn't stop her crying. After holding her and smoothing her hair for several minutes, she said, "Sarah, I don't think that there's anything that we can do about Sol and this woman. That's the way he is. But I'm worried about *you*. What I think that you need is some time away from Sol again, like last winter. And you need someone wise, someone you trust, to listen to you and to advise you. Let me take you to New York with me. We can check you into the Life Institute again. There you'll have time to think it all over, and you'll get good advice. I think that you should divorce Sol, but that's a sister talking. I'm no professional."

Sarah didn't answer, but her sobbing subsided. "Essie, what am I going to do about Jakie? He's our guest, and I don't think that I can even make dinner for you and him tonight. Before I saw Sumner, I bought some nice trout and fresh corn. I was going to make us a special dinner, trout almandine; I know Jakie likes it."

"Sarah, the last thing that I want you to worry about now is making dinner for us. I'll take care of that. I may be a business woman, but I can still pan fry a trout and steam some corn."

"Essie, I don't want Jakie to see me like this. I might start crying again. Just tell him that I have a headache, and the two of you, have a nice dinner."

"And what can I get for you?"

"I have no appetite. I couldn't eat anything. Just get me a glass of water and a couple of aspirin from the bathroom."

As Essie got up, Sarah added, "And you better get me a sleeping pill from the bathroom too. I don't want to go near the pills. I might do something stupid. Oh Essie, I don't know what to do. That no good *mamzer* who I love so much..... Essie, you never liked him. You knew better than me."

Essie went to the bathroom, found the pills and brought them back with a big glass of cold water. As she handed them to Sarah, she said, "I meant what I said before, about the Institute. I want to leave here tomorrow and take you with me. All right?"

"I think so. I can't stay in this lousy town. According to Sumner, everyone here knows about Sol and that woman. I can't lift up my head here." She took the glass of water from Essie, and downed the pills. "You'll explain to Jakie?"

"Yes, Sarah. I'll take care of everything. And tomorrow we'll drive to New York and you'll be in good hands." As Sarah lay down, Essie took her hand and said, "I'll sit here with you until you fall asleep. Everything will be better tomorrow. You'll see."

Fifteen minutes later Sarah was breathing evenly, and Essie left the room, carefully closing the door behind her. Justin was waiting for her in the hallway. "I heard some of that. She sounded terrible. And with everything that that idiot Sumner told her, she's still worried about being the gracious hostess. I wish that I could do something for her. She's always doing things for me."

"The best thing that you can do for Sarah is to say nothing. I'll rent a car tomorrow, and we'll drive to New York. Don't ask her any questions tomorrow; just give her a hug and say goodbye."

"Do you want me to come along? I'll do whatever you say."

"No, no! I'm sure that she doesn't want you to know that I'm checking her into the Institute again. As far as you know, I'm taking her back to New York with me for a nice shopping spree and a couple of plays. That's our cover story."

"And what about Uncle Sol? I'll be surprised if he doesn't come back tonight or tomorrow. He's never been away for more than a day when I'm here."

"If Sol shows up, I'll have a few choice things to say to him. Otherwise, you'll have to tell him. But come on now. Help me in the kitchen. We don't want to waste all that good food that Sarah bought for us. I promised her that I'd feed you. Come to think of it, you must be pretty hungry after our fishing expedition."

"I guess I still have my appetite. Love to help."

They were almost finished with dinner when Sol walked in with a big smile on his face. "Jakie, I'm so sorry that I had to be away today, but I'll make it up to you. Here, give me a hug."

As Justin got up hesitantly to go to his uncle, Essie cut him off. "Sol, stop playing the loving uncle! We've got some serious talking to do… Now!"

"What? I can't hug my favorite nephew? You're planning to make trouble between us? What…"

"Enough bullshit, Sol. Here it is. Sarah knows about you and the muffin lady and baby Isidore. God forbid that your father should ever hear about that!"

Sol paled and stood stock still staring from Essie to Justin and back. "What? How…? You told her, Jakie?"

"Forget about Jakie, you shit! It was Sumner who told Sarah, at lunch this afternoon in Bascomb's. According to Sumner, the whole town knows about you and your bastard. Poor Sumner is worried that little Isidore will take his place. But forget about Sumner. It's Sarah that I'm worried about. You didn't think that she would ever find out? How stupid can you be?"

Sol tried to find some words, but he could only hang his head and wait to hear whatever else Essie had to say.

"Sol, I'm taking Sarah back to New York with me tomorrow, and I'm checking her into the Life Institute again. They did a good job with her last time. She feels safe there. Right now she's sleeping soundly. I gave her a pill. That should take care of her until tomorrow morning. Here's what I want you to do…".

"But… but I've got to go in to see her, to explain…."

"EXPLAIN!! You're going to EXPLAIN!? She doesn't want to see you. If you go near her in this condition, she'll have a complete breakdown. Just stay away from her."

"But..."

"But nothing. Here's what you're going to do. You're going to arrange to have a limo with a driver here tomorrow morning at about ten. I can get her ready and put together a few of her things by then. And when the bills start coming from the Institute, you'll just pay them. No questions, however long it takes. And you'll get out of this house tonight. Go to your muffin lady if you want, but don't let Sarah see you."

When he could finally speak, he weakly assented, but then he asked, "What about Hope? Where is she, and does she know?"

"Hope, as usual, is in her own private little world. She didn't come down to dinner, so I brought a plate to her room. She was sitting there listening to some god-awful music and reading one of her books. She didn't even look up. What you should do about her? After we leave tomorrow, you come back here and take care of her, or get someone to do it for you."

"And, Jakie, what about you?" he asked softly.

"I'm not sure what I'll do, Uncle Sol. I may stay here another day or two, and then I'll go back to Winthrop until I have to get back to Cambridge. Don't worry about me. If you want, I can take Hope out for lunch and dinner tomorrow. Aunt Sarah's car will be here, I guess."

"Yes, yes, Jakie. You use the car. And maybe we can still have some time together. I... I wanted to go out fishing with you and take you to the summer theater and...".

Essie cut in. "Enough already, Sol. Just get a few things and clear out. I don't want to talk to you anymore. Just make sure that there's a car and driver here by ten." And with that, she turned away and headed for Sarah's room to check on her. She sat by her bed in the dark room and waited until she heard the front door close and Sol's car starting up. When she came out, she found Justin in the kitchen finishing up the dishes. He looked at her helplessly, and she came over, hugged him and said, "Sorry you had to be here for all of that, and thanks for cleaning up and volunteering to look after Hope for a day or two."

She thought for a moment and then said, "Let me make a pot of coffee. Then let's sit out on the porch. I have some things that I want to tell you."

When they were settled comfortably in their Adirondack chairs sipping their coffee, Essie said. "Beautiful night. Look at those stars out over the water. What a contrast! – what's going on with Sarah and Sol and this peaceful night with the sound of the waves lapping down there."

Justin breathed a pensive hmmmm and then said, "What a contrast! You and me out on the boat about five hours ago and that scene with Uncle Sol. I don't know what to think."

"Well, that's why I want to talk to you. I'll be leaving with Sarah tomorrow morning, and I don't know when we'll see each other again. Maybe never. But there's something I've got to tell you right now before you ever say the words 'in love' to me again, like you did out on the boat.

"Justin, I like you very much, and I'm happy that we made love this afternoon. Yes, I said '*made* love,' not '*in* love.' Justin, before I came up here, a very dear friend in New York asked me to marry him. I *think* that I'm in love with him; I know that he loves me. He's a professor at Columbia, and he's divorced. He was married for about twenty years, and he has two kids. He's a fine man, a real *mensch,* and he's brilliant. We go to concerts and plays together; we're both commited liberals; and we're both addicted to *Sunday Times* crossword puzzles. The reason that I came up here was to get some space between us so that I could decide whether or not to accept his proposal. I've already been burned twice, and I don't want it to happen again. Well, I've decided. And in very different ways you and that *mamzer* Sol helped me decide. I made mistakes in my two previous marriages, but I don't think that I'm making a mistake this time. After I get Sarah settled at the Institute, I'm going to tell Rob that I'll marry him. That's it."

Justin sat there silently, trying to absorb everything that Essie said. It was a long silence, and then, "Essie, I don't know what to say. You're a lot smarter… no, *wiser* than I am. Forget about all of that Harvard crap. Two days with you, and I feel that I've grown up, and I don't mean just the sex….Wow, the sex! It was fantastic!.... But I learned a lot more than that from you. Okay; I won't say I'm *in love* with you, but I do love you. So you're going to marry your professor. What can I say? I hope you'll be very happy. There's no one that I'd like to see happier than you. I mean it…. Is it all right for me to hope that we'll see each other again someday? Maybe not as lovers but as real friends?"

"Yes, dear Justin, as *best* friends. But now it's getting late, best friend. It's been a very long day, and I'm tired." Essie got up and took a step toward the door. Then she stopped and looked back at Justin who was still seated, pensive, his head down. Very quietly, almost in a whisper, she said, "One last thing, dear friend. Do you mind if I join you up in your attic tonight?"

Rowena

Justin had hoped that his zeyde and bobbe would have the pleasure of seeing him graduate from Harvard, especially his zeyde who had been his teacher since he was four. One of the great triumphs of his years at Harvard was a direct result of his zeyde's tutelage. It was during a survey course on the great books of Western Civilization that the world-renowned *litterateur*, I.A. Richards, made what was to Justin a startling remark during a lecture on the Hebrew prophets. In his high-pitched, British-accented voice, he stated matter-of-factly that Huldah was the only woman in the Bible identified as a *neviah* – a prophetess. It was on a Monday morning, just two days after Justin had been sitting in the Winthrop synagogue near his zeyde who, as usual, was standing during the reading of the Torah. Justin was following the chanting of the weekly portion from Exodus when his zeyde came over to him, as he often did to point out some interesting interpretation to his *einekl*.

"Yaakov, *zissinke,*" he asked in Yiddish, "did you notice what it says in the text about Miriam when she led all the Israelites in the Song of the Sea after they passed through the *Yam Suf*?"

Justin looked up at Reb Yisroel and answered: "You mean where it identifies her as the sister of Aaron rather than the sister of Moses? I remember you taught me about that."

"You're right, but that's not what I meant. Just before that. What does the Torah call her?"

"It calls her *Miriam ha-neviah*."

"Right; *Miriam ha-neviah* – Miriam the prophetess. Very unusual. Sarah wasn't a prophetess; Rebecca wasn't a prophetess; not Rachel either. In the whole Torah, only three people are called prophets. So who are they?"

"Well, Moses, of course, and ...," he thought for a moment, "wasn't Abraham called a prophet by somebody?"

"Right you are, *mein klugger*; you remember good. Avimelech called Abraham a prophet. So it's those two men, as you could expect, and the only other one in the whole Torah is Miriam. *Nu*, that's what I call equal rights! A woman, too, can be a prophet, according to our Torah. And then, later in the Bible, there are more. Tell that to your mother who thinks that everything in the Torah is old-fashioned. Tell her that the Torah came before Eleanor Roosevelt and Golda Meir."

As soon as Professor Richards completed his lecture, Justin went up to him and asked, "Professor Richards, did you say that Huldah was the only woman in the Bible who is called a prophetess?"

"Yes, that's right, my boy."

"But how about Miriam and Deborah?"

"They were not prophetesses. Only Huldah is identified by that Hebrew word *neviah*. No other."

"But..."

"You must not have read the text in the original Hebrew." And he turned away.

Justin stood there stunned. This man was teaching at *Harvard!* He was a distinguished professor, the author of several books, and he didn't know his Bible!! It was a liberation, an epiphany for Justin. "I know more Hebrew Bible than this master of English literature," Justin thought. "So he's written a bunch of books. So what? If I want, I'll write books too. Big deal!"

As it turned out, neither of Justin's grandparents attended his graduation. Bryna Forshtayn had died of a heart attack, complicated by diabetes, during his freshman year. At first Reb Yisroel continued to live by himself in their tenement apartment near Suffolk Square. He wanted to stay in Malden near his beloved *Litvishe* shul and the *schlachthoiz* where he had always made a decent living. But times were changing, and along with them the retail poultry business. The Jewish matrons who lived around Suffolk Square had discovered that they did not have to go to a slaughterhouse, pick out a live chicken, watch the *shochet* dispatch it, and then gossip with some old lady as she flicked it in order to put a decent kosher chicken on her table. Supermarkets had arrived on the scene, and some of them actually had packaged kosher birds, devoid of the ugly *penkes* that often escaped the notice of the chicken flickers.

These new economic developments, plus the fact that Bryna was no longer around to trade vital information about children and grandchildren with the customers, led to a severe reversal in Reb Yisroel's business. He kept the *schlachthoiz* open until 1948 when Justin left home for Cambridge, but then he had no excuse for staying in Malden. He considered acceding to his daughter-in-law Sarah's invitation to come live with them in the Maplehood section where he would still be able to walk to his shul, but he was not confident about her level of *kashrut.* After all, her parents were farmers in Melrose where there wasn't even a shul or a Hebrew school. And his son, Sol; what did he care about a proper Jewish home? And so Winthrop and Rowena's home was the only viable option.

Actually, it was not Rowena who first came up with the idea of inviting her father to live with them. It was Isaac's idea. It had been his deep respect for Reb Yisroel Forshtayn that convinced Isaac Ross in the first place that his daughter would be a good match. Raizel, who insisted on being called Rowena, was a voracious reader and a natural born teacher. Over the eight years that she had been on the English faculty of Malden High, she had succeeded in shepherding well over a score of her students into Harvard and Radcliffe. It was true that her high standards and often cutting remarks soured at least twice that number on academia, but the principal of the high school was in awe of her. She was his Roget and Bartlett combined, always ready with the word or the quotation that he needed.

Reb Yisroel yearned for a grandson who might inherit his love of learning and delight in the literature of ancient Israel. He was resigned to the fact that his son Sol would never produce such an heir, but Raizel was another story. If only.... a child with her intellect if not her acerb manners.... a child who might replace his sweet Ephraim who, if he had not been trampled to death so long ago in Vilna, might have been a rabbi or a professor.

When Reb Yisroel first brought Isaac Ross home to meet his Raizel, he feared that she would attempt to humiliate him, as she had done with other young men whom he considered suitable. And, in fact, the more that he praised Isaac's devotion to Torah, the more skeptical Rowena became. But when she, intending to brush him aside with an obscure quotation from St. Vincent Millay, was caught up short as he completed the verse, she was left gawking and the die was cast. She needed a husband, and he seemed intelligent enough – and meek enough – to fill the bill.

Isaac made a very modest salary in the Winthrop Hebrew school, but he was able to supplement it by preparing taxes and balancing books for more than a dozen of the shopkeepers on Shirley Street. With some help from Reb Yisroel, he and Rowena bought an old twelve-room house on Neptune Avenue, three houses removed from the beach. And it was in that house that Reb Yisroel lived out his final years. Rowena was initially opposed to her father's moving in with them; the last thing that she wanted was to take care of an old man still in mourning after three years for his Bryna. How could she invite the ladies of the Garden Club to their home with a grieving old man who spoke a broken Yinglish sitting around? But both Isaac and Justin insisted. They revered him. When they accompanied him to the synagogue, they were proud of the way that he stood erect at his lectern at a corner of the eastern wall praying with utter devotion. And they were even more proud on those frequent occasions when Rabbi Epstein came down from the *bimah* to share some esoteric gleaning from the Torah portion with their father-in-law and grandfather.

If Rowena resented the presence of her father in her home during the two years when he was in perfectly good health and kept his room immaculate, how much more so when he had an almost fatal stroke right after the family Passover *seder* of 1950. Sol and his family were in the foyer putting on their coats for the ride back to Malden. Reb Yisroel had expressed his disapproval of their driving on the festival. He wanted to know why they couldn't sleep over in that big house and go to synagogue with him the next morning. But Sol was insistent, assuring his dubious father that he would go to the Malden shul. Disgruntled, Reb Yisroel went back to his seat at the table and began softly chanting the traditional *Song of Songs. "Yishokeni min'shikos pihu ki tovim dodecho miyayin...."* Suddenly he stopped with a groaned *Oy!* and his head dropped onto his big *Haggadah.*

Justin, who had been listening to his gentle chanting, was the first to notice that something was amiss. He went over to his zeyde and prodded him lightly on the shoulder. No response. Then Isaac and Sol rushed over to him calling "Papa, Papa, what's the matter?" No response. They could hear labored breathing, but Reb Yisroel was otherwise lifeless. Isaac ran to the phone to call for an ambulance, but Sol intervened. "There may not be time. Sumner, run out to the car and start it up. Quick! Isaac, call your doctor and tell him to meet us at the hospital!" And with that he heaved his father up as he would a chicken coop, carried him out to the car, and carefully lay him down across the copious back seat of the Cadillac. Justin grabbed his coat and yelled, "I'm coming along." Less than fifteen minutes later, Reb Yisroel was lying in a bed in the Winthrop Memorial Hospital being attended to by Dr. Fleisher.

After a tense two days, Reb Yisroel who had suffered a stroke was stable enough to be transferred to Beth Israel Hospital in Boston. Sol insisted on round-the-clock nursing care and consultations with Boston's finest neurologists, making it clear to Rowena and Isaac that he would take care of whatever expenses were incurred. After two weeks the doctors informed the family that, while Mr. Forshtayn was out of any immediate danger, it was highly unlikely that he would regain the ability to communicate in any intelligible way. He had progressed from grunts and monosyllables to strings of two or three words, but it was painful to watch him struggling to express himself. He was also almost totally paralyzed on his right side and could not take care of his personal needs.

When the time came for Reb Yisroel to leave Beth Israel, Rowena wanted to put him in a nursing home, but Sol, Isaac and Justin felt certain that that would be a death sentence. He needed to see familiar faces and feel their loving concern. There was only one solution, and that was to go back to the Ross home in Winthrop. Rowena objected, insisting that she was incapable of handling her father in his current state. "He would be even more mortified than I if I had to take him to the bathroom or change his diapers. No! I can't do it. There has to be some other solution." And there was.

Sol made inquiries at the hospital and got the names of two male nurses who, for the price he offered, would put in ten-hour shifts caring for Reb Yisroel. There was plenty of room in the Ross home for live-in help, and again Sol assured his sister and brother-in-law that he would cover all the expenses for the nurses and medications. "And I'll throw in another hundred dollars a week for your trouble." Isaac said that that would not be necessary, but Sol insisted. "You're going to be there with him while I'm away in Maine. You deserve every penny. And I'll come to visit every week, and Sarah can drive in from Malden a few times a week to help."

Rowena was still doubtful, but the matter was settled when Justin added his voice to the discussion. "Mom, you can't say no.

This is Zeyde! Zeyde! I love him. He's the best teacher I ever had! You can't send him to a nursing home with *goyim*. He would die there in a week. I promise. I'll come home from Cambridge every weekend and once or twice during the week to help. Please, Mom."

It wasn't easy for Justin to give up his weekends and whatever spare time he had while finishing up his senior courses and writing his history honors thesis. And there was a further complication. He had begun dating a Radcliffe freshman whom he had met at a joint rehearsal of the Harvard Glee Club and the Radcliffe Choral Society. They were preparing to sing the Berlioz *Requiem* with the Boston Symphony, she with the altos and he with the baritones. He had heard her name, Shelley Newman, called during a roll call and decided that she must be Jewish. She had a pretty face with an upturned nose and her hair was a light brunette, reminding him of Essie who still featured prominently in his dreams. And so, during one of the rehearsal breaks, he approached her with a directness that he had never demonstrated B.E. (Before Essie).

"Hi, I'm Justin and you're Shelley. I'm a baritone and you're an alto, and we're both going to be singing at Symphony Hall next month, so I thought we should get to know each other." He extended his hand to her and, after a moment's hesitation, she giggled and took it.

"Justin what?" she asked as he held her hand.

"Justin Ross. I know your last name is Newman, because I heard it during roll call."

"Please don't take this the wrong way, but is Ross a Jewish name?"

"Yes, and I'm taking it for granted that Newman is a Jewish name too. There aren't many Jewish kids in the Glee Club or the Choral Society, so I thought that I'd take a chance with Newman."

"Well, you were right. But Justin? That's not very Jewish. Sounds like a name out of a romantic British novel, Sir Justin of Stonehenge! How's that? But seriously, how does a Jewish boy get a name like Justin?"

"Blame my mother. My Hebrew name is Yaakov, Jacob, named after my father's father. But you hit the nail on the head. My mother is addicted to all things British. Her own name was originally Raizel, but she changed it to Rowena, straight out of Sir Walter Scott. My father wanted to name me Jacob, but my mother insisted on Justin, so Justin it is."

Justin found that he enjoyed talking to Shelley and so after the rehearsal, he took her to Brigham's for ice cream, and that became their pattern over the following three weeks of rehearsals. By the second night they were holding hands as Justin walked her back to the Radcliffe dorms, and by the third they shared a brushed kiss. She was majoring in Music History and taking voice lessons at the Longy School of Music a few blocks from the Harvard Yard. She came from Philadelphia and was part of a family active in the Jewish community. By the week of the concert, a week before the fateful Passover of Reb Yisroel's stroke, they were sharing soulful hugs and kisses, but Shelley made it clear that Justin was not to let his hands stray. The first time he tried, she rebuffed him with, "Justin, we're not ready for that. We hardly know each other." The second time she surprised him with "Justin, you told me that you learned with your zeyde. Did he ever teach you about *tzniyut*, Yaakov?" She emphasized the name that he had told her his zeyde always used when they studied together."

Justin froze and then admitted shamefacedly that he knew about the traditions of female modesty. "Justin, we've become good friends in a short time, and I hope that we can become even better friends, but I'm not ready. You'll have to respect that or…".

He didn't let her finish. "Okay, Shelley, okay. I'm not going to risk ruining this. I like you a lot. Peace?"

"Peace." They had arrived at her dorm and she lifted up her face for a goodnight kiss, properly modest but lingering.

There were two performances of the Berlioz, Friday afternoon and Saturday night. Justin had raved to his parents about the way that the conductor, Charles Munch, not only directed the orchestra and the combined choirs, but how he turned around as the orchestra attacked the *Tuba mirum* and motioned in brass players in four corners of the second balcony for a wild crescendo. He insisted that they attend the Saturday night performance, but Rowena, using preparation for the Passover *seder* as an excuse, demurred. As so it was to his father alone that Justin introduced Shelley after the concert when they met as prearranged at the stage door. Isaac insisted on taking them to the Amalfi for some pasta and spumoni, and they spent a delightful hour re-experiencing the thrilling concert. The charter busses had already driven back to Cambridge with most of the choristers, and so Isaac drove Justin and Shelley back to their dorms. He made it a point to invite Shelley, to whom he had taken an immediate liking, to the *seder*, but Shelley was flying back to Philadelphia for two days to celebrate the holiday with her own family. As Justin sat in the hospital late that *seder* night, he thought how fortunate it was that Shelley had not joined them at their *seder*. He would not have wanted her to see him sitting in the waiting room crying.

There were two bedrooms, Justin's and the guest room, on the ground floor of the Ross home, in addition to a living room, dining room, family room, bathroom and kitchen. With Justin living in Cambridge, his room was available for Reb Yisroel, and the guest room became the nurses' room. There were two bedrooms on the second floor in addition to the master bedroom shared by Rowena and Isaac on those increasingly rare nights of marital harmony. One of the many reasons that Rowena did not want her father and his nurses taking over the two lower floor bedrooms was that she did not want Justin sharing the second floor with them when he could get away from Cambridge. In his downstairs room Rowena thought that Justin was unaware of the many nights when his father was relegated to one of the smaller upstairs rooms. But their house was an old one with creaky floors, and Justin could not help but be aware of the late night movements just above him, to say nothing of the muted sounds of his mother's scathing reproaches. Usually it was the tenuous state of their finances that inspired Rowena's tirades, but there were also shrewish remarks about this or that wife of one of Isaac's accountancy clients or one or another of the Hebrew School mothers who might have spent an extra minute talking to Isaac or who might have looked at him in some way that set off Rowena's internal alarm system. With a stranger in the guest room downstairs and Justin in an upstairs room two or three nights a week, Rowena had to censor both her tongue and her moods, increasing her resentment at the presence of her helpless father.

Within a few days of Reb Yisroel's invalidhood in the Ross home, a routine was established. His nurse had him out of his bed, washed, dressed in clean pajamas and a robe, his hair and beard neatly combed, his *yarmulke* perched on his head, and seated in his wheelchair facing the family room windows that looked out to the ocean. He made feeble attempts at feeding himself with his one good hand, but the slowness of his movements was frustrating both to himself and to the nurses who usually took over after a few minutes. The weather was pretty good that May, and so on most days his nurses would wrap him in a blanket and wheel him out to Shore Drive mornings and afternoons for some fresh sea air. On rainy days he just sat at the window mumbling incoherently.

On those days when Justin could get to Winthrop, he insisted on taking his zeyde out for his excursions down Neptune Avenue to the shore. He tried to figure out what it was that Reb Yisroel was trying to say, but it was mostly garbled syllables of Yiddish. There were two syllables, though, that were repeated over and over again and that were unmistakable. "Frayim, Frayim," he would cry, looking around and gesturing with his good left arm. "Frayim, Frayim," like a sob.

Justin asked his parents over dinner one night what Zeyde could possibly be saying or calling. They had no doubt. His mother explained with uncharacteristic gentleness and sympathy that he was calling for his baby son, Ephraim, who was trampled by tsarist cavalrymen almost half a century earlier. "I think that he wants to go to Ephraim. I'm sure he doesn't want to live the way he is now."

Isaac added, "He must really have loved Ephraim. I remember sitting near him on at least two occasions at *Selichot* services when the cantor began singing that beautiful passage from Jeremiah, "*Ha-ven yakir li Ephraim* – Ephraim is my dearly beloved son." Both times I remember him standing at his lectern with tears rolling down his cheeks. I think you're right, Rowena. He wants to be with Ephraim. This is no life."

In the third week of May, Justin was informed by the History Department that his thesis had been approved and that he would graduate with honors. He ran over to Agassiz to find Shelley before she could sit down to lunch there with her girlfriends. As soon as he saw her, he ran to her, grabbed her hand and said: "Let's have lunch at the Window Shop. I have some good news." He wouldn't tell her until they were seated at an outdoor table perusing the Viennese menu. As soon as they had ordered, he blurted it out: "They accepted my thesis! I'll be graduating with honors! And that means that I'll probably get into Yale or Chicago for my Ph.D." But he did not get the response that he had anticipated.

"Oh, congratulations," in a muted voice. "I'm happy for you."

"Gee, Shelley, can't you muster up a little more enthusiasm?"

"I'm sorry, Justin. I know how much this means to you, but…."

"But what? What's the matter?"

"Justin, sometimes you can be dense. Did you think for a minute about what this means to *me*? I knew that something like this was probably going to happen. You're going to go off to New Haven or, even worse, Chicago, and I'm going to be here in my sophomore year. I don't know; I thought maybe that you'd somehow be able to stay around Boston."

"Shelley, I applied to the grad school here; they accepted me, but no fellowship.. And if I stay around Boston doing something else next year, I'll be drafted. I've got to go to graduate school somewhere or else I'll be spending the next few years in Korea."

"God forbid! Don't even say that! I don't know. I'm sorry. Really, I'm happy for you. Forget what I said. Anyway, I've got a two o'clock. I've got to get going."

"Okay. Look, I don't have any classes this afternoon, so I'm going to Winthrop to tell my parents my good news and to sit with Zeyde for a while. I wish I could make him understand. He'd be even prouder than my mother and father."

"Are you coming back tonight?"

"Yes, I've got a nine o'clock tomorrow morning. I should be back before ten. Do you want to meet at Brigham's?"

"Sure. See you then." But, as it turned out, he didn't see her then or for the next three days.

Neither Rowena nor Isaac was home when Justin arrived, but he found his zeyde sitting in his wheel chair in the family room staring out at the sea with Bill Andrews, his nurse, sitting across the room reading. Justin had met Bill on a couple of occasions and, after exchanging a few pleasantries and learning that his mother would be back by about five, he told him that he could take a break if he wanted to. Justin would sit with Reb Yisroel until his mother returned. While the two of them were talking, Reb Yisroel kept repeating "Frayim, Frayim" followed by some syllables that Justin couldn't decipher at first. But when he pulled up a chair to sit next to Reb Yisroel and took his hand, he thought he recognized the words "vu ... vubitu...vubitu." Justin was pretty sure that he understood. Zeyde was calling out to his baby son, "*Vu bist du?* – Where are you?" That must be it.

Reb Yisroel dropped off for about half an hour, and when he awoke, he started again with his plaintive litany, "Frayim... Frayim.... Frayim....". Justin felt tears welling up in his eyes, and he gently squeezed his zeyde's hand. Reb Yisroel sat quietly for a few moments and then began again. "Frayim... Frayim...vu... vubitu... vubitu." Very softly, Justin answered him. "*Tateh, ich bin doh. Tateh, ich bin doh.*" Reb Yisroel slowly turned his head toward Justin and stared at him, trying to comprehend. "Frayim! Frayim!" Again, Justin squeezed his hand and answered, "*Tateh, ich bin doh, ich bin doh.*" There was no question about what Reb

Yisroel said next. It was as if he experienced a spasm of lucidity. Very clearly, he said, *"Frayimke, zissinke, ich kum, ich ….,"* and his head dropped to his chest.

Startled, Justin dropped his zeyde's hand and stared at him for a minute. Then, frightened, he called, "Bill! Bill! Come here!" Bill ran in from the next room, immediately grasped the situation and took Reb Yisroel's wrist, feeling for a pulse. Then he tried his neck. Nothing. And to Justin, "I'm afraid he's gone. I'm sorry. He was such a nice man. We've got to let your parents know."

Bill had the phone number of the Hebrew School where the secretary answered and ran to Isaac's classroom with the news. Five minutes later, Isaac was home comforting Justin who was in tears. Taking Justin by the hand, he stood with him next to Reb Yisroel and asked, "Jakie, you know what we say at a time like this?' Justin nodded; "Zeyde taught me. We can say it together." They both took *yarmulkes* out of their pockets and, looking at Reb Yisroel, recited, "*Baruch dayan ha-emet* – Blessed is the true judge."

There was no way to reach Rowena who, following the pattern that she had established as soon as her father was settled in their home, had gone into Boston for some shopping at Jordan's or Gilchrist's or Filene's. She arrived home just minutes before the men from Stanetsky's Funeral Home and didn't seem at all surprised at the death of her father. She took charge immediately, without shedding a tear or asking any questions. "I've got to call Sol. He's probably in Maine, but he might be in Malden. He's been spending more time there since Sarah came back from her asylum in New York. I'll try there first."

As it turned out, Sol was indeed in Malden. Unbeknownst to Rowena, Essie had demanded of Sol that he act like a dutiful husband if Sarah was to come back to Malden. She threatened to tell his father and his sister's family about his, as she put it, "priapism" if he did not begin behaving decently toward Sarah. She went so far as to imply that she would have no hesitation even about revealing what Sol had done with her all those years back. "And," she added, "I don't think that you want a divorce.

I've already spoken to my lawyer about it, and take my word for it, Sol, it will cost you!"

As it happened, Sol did *not* want a divorce, and it wasn't because he was afraid of the financial consequences. He had never stinted on Sarah or the kids. But he was contemptuous of people, Essie being his prime example, who divorced easily. And, truth be told, he did love Sarah in some warped way. He wanted to remain married and at the same time enjoy intimacy with other women. And so since Sarah returned from New York, he had been spending three or four dutiful nights a week with her in their Malden house, two or three nights with Claudette and little Izzy in Bath, and an occasional night either alone or with the wife of one of his truckers on a long haul assignment.

As soon as he hung up on Rowena, Sol was on his way to Winthrop. He got to the Ross home just as Stanetsky's men were getting ready to carry his father out to the hearse. The doctor had already been there to sign the death certificate, and Rowena, Isaac and Justin were sitting silently in the living room. Bill was packing up his few things, having already called his service and told them to cancel the next shift. As he passed through the living room to say goodbye and again express his sympathy, Sol handed him a fifty dollar bill. He protested that it wasn't necessary, but Sol clapped him on the shoulder and accompanied him to the door. Returning to the family, he went directly to Justin, hugged him and said, "You loved your zeyde more than anyone, even more than your mother and me. And he loved you like a son… like *more* than a son, because he wasn't so proud of me. Someday I hope you'll come up to Maine and join me in the business. But whatever you want, I'll help. I swear it on the memory of my father, Reb Yisroel Forshtayn."

The funeral took place in the Malden *Litvishe* shul with old Rabbi Boruchov officiating, assisted by Rabbi Epstein from the Winthrop synagogue. There were still enough elderly Jews living around Suffolk Square who remembered the way that Reb Yisroel had presided over the *schlachthoiz* that supplied them with their kosher *Shabbos* and *Yomtov* chickens and others who remembered seeing the bearded pietist standing at the east wall of the synagogue and still others who knew Sarah and Sol from Maplewood and Rowena and Isaac from Winthrop so that the synagogue was almost as crowded as on Yom Kippur. Sol had ordered Sumner down from Brunswick and had made it clear to Hope that she was to come along with them without one of her pulp romances, and so the seven of them – Rowena, Isaac, Justin, Sol, Sarah, Sumner and Hope – sat together in the front pew. Behind them sat the Dubrovskys and several distant cousins from Dorchester and Brookline.

Although the loss of his zeyde was foremost on his mind, Justin had hoped that Essie might come in from New York; he wanted to see her again and talk to her about Shelley. Just before the service, when the family was gathered in Rabbi Boruchov's study, Justin had asked Sarah if her sister was coming to the funeral. Sarah whispered that she didn't think so, but Rowena, ever alert, had overheard the brief exchange, and when Justin returned to her side, she gave him a disapproving look and asked him why he cared whether or not "that slut Essie" would be there. Justin reddened and murmured, "It's not important. I just wondered."

Rowena harrumphed and said, "I wouldn't want her here for my father's funeral. It would be an insult!" Justin was about to make a nasty retort when he thought better of it. He had never heard an angry word from his zeyde; this wasn't the time. So, after staring at his mother, he simply moved away and stood next to his Aunt Sarah, realizing – or possibly not realizing – that the simple act of moving four feet away from his mother was a stinging retort.

Rabbi Boruchov's eulogy was brief but eloquent. He had had a deep respect for Reb Yisroel who had been his friend and advocate for almost forty years. There had been several times during his tenure when members of the synagogue board had wanted to engage a younger rabbi with more modern ideas and unaccented English, but Reb Yisroel was always there to organize that hard core of loyalists who not only prayed with Rabbi Boruchov but who studied Talmud or *Ein Yaakov* with him and who depended on him to answer their *shayles* with empathy and erudition. He said that he considered Reb Yisroel to be a *lamed-vovnik*, one of those thirty-six hidden but saintly souls by whose virtue, according to mystical tradition, the world survives. He told the crowd of mourners what it meant to him personally to see Reb Yisroel at his lectern wrapped in his *tallit*. "I would see him standing there, quietly *davvening* with such devotion and concentration that I felt that my own prayers would ascend to the throne of glory on the wings of his prayers." Through his tears, Justin whispered "Amen."

During the chanting of various psalms and the *El Molei* prayer, Justin thought back to the precious times that he had shared with his zeyde. He smiled as he remembered how, whenever his parents took him to the Forshtayn apartment in Malden, Zeyde would take him by the hand, sit him down in his study, and open a Hebrew book, usually to the Torah portion of the week. When he was a tot, Reb Yisroel would point out the letters and explain their sounds, and as he grew up he taught him the meanings of the words, and then the verses, and then the commentaries. But what he remembered most vividly was the surprise that awaited him when the lesson was over and they closed the book. Somehow, under the cover, there would be some coins, usually eighteen cents – *chai* for life – when he was a little boy; then a dollar or two, and in more recent years, eighteen dollars. And Justin was surprised – or feigned surprise – every time he closed the Hebrew volume and found his reward.

He thought back also to those pre-Sukkot excursions to Melrose to cut down boughs of pine trees to use as *schach*, the leafy roof for the *sukkah*. His father would borrow a truck and driver from Dave Broman, the hardware proprietor, and they would first drive to Malden to pick up Reb Yisroel and then on to a wooded farm in Melrose where they would attack those trees with the thickest growth, chopping and sawing away, with the help of the driver. When Justin was a little boy, he would just watch the three men, standing safely clear of the cutting operation at the admonition of his zeyde. But as soon as he was old enough to handle a saw, he would work alongside the three men and help carry the boughs to the truck, where they were piled and tied down.

That operation, usually on a crisp autumn day, would conclude at about four when Reb Yisroel would call out, *"Mir hobben genug.* Dis is enough for our two *sukkahs* and for de shul too. Time for *Minchah.*" He would then look around, find the most beautiful tree, take his place in its shade and start to *davven* the afternoon prayers by heart. Isaac would join him while Justin and the *goy* looked on. And Justin recalled that when they went out to cut pine for the Sukkot following his bar mitzvah, Zeyde handed him a little prayer book from his pocket when they were done cutting and invited him to join his father and himself with the words, "Jakie, you're old enough to know you should tank Gott for all de trees He gave us. Here, stand by me."

When the funeral service was over and the family was gathered in the rabbi's study putting on their coats for the drive to the cemetery in Everett, a white-bearded and bent stranger walked in very hesitantly and introduced himself as Koppel Ganzfried, a childhood friend of Reb Yisroel's from back in Vilna. He explained that he was a Holocaust survivor and that he had lost track of his old friend. He spoke in Yiddish and told the family that Yisroel had been the brightest student in their gymnasium and that they had both fought in the tsar's army against the Japanese. He explained that he had been living in the *moshav zekenim* – the old folks home – in Mattapan since he arrived in America a few months earlier and that he was listening to the Yiddish hour on the radio that morning when he heard the announcement of Reb Yisroel's death and funeral. He just wanted to see Reb Yisroel's *mishpocha* and to tell them that their father and grandfather was his *chaver,* his very special friend, *an emesdike aidele bocher* – a truly genteel young man – and, here tears rolled down his sunken cheeks, that he loved him.

No, he could not drive out to the cemetery with them nor would he be able to visit during *shiva.* He wasn't well and had to get back to the *moshav zekenim.* Sol asked him how he had managed to get all the way to Malden from Mattapan. He answered that he had left early in the morning right after he heard the announcement and had taken the MTA. Sol calculated quickly and said "You had to take two street cars, an el train and a bus to get here. It must have taken you two hours!" Ganzfried shrugged and turned to leave, but Sol took him by the arm and said, "I will not let you go back the way you came. You were a friend of my father and you're not well. You sit down here and don't move. I'll arrange with one of Stanetsky's drivers to take you back to Mattapan, to the *moshav zekenim.* Jakie," he ordered, "you sit here by Mr. Ganzfried and make sure that he doesn't leave while I arrange with Stanetsky for a driver."

Justin complied willingly, and sat down next to the shrunken old man. He took his hand and asked, "You were really a friend of my zeyde?"

Ganzfried nodded and said, "We were *chaverim* in de gymnasium and in de army and in de *shomrim.*"

"What were the *shomrim*? I know it means guards, but what was it?"

"It vas a grup yong men to guard de *Yidden* in Vilna from de pogromists. Your zeyde and me, ve vas de liders. He had real coridge, your zeyde."

"Did you know about his little son who was killed by some soldiers?"

Ganzfried stiffened, "Vy you esk dat? He told you somting about Ephraim?"

"I just know that he loved him very much and was even thinking about him the day he died. I was with him."

"Yeh, he loved him very moch, yeh, very moch."

At that moment Sol came back into the room and told Ganzfried that it was all arranged; Stanetsky's man would drive him back to the door of the *moshav zekenim.* Ganzfried thanked him and then got up and solemnly shook hands with each member of the family, none of whom could have imagined in their wildest dreams that the hand that they were shaking – as well as the hand of their beloved and gentle Reb Yisroel – had in a far distant time and place committed murder. Justin was the last to shake his hand and accompanied him out to the foyer where the driver was waiting for him. As they were parting, Jacob held his hand for a moment and asked, "Would it be all right if I came out to the *moshav zekenim* to visit you some day? I'd like to hear more about my zeyde's early life."

Ganzfried nodded, "Yeh, Vood be nice." And he left with the driver.

It wasn't until the family returned to the Ross home to begin the observance of *shiva* that Justin called Shelley's dorm to explain why he had not shown up two nights earlier at Brigham's as promised. She wasn't in, and so he left a message explaining that his grandfather had died and asking that she call him at his parents' home. When two hours passed without a call, he tried again. This time she was in and, after a wait of several minutes, she came to the phone. Before Justin could say a word, Shelley told him how angry she was with him for not informing her immediately. She berated him for his insensitivity. "You didn't think that I would care to hear that your grandfather died? You didn't realize that I had no idea what happened to you? You just disappear without a word?" She began to cry and hung up.

There were family members around, and so Justin hung up the phone and went upstairs to his parents' room where he called Shelley again on the extension phone. After four rings, she answered and quietly asked Justin what he wanted. He apologized and explained that he couldn't figure out how to reach her that night at Brigham's and that he was completely involved with family and funeral preparations the next day. He went on to tell her that his zeyde had died peacefully holding his hand. "Shelley, I want to talk to you about it. There's no one here I can talk to. I think that Zeyde died thinking that I was his little son who was killed back in Vilna and that he was going to him. Shelley, I have to zip into Cambridge tomorrow for two classes that I can't miss, but then I've got to come straight home to be with the family for *shiva*. Could you.... Shelley, could you come here tonight or tomorrow night to visit? Even if you're angry with me, it's a *mitzvah* to visit for *shiva....* Please."

An hour or so later, as the family was finishing the traditional meal of consolation, people started arriving from the Winthrop and Malden congregations for the first *shiva* evening service. Isaac led the service, standing near Rowena and Sol who were seated next to each other on boxes in their stocking feet. The Ross living room was jammed to capacity with a few late arrivals standing in the doorway. When the service ended, the guests filed by Rowena and Sol reciting the traditional words of consolation, *"Ha-Makom y'nachem etchem....* – May God comfort you among all those who mourn for Zion and Jerusalem." Justin watched the solemn procession, and several of the guests, remembering Justin from his childhood years in Winthrop, stopped to exchange a few words with him. He was talking to Jim and Debbie Goldberg, when he felt a hand on his arm. It was Shelley.

Justin was so relieved to see her and so grateful that he was about to take her in his arms, but he controlled himself. The only people in the room who knew anything about Shelley were Justin's Aunt Sarah and his father who had met Shelley after the Berlioz concert. He and Shelley had driven over to Malden one night about a month earlier so that Justin could introduce her to "my favorite aunt." Sarah found her delightful and called Justin the next day to tell him how impressed she was with Shelley. As soon as Sarah spotted Shelley in the line of guests, she rushed over to greet her and tell her how happy she was to see her again. Rowena, sitting on her uncomfortably low perch, did not miss a moment of their exchange. She had no idea who the girl was, but she saw the effect that she had on her Justin, and a poisonous scowl crossed her face when she saw how Sarah greeted her. But she did not move from her low mourner's box, waiting to see what Justin would do.

Justin took Shelley's arm, whispered "Steel yourself" in her ear, and steered her through the crowd toward his mother and Sol. "Mom, Uncle Sol, I want you to meet Shelley Newman. She's a friend of mine from Radcliffe, and she was nice enough to come here for our *shiva minyan*."

Rowena looked up at Shelley for a noncommittal instant and then turned to Justin. "I see that your Aunt Sarah seems to know Miss Newman. How interesting. I had no idea…". But before she could finish her sentence, Isaac came over, extended his hand to Shelley and said, "How nice to see you again. Sorry it had to be on this sad occasion. The last time we met, it was such a beautiful evening…".

"Isaac! You know Miss Newman also? Strange how no one saw fit to tell *me* about her."

"Rowena, calm down. You remember when I went to Symphony Hall to hear Justin sing? Well, that's when I met Shelley. She was singing too. I forgot to mention it…"

"Oh shut up, Isaac!" Turning to her brother, "Sol, maybe you met her too?" she asked a bit too shrilly for the somber occasion.

Sol put his arm on his sister's shoulder and said, "Shh, Rowena, shh. No, I never met the young lady, but she looks very nice." And turning to Shelley, "Thank you for coming here tonight. We appreciate it. So where are you from, Shelley?"

Shelley was still trying to absorb the unexpected reaction of Justin's mother, and it took her a moment to answer. "I'm from Philadelphia, and I'm a freshman at Radcliffe. Justin and I met at a Glee Club rehearsal a few months ago."

Rowena was relentless. "You've known Justin for a few months, and you've met his aunt and my husband, and this is the first that I've heard about you? Sorry if I seem upset, but I just lost my father, and I wasn't ready for these surprises after a funeral."

Shelley didn't know how to respond. She looked toward Justin for some cue when Sarah spoke up. "Oh Rowena, wait till you get to know Shelley. She's a lovely girl."

"And you know this how? I'm supposed to trust your judgment," she spat out, "just a few months out of the asylum!"

Sarah recoiled, and Justin said in a low but determined voice, "Mother, that wasn't very nice. I know that you've had a rough day; we all have. But that was cruel." And turning to Sarah, "Aunt Sarah, I apologize for mother. She shouldn't have said that."

Shelley was deeply embarrassed to be in the middle of a family squabble when she had just come to extend sympathy. The visitors who had been waiting to say goodnight to Rowena and Sol were beating hasty retreats toward the door. Aware of the general exodus, Shelley said, "Justin, I think I had better be going. I've got classes tomorrow morning."

Justin had intended to spend the night in Winthrop with the family. He too had classes the next morning, but he was prepared to miss them so as not to leave the family on the first day of *shiva.* He took Shelley's arm and moved her away from the family group. "Shelley, I'm so sorry about my mother. She's not always like that. I'll explain later, but how did you get here?"

"By the MTA and the Winthrop bus. I probably shouldn't have come, but you sounded so alone…".

"You can't go back that way this late at night. No way! Wait a minute right here."

Justin went back to the family group and, ignoring his mother, addressed his uncle. "Uncle Sol, are you staying here through *shiva*?"

"I'll be staying here for four days. I'll stay over Shabbes, so I can say *Kaddish* in the shul with your mother and dad. But then I've got to get back to Maine. Why do you ask?"

"I know that Aunt Sarah has her car, and she's going back to Malden to be with Hope. But no one is using your car?"

"No, I won't be using my car until Sunday. You want it?"

"Yes, if that's all right with you. I was planning to stay here tonight, but mother changed my mind, and I don't want to send Shelley back to Cambridge on the MTA."

"No, you're a hundred percent right. You don't send a pretty girl on the subway late at night. Here are the keys. Go!" and with a chuckle, "Hey Jakie, tell her it's *your* Cadillac. She'll be impressed."

"She doesn't impress that easily, Uncle Sol, but thanks." He took the keys and then made it a point to say goodnight to his father and his aunt, ignoring his mother who sat stolidly alone.

Almost all of the cars that had been parked and double parked along Neptune Avenue were gone when Justin and Shelley stepped outside, so it was easy to find Sol's Caddy parked in front of the Rudovsky house next door. Justin opened the door for Shelley and made sure that she was seated comfortably before closing her door. When he was seated behind the wheel, he sat there silently for a minute or so. Neither said a word. And then Shelley, "I'm so sorry, Justin. I had no idea ...".

"*You're* sorry? I'm so sorry I could cry. I was so happy to see you. I felt like I was the only real mourner in the house, and then you showed up. I couldn't be more grateful. When you touched my arm and I realized you were there, I was so grateful. You came all the way from Cambridge to give me some comfort, and my bitch of a mother had to ...".

"Justin, don't talk about your mother like that. She was upset."

"Yeah, upset. Do you know why she was so upset? Because my Aunt Sarah met you before she did. My mother has had it in for Aunt Sarah because she knows that I like to talk to her. Ever since I was a baby, Aunt Sarah has always been there for me while my mother had her committees and her shopping trips to Boston. She has nothing but contempt for everyone, especially Aunt Sarah. It's good you didn't stay long enough for her to start quoting one of her favorite poems to you just to see if you could identify the poet."

"So how does your father deal with her?"

"My father? He's the proverbial *shlemazel*." And with that, Justin started the car and headed toward Shirley Street.

"*Shlemazel?* I don't know that word. I know *shlemiel*, but what's a *shlemazel?*"

Justin grinned. "Well, you know how a *schlemiel* is always doing stupid things? A *shlemazel* is the *shlemiel's* innocent victim. If a *schlemiel* is carrying a bowl of soup and he trips, the one he spills it on is the *shlemazel*. He's the simple guy that things happen to.

That's my father, the perfect *shlemazel.* I love him dearly, but he never should have married my mother."

Shelley didn't answer but just stared at the road ahead. Then, after a few minutes of silence, "Shelley, I don't know how to explain this, but another of the reasons that I've got to get out of here after I graduate is that my mother is sick jealous of anyone who I like or who likes me. What you saw tonight was mild. She treats my Aunt Sarah like shit because we love each other. I hate to think of the way she's going to treat the woman whom I bring home someday. Tonight was a good indication."

Shelley didn't respond immediately, but as they approached Storrow Drive, she spoke hesitantly, "I probably shouldn't ask this question. It's really none of my business, but … but why do your parents stay together?"

"Shelley, you can ask me whatever you want. And you have every right to ask after the display that you saw a half an hour ago. Why do they stay together? I could have given you a quick answer if you had asked that question a couple of years ago. They stayed together then because of *me,* I guess."

"So what's the answer today? Why doesn't your father just leave rather than endure all that abuse?"

"Well, I think it's because they've achieved a sort of *modus vivendi.* They don't spend much time together, and divorce isn't exactly acceptable in middle class Jewish communities, especially when the immigrant generation is still around." Justin paused for a moment and then went on. "You know? I hadn't thought about that. Now with Zeyde gone, all four of my grandparents are dead. Who knows? Maybe they *will* finally get a divorce…. but I doubt it."

"God! I don't think I could last for a week in a marriage like that. I hate conflict. My parents are nothing like that. They occasionally disagree about something or other, but they never raise their voices, at least not in front of my brothers and me. I wonder if I would be different if I had to listen to such… to such venom while I was growing up…. Justin, maybe this is a dangerous question, but how has it affected *you?* I care for you."

Justin thought for a few minutes as they drove along Memorial Drive. And then, realizing that Shelley was staring at him expectantly, he answered, a bit too lightly, "*Caveat emptor.* I'll make sure that any prospective wife meets my mother first. If she still wants me after that, well, she won't be able to say that she wasn't warned."

"Ha, ha; big joke. Okay, Justin; I'm not going to ask any more leading questions. You've had a hard day, and we're almost at Moors Hall. You can just drop me off; it's pretty late."

"Don't you want me to come in for a few minutes? We could sit and talk a bit more in the lobby."

"Not tonight, Justin. Please. I've got a lot to think over."

As he rolled to a stop in front of the dorm, he reached over and took her hand. "Wait just a minute. There's something I've got to tell you." She looked at him, half puzzled, half expectant. And then he blurted it out. "Shelley, I've decided about next year. There was a letter waiting for me at home from the University of Chicago. I've been accepted to a doctoral program in their history department with a full fellowship. That's where I'll be going in September. Let's go inside and talk. I don't want this to be the end for us."

There was a sharp intake of breathe from Shelley when he said those final words. It was obvious that she was stifling some kind of a response, but she sat there silent and unmoving. And then she leaned in Justin's direction and kissed him on the cheek. "Goodnight, Justin." And she was out the door and running toward the building. Justin sat behind the wheel, staring at Shelley's receding figure. When she disappeared through the Moors entrance, he kept staring at the building. A minute later, he saw a light go on in a second story window. He waited for another minute and then slowly aimed the car toward the river dorms and was fortunate enough to find a parking space not far from Dunster.

The next day was Friday – only a week remaining before Justin's graduation. He drove Sol's Caddy back to Winthrop for

Shabbat having resolved not to say a word to his mother about her conduct the previous night. As he drove homeward, he thought about his zeyde and how he would want his family to spend the *Shabbat* of his *shiva*. He remembered Reb Yisroel teaching him about *sh'lom bayit* – the ideal of peacefulness in the Jewish home. And what is the most ideal example of *sh'lom bayit*?" he could hear his zeyde asking rhetorically. The Shabbat table. Mother lights the candles, and then father recites the traditional tribute to his wife, *A woman of valor, who can find?* Then mother and father together bless their children with the numinous words first spoken by Aaron, the high priest in ancient days. Justin felt tears welling up as he conjured up the image of Reb Yisroel, waiting respectfully while his daughter and son-in-law blessed him, and then he in turn blessing the two of them. Justin was determined that this would be a Sabbath of complete *sh'lom bayit* in memory of Zeyde.

When the six of them sat down at the *Shabbat* table after he received the traditional blessing from his parents, Justin could sense that they were all on their best behavior. Even Hope seemed to sense the prevalent mood – no pulp romance, no slouch, no disagreeable comments; someone had had a serious talk with her. In fact, it was Hope who uncharacteristically asked Justin, as they were finishing the chopped liver, what he planned to do after graduation. That was the cue that Justin had been waiting for, though from an unexpected source.

"Mom, Dad, Aunt Sarah, Uncle Sol, we haven't had any time to talk this week because of Zeyde's funeral. That's been foremost on all our minds, and I didn't want to bring up anything else while we were observing *shiva,* while we were all thinking about Zeyde. But now it's *Shabbat,* and Zeyde taught me that we should have happy conversations around the *Shabbat* table. So a reminder, in case any of you have forgotten – this is my graduation week, and there are all kinds of events for the graduates on Tuesday and Wednesday, leading up to the main event in the Yard on Thursday. There's a Baccalaureate service, a dance, house banquets and a few more things. I've decided to skip all of the celebrations on Tuesday and Wednesday because of *shiva.* I wouldn't feel right celebrating in Cambridge while you were still observing *shiva.* I had hoped that Zeyde would be at my graduation, and so I'm going to be here with you."

Isaac jumped in before his son could continue. "Justin, this is your one and only graduation from Harvard. Zeyde would want you to be there for all of it." Sarah and Sol and even his mother joined in assuring him that they would not expect him to miss these once-in-a-lifetime events because of their observance of *shiva.* "After all," his mother added. "you're not officially an *avel.* Only Sol and I are *avelim,* and Sol," she shot him one of her patented withering glances, "and Sol is leaving here for business reasons after the Sunday morning *minyan.* He's reinterpreted *shiva* to mean four rather than seven."

Sol felt he had to justify himself. "Rowena, you should understand that a business like mine cannot go with the boss suddenly away without warning for a whole week. Isaac, Justin, you understand...".

Justin held up his hand, "Mother, Uncle Sol, this is what I hoped we could avoid here at the *Shabbat* table. Uncle Sol, you have to do what you think is right, and I have to do what I think is right. Anyway, I wasn't finished. May I go on, Mother?" She nodded silently as the others urged Justin to continue. "Two things. First, I hope that you will all come to the graduation ceremony on Thursday morning. It's almost as if Zeyde timed his death with us in mind. *Shiva* will be over after the Wednesday morning *minyan,* and so I don't know of any reason why we can't all celebrate together on Thursday. Hope, I'm sorry I can't invite you or Sumner to join us; each graduate only gets four tickets. Uncle Sol, can you come back for the graduation?"

"Jakie, I wouldn't miss it for the world! My one and only nephew graduates from Harvard, and I shouldn't be there? God forbid! Not only I'll be there, but I want all of us to have a nice lunch together afterward. I'm taking us all out to celebrate, and Aunt Sarah and I have a very special gift for you. A surprise; you'll see. And oh, bring along that pretty girl Shelley. You picked out a real nice one there."

Justin looked at his mother who was again staring disapprovingly at Sol. "I think that Shelley's probably on her way home to Philadelphia right now. I tried to call her at her dorm before I came here, but they told me that she had already moved out. She was a little upset the other night for a couple of reasons. I don't want to rehash the reception that she got here, but that wasn't the only thing that upset her – which brings me to the second bit of good news. Mom, Dad, you remember that letter that you were holding for me here? Well, it was an acceptance letter from the University of Chicago. They've offered me a full-tuition fellowship, and I've accepted. I'll be in Chicago for the next few years. Not only will I be working for my Ph.D. in a great department, but you won't have to worry about me being drafted and sent to Korea..... So, that's my news."

Sol was the first to respond. "So far away? Chicago? You couldn't continue here at Harvard?"

"I applied, and they actually accepted me, but without a fellowship. I wanted to stay here, but it would have cost too much...".

"Justin," Sol cut in, "who cares about the cost? Why didn't you tell me? I would have taken care of it. You know I'd do anything for you."

Rowena responded. "Sol, you've done enough for Justin, and we appreciate it – especially that trip to Paris last year. But I guess Justin's a man now, and he wants to take responsibility for his future." And then, trying to erase some of the rancor that she felt from her son after the Shelley episode, "Justin, I'm relieved that you won't have to go to Korea. I just wish that you could work on your doctorate somewhere closer to home. But you know what's best for you."

And from his father, "Your zeyde would be very proud of you." And he got up from the table and kissed his son.

The following Thursday morning, Isaac, Rowena, Sol and Sarah filled four of the thousands of seats set up in the Yard between Widener Library and Memorial Church. While awaiting the processional, they were leafing through the program booklets, and Sarah was the first to spot Justin's name, followed by those coveted words *magna cum laude.* She pointed to the words and asked Sol what they meant. He shrugged and turned to Rowena. "What's this mean? Looks like some Italian pasta."

Rowena gave him an exasperated look and explained the honorific, adding "But I had hoped he'd get a *summa."* Another puzzled look from Sol. "*Summa cum laude* is the highest honor. If Justin had spent more time in the library and less time with girls and that Glee Club, he could have graduated *summa* instead of just *magna.*"

Isaac, sitting to Rowena's left, shook his head in disgust. "Rowena, are you never satisfied? I'm so proud of our son, a *magna* from Harvard, going on for a Ph.D. at Chicago, and you throw cold water on it all because he didn't get a *summa*? Your father is up there *kvelling*, and you're sitting here complaining. I don't know what's the matter with you. Never, never satisfied..."

"Oh shut up, Isaac. I only wanted the best for Justin. If I pushed him, it was for his sake."

Sol put an arm on Rowena's shoulder. "Sorry I asked. I'm proud of Jakie too. I know you always want the best for him, but I think that this is pretty good. I'm only disappointed that he's going off to Chicago. I like it when he drops in to see us in Malden or in Maine. I just wish that he would come into the business with me. You know, the new generation of businessmen, they've all got college educations, not like me who quit high school. I would love to have Jakie with me, even without a whatchamacallit... a *sumer.*"

Before Rowena could correct Sol, the procession of faculty and graduates began, and the Rosses and Fairstones craned their necks searching the black-robed ranks for the object of their affections. Once all the front rows and the stage were filled, the program began and went on for close to three hours, including an oration in Latin by the valedictorian which elicited a few chuckles from the handful of cognoscenti. For most of those assembled, there were only about five minutes of genuine interest as their sources of pride rose to accept their various degrees.

When the ceremony ended, Justin met his quartet of admirers on the steps of Emerson as prearranged, and after hugs and kisses, they were off to the Window Shop with its tempting array of Viennese salads and confections as guests of Uncle Sol. And it was there in the Window Shop, which boasted of a visit by Eleanor Roosevelt a decade earlier in support of enterprising war refugees, that Reb Yisroel Forshtayn's son and daughter made startling pronouncements. When the five of them were comfortably seated around a garden table, Sol took a little leather pouch from his pocket and set it on Justin's plate. When Justin looked at him for some explication, Sol said: "A little gift from Aunt Sarah and me to show you how proud we are of you. Use it in good health."

Justin picked up the pouch not quite understanding, but when he unsnapped it, he found two keys that could only have been for a car. "You're giving me a car! I can't believe it. Wow! I don't know how to thank you." And he went over to Sol and Sarah and hugged them. Sarah was beaming as Sol said: "It's not a Caddy, but maybe you'll get a Caddy when you join me in the business." Sarah said: "This car is what a healthy young college graduate needs, an MG two-seat roadster. You know what the salesman said? He said it's a guaranteed chick magnet. Maybe with it you'll find a girl in Chicago even nicer than Shelley."

At the mention of Shelley's name, the scowl that had planted itself on Rowena's face during the presentation of a gift that she and Isaac could not compete with grew even darker. "Justin, your father and I have a very different kind of a gift for you. Ours is a gift of the intellect, not a 'chick magnet.'" – the last spoken with a condescending smile and nod in Sarah's direction. "You mentioned how sorry you were that Zeyde couldn't be here for your graduation, but our gift to you makes up for his absence in a way. You used to enjoy handling the books in his library, especially those big volumes of the Talmud. When we moved Zeyde to our house, we had his library boxed and stored away because we didn't have enough room in our bookcases. There are over a dozen boxes of Judaica which are now yours, a gift from Zeyde.

And our own personal gift to you is the entire set of the Harvard Classics. Needless to say, we didn't bring it along with us today, but the unopened boxes are waiting for you at home."

Justin got up again and hugged his mother and father. When he returned to his seat, he thought for a moment and then said, "Thank you all for making this a really unforgettable day for me. Look – there's something I've been thinking about all year, and I've finally made my decision. That gift of Zeyde'*s* library settles the matter for me. Mom, I hope that this doesn't bother you too much, but I've decided. I never liked the name Justin; I think it's pretentious and, well ... it's not me. Zeyde always called me Yaakov or Jakie, usually followed by *zissinke*." A tear ran down his face. "I'm going to register at Chicago as *Jacob* Ross, not Justin. I'm not a medieval knight; I hope someday to be a scholar and a *mensch* like Zeyde. Mom, you can still call me Justin, if you want to, but for everyone else, I'm Jacob... or Jakie, if you prefer. That's what the rest of you always call me anyway when Mom's not around. You won't have to get used to it."

Jacob knew that his mother would not be pleased. He had mulled over the idea of changing his first name ever since he first met Shelley. He recalled her puzzled reaction when he introduced himself to her as Justin – "Sir Justin of Stonehenge." But it was his reverence for his zeyde and his sense of loss at his death that finally convinced him to make the change, and what better time than before enrolling in a new school. It probably would have been more politic to inform his mother in private, but he had no idea of the impact of his words on her. She was apoplectic.

"Justin! Justin Ross, I forbid it!" carefully enunciating each syllable a bit too loudly. "I absolutely forbid it! You are my son, and I named you. I didn't want my son to be hobbled through life with an old-world, ethnic label. You can just forget this nonsense. Your name is Justin, now and always. And that's final!"

Isaac tried to calm her down. "Rowena, please lower your voice. Everybody is looking at us. Anyway, what's wrong with Jacob? It was my father's name. Jakie is old enough to decide for himself what he wants to be called." And then, grasping for a straw, "After all, in the Torah, Jacob was Isaac's son…"

"Isaac's son?! Isaac's son?!" she hissed. "Why don't you just shut up with your 'Isaac's son'? What was your father anyway? A peddler who never made a living. You *kunnyleml*! It's a miracle you could even have a son!"

The other guests in the restaurant were looking over at their table, as Rowena's family sat in embarrassed silence. She was seething, catching her breath and getting ready for some response from Justin when Isaac got up, folded his napkin neatly, laid it on the table, and faced his wife of twenty-three years. "*Raizel Forshtayn*!" he declared pointing at her. "It says on our *ketubah* that I married Raizel Forshtayn, not Rowena. So now I'm telling you, now that our son is a *mensch* and he's leaving our home, and now that the father-in-law whom I loved is gone…" He took a deep breath, took a step closer to her and announced, "Raizel Forshtayn, I've had enough of your abuse. I too have been thinking about this for a long time. I'm leaving you – finally! And I thank you, Jakie, for giving me the courage to do what I should have done long ago." And without another word, he walked out of the Window Shop and down Brattle Street toward the Harvard Square MTA station.

Sol got up from the table and ran after his brother-in-law, calling "Isaac, Isaac; wait; I'll drive you." But Isaac kept walking, hurriedly making his way through the dozens of proud family groups surrounding their robed and mortar-boarded sons.

Rowena broke the silence at the table. Aware of the fascinated audience, she spoke in a soft controlled voice. "Justin, he'll get over it. This has been a highly emotional week. Your father doesn't know what he's doing. He'll soon figure out that he can't function without me. He doesn't know his own mind."

"I think he does, Mother; I think he does, finally."

Sol walked back in and shrugged his shoulders. "He wouldn't take a ride. I'm sorry, Rowena, but you really went too far this time. A beautiful day ruined. Let's get out of here." Throwing two twenties on the table, "I'll drive you home. Jakie, how about you? Your car is waiting for you in our driveway in Malden."

"If it's all right with you, I'll go back to Dunster to get my diploma and a few things, and then I'll take the MTA to your house. Can I spend the night with you? Then tomorrow I'll come back here with my new car and pack all the rest of my stuff."

"You can stay with us whenever you want, here or in Maine. You know that."

"Thanks; I should be there around six. Goodbye, Aunt Sarah." He began to walk away, and then he turned, thought for a moment, and said, "Goodbye, Mother."

Jacob kept in close touch with his father, who was living in a couple of rooms at the rear of Rabbi Epstein's house on Wave Way Avenue. Isaac, recently turned fifty, was seeing Tamara Sandler, the widow of Justin's boyhood orthodontist who lived alone in a spacious home on River Road, far enough from the Shirley Street Jewish center of gravity that he didn't have to worry about being recognized when he slipped out of her house two or three early mornings a week. He had no hesitation in telling Jacob about his new arrangement and even gave him Mrs. Sandler's phone number as well as the Epstein's so that his son would have no trouble reaching him. Jacob made it a point to call his mother at least once a month. The calls were strained and rarely lasted beyond a few perfunctory questions about health and courses. Jacob tried to get some response as he spoke enthusiastically about his seminars in European political theory or about life in the tenuously integrated Hyde Park neighborhood, but Rowena, if she responded at all with more than monosyllables, spoke only about her miserable situation as a conspicuously abandoned wife in a gossipy community.

He didn't have to call Uncle Sol or Aunt Sarah; they each called him at his two-room Windermere apartment, she from Malden about twice a week and he from Maine at least once. The Windermere was a convenient address and would have been far beyond Jacob's means, but he lucked into a second-floor apartment that had formerly housed one of the domestics who served the occupants of the more gracious apartments on the upper floors. Sol had offered to pay for a more spacious apartment, but Jacob was determined to earn his Ph.D. on his own. He knew that his uncle desperately wanted him to join him in his trucking business, and although he had never outright abandoned the idea, he felt pretty certain that he wanted to pursue an academic career. If he could successfully earn a Ph.D. from Chicago in three or four years, write a significant dissertation, and impress a few faculty members along the way, he was confident that he could find a position and eventually tenure at one of the prominent northeastern universities, possibly even Harvard. And if he failed to make the grade, well, there was always Fairstone Farm Transport. His fellowship paid for most of his academic expenses, and he earned pocket money by teaching Hebrew two days a week at two of the Hyde Park synagogues.

Every call from Sol concluded with the reminder that a high-paying position was waiting for him in Maine, and every call from Sarah included questions about how he was eating, whether he dressed warmly enough to avoid Chicago's winter winds, and how he was making out with the girls. Actually, Jacob was doing rather well in the girl department. There was a wise and amiable rabbi at the University of Chicago Hillel, Shai Persky. Jacob and he hit it off from the first moment when they met at a welcoming brunch for new students, most of whom were freshmen. Very few of the Jewish graduate students made time for Hillel activities, but Jacob was still Reb Yisroel's grandson, and he enjoyed the warmth and the security of a Jewish ambience. The Sunday morning bagel and lox brunches and the presence of a genial host who was also a devoted social activist combined to make Jacob a regular visitor to Hillel House.

During his first two months in Chicago, Jacob tried to revive his relationship with Shelley in far off Cambridge by telephone. But they both longed for the warmth of a flesh-and-blood presence and ended most of their conversations in frustration, and so they agreed to put their relationship on hold until such time as they might get together again, possibly in the summer. In the meantime they would both feel free to have occasional dates. And so when Rabbi Persky introduced Jacob to an attractive junior majoring in Near Eastern studies and a graduate of the Chicago Hebrew High School, Trudy Friedland, Jacob finally had someone who could take his mind off Shelley. He was circumspect enough, though, not to mention to Shelley in their weekly telephone chats that Trudy was an overnight guest in his Windermere apartment after their very first date, a concert at Orchestra Hall featuring Rudolph Serkin with the Chicago Symphony. Trudy was a music lover and a passably good classical pianist, and as Jacob recognized how deeply immersed she was in Serkin's rendition of the Beethoven Second, he felt certain that she would want to relive the experience for at least few hours after the concert. It turned out that night that William Congreve was quite right about the effect of music on the breast, savage or otherwise.

Trudy, like Jacob, was not looking for an exclusive relationship. They were both in pursuit of academic careers which would involve several more years of study, but they each appreciated the gift of a goodlooking friend with whom, after a long day of research in the university stacks, one could discuss a Napoleonic decree or a Babylonian stele over a pizza and then enjoy the delights of the body in a private apartment. Jacob surprised himself at how coolly he could accept the fact that Trudy had occasional dates with other men, and he suppressed whatever pangs of guilt he might otherwise have felt when he romanced one or another coed who was thrilled at the idea of intimacy with a Harvard man. And so when he received the invitation from Sol to come up to Maine for a very special event, he decided, after giving it some thought, not to invite either Trudy or Shelley to accompany him.

Marie

Sol Fairstone decided during a frigid, snowbound February night in Claudette's home in Bath that he wanted to do something major in Maine in memory of his father and mother. He had already endowed a library in the Malden *Litvishe* shul in memory of his parents. But Sol had long felt that he wanted to do something more, something truly impressive, and something in the community of midcoast Maine which supplied his employees and the products that they delivered to markets all over New England.

It was his love for almost three-year-old, precocious Izzy as well as his reverence for his father that made him want to see the name Isidore on some significant building. Sol could not publically celebrate Isidore Potvin, not if he wanted to maintain his marriage to Sarah and his relationship with the rest of his family, but at least Claudette and Izzy would be aware of the fact that whatever it was that Sol chose to grace with the names of Isidore and Bryna Forshtayn was dedicated to Izzy's grandparents. That these grandparents would have been appalled to know that they had a Catholic grandson did not enter into Sol's calculations. What he had to decide was whether the building, whatever purpose it served, would bear the names of Isidore and Bryna

Forshtayn or Isidore and Bryna Fairstone. Claudette unremarkably preferred Fairstone.

Sol decided to focus his attention on the midcoast's most prestigious institution, Borden College in Brunswick, so he made an appointment to speak with President Coles, who he knew was attempting to expand the Borden campus. Coles had been in office for just over a year and had made it clear that he also intended to diversify the student body which was overwhelmingly drawn from New England Anglo-Saxon stock. Sol thought he might be able to accomplish two things by making a substantial gift to the college: first, to memorialize his parents, and second, to make the college community aware of Jewish philanthropy which, in turn, might lead to the admission of more Jewish students. There was also a more nebulous third motivating factor: his grandparents' names on a conspicuous building in Brunswick might influence his nephew Jacob's decision about where he would like to spend the rest of his life.

Considering his father's love of books, Sol's first choice would have been a new Borden library named after his parents. But President Coles, while welcoming Sol's idea of a new building on the campus, made it clear that the library would forever be named for the distinguished WASP alumnus who had endowed it.

It then occurred to Sol that Jacob was a music lover and that his father always loved to sing *zemirot* at their Sabbath table. He asked President Coles whether there was any place on campus for concerts and learned that the college had only makeshift locations for the occasional soloist or chamber group that visited Maine. He felt that a venue for small concerts and theatrical productions would be a lovely addition to the campus, and so a deal was struck. There was a perfect location at the northeast corner of the campus, just off the Bath Road, that could accommodate a concert hall with a capacity of about three hundred seats. It would take about a year to build and would be known as the Isidore and Bryna Fairstone Concert Hall. Groundbreaking was scheduled for late May or early June, around the time of

Reb Yisroel's first *yahrzeit.* By that time, President Coles assured Sol, the architect's plans would have been approved and work could begin.

As soon as Sol emerged from President Coles' office, he rushed back to his office to call Jacob. "Jakie, I want you to be the first one to know what I'm doing in honor of your zeyde and bobbe here in Maine. You know the college here? Borden?"

"Sure; good school."

"Well, I'm glad you approve of it, because I'm putting up a building there, a concert hall, in memory of your grandparents. I chose a concert hall because I know you love music, and so did my father, *his* kind of music, and I'm sure you'd love to see the names of Isidore and Bryna on a real Yankee school."

"Hey, that sounds like a great idea."

"That's what I thought. Anyway, the reason for this call is to make sure that you can be here for the groundbreaking. There'll probably be some silver shovels and hard hats, and I'd like you to be one of the shovelers. So when will your semester be over? I was told that the groundbreaking could take place around the end of May or beginning of June, around Papa's *yahrzeit.* By that time Aunt Sarah will be up here with Hope, and I'll invite your mother and also your father, if he'll come. It'll be a nice family reunion. So tell me; you'll be here?"

"I'd love to be there, Uncle Sol; of course. I'll be done here after Memorial Day." Jacob thought for a moment and then asked: "Uh, Uncle Sol, what about Claudette and little Isidore? I'm sure you thought of the fact that *his* name will be on the building also. I hope that you're not planning to have her there along with Aunt Sarah."

"God forbid, Jakie! How could you think such a thing. When my wife is here in Maine, she's my wife and my only wife. Claudette understands that. She'll have plenty of time to see the new building and to show it to Izzy after it's built. But this celebration is for our family."

"Uncle Sol, I don't know how you manage to keep these things separate in your mind. I feel uncomfortable if I'm just dating two different girls. Please be careful. You know how much I love Aunt Sarah. I don't want her hurt any more than she already has been. And oh, are you going to invite Essie and her new husband?"

"Between you and me, I'd rather not invite them. You know I don't get along too good with Essie, but I'll leave that to Sarah. If she wants her sister there, then I'll invite her.... And by the way, I got some good advice from Claudette that I think will make everybody happier around here this summer."

"I'm happy enough when I visit with you and Aunt Sarah, but what is it?"

"Well, you know how Hope always mopes around all summer. She hates it here, because she has no friends; never mind that she has no friends in Malden either. Well, Claudette, bless her, solved the problem, I think. She suggested that I hire a companion for Hope, someone around her age, someone who's upbeat and who knows a lot of young people. So that's what I'm going to do. I've been asking around from my drivers and some of the farms, and I'm going to check with the placement offices at a couple of colleges in Portland and Bangor. Maybe there's a young girl who could use some help with tuition. I'll check around, and by the time that the *mishpocha* is all here, I should have someone."

"That sounds like a great idea. I always feel guilty when I'm having a good time boating and fishing and driving around, and Hope just sits home wrapped up in some cheap paperback."

"And oh, Jakie, the usual question. I can't talk to you without asking...."

"I know; I know. Have I thought about joining you in the business? The answer is the usual, Uncle Sol. Yes and no. Yes, I think about it at least once a day. And no; if I think that I can have a real career in academia, I would prefer that. My answer doesn't change, much as I love you and appreciate everything that you're always doing for me."

"All right, Jakie; no harm in asking. You know I would do anything to have you here beside me. So just keep it in your mind ... up front in your mind. Okay, so I'll see you as soon as possible after Memorial Day. When I set the date with the Borden people, I'll let you know.

Groundbreaking for the new Borden concert hall – actually the foundation had already been dug – took place on the Monday two weeks after the Memorial Day commencement. In addition to the Fairstone and Ross families, there were President Coles, several members of the Board of Trustees, some members of the music faculty, and Sol's special guest and coup, Senator Margaret Chase Smith. After her speech chastising Joe McCarthy a few years earlier, she had become a hero to Sol. He became a major contributor to her campaign chest, and since her home was just a few miles away down the Cundy's Harbor peninsula, she was happy to return the favor.

Jacob arrived in Brunswick just in time for the ceremony, having driven from Chicago with just four hours of sleep in his car the previous night. There was barely time enough to hug the members of the family when President Coles called the assemblage to order and proceeded to welcome first Senator Smith and then the members of the Fairstone family. Obviously coached by Sol beforehand, he offered a special welcome to Jacob who, he explained, had driven all the way from the University of Chicago for the event. "Sol told me that your love of music was one of the reasons for his endowment of the Fairstone Concert Hall here at Borden. And so we thank you, Jacob, as well as Sol for this munificent act." Rowena winced at the mention of the name Jacob rather than Justin in this bastion of Yankee culture. She knew that she had lost that battle, along with the respect of her son, and she shot a glance in the direction of Isaac, filled with enough venom to convince him to forgo the festive family reunion that Sol had planned following the ceremony and to head back to Winthrop and the solicitude of the widow Sandler, taking time only to kiss his son and to shake Sol's hand.

Jacob couldn't help but notice a startlingly beautiful young woman at the ceremony, standing next to Hope. She had a golden blonde pageboy, deep blue eyes, and the kind of serene good looks that reminded him of Grace Kelly. He was, in fact, so focused on this lovely creature that it was only a few minutes later that he recognized Essie standing with a distinguished looking gentleman at the fringe of the crowd gathered around the site of the future concert hall. He guessed correctly that he must be Essie's new husband, the professor Rob something-or-other whom she had mentioned at the conclusion of the most memorable two days in his life. When he glanced in Essie's direction, she smiled and wafted an inconspicuous kiss in his direction. And then she nodded in the direction of the as yet unidentified blonde, raised her eyebrows and mouthed a silent "Wow!"

As soon as Jacob had dug his ceremonial spade of earth and set down his shovel and hard hat, he edged over to his uncle and whispered, "Who is *she*?" He didn't have to point her out or even look in her direction. Sol answered immediately, "That's the young woman who I hired to be Hope's companion. She looks pretty good, huh? She's been with us for two weeks already. I'll tell you about her later."

Sol had arranged a luncheon for the family in the garden of the Haraseeket Inn in Freeport, a fifteen-minute drive from the Borden campus. As they were leaving, Sol arranged the complement for each of the cars. To Jacob's relief, he directed Rowena into his own car with Sarah; Essie and Rob would drive in the car that they had driven from New York the previous day; and Sol asked Jacob if he would take the younger set in Sarah's convertible, since his MG could only accommodate one other passenger. Jacob readily agreed and had time only to ask the name of the stranger. "Marie Beaulieu. You'll like her."

"Like her!" Jacob thought; "My God, she's a knockout! She even impressed Essie."

They drove down Route 1 to Freeport with Sumner in the front next to Jacob and with the girls in the back. Sumner too was obviously taken with Marie and twisted around in his seat to make conversation. "I'm g…g…glad m…my father found you to b…be a friend for H…Hope. W…welcome to the family. You m…m…must be p…part of the family if you're g…going to the p...p....party. I'm Sumner, H...Hope's b...brother. I'm the chief m...m...mechanic at the Fairstone d...depot at C...C...Cook's Corner. I have m...my own ap...partment in town."

By the time that Sumner had got that all out, Jacob was in a sweat. He wanted desperately to talk to this lovely creature, but he didn't want to hurt Sumner's feelings by cutting in, and he wanted even less to ignore Hope, the purpose for Marie's presence. Given the situation, he could think of nothing to say to Marie other than to introduce himself. When Sumner was done talking, Jacob addressed himself to Hope with trivialities, and when he remarked that it would be nice having a new friend living in the house, she answered noncommitally, "I guess so. Dad found Marie in a college in Bangor a couple of weeks ago and thought that we could be friends. Maybe if we walk around together in Brunswick, we'll attract some attention. At least *she* will."

Marie responded quickly. "Hope, you look good enough to attract attention all by yourself. You just need some confidence, some chatter and... well, to lose a few more pounds. You'll see. We'll be buddies like the Andrews sisters," – she laughed – "and we'll have to chase the guys away."

As Jacob drove toward Freeport, he tried to figure out what the sleeping arrangement would be at the Fairstone home. Were Essie and Rob sleeping over? Probably; and they would most likely occupy the large guest room on the second floor, next to Aunt Sarah's and Uncle Sol's room. Sumner, of course, had his own place on Longfellow Street. Hope would be in her second floor room, and his mother would probably occupy the only other bedroom on that floor. Jacob had never slept in any of the second floor rooms; he always preferred the privacy of one of the two rustic attic rooms, with his own private bathroom. The only other sleeping room in the house was the one matching his, on the other side of the attic bathroom. Would Grace Kelly be sharing the attic with him? Where else could she sleep? In with Hope? But Hope's room was rather small and, as Jacob recalled, it had only one bed. Was it possible....? As Jacob was beginning to fantasize about the week that he would be spending on Bailey Island, he felt a familiar stirring. They were approaching the inn, and so he wrenched his mind away from visions of Grace K ... Marie Beaulieu ... at his door in a sheer nightie, and he began thinking of how he would interact with his mother over the next few days. That effectively quashed what might have been an embarrassment for him as he got out of the car and accompanied the younger set into the inn.

There was no way to avoid conversation with his mother as the nine members of the Fairstone party wandered around the lovely gardens of the inn sipping champagne while two waiters offered canapés. As soon as he walked into the garden, Rowena went over to him and presented her face for a kiss. Jacob complied dutifully and was encouraged to think that they might have a civil conversation. And, in fact, Rowena began by asking how he was enjoying his studies and whether he was tired after his long drive from Chicago. But then the tenor of the conversation changed abruptly and without warning.

Rowena's first salvo was unsurprisingly directed at her former husband. "Did you see how he ran away, Justin, as soon as the ceremony ended? He couldn't get rid of his shovel fast enough. He took one look at me, and he ran, the coward. By now he's probably on the Newburyport Turnpike, speeding back to his *nafke*, Tamara Sandler. There was plenty of talk when Dr. Sandler was still alive. She was always a tramp, and now she has your *kunnyl-eml* of a father to keep her warm at night. You would think that he would pay your uncle the courtesy of staying at least for this lunch. He told me he reserved for ten, and now there are just nine of us. I don't know why Sol didn't invite Senator Smith to come along. I was having a nice conversation with her. She didn't know that Vincent lived near her in Harpswell. Can you imagine? She's a senator, and she didn't know...."

"Mom, Mom, enough already about Dad and Senator Smith. I thought maybe you'd like to hear about my life in Chicago and about the people whom I've met this past year. Chicago's an exciting place."

"Chicago. What do I care about Chicago? I wanted my Justin to stay at Harvard. You could have done your graduate work in Cambridge and not deserted me when I needed someone around. Your father deserted me and then you, right after my own father died. Men… men just don't care. They're all the same, even you." And then, to Jacob's consternation, she began quoting Wordsworth in a voice loud enough to be heard by the other guests. *"Where art thou, my beloved Son, Where art thou, worse to me than dead."*

Everybody was looking at them. "Mom, stop it right now! If this is the way you're going to behave over the next…"

Before he could finish his threat to leave, the last thing that he wanted to do considering his fantasies of nights to come, Sol rushed over, took Rowena's arm, and hurried her away from Jacob, hushing her and warning her to behave. As he watched his uncle steering his mother away and taking a firm hand with her, Jacob thought back to the days not so long ago when his mother had nothing but contempt for her intellectually inept brother. She had learned over the decade since the war to appreciate his talent for making money and to defer to him. "God," he thought, "how this must stick in her craw."

Jacob was about to retreat to the men's room to compose himself when Marie walked over to him and said, "I've had mother problems too. That's why I agreed to live with the Fairstones and be Hope's companion. There's a lot more, but I'll spare you." And then, without missing a beat: "Hey, tell me about yourself. I heard from your uncle that you're studying in Chicago and that you graduated from Harvard." '

"Right. How about you? Hope said something about a college in Bangor. The U. of Maine?"

"No, that's the big school in Bangor, well, actually in Orono. I just finished my second year at Hudson College. It's mostly a business school. I'm studying to be either a legal secretary or a medical secretary."

Before Jacob could go on to ask how his uncle had found her, Essie came over to commiserate about Rowena's onslaught. She introduced herself to Marie and then took Jacob's hand. "I'm so sorry about that outburst. Your mother has no right to blame you for her misery. Whatever she's suffering, she brought it on herself. It has nothing to do with you. But tell me, who is this lovely young woman? Sarah said something about a friend for Hope?"

Marie extended her hand to Essie and introduced herself, adding "I was just telling Jacob that I had mother problems too. I guess it's tough on them when their kids grow up."

Essie looked at Marie appraisingly. "You seem to have survived in pretty good shape. If you can help Hope, you'll more than deserve whatever Mr. Fairstone is paying you. Hope has a pretty face, but she's too heavy and awkward, and as a result, she's not very sociable, as I guess you know. I hope you can help her."

"We're working on her weight first. It's only been two weeks and she's already lost almost eight pounds. We check every morning after a long walk along the shore. She's really into it, and I like her."

"Good for you!" Essie said, patting Marie on the arm. And then she turned to Jacob, "Jacob, I want you to meet Rob. He's a lovely man, and I think the two of you have a lot in common. I'd like you to be friends. Marie, let me steal this handsome young man away for a few minutes."

As she took Jacob's hand in hers to lead him toward her husband, Jacob couldn't help feeling a familiar stirring. He still had deep feelings for Essie, feelings that he could not express or even hint at given her present situation. But he couldn't help squeezing her hand, eliciting a smile and a whispered, "Let's behave" as they approached her husband.

It turned out that Rob Ruskin, a distinguished looking gentleman with graying hair, was a professor of modern American literature at Columbia University. He was interested in hearing about Jacob's experiences at Chicago and especially about his desire to go on to post-doctoral studies. It turned out that both of them were fans of Bernard Malamud and both Henry and Philip Roth. After no more than ten minutes of conversation,

Jacob developed a real affection for the man, even if his existence meant that he would never again experience the delight of a night with Essie. Impulsively he took Essie's hand and said, "My zeyde used to quote an axiom from the Talmud whenever I struggled to translate a verse and then figured it out. He would say, '*Yagata u-matzata* – You searched and you found it.' I think that that applies to you, Essie. *Mazal tov*! Rob, you've got a wonderful wife, to say nothing of an equally wonderful sister-in-law, my two favorite women."

Essie took Jacob's hand and gave him a light kiss on the cheek. "I think that you're pretty nice too. And talking about nice, what do you think about that companion that Sol found for Hope? Do her brains, by any chance, match her body?"

"I haven't found out yet. But if you insist, I'll look into it." The three of them were laughing when Sol came over and directed them to their tables.

By the time that the group sat down, Jacob had downed three flutes of champagne and was feeling a bit light-headed. He ended up sitting across from Marie at the young folks table with his cousins on either side. There was white wine at the table, and after a few sips Jacob found his thoughts bouncing back and forth between Essie and Marie. He compared them to Shelley and Trudy – 'no *chuppah,* no *shtuppah'* Shelley and bawdy, playful Trudy; both brainy, both more than attractive, but neither of them able to arouse him the way that even a sidelong glance at Essie or Marie did.

As he looked around the "elders" table, he was reminded of the Passover *seders* of his childhood years. From somewhere deep inside, he conjured up the song-riddle of numbers that his zeyde would address to him toward the end of the *seder*: "Who knows one? Who knows two? Who knows three? ….". And with a barely suppressed giggle, he thought of Essie and three of the four males in the room. Who knows only one of the men whom Essie has slept with? Rob! Who knows two of the men Essie has slept with? Sol! Who knows three of the men Essie has slept with? Me!! Only me! And he giggled again, this time out loud.

"A penny for your thoughts, Jacob?" Marie said with a smile. "Something must be pretty funny."

He shook himself out of his trance and answered, "Uh, well, there are some things that are better not talked about."

"Hmmm; so you're a man with secrets. Interesting. Maybe I can pry them out of you."

"Maybe, but we'll have to get to know each other a lot better before I start revealing any secrets. Hey, that sounds like a great idea!"

"Well, I do want to get to know the whole Fairstone family if I'm going to be living with them over this summer. I spend all of my time with Hope, and I haven't had much time to really get to know Mr. and Mrs. Fairstone. Hope and I are already good friends. But tell me about the others."

"Well, I can begin by telling you one of the things that struck me as funny a minute ago. We're sitting at the kiddie table, and they're the old folks over there. They're mostly in their forties. We're the pediatric table and they're the gerontologic table. My aunt Sarah's sister, Essie, is the youngest. She's a really nice person; she turned forty a few months ago. She lives in New York and is an executive at a fancy ladies' store there. She just got married to Rob Ruskin there. Ruskin, I just found out, is a professor of American lit at Columbia; he seems very nice. My aunt Sarah is a really wonderful woman; she's the one I could always go to when things got hairy at home. She's the main reason that I love to come up here. The Fairstone estate is really my second home. I've been coming up here just about every summer since I was fifteen. Uncle Sol and Aunt Sarah treat me like a son."

It was at that point that Jacob was reminded that he and Marie were not sitting alone. Sumner broke in with "Yeah, m…m…ore than m…m…me."

"Hey, Sumner, sorry; I didn't mean it that way. Aunt Sarah loves you and Hope more than anyone in the world, but she's always been there for me whenever I needed someone."

Hope spoke up for the first time, agreeing with Sumner. "Jakie, you know you're her favorite. So what! You're the smart one in the family; everybody loves you, … except for your mother." And she didn't even try to suppress a giggle.

There was nothing that Jacob could say to that, and so he resumed his rundown of the family. "You've already seen my mother in action. I think she's the oldest at the table, except maybe for Professor Ruskin. She's fifty, divorced from my father whom you may have noticed at the ground breaking. He knew better than to risk coming here and being abused by her. He's a very nice man, and I love him, but … well, enough about him. And then, finally, there's your boss, Uncle Sol. He's what they call a self-made man. He started out with nothing, and now he's one of the richest men in Maine. He's got a few skeletons in his closet…" – a guffaw from Sumner – "but he's very generous. I think you'll like them all."

"And tell me about the people that the new Borden building is named after. Who were they?"

"Isidore and Bryna were our – indicating Sumner and Hope – grandparents. Their last name was really Forshtayn but Uncle Sol Americanized it to Fairstone. My grandfather Isidore ran a chicken slaughterhouse near Boston, but he was a real scholar and very religious. He was the best teacher I ever had, and that includes Harvard. We all loved him very much. And his wife Bryna was a typical old-country wife, a wonderful cook and always cheerful. I'm really pleased that my uncle is endowing this memorial to them. They deserve it."

Jacob paused for a moment, but then quickly added, "But tell me more about you. All I know is that you're a student at … what's the name of that school in Bangor? I don't think I ever heard of it."

"Hudson College. It may not be Haahvud, but I like it. H-U-D-S-O-N; can you remember that?"

"I'm sorry. I'm sure it's a nice school."

"Yes, it *is* a *nice* school, nice enough for a hick from Presque Isle who's never been out of Maine but probably not for a *Haahvud* man with a rich uncle." She turned away from Jacob and began talking to Hope, leaving Jacob to consider the disadvantages of a Harvard education.

He would have to find some way to get around her sensitivity. Here she was, "a hick from Presque Isle," as she put it, in the midst of strangers. Strangers! More like Martians to a girl whose idea of the big city is Bangor and who probably never met a Jew before. No wonder that she felt offended that he had forgotten the name of the college which was her foremost credential. Beneath that beautiful veneer, she was obviously very touchy. If he was to have a chance with her, he would have to watch his words carefully.

A chance with her? What am I? he thought. A skirt-chaser? Had too much of his uncle Sol rubbed off on him? Why was he allowing himself to even think about Marie Beaulieu? To begin with, she's not Jewish. He was in Maine to help memorialize his zeyde and bobbe. What would they think if he started in with a *shikse*? But, God, she's so beautiful! And here she is, on a silver platter. He wasn't going to marry her, for God's sake, and he was only going to be in the Fairstone house for a week. So what if they fooled around a bit? But Sol hired her to be a companion for Hope. If he started messing around with her, wouldn't that interfere with or possibly endanger her relationship with Hope? But anyway, she was annoyed with him. He tried to think of the words that might mollify her. But why? A pretty *shikse* from Presque Isle, Maine. Forget it. Not for Reb Yisroel's *einikl.*

His mind jumped to Trudy and Shelley? He could have invited one of them to come up to Maine with him, but he was beginning to realize that he actually didn't want either of them spending a week with his family. Shelley? She might not even have agreed to come up. It was hard to believe that he hadn't seen her for almost a year; they had such good times together in Cambridge, especially those Friday afternoons when they went "rush" to hear the BSO. They would bring along that morning's *Times* crossword puzzle and work on it together while waiting to be admitted to the sixty-cent seats. But, truth be told, he didn't really miss her after meeting Trudy. So why not Trudy? She was always fun. But he had the uncomfortable feeling whenever he was with her that she could be having just as much fun with someone else, that she enjoyed good food, good music, good conversation and good sex, and he was always available and eager. As intimate as they had been over the past year, he had never really spoken to her about his family or she, as much as she loved to prattle, about hers. But now his mind was on the beautiful creature sitting across from him. How would he make it up with Marie?

When the luncheon ended, Jacob drove his tablemates home, dropping Sumner off at his apartment on the way. Marie made it a point to sit in the back seat with Hope, even after Sumner left them, and she directed all of her conversation to Hope. When they arrived at the Fairstone estate, Marie got right out of the car, took Hope's hand and led her into the house and up to Hope's bedroom. Neither of them appeared again until suppertime, and so Jacob went up to his attic room, unpacked his bag, and made up for some of the sleep that he missed during the long drive. When he did come down to watch the sunset across Merriconeag Sound, he spotted Sarah, Essie and Rob on the veranda, enjoying the view and drinking sherry. To his relief, his mother was in the living room, deep in discussion with Sol. He passed through with a "Hi" and a wave and joined the threesome on the veranda.

Sarah made room for Jacob on the glider next to her, and the conversation for the next few minutes focused on him. Sarah and Essie wanted to hear all about his life in Chicago and especially about any special friends that he had there. He mentioned Trudy in a noncommittal way, and then, when Sarah and Essie went inside to get supper together, he was left with Rob who was very concerned about the escalating hostility between Israel and Egypt. "You're a European historian," he said. "How do you think France and England are going to respond if Nasser nationalizes the canal?"

"I'm more concerned about his blockade of the Straits of Tiran," Jacob answered. "How is Israel supposed to react to that? Israel built up the port of Eilat to increase trade with the East, and now it's useless. I don't think the world gives a hoot. Israel doesn't have many friends, and I trust the French even less than I trust the English. You know that old saying "The sun never sets on the British Empire;" well, my zeyde used to add "Dat's because God don't trust dem in de dark." And the French; they're right up there with the Germans and the Poles when it comes to anti-Semitism. You've probably read the recent books about the Dreyfus trial. Anti-Semitism seems to be an inherited gene in France. I'm afraid that the only friend that Israel can depend on is the United States, and I'm not so sure about that with Dulles as Secretary of State."

Rob stared at the setting sun for a moment and then said: "I'm glad that you're so concerned about Israel. I went over there to fight in the War of Independence, and I teach a semester every couple of years at Hebrew University. Israel's my second home, and I'm trying to convince Essie to fly over with me next year. But she's got her job at Bonwit's, and she doesn't want to give it up. She's had some rough patches in her life, and she needs the security of that position. She did say, though, that she'd fly over with me for a week or so to give it a look. If anything breaks out in the next few months, I hope it won't change her mind."

"I'd love to visit Israel someday," Jacob responded wistfully. "My zeyde used to talk a lot about Israel. I remember him saying during the War of Independence that he wished that he could have fought in a Jewish army instead of fighting for the Jew-hating tsar. So you actually fought in the War of Independence! Wow! I wish that I had been old enough, but I was still in high school. You were an American, though. How come you were in the Israeli army?"

"Well, I was a forty-year-old, bored with the academic life. I had my Ph.D. and I was a non-tenured assistant at Columbia and not very satisfied by my situation. I went to Zionist camps when I was a kid, and so when the war broke out and I heard that there were Americans who were going over, I volunteered."

"I'm sorry I wasn't old enough. I would have gone."

"You mentioned your zeyde. Essie told me that the new concert hall is named after him and your grandmother. Tell me about him."

"You would have liked him. Did Essie tell you anything about him?"

"She told me that he was a wise and compassionate man and that you and he were very close. Don't take this the wrong way, but he didn't seem to have much influence on his two children."

"His children are sitting in the living room right now having a heart-to-heart. I think that Uncle Sol is telling her to cool it. I certainly don't want to spend a week here with her in the mood that she was in at the Haraseeket. It's such a shame. She's so bright, and she taught me so much, especially about your field, American lit. But she's bitter. Both she and Uncle Sol must have had problems when they were growing up. Did Essie tell you anything about the child who was killed?"

"No! I never heard anything about that. What's the story?"

"Maybe Essie doesn't know either. No one in the family ever talks about Ephraim. That was his name. I was with Zeyde when he died, and the last thing that he was thinking about, even with his mind so muddled, was his Ephraim. You know, when I was the boy alto in the Winthrop synagogue choir, I had the solo, "*Ha-ven yakir li Ephraim,*" each year at the *Selichot* service. Zeyde used to come to the Winthrop shul for *Selichot* instead of his own shul so that he could hear me singing that solo. And after the service, he would give me a kiss and thank me for singing about his Ephraim. I'm no psychologist, but I'm guessing that my mother and Uncle Sol grew up under the shadow of the dead brother whom they never knew. From what I've heard – and I've asked a few psychologists about this – parents tend to idealize a child who never had the chance to grow up. You know; he would have been a great scholar; he would have been a great musician; he would have been the best, the greatest, etc. etc. And there was his daughter, very smart, but a girl, and then his son who was certainly no scholar. That couldn't help but affect the atmosphere in their home."

"Thanks for telling me about Ephraim. That certainly helps me understand the family dynamic. I know that Essie doesn't much care for either your mother or Sol. Maybe if I tell her the story, she'll be easier on them."

"Well, don't count on it with Uncle Sol. As I'm sure you know, Essie loves Aunt Sarah very much, and she's very protective of her. You probably know about her visits to the Institute for Life. She had breakdowns twice because of Uncle Sol's affairs, and it was Essie who saw to it that she got the right care."

"I wanted to ask you about that. Essie thinks the world of you. Aside from wanting to see Sarah, you're the reason she convinced me that we should come up here for the groundbreaking. She said that I would enjoy meeting you, and she was right. And she said that the only reason that she was willing to spend a couple of nights under the same roof as Sol was because you and Sarah were here. But tell me; knowing what you do about your Uncle Sol, how is it that you seem to get along so well with him? Please excuse me if I seem to be prying, but, well, I don't see you and Sol operating on the same wave length. You don't have to answer if you don't want to. I won't hold it against you."

"No, no; that's all right. You're a member of the family now. It's something that I think about a lot. I don't think I'll ever forgive him for the misery that he's caused Aunt Sarah, but…." Jacob paused and thought for a moment.

"I'm sorry if I've touched a nerve,"

"It's hard to explain, but I do love Uncle Sol. Why? …. I guess the main reason is that during my childhood, he was very kind to me. He used to come to our house to play with me and to watch me showing off at the prompting of my mother and father. His excuse for coming to Winthrop so often was to visit with his sister and brother-in-law. He and my father enjoyed playing klabiash together. When I was old enough, he used to send me around the corner to buy his Lucky Strikes, and he always gave me a dollar bill and told me to use the change for an ice cream and a couple of comic books. My parents would never let me buy a comic book. And when I got a little older, especially when I was living in Cambridge, he would call me and arrange to pick me up so that we could go to the Café Rouge together for baked Alaska and conversation. He enjoyed talking to me and treated me like an adult. He even confided in me about his clandestine affairs. He trusted me. He didn't ask for my approval, but I guess he felt less guilty talking to a member of the family. And, as Essie may have told you, he wants me to join him here in the business. He promised me that it will be mine someday if I want it. Believe me, as much as I love the academic world, it's tempting. When my faculty sponsor at Chicago gives me a hard time, I think about what life would be like here." And then with a grin: "I guess I could do a lot worse than a Cadillac, a mansion overlooking Casco Bay, and a girl like Marie Beaulieu."

It was just then that the ladies announced supper. Sol and Rowena were sitting next to each other when Rob and Jacob walked into the dining room. Before Jacob, headed to a seat a safe distance from his mother, could sit down, he was startled to hear his mother invite him to sit next to her. He could hardly refuse, and so, hesitantly, he accepted her invitation. As soon as he was seated, Sol said in a low voice directed only to Jacob, "Your mother and I had a nice talk. She's feeling better now, so relax and enjoy your supper."

Rowena bent her head toward Jacob and said, "I'm sorry that I took my frustrations out on you. Can you forgive me? I promise; I'll behave."

Jacob gave her a long look and then leaned toward her and hesitantly kissed her on the cheek. "It's all right, Mother. Let's just try to enjoy the next few days."

Just then Hope and Marie came in. It was obvious that Marie had been working on Hope during the afternoon. Her hair was done up nicely, her lips unaccustomedly glossed, and her gait more confident. As for Marie – she was, in a word, radiant in a white dress with a blue scarf. Both of the young women greeted everyone in the room before sitting down, to the amazement of Sol and Sarah who were used to seeing Hope slouch in, plop into a chair and bury her head in a book. Sarah couldn't hide her delight and hurried over to give her daughter a kiss. "Hope, you look lovely, and you too, Marie."

Hope blushed and said: "Marie helped me. We're becoming good friends. Thanks for finding her, Dad. She's a doll." Marie said nothing but looked down demurely.

Rowena couldn't let the moment pass, and there was no doubt as to which of the two girls she was referring to as she declaimed:

"*She walks in beauty, like the night*
Of cloudless climes and starry skies;
And all that's best of dark and bright
Meet in her aspect and her eyes....

She would have continued, but Sol put his hand on her arm, and Essie broke in, "Rowena, let's not embarrass these *two* lovely girls. Let's all just relax and enjoy the lovely supper that Sarah prepared for us."

Rowena glared at her for a moment but then softened and said, "Right. No more poetry." And from Sol: "Jakie and Rob, we are surrounded by four beautiful women. It does wonders for the appetite. Let's eat."

The chit-chat at the table through supper was unremarkable or remarkable only in that Rowena was unnaturally pleasant. Jacob carefully addressed himself only to the older generation. He was trying to think of some way to ingratiate himself with Marie, but he could think of no way to approach her without including Hope. And then Sol came to the rescue: "Jakie, I have a great idea. Why don't you take Hope and Marie for a ride tomorrow? You know all the good spots along the coast, and Marie is new here. Show the girls around, and take them out for a nice lunch somewhere. My treat. What do you say?"

"I say, I'd love to. And hey, Aunt Sarah, if you let me take your convertible, it'll fulfill one of my more randy fantasies, driving two nubile women, a blonde and a brunette, with the top down. I'd take that lovely MG that you and Uncle Sol gave me, but one of them would have to sit on my lap."

Sarah laughed and said: "Take the convertible. But can we trust you with them?"

"I'm sorry to say yes. Hey, Hope and Marie, it should be fun. You up for it?"

Hope agreed readily, and Marie, rather than answering, just smiled and said to Hope, "Why don't you and I clear the table and do the dishes. You clear and I'll wash. I think that Mrs. Fairstone deserves a break. Okay?"

Sarah was about to protest, but she was so taken aback by Hope's ready acquiescence, that she graciously accepted and headed for the living room with Essie, Rowena and the three men. They were all about to sit down when Essie said, "Before Rob and I left New York, I was thinking about how we would spend our night here, and so I stopped at Macy's and bought two Scrabble sets. Do you know about Scrabble? I don't know if it's reached Maine yet."

Scrabble was one of Trudy's favorite games, and so Jacob knew how to play, as did Rob. Rowena preferred to go to her room and to read before going to sleep, but Sarah and Sol were game. "Okay," Essie said, "that leaves five of us. Sarah and Sol, you both play against me; I'll teach you how. And Rob and Jacob can play against each other. Agreed?" The threesome sat at the bridge table in one corner of the living room, and Rob and Jacob cleared the end table between their armchairs.

Essie had her work cut out for her. Sarah picked the game up fairly quickly, but Sol had a very low tolerance for accepting instruction, especially from Essie. They muddled though a game with Sol complaining about lousy letters after each pick-up and Sarah misspelling a couple of her words. After each outburst of frustration from Sol, Essie repeated that they were not playing for score but just learning the game. Sol, though, wanted to win and, as the game was approaching its conclusion, he laid down a seven-letter word with a blank tile and an x on a triple-score space, and laughed: "See! My first game and I beat you girls!"

Essie looked at Sol, as he began to get up from the table. "Just a minute, Mr. Tycoon. Would you mind turning over that blank tile? It seems to me that there are already two blanks out, and the set only has two." She didn't wait for him but turned it over herself to reveal a U on the other side.

Jacob and Rob looked up from their game as Sol spluttered and explained: "I thought that you could turn over any tile and make it a blank. That's what I thought. You didn't explain very well, Essie. Anyway, I'm going to bed; I have to work tomorrow. We'll call it a draw."

Essie looked at him in exasperation but didn't say a word. Sarah rose and said, "I think I'll go up too; it's getting late. I'll just take a look and see how the girls did in the kitchen."

Essie watched the two retreating figures with a mixture of incredulity and sympathy, and when they were out of earshot she exhaled and said, "A cheater is always a cheater." And with that she came over to Rob and Jacob and sat down on the carpet at their feet. Rob put his hand on her head and chuckled, "I thought you handled that very well, dear."

Rob and Jacob were in their second game. The first had ended in a quick victory for Rob, but the second was a duel of exotic words, and both players had amassed over four hundred points. When Jacob asked Essie whether he could turn over one of his tiles for the blank that he needed to win and end the game, all three of them had a good laugh. But then Essie got serious and said, "Jakie, I know that you love Sol, even with all his faults, and I don't begrudge your feelings for him. I know how much he's done for you. But please, don't let him suck you in to his way of life. You're a much better person. I would hate to see you throwing away what could be a promising academic career for a mess of pottage ...... even with Marie Beaulieu thrown in."

Rob couldn't help but append, "That's some pretty tempting pottage!" at which Essie picked up a pillow and threw it at him.

Jacob joined in the laughter and then said, "I appreciate what you're saying, and I know all about Uncle Sol's failings. I've got a lot of thinking to do." And he turned back to the game and to the five remaining tiles on his rack. He glanced at Rob's two remaining tiles and then saw an opening. He carefully put down 'olive,' attaching it to the end of 'envelop' and earned enough points to win the game.

"Good one!" Rob congratulated him. "Together we totaled over nine hundred."

"It's been a long day, guys. I think we should get to bed. Rob, do you mind if I give Jakie a little victory kiss?" Rob nodded his approval, and Essie brushed her lips lightly across Jacob's cheek. He thanked Rob for the game, suggesting that they play the rubber match the following night, and was disappointed to hear that they would be leaving for New York the next morning. As they headed for the stairs, Essie whispered, "I'd love to stay longer for Sarah's sake and so that you two could spend more time together, but I can't take very much of Sol. I get tense just sitting at the table with him."

Jacob nodded, and as Rob and Essie turned down the hall to their room, Jacob continued up the stairs to his room on tiptoe. He didn't know whether Marie was in the adjoining room or bunking in with Hope, and so he carefully turned the knob on his door and silently closed it behind him. As he stripped off his clothes, he remembered that Sarah always left two terrycloth robes hanging on hooks on the opposing bathroom doors. On the chance that Marie was sharing the attic with him and was in the room on the other side of the bathroom, he would have to make use of one of those robes. As soon as he entered the bathroom, he saw that the robe that was usually hanging on the opposite door was gone. Marie must have taken it for the same reason that he now unaccustomedly took his. He moved around the bathroom as noiselessly as possible, but there was no way that he could mute the rush of water from his flush. He just hoped that he had not awakened her; she was annoyed enough at him, and he couldn't help but think of the possibilities with the two of them alone in the attic separated only by a bathroom. The very thought of her lying on a bed no more than ten feet from him set off a familiar stirring.

As Jacob dropped onto his bed, he found himself mulling over Essie's condemnatory words in the wake of Sol's illegitimate

Scrabble move: "A cheater is always a cheater." Always? he wondered. He thought back to an incident at Harvard that had nagged at him virtually every day since. In his junior year, Ernest Hooton, his anthropology professor, had scheduled the final exam for a Saturday morning. Jacob – or more accurately in those years, Justin – carefully avoided Tuesday-Thursday-Saturday classes because of Shabbat. It wasn't until well into his senior year that he would use a pen or a pencil on the Sabbath, and so when he learned that he had a final scheduled for a Saturday morning, he asked the Hillel rabbi for advice. He was informed that one could take an exam at a later hour as long as one spent the time from the moment that the exam was given to the moment that one could take it with a proctor.

Jacob's friend, Sherm Notkin, also a Dunsterite and in Hooton's class, had no compunctions about taking an exam on Shabbat. When Justin told Sherm that he would be given the exam by a proctor as soon as Shabbat ended, Sherm offered to sneak a copy of his exam to Justin as soon as he was done taking it. Justin was doubtful at first; he was doing pretty well in anthropology and was pretty sure that he would get at least a B on the exam. "Yeah, but how about your shot at a *magna*? If you get a B, you'll probably end up with a *cum*. And, hey, let's see if we can beat the system."

"But what if we get caught? We could both be suspended."

"We won't be caught. Look, you'll be in your room with the proctor studying. At about twelve or so, tell him that you have to go to the john for a crap. I'll go to the john as soon as I finish the exam, probably at about eleven, and I'll tape the exam under the basin at the left end. You get it, take it into the booth with you, and then tear it up and flush it."

"And what if the proctor comes into the john with me?"

"Simple, you jerk. Then you just forget about getting the exam, and do the best you can without it. But if he doesn't come with you, you've got an A, guaranteed."

"And what do you get out of this?"

"Nothing. We're friends, and you've spent a lot of hours tutoring me in Hebrew. And, boy, how I'd like to put one over on this whole *farkakte* exam system with half your grade riding on one exam. I hate exams; they make me nervous."

Justin couldn't find any flaws in Sherm's plan, and it worked perfectly. He read over the three-question essay exam in the toilet booth and then carefully shredded it and flushed it away. He could have aced two of the questions without help, but the third one, about brachycephalic and dolichocephalic pre-humans, was totally unexpected. He would have had to bullshit his way through that one. He studied the relevant chapters in his text book that afternoon, and, after the requisite three stars appeared in the sky, he wrote a lucid essay on the long and short of prehistoric skulls. He received the expected A in anthropology, and his coveted *magna* at graduation the following year.

"A cheater is always a cheater." Essie's words rang in his head as he tried to sleep. This wasn't the first time that he had lain awake mulling over his three-year-old transgression. The fact of having cheated on an exam didn't bother him as much as his cheating against Judaism. He had used the Sabbath as a tool to get a better grade. His zeyde had taught him that a Jew had to guard the Sabbath; he could hear him chanting: *V'sham'ru b'nai Yisrael et ha-Shabbat...*". Guard it! And certainly don't use it to cheat. What would *Zeyde* have thought about his lust for Marie, sleeping just a few feet away? Was he following the path of Uncle Sol? Was he becoming a habitual cheat? Was that the kind of life he would lead if he accepted Sol's constantly repeated invitation? There was no way that he would ever allow himself to fall in love with a non-Jewish girl, but falling in love is not a requirement for sex. He and Trudy had always avoided any talk of love but they had a terrific time in bed together. Without sex, he felt closer to Shelley than to Trudy, but was that love? Why shouldn't he try to make out with Marie? When would he ever have an opportunity like this again, under the same roof with Grace Kelly. But why was he even thinking about that *shikse* in the next room? Why? But he was. How could he not?

He tried thinking about other things in order to settle his churning mind and fall asleep. The Scrabble game .... the outline of his dissertation on the Napoleonic Sanhedrin that he would have to present to his sponsor in September..... the Straits of Tiran..... Adlai Stevenson..... where he could take the girls tomorrow.... He was just about to drop off when he heard a soft knock on the bathroom door. It took him a moment to compose himself and to say "Come in." It was Marie, the light behind her revealing that she wearing the robe that he had noticed missing.

Marie stepped through the door but did not come in. She stood there for a moment and then spoke very softly. "I wasn't quite asleep, and I heard you come up. I just wanted to set things straight between us."

Jacob sat up on his bed and asked, "What do you mean?"

"Well, I was sort of bitchy to you at lunch today because you couldn't remember the name of my school. I'm sorry about that. There was no reason for you to remember Hudson. I guess.... Well, I guess I feel a little strange here. I've never lived with any people except family. And I'm sort of overwhelmed by everything here. Your uncle is so rich. I never had lunch in a place like that inn in Freeport. And I never met people from New York before. At Hudson the kids are always joking about snobs from schools like Borden and Harvard. I guess that I'm a little nervous about this job and your people, and so I took it out on you. I'm sorry."

"Hey, it's okay. No need to be sorry. I think that you're just the right person for Hope. You've only been here for two weeks and she looks better already."

"Well, we're supposed to go on a drive together tomorrow, and I don't want to ruin it for Hope. So can you forget about today, and let's be friends?"

"Sure, no problem. This must be tough for you, adjusting to a whole bunch of new people. I'm sorry if I annoyed you. I would certainly like us to be friends."

"Me too. Shake on it?"

"Sure." She walked over to the bed and held out her hand. He took it and held it for a bit longer than necessary. She gently withdrew it and turned to go, but then she stopped and turned toward Jacob again and said, "Oh, I hope I don't sound stupid, but what's nubile? I don't think I ever heard that word. At supper you said you had a fantasy about two nubile girls. I guess you meant Hope and me, but what's nubile? Was that some kind of a joke?"

"No, no; of course not. It was a compliment. The definition of nubile.... Well, it's a word that describes a young woman who is... who is... well, becoming mature, an attractive young woman on the verge of adulthood and.... well, sort of ready for love."

"Okay, you better stop there. G'night; sleep tight;" and she was gone. Jacob sat there staring after her through the darkness. Did he dare follow her into her room? Why not? She had come into his. Did she really not know what nubile meant, or was that a ploy to get him aroused? If it was, she had succeeded! But... "Once a cheater...". She was in the Fairstone home for Hope. She wasn't Jewish. Hands off! Reluctantly he lay down, knowing that there was no way that he would fall asleep without slipping the hand that had held hers into his shorts and giving himself a few moments of intense if solitary pleasure.

The next day was sunny and, for early June in Maine, a balmy 68 degrees, a perfect day for a drive along the coast. Sarah had prepared a lovely breakfast as a farewell to Essie and Rob, and Sol made it a point to sit down with the family for a quick cup of coffee before leaving for his office. On the way out the door, he called to Jacob and slipped him two twenty-dollar bills. "Show the girls a good time today, and take them for a nice lunch at one of those places you like overlooking the ocean. Oh, and one more thing, Jakie. I know it's not easy for a young fellow like you to take his eyes off someone like Marie, but remember why I hired her. She's here for Hope."

"Roger and out!" and Jacob went back to the table, making it a point to sit next to his mother.

Wistfully, Sarah turned to Essie "I wish that you and Rob could spend some more time here. We hardly had a chance to just sit and talk, and already you have to get back to New York. You two newlyweds should be taking a nice romantic drive up to Boothbay or Camden to look at the ocean and breathe the sea air. Maybe you'll come back later this summer? I love it when we're all here together. Otherwise it's just Sol and Hope, and now Marie, in this big house. At least Jakie is staying for the rest of the week."

Essie was about to reply when Rowena spoke up. "I think you're overlooking *me*, Sarah. Sol asked me to stay for a few days, so the place won't be that empty."

"Of course, you're here too, and you're very welcome, but there's nothing like having my little sister around. She knows how to make me happy."

"And I don't? Well, pardon me, dear sister-in-law, …"

Before she could continue with whatever sarcasm was on her tongue, Essie intervened as Jacob was putting an admonitory hand on his mother's arm. "Rowena, I'm sure that you and Sarah will have a nice visit together. Sarah, I'll call as soon as we get back to Manhattan, but I only arranged to take this long weekend off. We're just switching to our summer inventory, and the store's quite busy. They need me. But both Rob and I are planning to take some time off in August. Maybe we'll come back then…. That's *if* you invite us."

"Invite you? If I had my way, you'd move in, permanently. And you, too, Jakie. With you here and the girls, I feel great. The place is alive. Maybe I should open a B and B for select members of the family."

"Great idea, Aunt Sarah, as long as you don't rent out my attic room."

"Never! That attic room is yours, and I'm only sorry that you don't have a private bathroom any more. Marie, maybe you'd like to move down to the second floor. Maybe you and Hope could move into the big guest room now that Essie and Rob are leaving. Would you like that?"

Jacob held his breath waiting to hear what Marie would answer. She hesitated for a few moments and then said, "Well, all my things are already unpacked in the attic room, and the view from the window there is gorgeous. I don't know. If it's all right with you, Mrs. Fairstone, I'll stay up there for a while, at least until everyone is gone. Then we'll see."

Rob and Essie got up to leave. At the front door, they shared warm hugs and kisses with Sarah, Hope and Jacob, and shook hands with Rowena and Marie. Jacob accompanied them out to their car, carrying one of their small suitcases. As Essie got into the front seat next to Rob, she held Jacob's hand and said: "I'm so glad that you got to meet Rob. Let's keep in touch so that we can come up here at the same time in August. And if you find yourself in New York, well, you know. We'd love to have you visit.... Maybe with a girlfriend? That would be nice. And oh, while I'm thinking of girlfriends, I don't know what to say to you about Marie. I'm not surprised that Sol found a beauty. I just hope that he remembers that he brought her here for Hope and can keep his lecherous hands off."

Before closing the car door, Jacob leaned in to give Essie another kiss. And then, as an afterthought she added, "What I said about Sol does not apply to you. I've noticed how you look at Marie. Well, have fun, but be careful." And then with a grin, she lifted herself to his ear and whispered, "If you're feeling horny, just look at your mother, the sure cure for an erection." And slipping back into her seat: "Oh, I'm so bad!" And they were off.

As soon as Jacob sat down for a second cup of coffee, Rowena spoke up. "She did pretty well for herself.... a professor at Columbia. Hmmf. Maybe this one will stick around for a while, but I wouldn't put money on it."

Sarah responded quickly, "Don't give them a *kinnahora*, Rowena. Essie deserves a good husband and some happiness. She worked hard all her life, and she's as sweet and kind as a sister could be."

"Sweet and kind, hah! Not to me."

Again Jacob put his hand on his mother's arm. "Mother, sweet and kind works both ways."

"And what are you suggesting, young man?"

Jacob looked at the two girls who were sitting in embarrassed silence at the table, and, rather than answering his mother, he announced, "Hope and Marie, I think it's time for us to be on our way. Aunt Sarah, is there anything we can bring back for you for supper tonight?"

"No, no; I thought that we'd all eat out tonight. The girl is coming in today to clean. She should be here any minute, and I'll be working with her all day. Maybe we'll drive up to Ingrid's in Bath. That would be nice."

"And you, Mother? What are your plans for the day?"

"Well, it would have been nice if you had invited me to come along on your little jaunt up the coast, but I'll be all right. Don't worry about me, for heaven's sake. But there is one thing you can do for me. You can drop me at the Borden campus on your way through Brunswick. When I was discussing poetry with President Coles at the groundbreaking, he told me that the Borden Library has an excellent collection of American poetry, particularly St. Vincent Millay. So I think that I'll spend the day in the library. I'll walk into town for lunch, and I'll call Sol for a lift home."

As the four of them got into Sarah's convertible, the question of who would ride shotgun was peremptorily solved by Rowena who pulled down the front right seat and indicated to the two girls to climb into the back. When they dropped Rowena off at the campus, neither of the girls made a move to occupy the seat next to Jacob, and so he assumed the role of chauffeur intent on showing his two charges a pleasant afternoon. Driving north along the coast, he provided a running commentary on the places that they were passing, shouting to make himself heard over the rush of fresh sea air. As they drove over the narrow bridge connecting Bath to Woolwich, he pointed out the spot on the Kennebec River where he caught his first two bluefish.

A few miles after the bridge, he turned right and drove down the Boothbay peninsula, turning left toward Ocean Point and pointing out the old boatyard and the estates along Linekin Bay. He would have stopped the car for a more leisurely appreciation of the stunning views, but he had a more picturesque spot in mind as the goal of the day's drive. He chose the Fisherman's Wharf in the center of Boothbay Harbor for lunch and was pleased to see that they had already opened the outdoor dining patio overlooking the harbor.

As they were enjoying their shore lunch, two of the whale-watching boats nosed into the slips next to the patio, and a stream of excited and wind-blown excursioners passed by below them. To Jacob's surprise, Hope began to describe the whale-watch that she and Jacob had taken with her parents the summer before. As Jacob remembered that day, the thrill of spotting a pod of finbacks and a couple of minkes was dampened by Hope's mood of bored indifference. While the rest of the passengers crowded excitedly along the sides of the vessel in response to the guide's promptings, Hope sat huddled inside the cabin with one of her books. Yet, as she described the day to Marie, it was as if she had been the most enthusiastic of watchers. Jacob could only marvel at the metamorphosis that was taking place before his eyes. Was this really all Hope needed to draw her out? A companion who gave her undivided attention? If so, bless Uncle Sol for diagnosing the problem and acting.

Jacob's goal that afternoon was Pemaquid Point, a place that he had loved ever since he was first taken there as a teenager by Sol and Sarah. He parked the car facing the old lighthouse and, before releasing the girls from the back seat, shared what he knew about its history, going back to its commissioning by John Quincy Adams. He had made sure before they left home that they were both wearing sturdy rubber-soled shoes, and the reason became evident as soon as they walked past the lighthouse and viewed the huge rocky promontory extending out into the Atlantic. There was a moderate wind blowing from the northeast, causing the surf to pound against the natural breakwater and sending spumes of mist into the air. As they stood staring at the expanse of dramatically ridged rock in front of them, Hope took Jacob's hand. He remembered then that Hope had been with him and her parents on that first occasion, but she had chosen to stay in the car sulking for the entire time that the threesome had explored the rocky expanse. She looked up at Jacob and said, "Thanks, Jakie. And thanks, Marie. I … I …" and she brushed away the tear that was trickling down her cheek.

Jacob squeezed her hand and said, "Better late than never. C'mon, girls; let's explore." And they followed him down the promontory, jumping from one rocky layer to the next, marveling at the view of ragged rock ridges plunging into the sea. They skipped over rocks millions of years old, washed clean by the sea. Jacob explained to them how the thin stripes on the rock surfaces were the edges of layers of rock made up of combinations of minerals and how pressures of heat and sea caused the rock layers to rise up and fold over each other to produce the dramatic scene that lay before them. As they approached the tip of the promontory, a sudden swell caught them with a fine sea spray that made them retreat giggling to higher ground. They caught their breaths and sat down at the edge of a small tidal pool alive with tiny sea creatures.

They sat there silently for over half an hour, just looking out at the lobster buoys bobbing a few dozen yards from the rocks and at the boats further out to sea. Northward they could just make out the Camden Hills. Each of the three was wrapped in private thought: – Marie wondering about her new situation and the members of the Fairstone family, particularly Jacob, who were so markedly different from her family in Presque Isle or her classmates at Hudson. – Hope wondering if her new companion was really her friend or just a pretty girl whom her father was paying to make her presentable and to grace his table, and she wondered too about Jakie, whether he wouldn't rather be alone with a pretty girl like Marie rather than having her around as a fifth wheel. But he had squeezed her hand. Was it possible ....? He was being so nice to her and hardly talking to Marie. – And Jacob.... he couldn't get his mind off Marie. He looked northward toward Mount Battie and laughed inwardly as he imagined Marie crawling into his bed that night. You think *that's* a mountain! You ain't seen nothing yet!

The silence was broken by Marie who pointed toward the distant hills and asked about them. Jacob replied by promising to take them on a drive further up the coast toward Penobscot Bay on the next nice day. "And if you feel like it, we can hike up Mount Battie. That's one of the two mountains that you can just barely see there on the horizon. The other one is Megunticook."

"Sounds like fun. How about you, Hope? You interested in some mountain climbing? Your cousin seems to know his way around."

"Sure. If Jakie's willing, I'd love to."

"Ladies," Jacob said, as he got up reluctantly, "I'm willing and able, especially with you two by my side. But hey, it's getting late; we've got to get back and change for dinner at Ingrid's with the old folk." He extended a hand first to Hope to help her up from the rocks and then to Marie, the touch of her hand reminding him of the previous night. Tonight? To sleep, perchance to dream, ay, there's the rub... the rub... he shook his head to clear away the image, as Marie shot him a quizzical glance.

Dinner at Ingrid's was delicious and convivial. Again Hope amazed her parents by not only participating in the conversation but by describing the events of the day with enthusiasm. Sol asked the waiter to bring a bottle of white wine, and when the glasses were filled, he stood up and announced: "A toast! To our lovely daughter and to her... her, if I can use the expression, fellow travelers. May they always be happy and be good friends. *Le-chayim!*"

Marie smiled and asked, "What's *le-kayim?*"

Sol responded quickly, "It's a Jewish toast for happy occasions. It means that you should have a good life. Jakie's the expert on Hebrew. Maybe he should give you some lessons since you're living with a Jewish family. He wants to be a teacher, a professor. So maybe he can start with you. Hey, Jakie?"

Jacob smiled and agreed that he would be happy to teach Marie some of the fundamentals if she was interested. His own interest at the moment, though, was under the table. He was seated between Marie and Hope, and his left knee had "accidentally" found Marie's right thigh. He expected her to shift her leg away, but she didn't move a muscle, and so, encouraged, he maintained a slight pressure of thigh against thigh through the remainder of their dinner.

As soon as they arrived home, the girls went up to Hope's room to go through her closets and inventory her clothes in preparation for a shopping expedition to Freeport. Marie had managed to take Sarah aside and to suggest as tactfully as she could that Hope's clothes might be more suitable for the '40s than the '50s. Hope had never cared about her clothes, and Sarah had given up trying to make her more style-conscious or even to care about her appearance. But when Marie hinted to Hope that she might be more attractive if she had a few new ensembles, she responded by asking her mother if they could all go shopping together. The weather report for Wednesday was rainy and windy, a day more suitable for shopping than hiking through the Camden Hills, and so it was decided that the women would spend the day in Freeport and that Jacob would accompany Sol to his office for the morning and then, after lunch at Bascomb's, he would spend the afternoon making a dent in some of the reading that he had assigned himself for the summer.

As Jacob passed Hope's room on the way up to the attic, he could hear the girls in animated conversation. He paused at the door wondering when Marie might be coming up but thought better of knocking. Marie seemed to be making such amazing progress with Hope, it would have been inconsiderate and selfish of him to interrupt. And if he did knock on Hope's door, what could he possibly say? "When are you coming up, Marie? I'd like to resume our game of footsie?" He shrugged and went up to his room.

As tired as he was from the day's outing, Jacob couldn't just go to sleep after his pre-bed ablutions. He took one of the books from the stack that he had brought along, the final volume of Guizot's classic *History of France,* to take his mind off Marie and brought it to bed with him. He had decided before leaving Chicago that he would devote this summer to a study of French history before the two periods that were his primary focus, Napoleon's dealings with the Jews and the Dreyfus case almost a century later. He had mastered all the relevant nineteenth- and early twentieth-century literature, but he wanted to get to the roots of French anti-Semitism. The word *enraciné* had fascinated him ever since he learned that the eighteenth-century Comte de Mirabeau, in an essay in support of Jewish emancipation, had written that it would take a few generations to rid the Jews of their propensity for usury which, as he suggested, was *enraciné,* in the blood. Jacob wondered whether for the French anti-Semitism was actually *enraciné.* As enlightened a humanitarian as Voltaire had condemned the Jews as barbaric people and suggested that they be burnt. And so Jacob was devoting the summer to a study of pre-revolutionary French society in an attempt to isolate, as it were, the French anti-Semitism gene.

He was reading about the involvement of Louis XVI and his court in the American Revolution when there was a light tap on his bathroom door. He dropped the heavy Guizot volume on the floor with a noisy whack and sat bolt upright. "Yes?"

Marie opened the door and looked in. "Oh, I thought you might be asleep. I'm sorry if I'm disturbing you, but I'm glad you're not asleep. I want to talk to you. Okay?"

"Of course it's okay." He noticed that she was again wearing the same heavy bathrobe of the previous night.

"I don't want to make a habit of coming into your room at midnight, but, well, considering that leg game that you were playing with me at Ingrid's, I figured you wouldn't mind."

"Mind! No, of course I don't mind." He hesitated for a moment and then said with a nervous laugh, "You can even crawl into my bed if you'd like. Hah; I'm kidding."

"Yeah, I'm *sure* you're kidding. But that's what I want to talk about, that and a few other things. Mind if I sit down?"

He smoothed a place next to him on the bed, but she said, "I'll sit here on the chair, okay?"

"Yea, okay."

"Look, I don't want to sound conceited, but I know I'm good looking, and I know that guys are always trying to make out with me. I think that *you'd* like to make out with me. Am I right? Please, be honest."

"Honest? Wow! Okay, I won't deny it. I never expected to find a beautiful young woman sharing the Fairstone attic with me. It's like a fantasy come true. And hey, you're wrong, if we're going to be honest. You're not good looking; you're beautiful! I've never had a beautiful young woman in my room at midnight. Would I like to, as you put it, make out with you? Of course! I'm not a monk. You excite me….. but…."

"Yes? Remember, we're being honest."

"Well, but I don't want to throw a monkey wrench into what you're supposed to be doing with Hope. Sure, I'd love to see your gorgeous body and sleep with you,… Boy, am I being honest!.... but I'm a guest here, and the last thing that I want to do is to cause any trouble for Uncle Sol and Aunt Sarah. I love them. So let me reassure you. I will not try to force myself on you. I will not sneak through our bathroom and try to get under your covers. But I'm not made of ice. If you even hinted that it would be okay, then, yes, I'd want to make love to you. When you didn't push my leg away at Ingrid's, I thought that maybe we could bring it home….. Honest enough?"

"Yes, I appreciate that. Look, I want you to understand. I'm not a prude. There are a couple of guys that I've gone around with at Hudson, and …. I don't know quite how honest I can be with you without it coming back and biting me in the rear …. Okay, I'll admit it; I'm not exactly a virgin, but I don't sleep around either. There are a lot of guys at Hudson who I know would like to make out with me. They've tried. And there is one guy at Hudson who I like, and well, we got to know each other pretty well. We'll probably get together when I go back in September. Maybe; I don't know for sure; we'll see. But, well, I'm sort of uncomfortable about my body. It's gotten me into trouble that I don't want to talk about. The Hudson student organization wanted me to enter the Miss Maine contest last year, and I said no. No way! I don't want my body to govern my life. That's as honest and clear as I can be. I think that it's important for me to tell you all of this, because we're sharing this attic and bathroom So, how about you? Honest now. I'm guessing that you must have a girl … or girls?"

"Well, I've never talked to any girl about another girl, but, well, you're sure not *any* girl. You're Marie Beaulieu from Hudson College in my room at midnight being honest. I do have a girlfriend in Chicago. She's a student like me, and we have a lot of fun together. I doubt that we'll ever get married, but we enjoy each other's company. And there's another girl back in Cambridge at Radcliffe. She'll be a junior this September. I like her a lot, and I respect her. She's very smart and we both enjoy a lot of the same things, especially music. But…. I don't know how to say this and I may be wrong, but, well, you said *you're* not a prude, but *she is*. I've had some very frustrating dates with her. I think that I could be in love with her, but she always stops me when I get … horny. Boy, am I being honest! Now you know all about my sex life. Well, maybe not all, but enough; more than I ever told anyone else."

"Thanks; I think you are being honest, and I appreciate it. I think we can be more relaxed with each other now. But I'm curious about something else. Both of these girls, I'll call them Chicago and Radcliffe…."

"Okay, Hudson."

"Big joke: Chicago, Radcliffe and Hudson."

"Hey, you already taught me not to be a snob about Hudson. Don't *you* be."

"What I'd like to know, and maybe I shouldn't ask, because I'm not sure what it means, but... are both of these girls Jewish? Excuse me if I'm asking out of turn, because I don't even know what Jewish is. I thought about it when your uncle made a toast and said *l'kayim* or something like that. I guess if he's Jewish that means that you're Jewish and the whole family is Jewish. Am I right about that?"

"Right; we're a Jewish family, and the reason why we all came up here this week was to honor my grandparents who were *very* Jewish. Being good Jews was their whole life. And yes, you're right; both Miss Chicago and Miss Radcliffe are Jews."

"But what does that mean? What's Jewish and what's *very* Jewish? Do I sound stupid if I say that I never met a Jew before? I don't think that there are any Jews in Presque Isle, at least I never met any. I went to Catholic school with the nuns, and the only thing I ever learned about Jews was that way back they killed Christ. And oh yea, I remember when we read *Oliver Twist* there was a Jew who was a thief. And now I'm living in a Jewish home, and there's a Jewish Haahvud man who would like to climb into bed with me. Can you understand that I'm ... I'm upset. No, I don't mean that. I'm not upset; I'm confused, and I'm feeling sort of tense. That's not your fault, but I had to come in here to clear the air, so we can understand each other. If we're going to share this attic for the next few days, I want you to understand and not make it tougher for me." She got up. "Okay?"

"Okay. I understand. And I'm really grateful to you for coming in here and making us both be honest. Sure, I'd love to climb into bed with you, but I respect everything that you said. And I apologize in advance if I leer at you from time to time. It's not my fault that you're gorgeous."

"I'll take every leer as a compliment. Goodnight; sleep tight."

Wednesday was, as predicted, a rainy day. Sarah invited Rowena to join her and the two girls for their shopping expedition, but Rowena demurred. "I'd much rather spend the day with e.e. cummings than L.L. Bean." That earned her a good laugh, and so Sol and Jacob dropped her off again at the Borden campus while they went on to his offices in the massive Fort Andross complex.

Sol had decided that it was time for the hard sell. He was approaching fifty; he had given up on Sumner long ago, and he wanted Jacob to join him, to work with him for a few years so that he would be ready to take over when Sol reached fifty-five. Reb Yisroel, his father, had died at sixty-eight and his mother even earlier. Sol wanted to retire and enjoy life in some place like Florida or Arizona while he was still healthy. He told his secretary to bring in a couple of coffees, and rather than going to his desk, he sat down with Jacob in the two arm chairs facing out the floor-to-ceiling window overlooking the gushing Androscoggin River below. He decided to forego subtlety.

"Jakie, I'm going to make a speech, and I want you to listen carefully. You ready?" Jacob nodded his assent.

"Jakie, you noticed all the secretaries and bookkeepers working in the office outside; you've seen the truck depot over at Cooks Corner where Sumner works, and I've got four more depots like it in New Hampshire and Massachusetts. I've got over five hundred people working for me. I've got interests in almost fifty poultry farms and I own a dozen outright. I'm building a big chicken eviscerating plant in Lewiston, and I'm investing now in refrigerator trucks so I can send dressed poultry all over New England. This business grosses easily thirty million a year, Jakie. You understand what I'm saying? Jakie, it can all be yours, the whole thing. You could be a millionaire overnight. What are you going to make teaching at a college? *Bapkes,* that's what you'll make. I know; I know; you like the academic life, and I admire you for that. I wish I could read books and talk the way that you do. But it's people like me who pay for the colleges and the libraries and the concert halls. You could move up here and live like a king. And I'll tell you something else. I see the way that you look at Marie. If you were the president of Fairstone Trucking, you could have all the pretty *shikses* you wanted. They'd be fighting over you. So what do you say, Jakie. You know I love you. I want to give all of this to you. No more joking about it; no more 'let's wait and see'. *Toches af'n tisch.* What do you say?"

This was what Jacob was afraid of. He didn't want to make a decision just yet. What he wanted more than anything else was a tenured position at one of the Ivies or Chicago or Stanford. But what were the chances? One in a hundred? He was sure that he could get a lectureship or even an assistant professorship somewhere with a Ph.D. and some good recommendations from Chicago, but would he ever make it to a named seat at one of the great universities? It would mean years of struggling, publishing, ingratiating himself, and then *maybe, maybe.* And here he was being offered the good life on a silver platter. And it didn't necessarily mean turning his back on academe. As Sol said, he could be a patron of the arts; he could have someone like President Coles of Borden or even Nathan Pusey or Lawrence Kimpton romancing him to get an endowment. Sol wanted a commitment. Could he take a chance of losing all of this?

Funny that Sol had thrown in Marie as an inducement. Sol had this whole empire, and he had Aunt Sarah and Claudette and, according to Essie, several others. He didn't know why, but it bothered him that Sol referred to Marie as a *shikse.* His zeyde would have used the same term, but somehow from him it would not have been an insult. Funny, as he thought about it, how times and contexts change. Zeyde always referred to black people as *schvartzes* with no insult intended. That's what they were called by immigrant Jews, but today he would never use that word, nor would Uncle Sol or Aunt Sarah. What would Zeyde have thought about his lusting after Marie? But why was he thinking about his zeyde or Marie? Sol was waiting for a reaction, an answer. He had to be careful. Could he really renounce all of this?

"*Nu,* Jakie," Sol chided him. "You're just sitting there thinking while your coffee is getting cold. What do you say?"

"Uncle Sol, I can't tell you how much your offer means to me. You know that I love you and Aunt Sarah. I feel as close to you as to my mother and father, even closer sometimes. And I know that I can't put you off forever. You've been sort of making this offer ever since I started at Harvard, although you never quite spelled it out for me the way you just did. Wow! It's sort of overwhelming. Jacob Ross, president of Fairstone Trucking. Wow!"

"Not yet president. You'd start as vice-president and work with me for about five years. With a couple of degrees in French history, you're not quite ready to run a trucking business. But you've got smarts. It wouldn't even take you five years. And your starting salary? This I didn't mention. You'd start at maybe a hundred thousand. That's what President Eisenhower makes."

Jacob gulped. He was twenty-four years old, a struggling grad student teaching Hebrew on the side to make ends meet, and he was being offered a hundred thousand dollars! He could not simply say no. "Uncle Sol, my head is spinning. I've got to think..... Look, how about this? I've been working on the outline for my dissertation. I hope to have that ready for approval by the first week of September. Let me come up to visit again for a week or so around Labor Day. Take me around then to see your whole operation and to talk some more. Then I'll go back to Chicago to work on the dissertation, to get it ready for approval and maybe publication. And then I'll come back here a year from now, and I'll give you my answer, my final answer. President Coles said that the new building would probably be ready for dedication by the end of the next school year. You'll probably want to invite the family back up for that, and, well, maybe we can make an announcement then that I'll be joining you in the business."

"Maybe, Jakie; just maybe? What more can I offer you?"

"Uncle Sol, I have to be honest with you. I can't make that decision today. This is my future that we're talking about. If I said yes today, I could regret it and blame you for making me choose. I'll tell you this. I am very tempted by your generous offer and the faith that you have in me. I'm pretty sure I could make a life for myself up here. You know that I love Maine. I'll tell you this: right now I am more than slightly inclined to accept your offer. But please, give me a year. Please."

"Jakie, I hoped that we could settle this now. I'm offering you everything you could want. You know that Sumner can't run this business; he has no head for it. So if it's not going to be you, it'll be some *goy*, probably one of the vice-presidents from my bank. I've got an eye on one of them, a nice young man, but he's not family and he's a *goy*. Jakie, I built this business for the family, and you're the family. That's it. I've made my little speech."

They sat there in silence for a good couple of minutes, staring out over the Androscoggin to Topsham. Finally Jacob spoke. "Uncle Sol, please, can you give me a year? As I said, my inclination right now it to accept your wonderful offer, but I can't. Not today and not by Sunday when I'll be leaving. I promise you: I'll come back at the end of the summer if you and Aunt Sarah want me. We'll talk more then, and by a year from today at the latest, I'll give you my answer.'

"You could take a chance on losing a hundred thousand dollars?"

"I have to, Uncle Sol. I have to."

"I'm beginning to think that maybe you're more Ross than you are Forshtayn. Rosses and Forshtayns, they both love books, but at least Forshtayns know business. Your zeyde was a scholar *and* a businessman, a good businessman. He loved books more, like you, but he worked hard and made a nice living."

"I know. I wish I could ask Zeyde for his opinion .,.. but…" he shrugged. "Will you give me a year, Uncle Sol? Please."

"All right. One year. Not a day more. By the first week of June, 1956, *mirtzeshem*, I'll announce that Jacob Fairstone Ross is our new vice-president."

They shook hands, and then Sol suggested that they go to Claudette's in Bath for lunch. "I haven't seen little Izzy for over a week. You know, he's six years old now. If I could wait for him to graduate from college, I'd bring him into the business. He's a smart little boy; he's already beginning to read. But by the time he's ready, I'll be seventy. I can't wait that long."

"Uncle Sol, I'm not sure about going to Claudette's. I sort of feel uncomfortable about it, like sneaking around behind Aunt Sarah's back."

"Jakie, I want you to understand something. I have only one wife, my Sarah, and I love her. Since she got back from the Institute in New York, I've been treating her like a fragile China doll, and I think she's happy. But I'm a man with appetites. When I retire, it will be with Sarah. We'll grow old together. During the winter up here, I need someone. And I'll be honest; I always am with you, *only* you. If I see a woman and I talk to her and I like her, I want to be intimate with her. I've had relations with several other women since I got married. It used to be because I wanted to get away from the house, from Sumner and Hope. But that's not it now. I like women! What can I say? That's the way I am, and I'll make no apologies. Maybe I should see a psychiatrist, but I don't want to. The only thing bad about my… my, what would you call it…infidelity, is when I'm stupid and Sarah finds out and then gets so upset that she gets sick and has to go to the Institute. But that won't happen again. She knows about Claudette because your stupid cousin Sumner told her. That was cruel, and I can't forgive him. Claudette knows that I'm going to stay with Sarah, and she's satisfied. I even told her that if someone comes along and wants to marry her – why not? She's got a good business; she should go ahead. But I'll always do whatever I can for Izzy."

"Okay, Uncle Sol. You've talked me into it, or maybe it's those muffins. I dream about them in Chicago. So let's go have lunch at Claudette's."

Lunch at Claudette's was uneventful. They both had steaming bowls of clam chowder and muffins. The place was fairly crowded, but they were able to get a table looking out toward the Kennebec and the boats berthed at the marina. Claudette came out of the kitchen and joined them for just a couple of minutes. In reply to Sol's question, she told them that Izzy would be coming in from school any minute for lunch and that she would feed him in the kitchen. Yes, Sol could come in for a minute but only to look, not to touch. "Promise?" He promised, and she left.

Jacob was curious. "What did she mean by not to touch?"

"Claudette's afraid that Izzy will want to know why I always want to give him a hug and a kiss. She's afraid that he'll find out that I'm his father. She agrees with me that when he's older, he'll have to know. He'll be curious about where all the money is coming from for the things that I'll be paying for, like his tuition. And I've already created a trust fund for him, so he'll have to know sometime. She thinks that he's much too young now, and I can accept that. But he's such a lovely little kid; I just want to give him a hug or a pat on the head, but I mustn't."

"That must be tough, to love a child and not be able to show it."

"Tougher than you think. I want to be a real loving father to Izzy like I never was to Sumner and Hope. And it wasn't just that I was too busy for them and away from home so much. I hate to admit it but I could never make myself be affectionate with them. That's probably why I gave *you* so much affection. But you know, when I saw Hope at the table the other night, looking nice and smiling and taking part in the conversation instead of sulking and moping, I wanted to get up and give her a kiss."

"So why didn't you?"

"Why didn't I? Good question. I don't know; probably because if I did, it would have surprised everybody and led to a big scene. It's been so many years....".

"But isn't that the reason why you hired Marie? To get through to Hope and bring her out of her shell? So if she's successful, like you wanted, maybe it's time for you to take the next step. Maybe you can direct some of the affection that you have for Izzy to Hope."

"You're right; I know; you're right. Nu, we'll see."

Just then, a winsome little boy walked into the restaurant, took a quick peek at the guests, and continued into the kitchen.

"Did you see him, Jakie? Did you see that beautiful little boy? That's my Izzy. Wait here a minute."

Sol removed his napkin from his lap, neatened his jacket and tie, and followed in the wake of the boy. He spent less than a minute in the kitchen and emerged with a big grin. "Nu, Jakie; now we can go." The two men agreed that Jacob would drop his uncle off at his office while he drove the Caddy back to Bailey

Island where he could spend the afternoon reading. One of Sol's secretaries could drive him home for dinner.

When Jacob arrived back at the estate, he went up to his room and picked two volumes, the Guizot and Tcherikover's *Yid'n in Frankreich,* for the afternoon and took them down to the veranda. The rain had stopped, and the sun was dancing in glistening patterns around the rolling lawn. As soon Jacob had settled himself comfortably on the glider, his mind wandered back to his conversation with Sol. Was he being entirely honest when he told his uncle that he was inclined to accept his offer? And why had Sol mentioned Marie among the enticements of life in Maine? His thoughts kept returning to Marie. Was Sol right in hiring such a beautiful young woman as a companion for Hope? Not that Hope, though chubby, wasn't passably attractive, but her appearance was light years removed from Marie's. Jacob had noticed when the three of them were having lunch in Boothbay Harbor and when they were climbing around Pemaquid how people stared at Marie while paying no particular attention to Hope. The contrast in the appearance of the two of them together could only work to Hope's disadvantage. Jacob was sure that Sol could have chosen anyone of a number of young women who would have been happy to take on the socialization of Hope as a summer project. Was her beauty a determining factor in his choice? For Hope's sake or.... or, considering his history, for his own?

Marie had asked Jacob to be honest with her. Was he truly being honest? Didn't he, in fact, just want to get into bed with her? Sol was right. When Marie was in the room, Jacob couldn't take his eyes off her. She had nowhere near the intellect of Shelley or Trudy, but yet.... But what? She was a lovely young woman, even aside from her beauty. He had enjoyed their visit the night before immensely, even if it did not end up in her bed. She was pleasant to be with. She was more than just a pretty *shikse,* but how much more? He wanted to know; he *needed* to know. Why, as a rational man who was not lacking in female companionship, companionship with women who shared his religion, his devotion to scholarship, his love of music, his political liberalism, why was he so attracted to Marie Beaulieu from Presque Isle and Hudson? Was he his uncle's nephew? Did he belong in a trucking office in Maine or in a carrel in the university library?

He tried to make sense of Tcherikover's Yiddish, grateful that he had picked up a decent knowledge of the language from his zeyde, but his mind kept shifting back to his uncle's proposition, to Marie, to Trudy and Shelley, to tenure at an Ivy....and he gave up. The sun had warmed the air although there was still a fairly brisk wind, and Jacob thought that a couple of hours fishing out in Casco Bay might help clear his mind. He changed into shorts and boat shoes, picked out a sturdy rod and a couple of lures from the collection in the garage and went down to the dock.

Just stepping into the boat reminded him of Essie and his coming of age. He could use her advice now. She was wise and sympathetic, and she knew him better than he knew himself. But she was in New York with Rob. He revved up the engine and then headed out toward Ragged Island and beyond toward Seguin Light. He decided to troll for blues and stripers, back and forth on a straight course between Mark Island and Seguin. After about twenty minutes, he hooked a good sized blue and landed it after a decent fight. He had hoped to catch a striper for dinner that night; he and Aunt Sarah loved fresh striper, but no one in the family liked bluefish. And so he threw the blue back and watched it scoot away. Another ten minutes of trolling produced a second blue, and again he threw it back. It was probably too early in the season for stripers, and so he reeled in and just continued cruising around, watching the lobster boats with their soaring escorts of seagulls. After about an hour, he headed back to the Bailey Island dock having decided to talk to Marie that night.

A few minutes after Jacob returned to the house, Sarah, Hope and Marie walked in loaded down with more than a dozen bags and boxes with the logos of most of the apparel stores in Freeport. They were in high spirits, laughing together about the bargains and the salesgirls and some of the crazy outfits that they were shown. Sarah was the happiest of all. "Tonight, right after dinner, we're going to have a fashion show with my two beautiful models. We bought some nice new things for Marie too, because this was her idea. We don't have a runway, like at Dior or Chanel, but we'll sit around the living room, and they'll come down the stairs and sashay around the living room showing off all the new clothes. It'll be fun."

Dinner that night consisted of the veal parmesan, pasta and salad that Sarah had picked up at the Italian take-out on the way home from Freeport. Sol was delighted at the idea of a post prandial fashion show featuring his daughter, and he tried to kindle some enthusiasm in his sister, but Rowena announced that she would prefer to spend the evening in her room with the volume of Pound's *Cantos* that she had picked up in the library rather than ooh and aah over some silly clothes.

Against his better judgment, Jacob couldn't let that pass. "So, Mother, you'd rather spend the evening alone in your room with a notoriously insane anti-Semite than with two lovely young women? I simply don't understand you."

"You're right; you don't. And *I* don't understand how a supposedly brilliant young man can spend an evening watching two silly girls prance around showing off their clothes. That's what I call narcissism."

Jacob grimaced and was about to respond in kind, but Sol intervened. "Jakie, let's let your mother do whatever makes her happy. Rowena, we'll miss you, but you go do what you want. I thought that maybe you'd get some *nachas* seeing your niece looking so much better, but in my house, everybody should do what makes him happy. You're sure you don't want to sit with us?"

"I'm sure." And with nothing more than a withering glance at her son, she left the table and went up the stairs to her room.

Sarah shook her head, rolled her eyes, got up and announced: "You girls go up to your room and get ready. Jakie and I will take care of the dishes, and Sol, you arrange he chairs in the living room."

Marie and Sarah had selected some lovely outfits for Hope, and she displayed them with more animation than Jacob had ever seen in her. She was delighted to be the focus of their approving attention, and after she had modeled all of her new clothes, she insisted that Marie too display her new outfits. Marie demurred, not wanting to steal the spotlight from Hope, but it was Sol who insisted. "You're the one who deserves the credit for this – along with my lovely wife, of course – so come on, don't be shy. Let's see what you bought."

Reluctantly Marie complied with her employer's request. There was no way that she could minimize the impact of her exquisite body in the shorts and polo shirt that she agreed to model, but when Hope asked her to show off her new bathing suit, she agreed to pull the Jantzen out of its bag but not to put it on. "You can see me in this when we're at the beach. It's *you* that they're interested in tonight, Hope, not me. Anyway, show's over. Let's put all this stuff away now."

Sol jumped to his feet. "Hope, you look so lovely tonight. Would you let your old father give you a kiss?"

Hope reddened but agreed, and both Sarah and Jacob were delighted to see Sol embrace his daughter and give her an exuberant kiss before the two young women went up to Hope's room laden with skirts, shorts, blouses, polos, slacks, and bathing suits. As they were going up the stairs, Sarah said in a hushed voice, "It's like a miracle. Hope's like a new girl. That Marie is a wonderful influence. She's a real gem and so pretty. All day in Freeport, going from store to store, she kept looking for the right things for Hope. It was all I could do to make her chose a few things for herself. Jakie, what do you think of her?"

"She seems very nice. I just hope that she wasn't offended by what my mother said. She's anything but a silly girl, and she's certainly not a narcissist. Uncle Sol, you grew up with my mother. What makes her so nasty? She's intelligent, well-read, still pretty good looking for her age, but so damned nasty. What's with her? I'm her son, and sometimes it's like I don't even know her.... or even *want* to know her."

"I'm no psychiatrist, Jakie, so this is only my opinion. I think that my father was disappointed that she was a girl. He wanted a son who could learn with him and talk Torah, like he thought that Ephraim would do. Poor little Ephraim was always hanging over us. Sometimes I wonder what he would have been like if he lived. He'd be over fifty now. I don't want to say nothing bad about the dead, especially not about my brother who I never met, but I bet he'd be a school teacher like Rowena. And that's another thing – Rowena! She's *Raizel,* the daughter of greenhorns from Vilna, not Beacon Hill. No one was good enough for her. But she's my sister, and now she's divorced. She's not a happy lady. But don't you worry about her, Jakie. I'll always take care of her; sometimes she listens to me. But I wish that she'd be nicer to Sarah. She never said a kind word to my Sarah since the day that they met. Sarah came from a farm family in Melrose. That wasn't good enough for a Malden High English teacher. I don't know. She's a mystery."

As Jacob got up to go to his room, Sarah added, "And there's another thing, Jakie. She's very jealous of us. Not because of the money; no, that's not it. She's jealous because of *you.* She always thought that we wanted to steal you away from her, so she's angry with us, especially with me, and she's angry with you. We love you, but every time we did something nice for you, even when you were a little boy and Sol here would give you money for ice cream and comics, she would get mad. I know that Sol offered you a nice job here in Maine, but I wonder how Rowena would react if you agreed. Nu, better not to think about that now. You're here to have a good time, and now it's time for sleep. Good night, Jakie."

Jacob passed Hope's room on the way up to the attic and heard the girls laughing as they were trying to find space for all of Hope's new things. He paused for a moment, listening at the door. He wanted to talk to Marie. He had to talk to someone. His conversation with Sol earlier in the day kept repeating itself in his head. President of Fairstone Trucking…. as much money as President Eisenhower…. some *goy* from the bank…. family…. the way you look at Marie…. He headed up to the attic and decided to get into bed and read until he heard Marie go into her room and get ready for bed.

He dropped off after half a chapter of Guizot and then awoke abruptly as he heard a flush through the bathroom door. Would she be annoyed if he came uninvited into her room? But hadn't she casually come into his room the past two nights, as if they were dorm mates or family? I have to be cool, he thought, as he reached for the bathroom doorknob. He needed someone to talk to, someone of his own generation. No, not *someone*; he wanted to talk to *her*, to Marie.... seriously, but sex always got in the way.

How does a libidinous young man wearing nothing but a robe enter the room of a beautiful young woman around midnight casually, just to *talk*. But was that true? Did he really want just to talk? Honestly? That's what she wanted from him, honesty. Perhaps it would be better just to go to sleep. How could an unsophisticated *shikse* from Presque Isle and Hudson College understand all the things going through his mind? So maybe it was just sex impelling him to invade her privacy. How could she advise him about his future? What did she know? He turned back to his bed, took off his robe and climbed in.

But.... but.... He lay there thinking not about his future but about Marie. He really wanted to talk to her, and he couldn't sleep. Why do I want to talk with her? I want to go into her room and just be with her, he thought. There was no way that he could sleep. He had to apologize for his mother. His mother.... He laughed to himself as he thought of what *she* would say in his situation: "Beaulieu hath murdered sleep, and therefore Ross shall sleep no more." Goddammit! I'm not plotting a murder. I just want to talk to her. He got out of bed a second time, put on his robe, walked through their bathroom and gently knocked on Marie's door. No answer. He knocked again, with a bit more determination. No answer. He eased he door open and tried to look through the darkness to her bed, but he couldn't see anything. He hesitated and was about to close the door when he heard a sleepy "What is it?"

"I'm sorry if I woke you up. I didn't think that you'd fall asleep so quickly. I'm sorry. Forget it. Not important. G'night."

"Wait. It's all right. I was up and I heard you knock the first time. I just wasn't sure I wanted you to come in. I'm not up to wrestling, so if you have any of that stuff on your mind, please go back to bed. But if you want to visit for a while, at a safe distance, come on in. Just grab my robe from the hook and throw it to me so that I can put it on. Sorry; I'm not wearing anything. After I put it on, you can come in and turn on the light."

Relieved, he quickly followed her instructions. When she told him that he could come in, he switched on the light and saw her sitting on her bed waiting for him to say something. He made no attempt to sit on her bed but contented himself with the chair across the room. For a long minute he just looked at her, not quite knowing how to begin. She prompted him; "Well?"

"I… I wanted to talk to you about a few things. I know it's late, and if you want me to go back to my room, I will. I'm really sorry to keep you up, but after our talk last night, well…. I don't know, but when you left my room last night, I felt that I had a friend, someone who I could talk to, someone with good common sense…. Well, I was hoping that maybe you felt the same way."

"I do, sort of. I have to tell you, though, that sex gets in the way. I'd love to be your friend, but I sort of feel that I have to be on guard with you. You've already told me that you'd love to get in bed with me, and please, don't misunderstand what I'm saying. I don't blame you; you're a healthy attractive guy, and here I am, just a bathroom away. I'm sure that we could have a lot of fun together. But … but I'm not ready for that, and when I have to be careful of what I say to you or how I act when you're around, it makes me uncomfortable. It's hard for me to know whether you want to be friendly with *me* or with my body. Do you know what I'm saying?"

"There goes that honesty again. God, you're remarkable! I can't imagine having a conversation like this with any other woman. You really tell it like it is. You know I'd be lying if I said that I wasn't interested in your body. That's a given. But please give me some credit. I can control myself. I want to talk to you because…

well, because I just want to *talk* to you. Talk! You want honesty. So yes; there's another four-letter Anglo-Saxon word that keeps intruding, but all I want tonight is to *talk*. Okay?"

"Okay. Sorry for being so defensive. I'm all ears."

"There are a few things, but first I want to apologize for my mother. She can really be nasty, but I think you know that already. Every time that she opens her mouth nowadays, especially since my father walked out on her, she seems to get nastier and nastier. Don't worry that anything she says about you has any influence on Uncle Sol and your job. He's not the most perceptive person in the world, but he knows my mother. He and Aunt Sarah think that you're doing a great job with Hope. Me too. You're amazing! So don't worry about anything that my mother says. Just disregard her if that's possible. It took me a long time to be able to do that myself, but I've learned. So that's item number one."

"You don't have to apologize about your mother, but I appreciate it. Someday maybe I'll tell you about *my* mother. Some people just get screwed up and instead of facing their problems, they take it out on the people around them. Your mother is not your fault, and I understand now that my mother is not *my* fault. So, enough about our mothers, bless them. What else is on your mind?"

"Item number two. With Essie and Rob gone, there's a big bedroom available on the second floor, and it's right next to Hope's room and it has its own private bathroom. I… well, I was guessing that you'd want to move down there now that they're gone, but I was hoping…."

"Mrs. Fairstone already suggested that I move downstairs. We were talking about it over lunch in Freeport, but I told her that I really love this room. I told her that I love looking out the window and seeing the flashing light from the Halfway Rock lighthouse way out there. I didn't say anything about our nocturnal powwows. Anyway, I'm settled up here, and as long as you behave …."

"I promise; I'll behave. Please stay up here. I'm only going to be here for another three days. I'm leaving for Chicago on

Sunday morning. I usually have complete privacy up here, but I like having you as my next door neighbor. After I leave...."

"I didn't realize that you were leaving so soon. I'm sorry to hear that. I thought that we'd have more time to get to know each other. Mr. Fairstone told me when he hired me that his nephew was going to be visiting and that he thought I'd like you, but I thought that he meant that you'd be here for the whole summer."

"I wish, but I have to get back to Chicago. By the end of the summer I've got to present a pretty detailed outline of my dissertation to my advisor if I hope to finish it by next year. But I'm planning to come back after that for a week or so. I promised Uncle Sol that I'd come back and go visiting some of his farms and other business interests with him then. And that brings me to the main reason for my wanting to talk to you. This could take some time. Are you awake enough? I know you've had a long day, and I guess that this could wait. It's really not *your* problem. It's something that I've got to figure out for myself, but if you're willing to listen ...."

"This must be important to you or you wouldn't have come in. I'll be happy to listen. But first, do me a favor. Bring me a glass of really cold water from the bathroom. Let it run, okay? That'll wake me up."

"Sure." Jacob got up and went to the bathroom to get the water, while Marie quickly got up, grabbed her hairbrush from the top of the bureau, jumped back onto her bed, and with a few rushed strokes made herself as presentable as she could. As Jacob reentered he room with her water, she dropped the hairbrush onto the bed and covered it with a corner of her blanket. He let her take a few gulps before he went on.

"Uncle Sol wants me to chuck my hopes for an academic career and come to work for him here. He knows that I love Maine, and he's offered me a deal that's not easy for me to refuse. I'm twenty-four, and if I were to accept my uncle's offer, I would probably be a millionaire by the time I turned forty. We've talked about me coming to work for him before, many times, but now he's really turning the screws. He's trying everything to get me to agree to join him in the business, because he wants to retire in about five years. I usually answer him by telling him that I wouldn't be able to live the kind of a life that I want to live up here. I don't want to sound pompous, but I have friends in Chicago and in Cambridge with whom I can spend hours and hours discussing a Mahler symphony or the latest exhibit at the Art Institute or the situation in Israel or .... or the possibility of the Red Sox ever winning a world series. Okay; scratch that last one. I guess that there are plenty of Red Sox fans up here, but I don't know if I could really be happy living up here permanently. I don't know if there's a community here that I could be...."

"Whoa, whoa! Just how do you think that I could help you with a decision like that? You're talking about your whole future, your life. You've known me for three days, for God's sake! I mean, I'm complimented that you think that my advice would be helpful, especially after midnight, but I'm a nineteen-year-old college kid, Hudson College. Where do I get off giving you advice?"

"No, no. Don't get me wrong. It's really not advice that I'm looking for. You're right. This is *my* life, and no one can make this decision for me. No, relax. I'm not asking for advice. What I'm asking for is an ear, an ear with a heart. God, that sounds silly – an ear with a heart, a mixed anatomical metaphor. No, listen. It's easier for me to make decisions if I have a sounding board. When I verbalize a problem in a way that another person can understand it, I get to understand it better myself. Do you understand what I'm saying?"

"Well, I've been called a lot of things in my brief life but never a sounding board. Are you suggesting that I'm flat-chested? Well, compared to Mrs. Fairstone and her sister and Hope maybe I am, but.... Sorry, I don't mean to joke. And I'm sorry for the – as you put it – anatomical reference. We're trying to avoid my body, right?"

"Right. May I continue?"

"Jacob, I mean it; I'm sorry. I shouldn't have interrupted. Yes, I understand what you're saying. And yes, I'm happy to listen."

"That's okay. But you've asked me to be honest with you, and I take that seriously. There's another reason for my wanting to talk to you about this. It has to do with one of the things that my uncle mentioned during our talk this morning. He was trying to sell me on all of the attractions of life in Maine, aside from the great salary. And there were two things that he mentioned specifically. The new Fairstone Concert Hall and… you ready?" She nodded. "And *you*."

"What do you mean, and me? He mentioned *me* as an attraction for you? Are you kidding? I don't know whether to be complimented or insulted. What did he mean?"

"That's what I'm trying to figure out. You see, Uncle Sol has a rather devious mind. He sort of plays life like a chess game. He plans way ahead, and he's a good judge of people. I knew that he wanted to make a major contribution in memory of my grandparents. But a concert hall? He doesn't know anything about music, but he knows that *I* love music and that I love a collegiate atmosphere. I think that one of the reasons, maybe even the main reason, that he decided to contribute a concert hall to Borden College was to attract *me* here. And he often mentions that there's good music and a nice synagogue and nice restaurants in Portland – just a half-hour away, he always says."

"Yes, but what about *me*?"

"Well, he knows that… how can I put it? … he knows that I enjoy female company. He met the girl that I was going with at Harvard, and he knows that I have a girlfriend in Chicago. So he mentioned that there were plenty of nice women up here in Maine, and he mentioned you specifically. And that got me to thinking. Why did he choose *you* to work with Hope? There are lots of young women here in Brunswick and Topsham, and there are plenty of college girls in Portland, which is a lot closer than Bangor and Hudson. I think that you were a great choice to work with Hope, but he didn't know when he hired you how good you were going to be with her. I've got a sneaking suspicion that the motive behind the concert hall and the motive behind hiring you were the same. Maybe it's my ego talking, but I think that when he saw you at your interview in Bangor, he was thinking as much about *me* as about Hope. He wanted me to see up close that you don't have to be in Chicago or Cambridge to find a lovely young woman. Okay, now I've said it. What do you think?"

"Wow! Give me a minute."

They sat there silently for a minute, staring at each other. Marie opened her mouth a couple of times about to speak, but then changed her mind and shook her head. Then, very slowly, "So you think that Mr. Fairstone hired me sort of like bait, to reel you in? Like he's my pimp? Is that what you're saying?"

"God, the way that you say it sounds disgusting. No, that's not what I meant, not exactly. First, I'm not sure that my guess about his motives is correct. And second, if I am correct, that doesn't mean that it was the *primary* motive for what he did. He might have seen you and the concert hall as additional inducements for me. Do you know what I mean? Building a concert hall and hiring you to help Hope are good things, very good things in their own right. But he might have had, consciously or subconsciously, an additional reason. And no; I don't see Uncle Sol as a pimp. He doesn't wear a broad-brimmed fedora and he doesn't show off flashy jewelry."

"Ha, ha. Go ahead and make a joke. But this isn't a joke to me. It hurts. If you're right, if Mr. Fairstone hired me as sex bait for you, then I'll leave. I need this job but not enough so that I'd agree to be used like that. Sometimes I wish that I was ugly so that I could relate to people in a normal way. Be honest with me: would you be in my room right now if I looked like... like Hope? I know. Hope isn't bad looking; she's overweight and she's got normal looks, like hundreds of other girls. Would you be in here right now if I looked like Hope? Remember, be honest with me."

"Okay, I'll be honest. The answer is yes. Yes! And you know why? If this were two nights ago and we had not had the conversations that we had in my room those nights, and if I hadn't seen the influence that you've had on Hope and the way that you interact with my family, the answer would be No. The honest answer would be that I came in here to get into your bed. But I've learned a few things about you, Hudson girl, in the past three days. You're a very nice person. You're kind and you've got a good head. And yes, I'll never deny that I'd like to make love to you, but that's not the reason why I came in here tonight. I came in here because I respect you enough to overlook your beautiful body, as if that were possible. Whether my uncle had ulterior motives or not when he hired you, I enjoy talking to you. That's why I'm in here!"

"Wow! That was vehement. Okay, I believe you. And I enjoy talking to you too." She was about to continue, but she stopped and sat there thinking for a minute. Jacob looked at her expectantly.

"Look, I don't know if I should do this, but.... what the hell! Here goes. Do you want to know why I'm sort of sensitive on the matter of sex? You don't have to answer. You've talked a lot, so now it's my turn. Just like you need someone to listen so that you can think better, well, so do I, and you're it. You brought this on yourself." She sat still for another long minute and then went on.

"When you came in here, the first thing that you did was to apologize for your mother. And I said that someday I'd tell you about *my* mother. Well, I really hadn't expected to tell you or anyone else about my family, certainly not tonight, but here goes. You've told me a lot about yourself and I'm beginning to feel like we've known each other for a lot longer than three days, so..."

She paused, took a deep breath, and continued. "Jacob, I could have taken a summer job in Presque Isle or in Bangor, but I wanted to get as far away from home as possible. When Mr. Fairstone came up to Hudson to interview, it was like a godsend. I needed a place to live and a way to make some money for next year, and he showed up with an offer to move down to Brunswick, to live with what I hoped was a normal family and earn a good salary. I jumped at the chance so that I wouldn't have to go home to my family. I came here straight from Hudson even though Mr. Fairstone said that I could go home for a week before starting here. Now let me explain why I didn't want to see my family and... and..." – she was trying to keep herself from crying – "and why I really don't want to ever see them again, *any* of them.... O God!" She choked up. "I've never spoken about this to anyone."

She reached for a tissue on the bed table, sniffed a couple of times, and went on. "I've got two older brothers, Andre and Gil. They both dropped out of school after the seventh grade, and they work with my father on a potato farm. Andre is a big guy, a tough guy, and Gil, well, he's sort of slow in the head and harmless. He just follows Andre around and does whatever he says. We have a small house, nothing like this mansion. There are only two bedrooms in our house, one for my mother and father and one for us kids. Even I understood when I was about eleven or twelve that I shouldn't be sharing a bedroom with my brothers any more. I told my mother that I didn't want to be in there with my brothers, but she said that here was nothing that they could do. They couldn't afford to add on a room, and there was nowhere else to sleep. Well, I put up with it until that became impossible.

"Starting around when I was twlve, I couldn't pass Andre's bed without him grabbing at my nightie and trying to pull it up. At first it just seemed like fooling around, but then it became serious. I'm no Jane Russell; I'm not what they call full-figured, but it was about that time that my chest began to develop. And that's when Andre began trying to corner me every chance he got so that he could grab me and feel me up. He would lunge at me and try to unbutton my blouse and say, 'Hey, sis; let's see them little titties.' Somehow I always managed to get away, usually after a well-placed kick. I didn't want to tell my mother because I was embarrassed, but then it got really bad." There were tears in her eyes, and she dabbed at them.

She went on to tell Jacob about the day when her mother and father weren't home and she went bikeriding with some girlfriends. "I was putting my bike away in the barn when suddenly Andre appeared out of nowhere and grabbed me. I think that he had been hiding in the barn waiting for me. Anyway, he grabbed me and pushed me down on the dirt floor and pulled up my dress and climbed on top of me. I began screaming and trying to fight him off, and then Gil heard and came running in. He stood there sort of looking surprised and then he asked if we were wrestling. Andre laughed and said, 'Sure, Gil, and after I finish with her, you can wrestle her.' But Gil got down on his hands and knees and said, 'I want to wrestle now.' By then Andre had his pants down around his legs, and he tried to push Gil away. That put him off balance, and that gave me the chance to reach a pitchfork that was lying on the floor a couple of feet away. I grabbed it and jabbed it into Andre's thigh. He screamed bloody murder, and Gil just stood there puzzled. The pitchfork didn't go in very deep but enough to scare Andre. There was blood running down his leg, and after calling me a few nice names, he ran into the house. I was left lying on the floor panting and, believe it or not, Gil then asked me if it was okay for him to wrestle me or if I would stick him with the pitchfork too."

Jacob was listening to Marie's tortured recital with his mouth open. "O God! You poor kid!"

"Wait. You ain't heard nothin' yet! That wasn't the worst part for me. What was worse was when my parents came home. I waited until I could get my mother alone. There was no way that I could talk about what just happened to my father. When I told my mother what Andre had done to me, I was crying and shaking. She listened and then took my hands and said, 'Marie, darling, you shouldn't be so upset. You know, boys will be boys. I'm sure that Andre wouldn't have hurt you. He's your brother.' I tried to make her understand, but when I told her that I had to stick him with the pitchfork to get him off of me, she yelled, 'You shouldn'ta done that. That was wicked. He could get blood poisoning.' And she ran to find Andre who was in the bathroom trying to bandage up his thigh, and she took over, cleaning the wounds and putting on some antiseptic. I heard him yelling, 'That little bitch stuck me! That little bitch stuck me!' and my mother trying to calm him down. 'She won't do it again. You just shouldn't play so hard.'"

All of this came gushing out of Marie as she looked away from Jacob. Before he could offer any comment, she took a few deep breaths and went on. "That night I refused to go to bed in the room with my brothers. I took an old sleeping bag that I found in the cellar, and I slept on the living room floor, and I told my parents that I was never going to sleep in the same room with my brothers again, that I was too old for that. It took about a month of my sleeping on the floor in that ratty old sleeping bag before my father agreed to partition off a part of their bedroom to make a space big enough for my bed. So that was the Beaulieu sleeping arrangement until the next incident. This will give you a good idea of the kind of family that I come from."

What followed came spilling out of Marie in an almost hysterical torrent. "My father built a plywood partition across a corner of their bedroom, and I moved in. There wasn't any room for a dresser, just my bed, a chair for my clothes, and a little bed table with a lamp. There was hardly any room to move around, but at least I had my privacy. I also began carrying a small knife in a leather sheath from then on, and I let Andre know it. He never stopped making dirty remarks to me when my parents weren't around, but he knew enough to stop molesting me. So things went along okay for a couple of years until one night I noticed something strange. I had gone to bed and was just lying there not asleep yet when I noticed some light shining through a hole on the plywood wall. It was the light from my parents' room. They usually went to bed while I was still doing homework in the kitchen, and I would sneak through their room to mine after they were asleep. But one of them must have gotten up for some reason and turned on the light, and I saw it shining through this hole. I didn't think much about it, and I fell asleep. But the next morning I took a good look at the hole, figuring it must be some kind of knothole or something. It was about five feet up from the floor, and as I looked at it, I saw that it was a drilled hole, maybe an inch across and hardly noticeable. I thought that it was strange, but I figured that my father had used some old wood for the partition and that it must have had a hole drilled in it for some reason. But now that I was aware of the hole, I kept looking at it each night as I got ready for bed.

"And then one night a couple of years ago, I was undressing, and when I was naked I thought I heard something, something like a gasp or heavy breathing on the other side of the partition. I didn't know what it was, and so I just climbed into bed and lay there for a while thinking. Was it possible? My father? No way. But what if…? I decided that I had to know. And so the next day I went looking in the refrigerator and I found a bottle of hot barbecue sauce with a squeeze top. I took it into my room and put it on the chair right next to the hole. That night I finished my homework and as usual sneaked through my parents' room to mine; they were asleep, or at least it looked that way. When I got into my room, I put on the light and then just stood there for a minute listening. And then I heard it, a tiny sound of movement from the other side of the partition. I began undressing very slowly. When my bra and panties were off, I took a little step toward the hole, and then I grabbed the bottle, shoved the top into the hole and squeezed. There was a scream from the other side, and I heard my mother yell, 'What's wrong, Denis? Where are you?' I grabbed my robe and stormed into their room and began screaming at my father who was crumpled to the ground with his hands over his right eye. My mother wanted to know what was going on, and I told her. As calmly as I could, I told her that her husband was a pervert who got his jollies by spying on his naked daughter. With all the evidence right in front of her, she refused to believe it. She asked him what happened, and he said that he had just got up to take a piss when something stung his eye. I called him a liar, and my mother slapped me and called me a trouble-maker.

"Anyway, to make a long sick story short, we agreed that I would move in with my grandmother from then on. My mother told everyone that it was because my grandmother lived closer to the high school, which was true. Neither of my parents came to my graduation, and I continued living with my grandmother – who, by the way, also blamed me for the incident with my father, her son –until I left for Hudson. I got straight A's in high school, and the principal arranged a scholarship for me. Otherwise there is no way that I could go to college. My parents wouldn't give me a penny, and I don't care if I ever see either of them again. You think *your* mother's a problem? I'd trade you any time." And with that, Marie began crying, at first quietly and then with heaving sobs. She tried to control herself, afraid that she'd be heard by someone downstairs, As she began to regain her composure, she said, "Jacob, I think that you'd better go back to your room now. I think that maybe I made a mistake telling you all of this. This wasn't what you expected when you came in."

Jacob got up and hesitated, looking at Marie crouched in a corner of her bed, sobbing. Then he went over to the bed, sat down next to her and took her in his arms. "It's okay; it's okay. I'll just hold you until you feel better. Nothing intimate. Just a friendly hug. Okay?"

She shook her head affirmatively, and they sat there rocking together until she stopped crying. "Are you okay?"

"I'm okay now. I guess I needed that. I never told anyone that story. Whew! I feel a lot better now." She extricated herself from Jacob's arms and looked into his eyes. "I'm okay now, really." And then she smiled and sniffled, "I guess instead of helping you with *your* problem, I laid *mine* on you. Sorry."

"Don't be sorry, please. You helped me a lot. You trusted me with your story. I know you better now. You've sort of become more real for me. You're a lot more than a lovely body. I've learned something… about myself." He got up. "Do you want me to go back to my room?"

"Yes, thanks. I'd like to hold onto you for the rest of the night, but… well, it's not a good idea."

He gave her a final reassuring hug and turned toward the door. Then he turned back and asked, "Can I give you a kiss goodnight?"

"Well, since you asked like a gentleman…" And she lifted up her head to him and smiled. Jacob bent down and gave her a kiss on the forehead and then kissed one of the tears off her cheek. "Good night." And he left.

Thursday was a beautiful day, and when the girls came down for breakfast, he told them that it would be a perfect day for a ride up the coast and for the hike up Mount Battie that he had mentioned when they were at Pemaquid. Before they could answer, Rowena observed pointedly that she had never had the opportunity to climb up Mount Battie and suggested that they might like to take her along. Jacob looked at his mother not knowing how to respond. The last thing that he wanted driving up the coast with the top down and two enthusiastic girls was his *kvetch* of a mother, who seemed to be in a particularly foul mood.

He was searching for some reply when Sarah said, "Rowena, ask Sol to take us up to Mount Battie someday soon. I'm sure he'll be happy to. Jakie and the girls are young and they've got good strong legs. We'd probably hold them back. And anyway, Rowena, I thought that maybe you'd like to go with me to do the shopping for tomorrow night. With Jacob here, I'd like us to have a real Shabbes. I've got to get some *Kiddush* wine and a big chicken for roasting for Shabbes dinner; and maybe in the bakery we'll find something that looks like a challah. Better you and I should go shopping than go mountain climbing."

Jacob looked at his aunt gratefully, remembering that it was Sol and Sarah who first took him to the Camden Hills Park a couple of years back. He recalled that Mount Battie was a pretty easy climb and that Sarah had had no trouble at all keeping up. But he nodded at what his aunt had said and added, "She's right, Mother. It's a pretty rugged climb. I think that you should wait for another time."

Rowena humphed and said, "I thank you both for your concern. I know when I'm not wanted. I just thought that Justin would appreciate someone along who could provide some intelligent conversation."

"I guess that we'll have to save that for some other time, Mother. And I think that I can depend on Hope and Marie for conversation." He turned his attention to the girls. "You'll both need sturdy walking shoes and long pants for the climb." Turning back to his mother: "Do you want to go shopping along with Aunt Sarah or would you prefer that I take you to the library again."

"Well I certainly don't want to spend my time here in a grocery store. I can do that back in Winthrop, although now that

I'm alone, I don't do very much grocery shopping. Justin, you can take me to the library while the girls are getting ready. There's something that I need to talk over with you.... alone."

Jacob hurried his mother into the car so that he could get back to the girls as quickly as possible. He had no sooner started the engine and begun driving down the long driveway when Rowena went on the attack. "Justin, you're a fool. With all your education, you're a fool. You're no better than your father."

"What suddenly brought this on?"

"What brought this on? You don't know? Why do you think that I wanted to go along with you and the girls? In order to climb a mountain? Sometimes you seem as stupid as Sarah. Justin, I heard you last night. I heard you in that slut Marie's room, and I heard her moaning. What's got into you? She's a *shikse*! Worse; she's a low-class Canuck and a Catholic. That's what I sent you to Harvard for? You should be ashamed of yourself!"

Jacob had all he could do to keep the car on a straight course. He was ready to explode, and after about a half-mile of rigid restraint, he did. "How dare you talk about a decent person like that! You're a real shrew and a bigot to boot! Yes, I was in Marie's room last night, and no, we did not have sex. Believe it or not, we were commiserating with each other about our problem mothers!"

"Watch your tongue, young man! All that moaning and groaning last night and you were just talking? I don't believe you. So you had to *shtup* a *shikse,* just like your uncle. He's a notorious *shikse-shtupper.*"

"Mother, how did you happen to hear all this 'moaning and groaning?' From your room downstairs? You weren't by any chance eavesdropping, were you?"

"I was *not* eavesdropping. I was lying in bed reading, and I heard Marie leaving Hope's room and going upstairs. I think that Sarah made a big mistake putting Marie next to your room, and I told her so right after that whore Essie left with her latest *schlemiel.*"

"Mother, I asked you how you heard what was going on in Marie's room. Enough about sluts and whores. How could you hear from your room with two closed doors and a flight of stairs in between? Tell me the truth!"

"All right; the truth. I'm your mother and I have an obligation to protect you from someone who could ruin your life. I'm not ashamed to admit it. I got out of bed and listened from the stairs. At first I didn't hear anything, and I thought that you must be asleep, but then, when I was about to go back to my room, I heard you moving. So I waited. All I heard for a while was some muted conversation that I couldn't make out, and then the moaning started. I was disgusted, but the last thing that I wanted was to burst in on you and make a scene and wake up Sol and Sarah. So I went back to bed determined to have a talk with you, to make you come to your senses before it's too late. All right, so you *shtup* a *shikse* who has her eyes on you once or twice. I guess that every healthy Jewish boy has to give it a try. It's a notch in your male belt. Now that you've done it, you can be man enough to admit it and stop it. I'm telling you this for your own good because I'm your mother, and I care about you even if you've forgotten that."

"Mother, all you care about is ripping apart other people, *good* people like Aunt Sarah and Essie and Dad and now Marie. Your own life is so totally screwed up that you've got to try to ruin other people's lives. The only reason that you get along with Uncle Sol is because he has money, and you know that he'll take care of you no matter how nasty you are. Mother, Marie Beaulieu is a nicer person than you could ever hope to be. I enjoy her company. It's refreshing; it's honest. She's not a *shikse,* she's a decent human being who shared some of her personal history with me last night. We did not make love, although that's none of your business. And I think that it's really grotesque that you stood on the stairs in the middle of the night listening to us. You're so dried up and frustrated that it probably gave you a perverted thrill to imagine your son *fucking!*"

Jacob had never used that word within the hearing of a member of the older generation, certainly not with his mother. He almost shouted it, and it had had desired effect. As they drove past the Borden field house and into Brunswick, Rowena stared straight ahead in silence. But then, as Jacob slowed down on College Avenue near the library, she snapped, "I changed my mind. I don't want to go to the library. Take me to Sol's office. I'm going to tell him to get rid of that *shikse,* and I'm going to have him get me a driver to take me back to Winthrop. I can't stay another minute under the same roof with stupid Sarah and that *nafke* who obviously has you under her spell."

"Mother ...." He was about to respond in kind, but then, "You know, I don't even want to call you mother. I'm beginning to sympathize with Lizzie Borden. I'll be happy to take you to Uncle Sol's office and to see the last of you."

Not another word passed between them as Jacob made his way up Maine Street to Fort Andross. Before the car came to a complete stop in the parking lot, Rowena pushed open the door. She jumped out and headed for the entrance. Then she stopped, turned and yelled, "Tell that cow Sarah to pack up my things and give the bag to Sol. He'll send it to me. And you can tell your *shikse* that I hope she breaks a leg on the way up Mount Battie."

Jacob sat in the parking lot looking after his mother as she disappeared into Fort Andross, his heart pounding. For a moment he wondered whether she could actually convince her brother to get rid of Marie, but it took him only a moment to decide that that would not happen. Sol was used to his sister's venom. Would he believe that Jacob was sexually involved with Marie? Possibly. And if he did believe it, would it really matter to him? Wasn't it possible that that was actually what Sol wanted? Jacob shrugged and headed back to the Fairstone estate. He resolved not to say a word about his mother's rant and her decision to leave, which he welcomed. It was too beautiful a day to spend even one more minute thinking about his mother.

As they got into the car, Marie made it a point to seat Hope in the front next to Jacob, and she slid into the rear seat. With the top down, they had to shout as they drove through Bath, over the rusty bridge spanning the Kennebec, and into the quaint village of Wiscasset. Jacob had considered that nice restaurant in Wiscasset for lunch, but it was just after eleven-thirty, and no one was quite hungry yet. And then he remembered the old diner in Nobleboro that was one of Sol's favorites. Sol could easily afford the finest restaurants in Boston and New York, and he often patronized them, but he insisted that rough-hewn, unpretentious Moody's Diner in Nobleboro served the best berry pies west of Vilna. Shouting over the wind as they drove through Damariscotta, he informed the girls that they were going to eat where ordinary Mainers ate and not to be put off by the décor.

After a delicious haddock lunch topped off with three oozing portions of mixed berry pie a la mode, they continued up Route 1 through Waldoboro to Thomaston where Jacob pointed out the state prison and the gift shop that featured creations by the inmates. When he explained that some of the salesmen were actually prisoners on good behavior, the girls were curious and insisted on stopping there. After a few minutes of rifling through a profusion of wood-carved souvenirs and staring at the personnel, Hope bought a small model of a lobster boat, and Marie bought a tiny rowboat with three frogs sitting on the gunnels with fishing poles in their hands. That kept them all giggling through the Camden bottleneck and on to the entrance to Camden Hills State Park.

Jacob was about to make a left turn into the park when he changed his mind. He slowed down and said, "It's still pretty early; would you mind if I took a couple of minutes to perform an act of homage?"

"Homage to what?" Hope asked.

"Well, it's a long story that might not interest you, but it has to do with an estate a little way past here toward Lincolnville. It's called Casa Bidu. Whenever I drive up this way, I slow down at Casa Bidu and honk the horn a few times."

"What in heaven's name for?" Marie wanted to know.

"I don't suppose that either of you has heard of the soprano, Bidu Sayao? Well, ..."

Before he could continue, Marie said, “I’ve heard of her. A few of us Hudson students who like classical music meet on Monday nights at the house of this guy Hank who has a hi-fi system hooked up in the rec room in his cellar. He’s a real music lover and he knows a lot. His parents always go to the movies on Monday nights, and so that’s our music night. I love it. I didn’t even know that there was such a thing as classical music when I was living at home. Anyway, this past year we’ve been listening mostly to operas, and a few of his records had Bidu Sayao as the soprano. She’s great. I think that she’s from Brazil.”

Jacob broke into a broad grin. “I had no idea that you liked classical music. We’ve really got to get to know each other better.”

Hope began snickering. When they both asked her what was so funny, she shook her head. But after a few “come-ons” and “let-us-in-on-the-jokes”, she blushed and blurted, “I thought that you would be getting to know each other a lot better up there in the attic.”

Marie answered quickly, “Hope, I want you to know that your cousin is a perfect gentleman. I think of him as the guardian of my virtue. All we do up there is talk. Okay?”

“Okay. Sorry. So what about this Bidu Say Ow?” And she laughed again.

“One night Hank played a recording of a little Puccini opera, and I remember that there was a beautiful aria in it that was sung by Bidu Sayao. We liked it so much that we asked Hank to play it again, just that aria. I can’t remember the name of it.”

“That must have been *O Mio Babbino Caro* from *Gianni Schicchi.* It’s a really beautiful aria and one of her favorites. God, I can’t tell you how happy I am that you like music and that you know about Bidu Sayao. Maybe now you won’t think that I’m crazy when I tell you why I want to drive a little further up this road.

“I’ve loved Bidu Sayao ever since I heard a recording of her singing a song that was written by another Brazilian, Villa Lobos. He wrote a group of pieces in honor of Johann Sebastian Bach that he called *Bachianas Brasileiras.* The recording was of Sayao singing *Bachianas Brasileiras* number 5, and it was absolutely exquisite. That was the first I ever heard of Sayao, back around when I was about fifteen. And since then I've been to a couple of her recitals. She retired from the Met in '52, the same year that I graduated from Harvard. I actually hitched from Boston to New York to attend her final performance there. Believe it or not, I sneaked in holding an old Met program, and I stood in the back of the first balcony through the performance. The audience went wild when she took her final curtain call. I'll never forget that night. After the performance I actually walked from the Met to the West Side Highway, and I hitched back to Cambridge so that I wouldn't miss a nine-o'clock class."

"So where are we going now?" Hope asked.

"Well, Bidu Sayao loves the coast of Maine, like I do, and she bought an estate just beyond here, between Route 1 and the ocean. She's been living here since her retirement, and you can tell which is her house because there's a sign out front that says 'Casa Bidu.' Whenever I'm up this way, I drive by there slowly, and I make five short beeps on the horn, five beeps in honor of her *Bachianas Brasileiras* number 5. I don't know whether she's ever heard my beeps or whether she knows why five, but it makes me feel good, like I owe it to her."

Hope said, "Okay, I'm riding shotgun, so I'll look for the sign." And about two minutes later, she yelled, "I think I see it. That red and white sign?"

"That's it." He slowed down, beeped the horn lightly five times, and then found a driveway where he could turn the car around and head back toward Camden.

Climbing up Mount Battie, Jacob wanted desperately to talk more to Marie about her love for music. Which composers? Which conductors? Which soloists? More and more he was feeling a bond developing between them. She had actually heard of Bidu Sayao! She was brought up in a miserable family in rural Maine; she attended a college that he had never heard of; she was not Jewish; but.... She was intelligent and sensitive; she loved music; his mother was utterly contemptuous of her; she was beautiful....

About half way up the trail, Hope began to flag. The extra thirty or so pounds that she was carrying were not helpful. The trail was rated as moderate, and Hope had said that she wanted to climb, so they had set out together at a rather brisk pace. After Hope had stopped a second time, pouring sweat and panting, Jacob asked her if she really wanted to continue to the top and offered to stay with her while Marie went up alone. But Hope insisted that she could make it. Jacob looked at Marie who clearly did not want to see Hope fail. She stood there thinking for a moment and then said "Look, Hope, why don't you sort of lean on Jacob and me. We'll get on either side of you, and you put your hands around our waists, and we'll go up like the three musketeers, all for one and one for all. Okay?"

Hope nodded and after an hour's struggle, they made it to the top where the three of them dropped onto the ground. Hope was exultant. "We made it! We made it! I promise I'm going to get rid of all this fat. I promise! When you're here next year, Jacob, I'll race you to the top, and I'll beat you."

The three of them lay there at the base of the stone tower laughing and catching their breath until Jacob said, "We came up here to see the view. You both okay to climb up the tower?" Hope said that she was satisfied with the view that they had from where they were, but Marie wanted to go up with Jacob. The view from the top was spectacular – the boats bobbing in Camden harbor, the sweep of Penobscot Bay with Cadillac Mountain just barely visible on the northeast horizon, the rock-bound piney coast. They stood there soaking it in and breathing the cool mountain air. Without a word, they joined hands and just stood there until Marie abruptly looked at Jacob and asked: "Jacob, what's Shabbes?"

"What?"

"I said, What's Shabbes?"

"Where did that come from? We're standing here on the top of Mount Battie looking at one of the most spectacular views on the Maine coast, and suddenly you ask 'What's Shabbes?!"

Marie dropped Jacob's hand, looked him in the eye, and said, "Jacob Ross, don't make fun of me. Just before we left this morning, Mrs. Fairstone said that she wanted to go shopping for Shabbes. She mentioned something that sounded like holly and something else that I didn't understand. It must be something Jewish, and I don't want to look like an ignoramus. I want to feel comfortable with the Fairstones, and I can't be comfortable if I don't know what they're talking about. I thought that you could help me understand, but if you don't …."

"Whoa, I didn't say that I didn't want to help you. Of course, I do. It was just that your question came out of left field while we were enjoying this great view."

"Well, I'll admit it. It's been bothering me since we left Harpswell, but I didn't want to sound stupid in front of Hope. So are you going to tell me or not?"

"Sure. Okay, I understand. There are probably a lot of things that Uncle Sol and Aunt Sarah say that are strange to you. Sometimes, coming from Boston and Chicago, it's hard for me to believe that there are people who aren't familiar with some basic Jewish words. But I guess that there aren't many people in Presque Isle who celebrate Shabbes.

"Okay; to begin with, it's actually Shabbat, not Shabbes. Shabbes is the old Yiddish…." Marie looked at him blankly. "Wow. Okay, Yiddish. Yiddish is the language that Jews spoke in Eastern Europe where Aunt Sarah's and Uncle Sol's parents came from. The Hebrew or Israeli pronunciation is Shabbat. That's the way that most younger Jews, including me, say it."

"So what's Shabbat?"

"Shabbat is the Sabbath day. We call the period from sunset on Friday to sunset on Saturday, Shabbat, and we celebrate it with special prayers and songs and foods. It's a day to sort of step back from the hustle and bustle of everyday life and take a deep breath, relax and think about what's important and what's not so important. What we're doing now is sort of like Shabbat. We're standing at a high place and looking out at the view and soaking it in. Well, Shabbat is like a high place at the end of every week. It gives us a chance to separate ourselves from ordinary life and evaluate."

"Sounds sort of heavy. Is that what you and the Fairstones are going to be doing tomorrow night and Saturday? So what should *I* do?"

"No, no. I don't want you to get the wrong idea. Shabbat isn't heavy. Actually, it's a very joyous day. One of the prophets said that we should call Shabbat *oneg* – a pleasure. The reason that Aunt Sarah is going shopping for special things like *challah* – that's a special twisted loaf of bread that we say a prayer over – is that the Shabbat dinner is supposed to be very festive. There are even special songs that we sing at the table. I used to love going to my grandparents' house for Shabbat. It was beautiful, and my zeyde – my grandfather – would always put his hands on my head and give me a blessing. Believe it or not, even my mother usually behaved nicely on Shabbat. She wasn't as religious as my grandparents or my father, but she did make Shabbat special in our home."

"Your mother! The same mother that you were complaining about last night. She doesn't seem to like me much. I can see it the way she looks at me. Do you think that she'll be nice during Shabbat? There; I said it – Shabbat."

"My mother, I am happy to report, will not be with us. We had a big fight while I was driving her into town this morning, and she decided to go home to Winthrop. Good riddance!"

"Jacob, you shouldn't say that about your … Hey, scratch that. As you know, I've said a lot worse about my mother. So here we stand, at the top of Mount Battie, a couple of motherless children." She took his hand again, thought for a minute and then said, "Wouldn't it be nice to hear Bidu Sayao singing *Sometimes I feel like a motherless child*? Maybe we should drive back up to her house and ask her."

Jacob looked at her in amazement and then took both her hands and kissed her on the lips. She didn't push him away, but she didn't respond either. "I wasn't expecting that. Please…. I'm already confused enough. Don't make it worse. Let's climb back down and get Hope. She's been alone long enough."

The trio of mountain climbers got back to the Fairstone estate just in time for supper. Sol had arrived about an hour before them and was delighted to hear that Hope had climbed Mount Battie. More important, she reported on the events of the day to her parents with unwonted enthusiasm, as Jacob and Marie stood by smiling.

Later at the supper table Sarah reported on her shopping expedition. "You think that climbing Mount Battie was something? How about trying to find a *challah* for Shabbes in Brunswick? They never heard of it. I was going to settle for a nice looking Italian bread, but then I thought: this will be Jacob's only Shabbes with us until September; we've got to have a beautiful *challah.* And so I drove all the way down to Portland, and while I was there, I found some whitefish and carp that I can grind up for *gefilte* fish. And I bought *chrain* too. Jakie, it's going to be just like at Zeyde and Bobbe's in Malden. I'll make a nice chicken soup and a roasted chicken with *kompot,* and what you like best, Jakie, a potato kugel! And Sumner will join us; I already called him. It will be a real family Shabbes… except I was sorry to hear that your mother won't be with us. Sol said that she decided to go back to Winthrop. She has some kind of a meeting there that she didn't want to miss. But she left so quickly. She didn't even come back for her things. We'll have to send them to her. Nu, maybe it's for the best."

Sol chimed in. "Jakie, you'll make *Kiddush* and we'll even sing some of my father's *zemires.* That would make him very happy, and it's his *yahrzeit* this week."

Marie had been sitting very quietly absorbing all of the ethnic code swirling around the table, but finally she shrugged her shoulders and said, "Jacob explained Shabbes or Shabbat to me, but I'm afraid that a lot of what you're talking about is new to me. I'm not complaining, but you'll have to help me with a lot of the other words that you're using. Remember, I'm from Presque Isle. If you couldn't find a holly… no, that's not it – a *chcholly* – in Brunswick, how about Presque Isle?"

Sol answered immediately. "Marie, you're a hundred percent right. We shouldn't use language that you don't understand. Jakie, I've got a job for you, your first assignment as my right-hand man. I want you to spend a couple of hours giving Marie a basic course on Judaism, enough so that she can feel at home living with a Jewish family. Marie, I want you to be comfortable here. I want you to stay with us for a long time. Hope likes you, and Jakie likes you, and *we* like you. So, Jakie, you'll accept the assignment?"

"Hmm, I'll have to think it over," he answered with a smile. .... Okay, I've thought. I'll accept on one condition."

"Nu?"

"I'm very happy that we're going to have a nice traditional Shabbat dinner tomorrow night. Thank you very much, Aunt Sarah, for all that you're doing to make it really nice..."

Before he could continue with his condition, Hope interrupted. "Mom, I'll help you tomorrow. I'd like to help make it nice in memory of Zayde and because it's Jakie's only Shabbat with us."

Sarah's mouth fell open. When she regained her composure, she said, "Hope, that was a very lovely offer. You're making me and Daddy very happy."

Sol too was impressed. "Very nice, Hope. So Jakie, what's the condition already."

"Seriously, I don't have any conditions; I'll be happy to brief Marie about Shabbat and other Jewish things, but there is one thing that I would like to do on Shabbat morning. I'd like the two of us to go to shul in Portland so that we can say *Kaddish* for Zeyde. Is that all right? I could drive down myself. I know where the shul is, but I'd love you to come along. Okay?"

"Okay? Sure it's okay. We'll drive down together, and maybe I'll get an *aliyah* and they'll make a *hazkore* for Zeyde. Jakie boy, I should have known that you'd have a condition like that. I love you; me and Sarah and Hope, we all love you. You should only know how much I want you to move up here to Maine with us. Okay; okay; I know. Enough said."

Toward the end of a very pleasant supper of broiled salmon, sweet corn and salad along with a delicious Vouvray, Sol suddenly laughed. "Hey, Jakie, when you're teaching Marie about Shabbes, one thing you can skip." A wink. "You know what I mean?"

Jacob looked puzzled. "What's the matter, Jakie, you don't remember the big *mitzvah* for Shabbes? You're going to get a Ph.D. and you don't remember about the real *oneg Shabbes*? It's a *mitzvah* that I can't mention at the table?" He laughed again as Jacob turned red.

"I think that we'll skip over that, but thanks for reminding me. This crash course will be Judaism 101. That particular *mitzvah* is in 102." And they both laughed while the ladies looked mystified.

When supper ended, Jacob turned to Marie and said, "We may as well start your tutorial now. Let's sit in the living room where it's comfortable. You can curl up on the sofa."

"Great! Hey, Hope, you want to join us?"

To Jacob's surprise, and even more so Sarah's and Sol's, Hope assented enthusiastically. "I only went to Hebrew school for a couple of years when I was about seven or eight, and I don't remember anything from that. So yup; me too."

For an hour and more, Jacob went through the fundamentals of Judaism – the holidays, the life cycle, a quick review of history, and even a bit of theology, all punctuated by probing questions from Marie. She started asking about the words that Sol and Sarah had used at the table – *Kiddush, mitzvah,* and a few others that she wasn't sure how to pronounce. She found it hard to believe that there was no place for Jesus in Judaism, and she was particularly interested in the way that Jacob described joyous family celebrations like the Sabbath eve meal and the Passover *seder.* From the little that she had garnered from the nuns in high school, she had an image of Jews as being doomed to suffering for their rejection of Jesus. She envisioned the synagogue as a place where Jews lamented over their guilt, and Jacob was taken aback when she asked if it was true that blood was used in the manufacture of "those wafers that Jews use on Passover."

He hadn't intended to bring up subjects like the blood libel and anti-Semitism, but he was so immersed in the study of

French anti-Semitism and so angered by it, especially the French cooperation with Hitler's attempt to exterminate the Jews of Europe within his lifetime, that he pounced on Marie's question. He denounced Christianity in general and the Catholic Church, Marie's church, in particular. He said that it was because simple people believed such nonsense as the use of blood in matzah and Jewish complicity in the crucifixion of Jesus and hundreds of other lies preached from church pulpits that it was possible for Hitler to enlist tens of thousands in his program of extermination. When he saw that he was making Marie uncomfortable, he caught his breath and said, "I'm sorry, Marie. I wasn't aiming this diatribe at you. I just get carried away when I hear anyone repeating one of those old lies that caused Jews so much suffering."

Looking down, Marie whispered sarcastically, "I'm sorry I said anything. I'll just sit here like a good little girl and listen."

Jacob looked at her and said, "No, *I'm* sorry. I *want* you to ask questions, and you too, Hope. It's just that I sort of lose it when I come across traces of Christian anti-Semitism. What you were taught by the nuns at your school is certainly not your fault. But whenever I hear that kind of stuff, I think of the family that my grandfather left in Lithuania. They were all wiped out because Christians believed ugly lies about Jews.

"Anyway, that's not what I wanted to talk about tonight, because Judaism is a religion that teaches us to enjoy life. There have been a lot of tragedies in Jewish history, the latest being the Holocaust, but if you really study the whole sweep of Jewish history, it's very positive. There were great Jewish thinkers, authors and poets and philosophers in every generation. You know, there's actually a teaching in one of the early Jewish law codes that says that God will call you to account for any legitimate pleasure that you didn't experience. God gave us bodies that can experience pleasure and a whole world full of gifts for us to enjoy. That's why we don't have any Jewish monks. Asceticism is not considered a good thing in Judaism."

He was about to go on when he noticed Hope yawning. He looked at his watch and saw that it was after eleven. Sol and Sarah had already gone up to their room. "I guess that we'd better stop here. If you want, we can continue tomorrow. The weather's supposed to be a bit iffy tomorrow. I thought that I'd go out on the boat for a while, but that may not be possible. We'll see. Okay?"

They exchanged "good nights," and on the way up to their rooms, Marie asked Hope if she wanted her to stop in for a few minutes. Hope answered that she was tuckered out from the day's climb and that she just wanted to get to sleep. "See ya tomorrow."

Jacob couldn't decide whether it would be wise to knock on Marie's door after she finished in the bathroom. She had been clearly annoyed by the vehemence of his response to her question about "those wafers that Jews use." He could only smile at her choice of the word "wafer". Of course, she got that from Communion in her church. The wafer was the symbolic body of Christ. She had almost twenty years of exposure to the teachings of her church, and he was going to give her a crash course in Judaism? Good luck! But.... but she had rejected her family; she hadn't mentioned anything about going to church in Brunswick; she seemed to have an appreciation of music; and she was curious. She wanted to learn. He decided that it would be best not to bother Marie. He'd try to make it up with her the next morning. If the weather was good, maybe she'd go out on the boat with him ... with Hope along, of course. He brushed his teeth at the washstand in his room rather than using the bathroom and possibly bothering Marie, and reluctantly he climbed into bed and closed his eyes. But ....

He wanted to talk to her; he wanted to be with her for at least a few minutes without Hope or Sol or Sarah around. Had he hurt her by talking the way he did about her church? Did she feel that she was in alien if not hostile territory? She was cut off from family and friends. She needed someone whom she could trust, and the previous night she had chosen him. He thought about how it had felt to hold her in his arms in her bedroom. But she had not responded to his kiss on Mount Battie. That was a mistake. If only he could hold her now. He took the pillow from under his head, and he hugged it. He could feel the blood rushing to his loins, and as his hand went under the covers to his shorts, there was a knock on the bathroom door. Quickly he extricated his hand, replaced his pillow and said, "Come in."

Marie stood at the door outlined by the bathroom light, the terry bathrobe cinched tightly around her waist. "You awake?"

"Sure; come in."

"No, I'd better stand here. I just wanted you to know that I'm not angry at you. You were sharing your feelings honestly, like I want you to. But … well, when you were talking about the Holocaust and Christianity, I realized how big a gulf here is between us. All that I know about the Holocaust is what I read in *The Diary of Anne Frank* in high school. I like you, very much. It was great talking to you last night and … and holding you. That was nice but … but you shouldn't have kissed me this afternoon. You're getting me even more confused. I don't know if you have real feelings for me or if it's your hormones." He began to object, but she cut him off. "I know… I know…. It all has to do with my suspicions about the motives of men. I don't have to explain that to you; I already did. But anyway, I wanted you to know that I'm not angry at you, and I do want to learn more about Judaism. Friends?"

"Sure; friends. *Good* friends."

She blew him a kiss from the doorway and was about to step through when she stopped and turned back to him. "One more thing. Another question. And remember, you promised to be honest with me."

"Shoot."

"You and Mr. Fairstone shared some kind of a joke at the table, and I think it might have been about me. You turned red and said that I wasn't ready for whatever it was that you both knew. Mr. Fairstone said something about a special *mitzvah* on Shabbat. You already explained about a *mitzvah.* I know that a *mitzvah* is a commandment or a custom that you're supposed to do, like celebrating Shabbat. So what's this special Shabbat *mitzvah* that I'm not old enough to know about?"

"Wow! Now you're going to embarrass me, like a couple of nights ago when you asked me what nubile means. Are you sure you want to know?"

"Uh huh; come on now; no secrets. I'm a big girl."

"I've noticed that." If the light were on in his room, she would have noticed that his face was red. "Okay; you asked for it. You'd better sit down."

As she sat down on the chair at his book-laden table, he said, "I've already explained that Shabbat is a day for enjoyment and relaxation. And I told you about prayers in the synagogue and reading the Torah and delicious meals with wine and songs. All of that is a part of *oneg Shabbat,* the special joy of Shabbat. But that's only part of it."

"So what else?"

"Well, there's a custom that probably goes back to the mystics of sixteenth-century Palestine or maybe even earlier. They used to go out into the fields toward sunset on Fridays to welcome *Shabbat ha-malkah* – the Sabbath queen. They thought of Shabbat as the day of union between God and the people of Israel. And they composed a beautiful hymn to celebrate that union, it's called '*L'cha Dodi* – Come, my beloved.' Uncle Sol and I won't be going to synagogue tomorrow night; we'll go on Saturday morning, but maybe I'll sing *L'cha Dodi* at our Shabbat table. And Uncle Sol, if he remembers how, will recite a few verses from the end of the book of Proverbs that describes a virtuous woman. Every Jewish husband is supposed to recite those verses to his wife, sort of to create an amorous atmosphere that's connected to the union between God and Israel."

"This is getting interesting."

"Patience; I'm getting to the good part. In that hymn that I mentioned, *L'cha Dodi,* one of the verses describes how God rejoices over Israel on Shabbat: 'as a bridegroom rejoices over his bride.' Are you getting the picture?"

"I… I think so. It's beginning to sound X-rated?"

"Well, sort of. To make a long explanation short, based on all of what I've described, husbands and wives are supposed to make love on Shabbat. That's the *mitzvah* that Uncle Sol was referring to. It's certainly not one of the essentials of Judaism, but it's the kind of tradition that would stick in the mind of someone like my Uncle Sol."

Marie sat there quietly for a long minute, and then she said slowly, "So you're saying that making love, sex, is a *mitzvah* in Judaism? I can't believe it! The sisters always taught us that sex is dirty, that it's giving in to the lusts of the flesh. They taught us that we should be chaste, and that taking vows of chastity, like the priests and the nuns do, is what God wants. Hmmm....".

She was quiet for a moment and then laughed and said, "Do you know that one of the nuns, Sister Evangelista, tried to convince me to become a nun? And she almost succeeded. That was around the same time that my brother Andre attacked me. I was about fifteen, and I guess that I was beginning to look pretty good. I complained to Sister Evangelista that boys were trying to mess around with me, and I asked her what I should do. So she told me to dress more modestly and to pray a lot and that if I really wanted to put off the boys, I should tell them that I was going to be a nun. And from then on until I graduated, she kept urging me to take vows. She even made me watch a movie with her in the school chapel, *The Bells of Saint Mary's*, with Ingrid Bergman. She said that if someone as beautiful as Ingrid Bergman could be a nun, so could I. It was as if she actually believed that Ingrid Bergman was a nun. Anyway, I really thought about it, but then I got that scholarship to Hudson and I stopped thinking about it. I would have hated that life." She got up to leave but then paused and said, "So making love is a *mitzvah* in Judaism! Wow! I can't believe it! On the holy day, on Shabbat? Wow again! I want to learn more about your religion."

"Always happy to share information."

"So tell me. How come you know so much about Judaism? You're not a rabbi" – she pronounced the unfamiliar word as rabbie – "but you seem to know a lot more than Mr. and Mrs. Fairstone."

"Don't be so impressed. I've got a lot more to learn. But I used to study with my zeyde who knew a lot more than most rabbis.

And oh, it's pronounced rabbi, with a long i. Anyway, I went to a Hebrew high school in Boston for four years and during my first two years at Harvard, I took courses at Hebrew Teachers College. So I've got a pretty good Jewish education."

She got up to leave and then paused and asked: "Hey, can I call you Jakie, like your uncle and aunt, or maybe Jake?"

"Sure; I'd like that."

"I like talking to you, Jake. I'll miss you when you leave."

"I'll be back at the end of the summer."

"By that time you'll probably be engaged to Miss Chicago or Miss Radcliffe."

He laughed. "Not very likely; I haven't decided yet what I want to be when I grow up. When I make *that* decision, I'll probably ask some nice young woman to share my life."

"A nice *Jewish* young woman?"

Jacob was struck dumb by the question. He looked at Marie, opened his mouth and closed it again. "I... I...."

"I shouldn't have asked that. Sorry."

"No, that's okay. Really, it's okay."

"Good night, Jake. Sweet dreams."

"Good night, Marie. And ... and thanks for coming in."

Jacob knew that he wouldn't be able to fall asleep just yet. He lay in his bed thinking. Had he really not yet decided what he wanted to be? Why had he jokingly said "when I grow up?" He had decided during his freshman year at Harvard that he wanted to be a professor. He loved teaching, and he loved history, especially Jewish history. He wanted to make other people love it too. That's why he read so voraciously; that's what he wanted to do with his life, to teach. But what about that offer from Uncle Sol? How could he pass that up? How many other people his age were offered a future of guaranteed wealth in a place that was so beautiful. But to give up academe? How could he even consider that?

Maybe, he thought, I haven't really grown up yet if I can be tempted by what Uncle Sol has to offer. He thought of Faust and Mephistopheles and laughed. Mephistopheles Fairstone, tempting him with the pleasures of the flesh. Ah, but there was Faust's beautiful Marguerite.... Marguerite.... Marguerite.... And suddenly he sat bolt upright. My God, he thought; "your golden hair Margarete...," that amazing poem by Paul Celan, *Death Fugue*! Over and over again in that frightening poem about the seductions of Nazi Germany, the symbol of the golden-haired Margarete. Was there a connection between Faust's Marguerite and Celan's Margarete? Between those two golden-haired sirens and ... and Marie? Your golden hair Margarete, your golden hair Margarete... your golden hair Marie....Marie.... Marie.... God, she's so lovely! And finally, his hand an inadequate substitute, he fell asleep.

The next morning at breakfast, Marie offered to help Sarah and Hope with the preparations for Shabbat, but Sarah said that she was looking forward to spending the day working with Hope. "It's such a beautiful day; it would be a shame for all of us to spend it in the house. Jakie, what are you planning to do today, more reading?"

"Some. I'm working my way through a Yiddish book about France, and I'd like to finish it this morning. That should take me two or three more hours, and then I thought that I'd take the boat and do a little cruising around Eagle Island, maybe fish a little too. But if you have any chores for me to do for tonight, just say the word. I'd like to help too."

"No need," Sarah was emphatic. "You're not here to work. Anyway I have a great idea. Why don't you take Marie out on the boat with you. She spends all her time with Hope; she deserves a little time for herself. And you can take her to one of those seaside restaurants that you love for lunch. And if you catch any fish, don't bring them home. I've got the whitefish and carp for my special *gefilte* fish, and we're going to have a nice roast capon. What do you say?"

"Marie, I'd love to take you out on the boat. You interested?"

For a moment she weighed the wisdom of being out on Casco Bay alone with Jacob, but then quickly agreed. "Sounds nice. You sure that you don't need me, Mrs. Fairstone? Hope, okay with you?"

They both agreed that she deserved some time for herself. "Okay, Jacob, I accept your invitation, but I've got to warn you. I've never been on a boat out in the ocean. I've been in canoes a few times on the Aroostook River, but I'm mostly a landlubber. I've been looking at that lovely boat since I arrived here and wondered if I'd ever have the nerve to go out on it. I guess that now's as good a time as any."

"Great. I should be ready around noon. You'll need boat shoes or sneakers. I know a great place where we can pull in for lunch." As he spoke, he thought back to the last time – the *only* time – that he had been out on a boat alone with a woman – the most memorable day of his life. Was it possible…? It was hard for him to concentrate on Tcherikover over the next three hours, but he did manage somehow to finish the book. He was about to leave his room when he had a thought. He opened the second drawer of his bureau, looked at the small box labeled Trojans hidden under his socks and reached for them. Maybe? Out around Halfway Rock? Why not take a chance? If she said no, he certainly wouldn't try to force her. And he was leaving on Sunday; no harm done. He stood there hesitating, and then he slapped his hand. Wrong! I'm not my Uncle Sol. He left the room empty-handed … with regret.

When he went down to the dock to get the boat ready, Marie was already there. She was wearing Bermudas and a Ship 'n Shore blouse, newly acquired during Sarah's Freeport spree, along with a kerchief that hid most of her golden hair. After they had donned their life preservers, they were off. Jacob carefully threaded the boat through the maze of lobster buoys in Wills Gut and then headed south toward Lands End and Jaquish Island, pointing out the Giant Steps and the monument on Little Mark. There was a mild chop to the water and so he checked with Marie before heading out into Casco Bay. She said that she was feeling fine, and so he revved up the engine and headed out. "Is it all right with you if we cruise around for a while before lunch? I'd like to show you that lighthouse that you like to look at through your window close up."

Twenty minutes later they did a couple of loops around Halfway Rock Lighthouse with Jacob pointing out the keeper's house and explaining some of the history. "You can see how rocky it is around the ledges. I once tried to pull the boat in, but it's almost impossible. I'm afraid that Uncle Sol had to replace the propeller after that experience. So I won't dare bring us any closer than this."

Marie was enjoying herself tremendously. "Wow! I've never been this close to a lighthouse. I can see why they need one here. All these ledges must be a real hazard to ships. And look at that little house! I guess that's where the keeper lives. Must be pretty lonely, especially in the winter."

"You're right about needing a lighthouse here. A couple of ships came aground on these ledges before the government agreed to build it back in the 1870's."

"Why do they call it Halfway Rock? Halfway from what?"

"Good question, especially because I know the answer. Just keep asking questions that I can answer. Makes me feel good."

"Okay, so what's the answer, wise guy?"

"Well, you've heard of Casco Bay?" She nodded. "The southern end of Casco Bay is Cape Elizabeth below Portland, and the northern end is Cape Small which you can just barely see there." He pointed toward the northeastern horizon. "This light is almost exactly halfway from one cape to the other."

Marie was staring off in the direction indicated by Jacob. "Don't I see another lighthouse way off there, or is in my imagination."

"Wow! You've got pretty sharp eyes. I can't see it, but I know it's there, because I pass it whenever I go trolling on the Kennebec. That's Seguin Light. It's one of the tallest lights on the Maine coast and it goes all the way back to George Washington."

"So tell me Jake. I know that you know a lot about Judaism and French history, but how do you know all this stuff about the Maine coast and lighthouses?"

He shrugged. "Just curiosity, I guess. I've loved Maine ever since I first came up here to visit with Uncle Sol and Aunt Sarah when I was a kid. I've been lucky. Uncle Sol used to take me out fishing occasionally. He had a smaller boat then, a Boston Whaler. And Aunt Sarah used to enjoy driving me around to places along the coast. It was she who first pointed out Casa Bidu to me. So I guess I picked up a lot from them and then from tooling around myself."

"But you never got to Presque Isle."

"Sorry; guilty as charged. I'm pretty good up to Bar Harbor and the Schoodic Peninsula, but I've never gone beyond there. Someday."

"Don't bother. There's nothing to see in Presque Isle, and I don't ever want to go back there. Bad subject. Let's talk about something else."

"Okay," he said, as he turned the boat northward. "Let's talk about what we want to eat for lunch. I'm hungry. You?"

"Yuh, I'm surprised. I thought I might feel a little seasick, but I'm feeling great. I love it out here! I wish that you were staying a few more days so that we could sail out toward Seguin Light. I'd like to see that one close up too."

"I wish I could stay here longer myself. I'd really love to get to know you better. But I've got an appointment with my dissertation advisor next Wednesday. It'll take me a good two or three days for the drive, and I want to make a stop in Boston."

"To see Miss Radcliffe?"

"No, no; forget about Miss Radcliffe. She's in Philadelphia for the summer, and I don't plan to stop there. I'm not even sure I want to. No, I want to spend some time with my father in Winthrop, and then I'm thinking of visiting with an old man whom I met at my grandfather's funeral three years ago. He knew my grandfather when they were students together in Lithuania. I'm not sure he's still alive, but if he is, I'd like to talk to him. I should have found some way to get to him before this."

"He must be pretty old if he was a friend of your grandfather's. What is it that you want to talk to him about?"

"Well, my grandfather ... I always called him Zeyde ... Anyway Zeyde was a great influence on me. I got my love of learning and my love of being Jewish from him. I'd just like to know more about how he grew up, and I think that this old man, if he's alive and with it, might help. He's probably not terribly old. When my zeyde died, he wasn't quite seventy. From the little that this guy told us at the funeral, I think that they were very close. Anyway, I'd like to talk to him."

They didn't say anything for a while, enjoying the sun and salt air as it whipped around them, and then Marie said, "You know, Jake, you're a very lucky fellow."

"How do you mean?"

"Well, you had a gran... a zeyde whom you loved and who loved you. You've got Mr. and Mrs. Fairstone who love you and would probably do anything for you, and you've got your father. Okay, your mother's not a winner, but still, you're lucky. You have people who love you, and from what you told me, you could be rich if you wanted to. Would it be wrong of me to be a little jealous?"

"Marie, please don't be jealous of me. You have so much going for you. Okay, your family from what you told me is pretty miserable, but you're beautiful; you're smart; and what I find so great about you is that you're fun to be with. You're kind, and you speak your mind. I see the way you work with Hope and the way you act with Aunt Sarah. And you're a great listener. I've never enjoyed talking with anyone the way I enjoy talking to you. I don't know where you get it from, but you're just plain a nice person." He stopped and thought for a moment. "You want honest? Okay. We've only known each other for less than a week, and I'm afraid that if I stay here much longer, I might fall in love with you. I think you're terrific! There; I said it!"

She looked startled for a moment and then said slowly, "But you don't *want* to fall in love with me. You'd like to *make* love to me, but not fall in love with me. Right? That's what you mean by honest?"

Jacob was beginning to feel uncomfortable with the turn of the conversation. They were heading into Merriconeag Sound, and he slowed the engine down to avoid making a wake. "Look, when you told me that you'd like to come along this morning, I thought, Wow! Here's my big chance. I actually went to my drawer to get a safe to bring along. I thought that when we were alone out there near the lighthouse, maybe we could... well, we could make out. But I decided *not* to bring the safe along, because... because it would be wrong. That's what I decided – it would be wrong! Three days ago, all I wanted was to get into your pants, but... well I *still* would love to, but I *know* you now, at least as well as you can get to know someone in such a short time. If we do ever make love, it will be because that's what *both* of us want, not because I'm horny and it's what *I* want. I'm your boss's nephew, and sometimes I impress you with the things that I know. But I'm not going to try to snow you. I'm going away on Sunday, and maybe when I'm a thousand miles away, you won't be as much on my mind as you are now. The last thing that I want to do is to hurt you. You've been hurt enough."

Marie didn't answer but sat there next to him at the helm thinking. He steered the boat around the southern tip of Bailey Island and into a cove leading to Cook's Lobster House and asked, "Hungry?"

A whisper: "I guess so." He eased the boat smoothly into the dock and threw a line over a cleat. "Can I do the other one?" she asked meekly.

"Sure."

She managed to get the line over the cleat on her second try, and Jacob got out and gave her a hand up onto the dock. "You'll make a good sailor. By the time I get back here in September, you'll be a pro." She nodded but didn't say anything.

As they walked into the restaurant and waited to be seated, Marie turned to Jacob and said: "Let's have a nice pleasant lunch. No serious talk. You can tell me more about what this Catholic girl can expect at Shabbat dinner tonight."

Jacob was relieved. "Happy to." When they were seated at a table with a view of the Cribstone Bridge, Jacob said, "This place is new; they just opened a few months ago, and they specialize in seafood, as you can tell from the name. We'll be having a big dinner tonight, so all I'm going to have now is a lobster roll with some of their great cole slaw. You?"

"I guess I'll have the same."

After they gave their order to the waitress, they sat there for a few minutes in awkward silence looking out at the bridge and the build-up of weekend traffic headed for the Bailey Island motels.

"What's going to happen tonight at dinner? Describe it to me."

"Well, our dinner will start with Aunt Sarah lighting the Shabbat candles and saying a prayer over them. And then ..."

"What kind of a prayer? Is it like lighting a candle in church when you're praying for someone who's sick or for something special that you want?"

"No; it's not like that at all. The women of the house always light candles and say a prayer to welcome Shabbat. It's like they're setting the mood by bringing a special light, sort of a holy light, into the home and the family circle. I remember when my grandmother – I called her Bobbe – lit the candles, she would put a kerchief over her head, light the candles and then, after reciting the prayer aloud, she would stand there with her eyes closed, whispering something over the candles for two or three minutes. When I was a little boy, I used to watch her lips trying to figure out what she was saying. She never would tell me; she would just look at me, kiss me, and say that I was going to grow up to be a good Jew and a scholar."

"God! I would love to have memories like that. My grandmother, the one I lived with after I got away from my family, was a pretty mean old woman. She never forgave me for accusing her son of being a pervert. She used to tell me that I was over-sexed, and she wouldn't allow me to go out with any boys. She told me a dozen times that if I got 'knocked up,' she'd throw me out. Doesn't sound much like your *bobbie.* Anyway, I asked you about the prayer that Mrs. Fairstone will say tonight over the candles. Is it all right to tell someone who's not Jewish what's in a Jewish prayer or is it just for Jews?"

"No, no. There's nothing secret in the Jewish religion. Non-Jews are always welcome in the synagogue, and there are really no prayers that we say that a non-Jew couldn't say, except maybe those prayers that thank God for giving us the Torah and giving us certain *mitzvot.* Anyway, the prayer over the candles simply thanks God for making us holy with the *mitzvah* of lighting the Shabbat candles."

"There's that word *mitzvah* again, like the *mitzvah* that Mr. Fairstone and you were laughing about, making love on Shabbat. I still can't get over that one after what the sisters taught us about sex being sinful. Wow!"

As they ate, Jacob went on to describe the rest of the Shabbat table ritual, the *Kiddush, motzi, zemirot* and the grace after dinner. Marie was fascinated by her crash-course into a culture so foreign to her upbringing in Presque Isle. "I just hope that I don't feel like a fifth wheel tonight when you're doing all that. I don't want to look stupid."

After lunch they sailed under the Cribstone Bridge and were back at the Fairstone dock by three. They found Sarah and Hope in the kitchen working on the *gefilte* fish. Hope was chopping the fish in a big brown wooden bowl with what Sarah called a *hakmesser,* while Sarah put the finishing touches on a large capon. Marie asked if she could make a salad, and the two ladies were happy to welcome her to the kitchen crew.

Sol came home earlier than usual. He was looking forward to the Shabbat dinner, and he brought Sarah a big bouquet of spring flowers interspersed with a dozen red roses. He found Jacob on the veranda reading and joined him for some chit-chat about the hapless Red Sox. Things were looking up at the beginning of the season with their new manager, Pinky Higgins, but they had just lost three games and were in fourth place. Jacob said, "I've been a Red Sox fan ever since you took me to my first game at Fenway. And this year I'm even more of a fan because of Harry Agganis at first. He's from Lynn, right near Winthrop. It's nice having a local guy on the team."

"Local, shmokel. He's batting over .300 now. I don't care if he came from Oshkosh. It's just too bad that Williams is getting old. With him in his prime, along with Piersall and Malzone, the Sox would have a shot at the pennant."

"Dream on, Uncle Sol. You're forgetting about the Yankees. They're running away with it, as usual."

"I always forget about the Yankees, those anti-Semites! Anyway Aunt Sarah says that you took Marie out on the boat. D'you have a good time? She a good sailor?"

"I think she really enjoyed it. After I'm gone, maybe you can find some time to take the girls out on the boat. It's great out there."

"Maybe I will. Hey," with a lascivious grin, "when you had her out there, you didn't…."

"No, I didn't! I'm not going to start anything that I can't finish, and she's really a very nice girl."

"Okay; don't get huffy. She's awfully pretty, and I thought maybe you were developing a thing for her. According to your mother, you're almost married. You should have heard her carrying on about the *shikse* that I brought into our house. Anyway, she's gone now. I really don't know what I'm going to do about her. The more she's alone in that big house in Winthrop, the worse she gets. Are you going to visit her on your way back to Chicago?"

"No; I've really had it with her. She's nastier than ever. I'll stop by to see my father, and then, you know what I want to do?" He reminded Sol about the old man, Koppel Ganzfried, who they met at Reb Yisroel's funeral. "I'm going to stop by the old folks' home in Mattapan where he said he lived, if he's still alive. I'd want to ask him about Zeyde's younger years in Vilna."

"You sure you want to do that? Maybe he'll try to touch you up for some money. You never know with these Holocaust survivors. It's like we owe them."

"Uncle Sol, come on! We *do* owe them. When we met him, he didn't ask for anything from us. He just wanted to make contact with the family of his old *chaver* from Vilna. One of us should have contacted him before this. I guess the fact that this is Zeyde's *yahrzeit* week made me think of him. So I'll call the home, and if he's there I'll visit with him for a while."

"I guess you're right, Jakie. You've got a good heart. Nu, it's time to get ready for Shabbes. For this occasion with you here, I'm going to wear a jacket and tie."

"Me too. And could you do me a big favor?"

"Anything, Jakie."

"I saw the beautiful Shabbat bouquet that you brought for Aunt Sarah. That was very nice. And you know what would be even nicer?" Sol looked at him quizzically. "If you recited the *Eshet Hayil* for her before I make *Kiddush.*"

"Jakie, I haven't recited *Eshes Hayil* for almost twenty years! I don't even remember how to say it."

"What if I find it for you in the Bible, in English? Will you at least recite the first few verses?"

"If it'll make you happy, Jakie, I'll do it."

"Never mind *me;* I think that it will make Aunt Sarah very happy."

Sumner arrived just after six in a clean shirt and trousers, kissed his mother and sister and was re-introduced to Marie. "C… can I k…k…kiss her t… too?" Marie smiled and presented her cheek.

Sarah looked pleased. "It's so nice to have the whole family together for Shabbes. Let's all sit down now. Jakie, I put you at the head of the table because you're going to lead the *Kiddush* and *Motzi*. Okay?"

Jacob was about to take the indicated seat but then thought better of it. "No, Aunt Sarah; I think that Uncle Sol should sit at the head; he's the *baal ha-bayit.* That's his place. I can lead the *Kiddush* from another seat."

Sarah shrugged and then put a kerchief over her head. There was a beautiful three-branched silver candelabrum on the table, fitted with long white tapers. She lit them and then recited the blessing. As she removed her kerchief, she turned to Marie and said, "That was a Hebrew prayer thanking God for giving us the *mitzvah*…."

"I know," Marie interrupted. "… the holy *mitzvah* of lighting the candles. Jacob told me. And he told me that the husband recites a loving appreciation of his wife."

Sarah looked doubtful, and said, "Well, I don't think….".

But Sol cut her off. "Of course I'm going to say it. I can't say it in Hebrew, but I can read the English from Jakie's Bible. But first, let's sing *Sholom Alaichem* like at Zeyde's."

Jacob explained that *Shalom Alaichem* was a hymn welcoming the angels of peace to the family circle for the celebration of Shabbat. "I learned a new custom from Rabbi Persky in Chicago. At his Shabbat table, when they sing *Shalom Alaichem,* the family and guests join hands around the table. Let's do that." Even Hope and Sumner knew *Shalom Alaichem,* and so they all sang together with gusto, holding hands. By the third stanza, Marie was la-la-ing in an enthusiastic soprano along with the others.

Then Jacob handed his Bible to Sol, opened to Proverbs 31, and Sol began to read in a faltering voice. But as he got beyond the first two verses, his voice strengthened and he began reading with conviction. He didn't stop after the first few verses but continued on, stopping only after reading verse 28. "I want to repeat that verse; it's just right for my Sarah. And I want you kids to say it after me. '*Her children rise up and call her blessed…*' – they repeated if after him, with Jacob and Marie joining in – '*her husband also, and he praises her*' and again they all repeated it. There was a lump in Sol's throat and tears running down Sarah's cheek. Sol got up from his chair and went over to Sarah and kissed her. And then, holding her hand, he asked Jacob, "I remember my father used to give us a blessing after he recited *Eshes Hayil.* I want to give my three kids a Shabbes blessing. Do you know the words, Jakie?"

"Sure; that would be very nice. Let me turn to it; it's in the book of Numbers, chapter 6. Here it is, Uncle Sol." And he handed him the Bible again.

"Okay; Sumner and Hope, and you, too, Jakie; you stand by me and I'll say the blessing."

As Jacob went to stand by his uncle, he whispered something in his ear. "You're sure it's all right, Jakie?" Jacob nodded. "Marie,

Jakie said it's all right to give this blessing to someone who isn't Jewish. I didn't want to make a mistake."

Jacob went to Marie's seat and took her hand. "Marie is almost like a member of the family. I think that she deserves to be blessed too."

Hesitantly, Marie joined Sumner, Hope and Jacob as Sol raised his hands over them and recited the ancient priestly benediction. When he finished, Sarah was awash in tears. Sol kissed her again and said, "It'll be all right, Soreh'le; it'll be all right. Now Jakie, you make *Kiddush* for us."

After Jacob chanted the *Kiddush,* he poured the wine from his silver beaker into six smaller goblets. Marie was not sure that she should drink, and she looked questioningly at Jacob. He understood immediately. "I know; at Mass only the priest drinks the wine, but this isn't like communion wine. We use wine on all our holidays as a symbol of God's blessings. It's supposed to bring joy to the table. There's nothing mystical about *Kiddush* wine. So drink up."

Sol issued a hearty *le-chayim,* and they all drank. After the *motzi,* recited over two large braided *challot,* Sarah went to the kitchen and brought out the *gefilte* fish, another first for Marie. She loved it especially after Hope showed her how to flavor it with horseradish. When they had all finished the golden chicken soup and Sarah, accompanied by Hope, went back to the kitchen for the roast capon and the *kugel,* Sol asked Jacob if he would lead them in singing some of the *zemirot* that he remembered from Shabbat dinners with his parents. Jacob remembered most of the verses of *Tzur Mishelo* and *Yah Ribon,* and Sol and Sarah were able to join in the refrains.

When they had finished and were complimenting themselves on how much they remembered, Jacob said, "I'd like to sing one other Shabbat song, a melody that I learned from the Hillel rabbi at Chicago. It's a beautiful setting of *L'cha Dodi.* I was telling Marie about *L'cha Dodi* the other night, how it's sort of a love song between God and Israel. I want to sing it because of what I'm feeling around this table tonight. Uncle Sol, Aunt Sarah, this is for you." He sang it softly and lovingly, and then, before singing it a second time, he taught them all to join in the refrain.

They were all delighted to see Marie trying to join in the singing, and when the dinner ended, she went over to Sarah and gave her an exuberant kiss and a hug. There were tears in her eyes as she said, "I don't know how to thank you. This was the most wonderful dinner that I ever had. It was so full of love, and... and..." she laughed, "it was delicious too." Then she paused for a moment and added, "Would it be all right if I call you Aunt Sarah like Jacob does? You've just made me feel so welcome here. Please?"

Sarah returned her hug and said, "Of course; I'd love it if you called me Aunt Sarah. You're like a cousin to Hope and to Sumner and Jakie too, so, sure; call me Aunt Sarah."

Marie joined Hope in the kitchen to do the dishes while Jacob, along with a somewhat reluctant Sumner, cleared the table. When they were done and all the dishes were put away, they joined Sol who was sitting in the living room watching television. Sumner left after a few minutes, explaining that he had arranged to meet with a couple of the guys at Moriarty's while the others went on watching the *Schlitz Playhouse of Stars* and *Our Miss Brooks.* Marie and Hope excused themselves as soon as Eve Arden had her last word, and Jacob remained watching with his aunt and uncle. After about fifteen minutes of an inane mystery, he began yawning, and he, too, excused himself. But before going up to the attic, he thanked Sol and Sarah for making their Shabbat together so lovely and *haimish.* He exchanged a few more words with his uncle about their drive to the Portland synagogue the next morning, and they decided they would leave at about eight to get to the service on time.

When Jacob arrived in his room, he listened for some sound of Marie but heard only silence. He went into their bathroom and used the facilities as quietly as he could so as not to awaken her, and then, closing the door silently behind him, he crept into bed. He lay there for a while going over the events of the day, especially his conversations with Marie on the boat and at Cook's. He thought about her initial hesitation at the dinner table and then her enthusiastic participation and decided that she was really a remarkable woman. He wondered whether he should keep in contact with her from Chicago. It was just so pleasant to talk to her. He would miss her.

As he was dropping off, he sensed that there was someone in his room. He whispered, "Marie?" and heard a shhh in response. "What…!"

"Shhh. Just shift over."

He sat up and could just make out, by the dim light from the bathroom, the silhouette of Marie at his bedside. She was wearing her terry-cloth robe, but as he stared in disbelief, she took it off and slipped into his bed naked.

"Are you sure…?"

"Shhh. It's a *mitzvah*!" And she pressed her body next to his, her arm reaching behind his back. He was rock hard in an instant but had to extricate himself from her embrace in order to get his shorts off.

Again he asked, "Are you sure?"

"No, I'm not. I'm not sure of anything. I just know that I want you to make love to me tonight. Remember? 'As a bridegroom rejoices over his bride?' That's what you taught me. I'm a good student."

He felt for her breasts and was surprised by how small and firm they were. He pictured Trudy who took pride in the fact that she could hold a pencil under each breast. Marie's were like a ballerina's, but they produced the same response as he fondled and tongued them. She moaned and reached for his throbbing penis. He was about to enter her, when he caught himself. "Wait! I need a safe! I don't know how you feel about birth con…."

"Don't worry. I put in my diaphragm before I came in."

"You have a diaphragm? A good Catholic girl? How come?"

"You talk too much. I was fitted for it at Planned Parenthood in Bangor when I thought I might be getting serious with a guy I was dating. Satisfied?"

"Ecstatic!" He ran his hands over her cool lithe body and then slipped into her. For as long as he could, he just lay astride her not moving, just reveling in the intimacy of the moment. But then, when she stirred beneath him, he began slowly thrusting. He wanted to control his ejaculation; he wanted her to have as much pleasure as he was having. He tried to shift his mind from what he was doing – the Straits of Tiran, Nasser, Ted Williams, Harry Agganis.... Can't let go yet....

"Slowly, slowly," she moaned, and then he felt a slight spasm, and then a more frenzied one and then a cry. He lost control and came as her body heaved in a throe of ecstasy. They both lay there panting for a while, and then she began laughing and kissing him all over his body.

"O God, that was so good! I had no idea. I only did this twice before, and I didn't enjoy it either time. It was like one-two-three, he came, and that was it. I thought I was just doing this for you, to show you how much I lo... like you. I didn't expect to have so much .... I don't know... so much wow! I think I actually had an orgasm! Was that an orgasm? Could you tell?"

"I'm no expert on female orgasms, but if it wasn't, it was the next best thing. God, you're fantastic."

They lay there side by side for a few minutes, not saying a word, and then Jacob said: "Don't think that I'm kinkie or anything, but would you do me a favor?"

"Oh, oh. What?"

"I want to see you naked. I've been dreaming about seeing your body for five days. Can I put on the light?"

"I don't like to show off my body, but... okay, I guess I don't have anything to hide from you now."

Jacob reached back to his bed table and snapped on the lamp. "Would you get out of bed and just stand there for a minute?"

She hesitated but then shrugged and complied.

He stared at her and said, "Marie Beaulieu, you are gorgeous! If I could paint, I'd want to paint you just as you are right now so that I could always remember. You are so blonde, and your body is so smooth and lovely, and... and the sensuous curve of your hips. And your breasts! *Shadayich kish'nai afarim.* God, I can't stand it. Come back into bed."

She jumped into the bed with unexpected abandon and climbed on top of him. He groaned and said, "I don't think I'm ready yet. Give me a minute."

"Okay; a minute. That'll give you time to tell me what you just said in… was that Hebrew?"

"I was quoting King Solomon when he gazed at his beloved. It's in the Song of Songs in the Bible. '*Your breasts are like two fawns, twins of a gazelle that feed among the lilies.*' I've always loved that verse, but I never thought I'd actually see breasts like fawns."

"That's in the *Bible!* Wow. The sisters never read *that* part to us. King Solomon, huh? Okay, King Solomon. You ready yet?

"I'm ready. Oh, am I ready!"

This time Marie took control, gently guiding him into her and then slowly rising and falling, rising and falling until he came. And then they both just lay in each other's arms exhausted. Jacob arranged their bodies like spoons with his hands cupping her diminutive breasts, and soon they were asleep. About an hour later, Marie awoke and lay there thinking. She was amazed at her brazenness. How could she have…? But it was so wonderful. Jacob had said that one of the ancient sages had taught that God wants people to enjoy their bodies. But she had been taught that what she did was a sin, not only the intercourse but the planning ahead, the diaphragm. And Jake; what would he think of her after this? He was leaving on Sunday. Would he ever want to see her again after he was back with Miss Chicago? She stirred and removed his hands from her breasts, and he woke up.

"You okay?"

"Yuh, fine; just thinking."

"Penny?"

"Jake, you know how the great thing about us is that we're honest with each other. You agreed to be honest with me that first night when I came in here. Honest?"

"Okay."

"Jake, I don't know quite how to put it but .... but it's important to me." She hesitated, searching for the right words. He put his arms around her, but she shook her head. "Jake, tell me: what we did, was that making love or was it ..." She didn't want to say the word. She whispered, "Or was it fucking? See, you told me that making love on Shabbat was a *mitzvah,* but I don't know if that applies to plain, old-fashioned fucking." She spit out the word. "Tell me what we did before."

Jacob didn't know how to answer. Was she asking him for some commitment, a commitment that he was far from ready to make? Did he love her? A small-town Catholic girl from a cretinous family? He lay there not answering for a moment too long, and Marie slowly climbed out of his bed. She grabbed her robe and quickly hid herself from his eyes. "It's very late, and we've got to get some sleep." And she went through the bathroom door.

He lay there bereft. How could he not have answered her? That was treating her like a whore. That's what his mother had called her, a *shikse* whore. But she was so lovely, so decent, so genuine.... He was a fool. He got up and went quickly through the bathroom to her room, not bothering to knock. He found her lying in the dark weeping. As he approached, she said, "Go away. It's late. The shop is closed."

"No, I won't go away. You mean too much to me. I should have answered you right away, but you.... well, you sort of caught me off guard. I could have answered with something dodgy, but you want honesty. And so here's my answer, my honest answer that I should have given you while you were in my arms."

He paused for a moment wanting to get it right. "Marie, yes, we made love. We made love! I think that that was only the second time that I ever truly made love, and the first time was with somebody much older who was very kind to me when I needed someone to be kind. Marie, do you want me to tell you that I'm in love with you? I could say it, but I'm not sure it would be true. Now you've got *me* all confused. I was making love to you, not fucking you. I was making love to you, because I think that you're wonderful, because I think that you're the most fantastic woman that I've ever met. And I think that *you* were making love too. I felt it. It wasn't a roll in the hay. It wasn't because we needed some titillation. Marie, we made love. I want you to believe that."

"I... I do... and I shouldn't have asked you that, and I shouldn't have walked out like I did. I guess I'm not very secure when it comes to intimacy."

She had stopped crying and was lying there very still. Jacob just stood there, looking down at her. "Jake, will you do me a favor?"

"Sure."

"Go back to your room and put on your shorts while I put on my nightie, and then come back. Please come back."

He was back at her bedside in less than a minute with his shorts on.

"Jake, do you think that we could sleep together for the rest of the night, just sleeping together, no sex?"

"I'd love to."

She pushed over and lifted up the covers for him. He climbed in and turned facing her.

"Can we kiss goodnight without your little friend getting all excited?"

"I can't guarantee it, but we can try." He gave her a gentle kiss on the lips, and she responded, holding him tightly. "Goodnight, King Solomon." "Goodnight." And they slept.

The light was streaming through Marie's window when Jacob jumped up. "I think it's late!" He looked at the clock-radio on Marie's bed table and it read seven-thirty. "Sorry, Marie; got to run. Uncle Sol and I are leaving for the Portland synagogue in half an hour, and I've got to shower and everything. God, I hate to leave you. I wish I could spend the day just lying in bed with you."

She smiled up at him through the fog of sleep and whispered, "I'll be here."

He took a long look at her, her thick blonde hair like a halo around her head, and he leaned down and kissed her forehead. "Mmmm. That was nice." And she slept.

Twenty minutes later Jacob joined his uncle at the breakfast table for the coffee and toast that Sarah had ready for them. As they were about to leave, Jacob said, "Whoops, I forgot my wallet; be back in a minute." He actually had his wallet in his pocket, but he had to see Marie again before leaving. He eased open her door and watched her sleeping for a moment before tip-toeing into her room and kissing her lightly on the lips. She smiled, and as he tip-toed out, he whispered, "We made love."

As soon as they had driven out the long driveway and turned up Route 24, Sol said, "Are you sure you want to go to shul? Maybe we could go instead to Bath for a nice breakfast? What do you say?"

"Uncle Sol, I can't believe you! Last night you were such a *mensch.* You were so loving to Aunt Sarah and the kids. You actually made me think that maybe you had given up on Claudette and were going to be a faithful husband. We're going to shul to say *Kaddish* and make a *hazkore* for Zeyde. Look, if you don't want to go, drive me back and I'll go in my own car."

"All right, all right. Don't get upset. I'll go. And look, I want you to know… I've told you this before. I love my Sarah. I meant every word that I said to her last night, but I love my nights with Claudette too. And I love my Izzy. It's like an addiction with me, and I can't do anything about it. I will stay with my Sarah for the rest of my life. I'm not going to leave her for a Catholic, but… Well, I think *you know* how it is when you're attracted to a lovely person who you shouldn't be attracted to. Am I right?"

Jacob reddened. "What do you mean?"

"Look, Jakie; I love you like a son, and I'm not going to tell you who you should play around with, but … how can I say it? Well, there were *two* couples in our house doing the *Shabbes mitzvah* last night. I know; I heard."

"You heard?!"

"Don't get huffy with me; I wasn't spying on you. I'm not as young as you. Sometimes I have to get up at night and go to the bathroom. After Sarah and I finished and she was asleep, I got up and went out in the hall to the bathroom. When I came out,

I heard something moving up in the attic, so I went to the stairs and listened. I heard someone going from one room to the other, so I said to myself 'Good Shabbes!' and I went back to sleep. Look, Marie's a beautiful girl, so why not? It's not like you're going to marry her. You're two young people with urges, natural urges. When I was your age, I had lots of urges, and," – he smiled – "not all of them were natural; I'll admit that to you and only you. So if you want to play around with Marie in my house, go right ahead. I'm not her father, and she's not a minor. When she said after Essie and Rob left that she didn't want to move downstairs, I thought that something might be going on. Look, you're young and you shouldn't be spending all your time with books. Have some fun! That's why God created *shikses.* Just be careful; don't get her pregnant."

Jacob didn't know what to say. He bristled at the word *shikse* but saw no point in lecturing his uncle about bigotry. He sat silently for a few minutes as they drove through Orr's Island, and then he said, "Uncle Sol, this is important. Please don't let Marie know that you know about last night; please. She's a very nice person and she's certainly not promiscuous. In fact, she's sort of shy. She'd be very upset if she thought that you or Aunt Sarah knew that we … that we…" He was hard-pressed to find the right word.

"That you *shtupped*! Say it like it is. You *shtupped*; it's not a crime. You're a single young man and she's a single girl of the right age, so you *shtupped.* I don't blame you."

"You don't understand."

"So what don't I understand?"

"Look, Uncle Sol; I have feelings for her. I like her very much, and I don't want her hurt. So please, just promise me that you won't make any remarks or give her any looks that indicate that you know about what we did. Maybe it won't happen again. I don't know…"

"Why shouldn't it happen again? Like I said, it's natural. I don't blame you."

"Please promise me."

"Okay, *boychik*." He reached over and patted Jacob on the leg. "I promise. Happy now?"

"Yes, and I trust you. And that promise goes for after I'm gone too. I may keep in touch with her from Chicago. She's just a really nice person, and I enjoy talking to her."

"Now you've got me worried. Be careful, *boychik*. She's a Catholic. Remember; we're going to shul to say *Kaddish* for your zeyde. What would he say if he thought that his favorite *einekl* was getting involved with a Catholic? It was those Lithuanian Catholics that made his life miserable in Vilna and that wiped out his family during the war. You don't get serious with someone like Marie, no matter how nice she is."

"Okay, I heard you, Uncle Sol. Let's change the subject. You seemed not to be very enthusiastic about going to shul when we started out. Am I right? Have you given up on shul?"

"No, I haven't given up on shul. I used to go to the shul in Portland occasionally until about two years ago when Berel Glick became president. I still contribute because it's the only real shul around here. You wanted to go because we have *yahrzeit*, so we're going."

"What have you got against this Glick guy?"

"You want the whole story?"

"Why not? It'll take us another half hour to get there, and if there's something I should know about someone who might be there, you'd better tell me."

"Nu, if someday you're going to be my right-hand man, you'd better know the story with Glick. It goes back to when I was expanding Fairstone Trucking from just around the counties north of Boston to southern Maine. Berel Glick had a small poultry business in Portland, and he had less than a dozen trucks that he used to haul poultry. His trucks were mostly pretty old, and they broke down a lot. At that time I had about twenty trucks, and they were mostly new. I took out a bank loan for another dozen trucks, ten of them refrigerated, and I had to get a lot of new business if I was going to be able to pay the bank. So I began soliciting a lot of the farmers in Biddeford and Scarborough and

Cumberland counties, where Glick did his business. When they saw the kind of trucks I had, a lot of his farmers decided to ship with me. Within two years, Glick was out of the trucking business, and I had signed up almost all of the farmers from Kittery to Damariscotta. I was able to pay off my loan before it was due, and I bought another twenty trucks to handle all the business. That's when I relocated my offices to Brunswick and bought the estate on Bailey Island."

"So what happened to Glick?"

"Nothing happened to him. He lost his trucking business, but he still had a few farms and two slaughterhouses in Portland. He doesn't have to worry about where his next meal is coming from, but he never forgave me for ruining his trucking operation."

"It doesn't sound like you did anything dishonest. You didn't cheat him, so why do you feel uncomfortable about going to his shul?"

"Not only did I not cheat him, but I made him a good offer for his trucks before I took away his customers. He wouldn't listen. He thought those farmers were his friends and that he could keep them, but business is business. They all deserted him and came over to me. But that's not the end of the story."

"What else?"

"Well, you know, people like to gossip, and Glick knows a lot of people around here, especially truckers. So somehow he heard about me and Claudette, and when he heard that she was having a baby, he went to Rabbi Himmel – he's been the rabbi at the Portland shul for a long time – and he told him that I was guilty of breaking the seventh commandment. That's how Rabbi Himmel put it to me when he was explaining why I wasn't called to the Torah on your zeyde's first *yahrzeit.* He said that if he gave me an *aliyah,* Glick would stand up in the shul in front of the congregation and call me an adulterer. Himmel didn't want to offend me, because he knows that I could buy and sell both him and his shul, and so he sort of pleaded with me to understand that he was stuck. If it was up to *him,* beh beh beh beh, but he couldn't take a chance on Glick. So you understand why I don't particularly want to go to shul? But for you, Jakie, I'll do it. For you and my father, but I'm pretty sure that they won't give me an *aliyah*."

"Gee, Uncle Sol, I'm really sorry to hear that. That Glick guy must be pretty bitter. I'm sorry that I asked you to go to the shul; I could have gone alone, but I didn't know."

"It's all right; it's all right. Not your fault. Maybe if we're lucky, Glick won't be there today. We'll see. And if he is, I'll ask Rabbi Himmel to call *you* to the Torah, and you can make the *hazkore*. He can't refuse that. If he does, not one more penny will I give to that shul."

They arrived at the shul during the chanting of the introductory psalms. Sol had brought his own *tallit*, and Jacob took one from a receptacle at the entrance. Sol chose two seats about midway up the center aisle, and as soon as they were seated with prayer books in their hands, he whispered to Jacob, "There's Glick, sitting on the *bimah* next to Rabbi Himmel. No *aliyah* for me this morning. Nu, let's see if the *shammes* offers one to you."

Within a few minutes of their arrival, as the cantor was chanting *Shochein Ad*, they saw the *shammes* going up onto the *bimah* to consult with the rabbi and the president about which of the worshippers would be called to the Torah. The three of them scanned the thirty or so men in the congregation, and then the *shammes* came down and began whispering in the ears of several of the men. He was clearly hesitant about approaching Sol, and he saved him for last. When he did arrive, he shook hands with Sol and whispered, "Who's the young fellow with you?"

"My nephew."

"Rabbi Himmel wants to know if we can give him an *aliyah.*"

"Glick, that *mamzer* told you no *aliyah* for *me*, right?"

"Look, Mr. Fairstone; that's not my business. Rabbi Himmel said that if this fellow with you is a relative and if he knows how to say the *broches*, I should give him an *aliyah*. It isn't my fault whatever is between you and Glick. So?"

"Your right; it isn't your business. Okay, tell Rabbi Himmel that this is my nephew and that he probably knows more Hebrew than anyone else in this shul. Which *aliyah*?"

"*Shishi.*"

Sol looked at Jacob and he nodded his assent. But as the *shammes* was leaving to report back to Glick and the rabbi, Sol grabbed his arm. "Tell me, do you have anyone to chant the *haftorah?*"

"No, there's no one here this *Shabbes* who knows how to do it. When that happens, which is most of the time unless there's a bar mitzvah, Rabbi Himmel chants the *haftorah* himself."

"Tell Rabbi Himmel that I'd like my nephew to chant the *haftorah.* He's a scholar, and he has a beautiful voice. Tell him."

The *shammes* shrugged and said, "I'll ask." He went back up to the *bimah,* waited for a respectful minute while the congregation joined the cantor in singing the *Shema,* and then whispered in the rabbi's ear with Glick leaning in to overhear. Rabbi Himmel thought a minute and then smiled, looked in the direction of Sol and Jacob, and gave the thumbs up sign.

Sol turned to Jacob and crowed, "We got him! Jakie, I want you to chant the most beautiful *haftorah* you ever chanted. Make like it's your bar mitzvah. That'll take care of Glick."

"Uncle Sol, I'll be happy to chant the *haftarah,* but not because of your feud with Mr. Glick. This week's *haftarah* is that really beautiful one from Zechariah that tells about the vision that the prophet has of the *menorah* from the destroyed temple of Solomon. It's one of my favorites. I'll chant it the way that Zeyde taught me. That'll be a nice *hazkarah* for him."

"That's my boy!" And he squeezed Jacob's hand.

About a half-hour into the Torah reading, Rabbi Himmel crooked his finger in the direction of Jacob who responded immediately and made his way up to the *bimah.* Rabbi Himmel extended his hand and asked him for his Hebrew name. "Yaakov ben Yitzhak Meir." The rabbi repeated the name aloud and indicated the place in the Torah for Jacob to touch with the fringes of his *tallit.* As he kissed the fringes, he suddenly reddened, recalling the passionate kisses of the previous night. Fleetingly, he wondered whether he had the right to kiss the Torah just a few hours after making love to a Catholic. He quickly drove that thought out of his mind and chanted the Torah blessing. He followed closely as Rabbi Himmel read the final few verses of the portion, and then chanted the concluding blessing, after which the Torah was raised high for all to see and then set down and dressed. Rabbi Himmel then announced the page where the congregation could find the prophetic reading and informed the congregation that the *haftarah* would be chanted by a newcomer to the shul, a nephew of Mr. Sol Fairstone.

Jacob opened the *haftarah* book to the prophecy of Zechariah, and as he was about to begin with the recital of the special *haftarah* blessings, he thought that it would be wrong to simply chant that exquisite prophecy without an introduction. He was surprised that Rabbi Himmel hadn't done it himself and then decided that the rabbi might not have wanted to draw too much attention to the fact that the honor of this particular *haftarah* was being given to a member of the Fairstone family.

Jacob looked up at the congregation and then said, "With your permission, Rabbi Himmel, I'd just like to point out a few of the more beautiful and significant passages in this prophecy before chanting it." He looked in the direction of the rabbi, now reseated next to Berel Glick, and the rabbi nodded.

Jacob then explained how the prophet Zechariah was trying to encourage his desperate people on their return from exile to a devastated land. He emphasized the beauty of the prophet's opening words of encouragement: *"Roni v'simhi bat tziyon… – Sing and rejoice, daughter of Zion,"* and then pointed out a few other verses, concluding with the well-known *"Not by might, nor by power, but by my spirit…"*. As Jacob spoke, the congregants, most of whom were used to napping or schmoozing during the Torah and *haftarah* chants, were fully engaged. It was obvious to them that this young stranger loved the text and was attempting to transmit that love to them. And then he began chanting in the sonorous baritone that had made him an occasional soloist in his Harvard Glee Club days. When he finished chanting the final *b'rachah,* he began walking back to his seat next to Sol. On the way there, he shook about a dozen outstretched hands and responded individually to the traditional *yasher koach* blessings of strength. Sol hugged and kissed him and then shot a withering glance toward Glick whose eyes were focused on his prayer book, anxious for the service to resume.

On the drive back to Bailey Island, Sol was exuberant. "You showed him! You showed that *mamzer* what kind of a family I've got. You were terrific. Oy, am I going to be happy when you come up here for good. What a team! Fairstone and Ross. Boychik, we'll take over all of New England!" And then he had a thought. "Jakie, I'm going to do you a big favor this afternoon."

"What do you have in mind?"

"No, it'll be a surprise. You'll see."

Sarah had prepared a lovely cold lunch for the five of them, including one of Jacob's favorites – cold borscht with a boiled potato, sour cream, diced vegetables and crumbled egg yolk, along with thick slices of *challah* from the night before. She had found a beautiful cinnamon and raisin babke in Portland to go along with the coffee, and, as they were finishing it off, Sol got up to make an announcement.

"Sarah, this has been such a lovely lunch that I think we should do something nice this afternoon. I want to take you and Hope for a nice drive to Popham Beach. We can take a walk along the dunes there and then have something to drink at Spinney's. What do you say?"

"It sounds very nice, but aren't you forgetting something? How about Jakie and Marie? Can't they come along?"

"You're absolutely right, Sarah. But Jakie and I were talking in the car, and he told me that he has to finish another of his books before he leaves tomorrow. So this will give him a chance to finish his reading."

"And what about Marie? She always goes with Hope."

"You know, Sarah, I think that Marie deserves a day off. We never talked about that, but everybody gets a day off. In fact, in the Ten Commandments it says that everyone should get a day off. That's what Shabbes is all about."

Sarah looked at Marie and asked her whether she wanted to accompany them to Popham. She thought for a moment and then said: "You know, I think that the three of you should have some family time together without me. Anyway, I've got some laundry to do. I'll be fine here; you go and enjoy yourselves."

Sarah shrugged and said, "Okay; if that's what you want. Sol, it's such a lovely day; let's take my convertible."

Sol shepherded Sarah and Hope out the front door and then he went over to Jacob who was watching them leave with a puzzled look on his face. He came close and whispered in his ear, "This is the favor I mentioned in the car. Have fun!" He poked him in the arm and walked out with a big smile on his face.

As soon as the door closed behind the three of them, Marie looked at Jacob. "Jacob Ross, tell me the truth; did you plan this with your uncle?"

"Scout's honor. This came as a complete surprise."

"Are you going to spend the rest of the day finishing one of your books?"

"Are you going to spend the rest of the day doing laundry?"

They both ran to the window and watched Sarah's convertible emerging from the driveway and turning right onto Route 24. When it was out of sight, they stared at each other with the look of children who had just been handed big ice cream cones covered with jimmies. A minute later they were both lying stark naked on the living room rug giggling. Jacob reached for her, but she jumped up with an urgent, "Wait! Wait!" and ran up to the attic. She was back in two minutes and lay down next to him again. As he reached for her again, she said, "Wow! I couldn't really see you last night. Your little friend down there looks mighty excited."

"My little friend is feeling cold. He told me he wants a nice warm, moist place to slip into."

"I think I know just the place;" and she climbed on top of him. And thus began an afternoon of utter and uninhibited abandon, from the living room floor to a chair in the dining room to the veranda glider to the secluded front lawn and then up to Jacob's bedroom where they lay, utterly spent, for almost an hour.

"Hey," Jacob said, nudging her. "You know, this is the warmest early June that I can ever remember here in Maine. I bet the water's warm enough for a swim."

"You think so?"

"Come on! Let's give it a try."

"Okay; I'll get my bathing suit."

"Forget your bathing suit. There's no way any of the neighbors could see us. There are thick pines and sumac on either side of our beach. It's totally private."

"You mean…?"

"Yes, I mean skinny dipping unless you've suddenly gone shy. But let's take along a blanket and our bathrobes, just in case Uncle Sol and the ladies come back while we're down there

"A few minutes later they were splashing and shrieking in the sixty degree water of Casco Bay. Jacob put his arms around her and tried to enter her, but he found it impossible. By that time they knew each other well enough to be able to make fun of what had been an impressive staff, now a shriveled anchovy roll. Jacob licked the salt off her breasts, and when she moaned, they ran out of the water hand in hand and up onto the beach where they fell onto the blanket and summoned their ebbing vigor for a final languid but sweet bundling.

As they lay there Marie whispered, "Jake, tell me about you. I feel I know you so well now, but I really *don't* know you. Where do you come from, Jacob Ross, and where are you going?"

"I guess you've told me more about yourself than I've told you about me. And I *want* you to know me better. I may be going away tomorrow, but I feel like I'm leaving a piece of myself here with you. You must be a witch, Marie Beaulieu; you've totally enchanted me."

She leaned over and kissed him on the lips. He thought for a while and then went on: "You know, this morning in the synagogue, I discovered something about myself. I was given the honor of chanting the weekly prophetic portion, and I decided to explain it to the congregation before I began the chanting, to sort of teach them what I was going to chant. I've done that before in student groups, like in my father's junior congregation in Winthrop and in the student congregations at Harvard and Chicago, but this was the first time that I ever had the nerve to do it in a real synagogue. And I enjoyed it. I really enjoyed it! My uncle thought that I did it to help him show up a guy there who doesn't like him, but that wasn't the reason. I love that particular text, and I wanted to share that love with the congregation."

He paused, thinking, and Marie said, "I wish I could have been with you in the synagogue. I would have liked to listen to you in front of a congregation. You really love your religion, don't you."

"Yes, I do."

"And how does what we're doing fit in with your religion? Remember; honest."

"In a way it does, and in a way it doesn't. You know what happened to me for just a second in the synagogue? Well, a man who's called up to the reading of the Torah is supposed to touch the spot in the scroll where the reading begins with the fringe of his prayer shawl and kiss it. When I did that, I thought of how it felt to kiss you last night. I sort of stood there for a moment in shock – you and the Torah! Blasphemy! But then I told myself, love equals love, sacred or profane."

"What we're doing, Jake; is it profane? Did you insult your Torah by thinking of me? Am I insulting my Jesus?"

He was taken aback by her mention of Jesus and didn't know quite how to answer. Jesus and the Torah! He was deeply bothered by the juxtaposition. He leaned up on an elbow and asked, "Marie, we're getting to know each other. Tell me. How important is Jesus to you? I know that that's a tough question, and I'm not testing you, but I sort want to know, if that's okay with you."

"Wow! That's a complicated question. I haven't gone to church since I left my grandmother's house. It's over two years since my last confession, and boy" she said with a chuckle, "have I got some stuff to confess now! No, seriously, I haven't wanted to go into a church since what my brother and then my father did to me. When I look at a priest, I see my father, and I almost feel sick. But Jesus.... That's different. When I decided to leave my house, I felt that Jesus – you know, the Jesus who *cares* about us – well, that Jesus was helping me with my decision. And when I was offered that scholarship to Hudson, I felt that Jesus was encouraging me. In fact, when Mr. Fairstone offered me this job so that I wouldn't have to go back to Presque Isle, I thanked Jesus. So I guess that I should thank Jesus for you too." She leaned over and gave him another kiss. And then she asked, "Was Jesus really a Jew?"

Jacob felt almost dizzy as he heard her talking about Jesus. Would there be anti-Semitism without Jesus? Would there have been expulsions and pogroms and a Holocaust without Jesus? Inwardly, he slapped himself. He told himself not to go down that path again, remembering how she reacted to his emotional attack on Christianity when he was teaching her the fundamentals of Judaism. And so he answered blandly, "Historically, we really don't know very much about Jesus. Most of the liberal Bible scholars believe that he was a mystic and a teacher, sort of a Gandhi-like person, who went around Judea preaching a message of social justice. A lot of what he taught is what any rabbi of that time would have taught. So sure, he was a Jew."

"So why don't the Jews accept him?"

"Well, that's because his disciples claimed that he was the son of God and because, in the name of Jesus, they dismissed a lot of the essentials of Judaism in order to attract Greeks and Romans to their new faith. So no; Jews can't accept Jesus."

"Boy, I've got to do a lot of studying. I don't think that I could ever give up Jesus. Maybe I'll take a course in religion at Hudson next semester. Jake, could you recommend some books to me? I love to read."

"No, I won't recommend them." She was startled for a moment. "I'll send them to you."

"You scared me for a minute;" and she gave him a dig in the ribs. "Now tell me more about yourself. You like being Jewish, and you like to teach. What else?"

"Well, I was brought up to believe that I had a sort of responsibility to learn and to be a good Jew. You see, I have a lot of what's called *yiches. Yiches* means a connection."

"So what are you connected to? Sounds like the Mafia." She giggled. "So you're a guy with connections." She saw him frown. "No, no; sorry. Go on. So you've got *yikkies.* Explain."

"I don't usually tell people about my *yiches* because it sounds like bragging, but I'm descended from a couple of very great rabbis. My grandmother Bryna was a great-great-granddaughter of probably the greatest rabbi of eighteenth-century Europe, Rabbi Elijah of Vilna. People called him the *Gaon*; that's sort of like 'Your Highness.' And my father is supposed to be a descendant of one of the greatest sages of medieval Jewry, Rabbi Meir of Rothenberg. Those names don't mean anything to you and to most people today, but if you mention them to any Jewish scholar, they're very impressed. So I usually don't."

"Why not?"

"Well, first, because I would feel like a fraud. I don't observe a lot of the laws of Judaism, and occasionally I do things that they certainly wouldn't have approved of, so…"

"Like making love to a Catholic, huh?"

"That for sure. But I don't keep kosher. You remember; I told you about kosher – the Jewish dietary laws?" She nodded. "And I don't keep all the *mitzvot* of Shabbat…."

"You sure went all out with *one* of them, Studs!"

"Okay, okay. You got me. But no, seriously; there are dozens of laws about Shabbat and the holidays that I don't observe. Don't get me wrong. I observe a lot of Jewish laws and customs, but I'm sort of selective, and I don't think that either the Vilna Gaon or Rabbi Meir would approve of my selectivity."

"I think I understand. *Yikkies!* Hmmm. Do you want to know about *my yikkies?*"

"*Yiches,*" he corrected her. "Go ahead; I'm all ears."

"Well, around the same time that your *Gaon* great-great-whatever grandfather was holding court in Vilna, *my* great-great whatever grandparents were being expelled from the area around the Bay of Fundy, what was called Acadia. When the British conquered that area from the French, they expelled thousands of Acadians, mostly to Louisiana."

"I read about that! So you're an Acadian, like Evangeline! My mother made me memorize the Introduction to *Evangeline.* You know: *This is the forest primeval. The murmuring pines and the hemlocks…*".

"We had to memorize that first part in seventh grade, because there were a few of us in the class who were actually descended from the Acadians. After our great-greats were thrown out of Acadia, some of them managed to settle in northern Maine. My parents weren't much interested in where our family came from, but I've always thought of Evangeline as sort of my great-great grandmother. Boy, what if Evangeline met your *Gaon.* Do you think they would have fallen in love?"

Jacob laughed. "Well, you never know. There's a line toward the end of that intro that tells about '*the beauty and strength of a woman's devotion;"* sort of like the Woman of Valor that Uncle Sol read about at the Shabbat table last night. Wouldn't that be a scene, the *Gaon* with Evangeline in his lap."

"Almost as strange as *me* in *your* lap."

"Yup. Strange…. But nice, very nice. I wish that this could last forever, but we'd better get back to the house and get dressed. The sun is going down, and they'll probably be back any minute. We'd better put on our robes."

As they walked up the stairs from the beach holding hands, they heard the sound of a car approaching the house. Guiltily they dropped hands and walked up the lawn to greet the threesome as they were getting out of the convertible. Sarah looked at them and said: "I guess you finished your book, Jakie, and you finished your laundry, Marie." Sol just stood there grinning, and Hope looked puzzled.

Jacob answered quickly. "Yuh, we both finished a little while ago and decided to go down to the beach for a swim. The water's still pretty cold, so we just waded a little and then sat on the blanket and talked. Did you know that Marie is descended from the Acadians in Nova Scotia? Do you remember *Evangeline?*"

Sol and Sarah looked blank, but Hope spoke up. "Sure, I remember *Evangeline* from high school. Wasn't that by Longfellow, the guy they named the street where Sumner lives for? So are you an Acadian? I thought you were French."

Marie, a bit flustered, answered, "Yup, I'm an Acadian. I'll explain it to you in your room after I get out of my bathing suit." She emphasized the last phrase.

Sol couldn't help but say with a grin, "So maybe now we can see you in a bathing suit? You were too shy the other night when you girls were modeling, but maybe now that you've been swimming…?"

Marie turned crimson, but Sarah stepped in. "Sol, don't embarrass the girl. She's not an exhibitionist and this isn't a burlesque show. We found out the other night that Marie doesn't like to show off. She's modest, like a nice girl should be. I think that's very sweet. Marie, you just ignore him and go up and get into some clothes."

Marie didn't need any prompting but quickly disappeared into the house. Jacob decided that it would look better if he didn't follow right after her. "So did the three of you have a nice drive?"

Sarah answered, "It was really very nice. We took a leisurely walk on the dunes at Popham Beach, and then we sat on the sand looking out to Seguin Light, and then we had pie and coffee and ice cream at Spinney's, a perfect day with my very considerate husband who didn't have to go running around today, and with my lovely daughter, my *new* lovely daughter who didn't mind spending some time with her parents. But we missed having you along, Jakie."

"I didn't miss him," Sol said gruffly. "I had him all morning. And he had to finish his book. Did you finish it, Jakie?"

"Oh yes," he lied. "I brought along four books this week, and I finished them all. This was a great week."

"I'll bet it was," Sol said with a laugh, clapping Jacob on the back, and the four of them went back into the house. Before

Jacob could go up the stairs to his room, Sol said: "Sarah, let's end the day at a nice restaurant. It's Jakie's last night, so let's send him off with a nice Maine lobster dinner. We'll go to that new place, Cook's. Jakie, have you been there yet?"

"I tried it out for lunch with Marie yesterday. It's nice."

"Okay with you, Sarah?"

"Fine, now that Jakie eats lobster. I remember a few years ago you wouldn't touch it. So what changed your mind?"

"That's a very long story, Aunt Sarah. Someday I'll tell you."

Sol laughed. "*Haftorah* in the morning and lobster at night. That's what I call a well-rounded boy. *Nu,* let's leave in about half an hour. Tell Marie to be ready."

"Will do."

As soon as Jacob reached his room, Marie came in giggling. "You and your great ideas! Skinny dipping! I didn't know what to say when Mr. Fairstone asked me to show off my bathing suit. I'm just glad that he didn't grab the belt on my robe and undo it."

"I would have slapped his hand."

"I'll bet. O Jakie, it was such a lovely day, and you're leaving tomorrow. I'm going to miss you terribly."

"And I'm going to miss you terriblier, much much terriblier."

"Couldn't you stay just one more day?"

"How I wish. But I've got to be back to the university for an appointment on Wednesday morning, and I've got to stop to see my father and do a couple of other things in Boston. I'd love to stay another day… another week, but remember: I'll be back the first week of September, less than three months away."

"That's about when I'll be finished working with Hope and getting ready to go back to Hudson. A lot can happen in three months. Wait 'til Miss Chicago gets ahold of you."

"Forget about her; I'm sorry I even mentioned her. We've been good friends, but she's not the kind of woman I would ever think of seriously."

"Does she have *yikkies* like you?"

He took her in his arms. "You are a riot. I don't know if she has *yikkies*; that's what I'm going to call it from now on, *yikkies.*

Anyway, I never asked her. I don't think I ever had a really serious conversation with her."

They kissed, and Jacob said, "You go down to the family. I'll get dressed quickly. We're going back to Cook's for lobster tonight. Okay?"

"Okay. I better get out of here before you take off your bathrobe. I'd be terribly embarrassed."

"Yea, right. Go!"

As they sat down at their table at Cook's, Sol referred to the meal that they were about to eat as "the last supper" which brought a laugh to the small group. But then, after they had ordered their lobsters, he expanded on the theme. "You remember what happened to Yoshke after the last supper, so you be careful, Jakie. If you meet any Romans on the road to Chicago, run."

Puzzled by the laughter, Marie asked, "Who's this Yoshke? Some relative?"

Sol was about to answer when Jacob gave him a sharp look and intervened. "It's an old family joke, Marie, about a cousin named Yoshke who got into some trouble in Rome. Not important. Forget it."

Sarah and Hope got the clue and kept silent while Sol chuckled and said, "Right. Yoshke got sick after a big pasta dinner his last night in Rome." To Jacob's relief, Marie seemed to accept the explanation.

A few minutes later, five pound-and-a-half red lobsters arrived, along with bibs, bucket, nutcrackers, extra napkins, dishes of melted butter and sides of corn and cole slaw. They were surprised to learn that this was Marie's first experience with a whole boiled lobster and all the attendant paraphernalia. She didn't know how to attack her lobster, and so Sol began instructing her in the exotic art of lobster eating. He reminded Jacob that he had given him the same instructions a few years earlier when Jacob, as Sol put it, "went off the kosher standard."

Marie looked confused, and Jacob explained to her that lobster wasn't kosher. "You remember when I was telling you and

Hope about Jewish customs, and I explained that there were certain dietary laws that are followed by some Jews? Well, lobsters and other shellfish are among those foods that are not kosher."

"Now you've got me really confused. I thought that the dinner that we had on Friday night was a kosher dinner and that Jews were supposed to eat kosher. But you all eat lobsters?"

At this point, Sol took over. "We're not Orthodox Jews. They observe all the rules, like my father and mother did. But we're not so strict. We eat shellfish, but I would never eat bacon or ham or pork."

Hope offered: "Neither would I. Gross!"

Marie continued probing. "Jacob, do you eat bacon?"

"No; that's where I draw the line, not so much because it's not kosher, but because there were times when Jews were persecuted because they wouldn't eat pig meat."

"So I guess that's what you meant when you told me that you were selective about what Jewish laws you follow and what laws you don't."

"Right."

Sol proceeded with his instructions about the proper way to attack a lobster. She was doing very well under his tutelage until she uncovered a green mass and made a face. Sol explained that it was the tomalley and that it was a particular delicacy. "Tomalley?" she asked innocently. "Is that a Jewish word?" That produced gales of laughter from the other four, and Marie looked embarrassed.

Sarah said, "Marie, dear, we're not laughing *at* you; we're laughing *with* you. You're a darling to be so interested in Jewish things; I love it. It's too bad that Jakie is leaving tomorrow morning. He's a good teacher."

The rest of the dinner was uneventful, and they all left sated. When they got back to the house, the girls went up to Hope's room and Sol, Sarah and Jacob went into the living room to watch television. They caught only the end of the Jackie Gleason show but were in time to see all of their favorite, the Sid Caesar Hour. Sol and Sarah remained to watch the George Gobel show, but Jacob announced that he wanted to get a good night's sleep before leaving the next morning. As he was going up the stairs, Sarah said, "Jakie, leave time for a good breakfast tomorrow before you go. When I was in Portland, I got bagels and lox. We'll have a nice brunch. Tell the girls."

Sol winked at Jacob and said, "Sleep well; pleasant dreams."

Jacob stopped by Hope's room and knocked on her door, expecting to find both girls there, but Hope was alone and already in bed, with the light on. "Sorry; I didn't wake you, did I?"

"No, I'm not asleep yet. I was reading until a minute ago. Were you looking for Marie? She went up about fifteen minutes ago."

"No, no. Actually I was looking for both of you. Message from your mother: She's got a nice bagel brunch for tomorrow morning before I leave, and she wanted all of us to know so we can eat together and say goodbye."

"I'll miss you, Jakie. It's nice to have you here. Can you give me my goodbye kiss *now*?"

"Sure; I guess so."

He walked over to her bed and leaned down to kiss her on the cheek, but to his surprise she flung her arms around his neck and gave him a long wet kiss on the lips. He didn't want to offend her, and so he very gently extricated himself and said, "That was nice; not very cousinly, but nice."

"Jakie, I'm going to miss you a lot. We could be good friends, even though we're cousins. Give me your hand."

Puzzled but careful not to offend her, he gave her his hand. She looked at him meaningfully, and then slowly drew his hand to her left breast, breathing heavily. "Jakie, feel me."

He didn't know what to do or say. All he knew was that he desperately wanted to get out of Hope's room without a scene. "Hope, please," he said as he drew back his hand. "I love you very much as a cousin. But cousins shouldn't get involved with each other; it's not a good idea. You're a really lovely woman, and if we weren't cousins, I'd probably fall for you."

"I'm not as pretty as Marie, huh? I know she wasn't wearing a bathing suit under her bathrobe when we came back from Popham. She probably forgot that her bathing suit was in my room. I found it there. Whatever you do with her, you could do with me too. You could stay here with me for a while, just a few minutes before you go up. I wouldn't tell anyone. Here; I'll open my pajama tops. You'll see; my titties are a lot bigger than Marie's."

"No, no! Please, Hope. This is a bad idea, a really bad idea. Your mother and father would be very angry with me if they thought I took advantage of you. Please; if you really like me, let me go to my room. You're getting prettier and prettier every day. And Marie is your friend; she told me that she really loves you like a sister. You'll find some nice guy to love you when you get back to Malden, I'm sure. But I'm your cousin. I can't. I just can't. Okay? Can I go without you being upset?"

"Oh shit! You know, I've got feelings too, Jakie. How do you think I feel when the three of us are together and you're always looking at Marie? Okay; get out and go back up to her."

"Hope, she's your friend. She really enjoys being with you. Don't let this ruin things. Please."

"Go! Go! I'm not stopping you. But do me favor and don't tell anyone about this. Not Marie and not my folks."

"I promise; I won't. Still loving cousins?"

"I guess so. Get out before I start crying."

Jacob closed her door gently, staggered up to his room and flopped on his bed in a sweat. He just lay there for a few minutes trying to regain his equilibrium when Marie came in wearing her robe. "I was waiting for you. I thought you'd come right in. Something wrong?"

"No, no; nothing." He sat up. "I was just trying to figure out tomorrow morning. I've got to pack up, and Aunt Sarah has a special brunch that she's been planning for us. She wanted you and Hope to be sure to come down so we can all eat together before I leave."

"Do you want to pack now or later? I could help you, if you want."

His mind was spinning. He wanted to tell her about Hope, to warn her that Hope knew about her bathing suit or lack thereof, to let her know about Hope's resentment, but he thought better of it. He felt pretty sure that Hope liked Marie enough to keep up their good relationship after he was gone. "Okay; I'd love you to help. My suitcase is right here under the bed; I'll get it out."

"Are you a neat packer, or do you just throw the stuff in."

"Hey, I'm not a slob. I really don't have much, just what's in these drawers."

As he bent to pull his suitcase out from under the bed, Marie opened the top drawer of his dresser which had just a few polo shirts and a belt. She quickly threw them on the bed for Jacob to take care of, and she attacked the second drawer. As she was pulling out his few remaining pairs of socks, she spotted the box of Trojans. She looked at it for a moment and then lifted it out. "Uh, Jake," she held them up, "are you planning to use these any time soon?"

He turned red and stammered. "Not now I'm not. Don't get the wrong idea. I didn't have anyone in mind when I packed them. It's just… well, you never know what might come up, and it's better to be prepared."

"Okay, Studs. Don't be so defensive. You know that I carry a diaphragm with me, just in case. But… I don't know. I sort of wish that I hadn't seen these."

"I'll throw them away if you want."

"Don't be silly. Where would you throw them? Somewhere where Mrs. Fairstone or her cleaning lady would find them when they came up here? No, you pack them away like a good boy. I have no right to tell you what to do when you're back in Chicago." And she turned away and faced the wall.

He went over to her, turned her around and took her in his arms. "You *do* have the right to expect me to behave myself when I'm away from you. Right now, I give you that right." And he kissed her.

"Are you telling me the truth? You're not going to have sex with Miss Chicago or Miss Radcliffe? No, I take that back. Please, *don't* tell me the truth. I don't want to know, and I'm not holding you to any rash promises. We're not engaged or anything. I hope… no, I *pray* that you'll come back to me in September before I leave for Hudson, but between now and then, you can do whatever you think is right."

He kissed her again and opened her robe. "No, not now, Jake; not now. Please. I'm just feeling a little weepy." She moved away from him and back to the dresser. "Okay if I open the third drawer? No surprises?"

He laughed. "No surprises." And he began packing the things that she handed to him. When the dresser was empty, she went to the closet and took out the few things that were hanging there. They were done in a few minutes, and he closed the suitcase and lay it on the floor next to the door. Sarah had provided him with a laundry bag which had a few things in it. He took it off its hook and set it on the suitcase. "I guess that's about it. I'm really tired. You?"

"Very. It's been a long and unbelievable day. Shall I go to my room now?"

"Are you kidding? As one of my ancestors said, *Whither thou goest, I will go.* Your room or mine?"

"I guess yours. I got ready for bed before you came up. I'll take off my robe and climb in and wait for you, okay? Mind if I watch you?"

"I guess I'd be insulted if you didn't." He proceeded to strip down to his shorts and then went into their bathroom for a couple of minutes. When he came back, he shut the light and then took off his shorts.

Marie laughed. "Getting modest on me?"

"No, no. Just a natural reflex. Anything you want to see, just say the word." He climbed into the bed next to her and took her in his arms.

"Jake, wait a minute. Please?" She could feel his stiffness on her thigh. "Jake, this is our last night together… maybe for a couple of months and maybe forever; God knows what can happen between now and September. I'm pretty sure I'll be here waiting for you, but …., but…."

"But what?"

"You know, back in the restaurant when I was asking you about kosher and eating lobster, I got to thinking. Am I… how can I put it?... Am I like your lobster?"

"Like what!?"

"I'll tell you what I mean. You said that Jews aren't supposed to eat lobster, but you and the Fairstones do. You've got all those *yikkies* that you told me about. Those great-greats of yours probably wouldn't approve of your eating lobster, and they wouldn't approve of me; I'm pretty sure of that. But you're selective, like you told me. So I'll ask you again; am I like your lobster?"

"God, you are something! How do you come up with this stuff? If you were my lobster," he guffawed, "you'd probably snap off my penis with your claw." And he hugged her.

"Jake, will you do me a favor? A very *big* favor?"

"What?"

"I know that this is a lot to ask. I can feel how stiff you are. Jake, I want you to do this for me." She hesitated, and he whispered into her ear, "What?"

"It would make me very happy if we could just hold each other and fall asleep in each other's arms like last night. No sex, just love … like an old married couple. Would you do that for me?"

"Wow! Are you sure that's what you want?" And then in a pleading tone, "This is our last night together."

"I hope not." And she whispered again, "I hope not."

"May I kiss you?"

"That you may."

He hugged and kissed her passionately, his stiffness throbbing between her legs. "Jake…, please."

"Okay. I'm only agreeing because I love you."

"Do you know what you just said?"

"Yes, and I meant it."

"And I love you, Jacob Ross. I love you." And she turned her back.

He slipped his arms around her, pressed against her unbelievably desirable body and eventually slept. As soon as she heard him breathing regularly, she began weeping quietly. The weeping relieved her, and she whispered into her pillow, "I love you, Jacob Ross; I love you, Jacob Ross; I love....". She tried to drift off, but she simply could not ignore the body pressed against her. She turned and kissed his lips lightly. If he had been asleep, he was no longer. He whispered: "I do love you; I do..." and he found her more than ready to receive him. Then they slept until awakened by the smell of coffee brewing below.

Persons and Places

Jacob arrived at his father's – or, rather, the widow Sandler's – house at about three that afternoon. Tamara Sandler welcomed Jacob, and he was pleased to hear her refer to her lovely home on River Road as "*our* home" even though his father was supposedly still living with the Epsteins. She had prepared a delicious dinner for the three of them for that evening, and she had no objection when Jacob asked his father if he'd like to talk a walk with him on Shore Drive. The afternoon was slightly overcast and windy with a threat of rain, the kind of a day that Jacob loved in Winthrop – not many people on the beach and the breakers roaring. They walked along Shore Drive toward the Highlands as Jacob recalled the many days when he had slammed out of their house on Neptune Avenue to escape his mother's rants and walked up and down along the shore until he felt calm enough to go home.

"How are you doing, Dad. Happy?"

"Very. Tamara is a lovely woman. We're planning to get married before Rosh HaShanah. Is that all right with you?"

"You certainly don't need my permission, Dad; she seems like a lovely woman, and her home is beautiful. I think you'll be very happy with her."

"But your mother… you don't mind…"

"I've had it with mother. I don't know how you lived with her as long as you did. Forgive me for saying it, but she's a shrew, a real shrew. She was insufferable in Maine, spouting her poetry and insulting everyone, especially Essie and the young lady Uncle Sol hired to be Hope's companion, Marie. I'm not planning to see her before I leave tomorrow."

"You're not going to see your mother? Even to say hello? Jacob, that's not right."

"Dad, I'm sorry. I just can't. I don't even think of her as my mother anymore."

Isaac thought for a minute and then shrugged and said, "I don't know what to say to you. Who am *I* to talk? I abandoned her."

"Dad, you didn't abandon her. She was cruel to you, really cruel. She brought it on herself."

"I don't know. I feel bad about it. You know, Winthrop is a small town and people see her every day on Shirley Street, and they talk, not to me, of course, but Tamara hears from her friends. They say that she's… how can I put it? They say she's… crazy, Jacob; crazy! I don't know what to do. I'm afraid of what she might do if she hears that you were here and didn't go to see her."

They were at Coral Avenue, just two short blocks from Neptune and the home where Jacob grew up. "We'd better turn around. She might see us if she's out on the porch. Look, no one is going to know that I was here except you and Mrs. Sandler. I'm planning to leave before ten tomorrow, and I'll drive straight out of town. So if you and Mrs. Sandler don't say anything, she'll never know. And anyway, the way that she spoke to me the last time we were together, I'm not so sure that she wants to see me. So let's forget about Mother. If what you say is true and she's really losing it, talk to Uncle Sol. He told me that he would always take care of her."

"We were married twenty-two years…"

"How many happy years, Dad?"

"Maybe two, three, when you were a little boy. I was always happy with you and that wonderful head of yours, but with her? Not very much."

"All right; enough about mother. There are a couple of things I want to talk over with you, and I'd prefer that we talk alone, without Mrs. Sandler. By the way, I think that she's very nice. She seems devoted to you."

"You're right. I don't know how I deserve her, but she's making me very happy. She's active in the shul, and everyone likes her. She even helps me with the junior congregation. What a difference! So what do you want to talk about, *zunnele*?"

"Well, first I want to talk about Uncle Sol. Dad, talking man to man; what do you think of Uncle Sol."

"That's a strange question. Why suddenly Uncle Sol?"

"Something has come up. He made me a very tempting offer to work with him in Maine. Believe it or not, he wants me to take over from him in a few years, and the salary that he offered me is fantastic. But I don't know if I could devote my life to business, especially in a place like Maine. But Uncle Sol has always been so good to me, ever since I was a little kid. I know a lot about Uncle Sol that I wish I didn't know, but what do you think of him? Do you think I could be happy working with him and living in Maine?"

"What do *I* think? Jacob, this is a very big decision, and you're a man now. But think: you're just a couple of years away from your Ph.D. at a great university. With your head and your personality – you see, I'm very biased, *zunnele* – you could probably end up as a professor at some good university. And Uncle Sol? What can I say? I love him like a brother. He has always been very generous with us, and he knows how to handle your mother. I used to enjoy playing cards with him and swapping jokes, but..."

"That's what I want to know, Dad, the *but*."

"But he's a driven man. He's driven about money, and he's driven about women. I can't excuse him for what he's done to your Aunt Sarah. Twice already she had to go to a psychiatric hospital in New York after finding out about his peccadillos. She's such a lovely woman, and beautiful, too, but he's never satisfied."

"I know. I love Aunt Sarah very much, and it hurts me when I see that she's hurting. It's a good thing that she has her sister when she needs her. So what you're telling me is that I should forget about going into business with Uncle Sol, and I should continue working on an academic career."

"Jakie, I'm not telling you anything. It's your decision. I'm just giving information to help, like you asked." They had reached the end of the Crest, below the water tower, and they turned around retracing their steps. "You said there were a couple of things. So what else?"

"I want to tell you about a girl…."

"You mean Shelley? That nice girl from Radcliffe? Did you stop by Cambridge to see her?"

"No, school is over for the summer. I think that she's at home in Philadelphia. I probably won't see her. No, the girl I want to talk to you about is Marie."

"Marie? Who's Marie? That doesn't sound like a Jewish name."

"I mentioned Marie a few minutes ago. She's the young lady that Uncle Sol hired to be Hope's companion. Remember?"

"Oh, I think maybe I remember seeing her at the groundbreaking at Borden before I left. She was the very pretty one?"

"Right. She's not just pretty; she's very nice and we spent a lot of time together last week."

"What? *You* getting involved with a Christian? *You* who love everything Jewish? *You* who loved to learn with your zeyde? *You* would get involved with a Christian girl? Impossible!"

"I thought that's what you would say. Dad, I've got a problem. I really fell for Marie during this past week at Uncle Sol's. She's a lovely girl…"

"Jakie, my only dear son, Jakie. How could you talk like that about a… a *shikse*? How?"

"Dad, please don't use that word; please."

"All right; I won't call her a *shikse*; Christian is bad enough. Last time that we had a long talk, you were telling me all about anti-Semitism. You know what happened to our family during the Holocaust. And now you're talking about a lovely Christian girl? I can't believe it."

"Dad, it's not like I'm marrying her. I just want to talk to you about how I feel. I know all the arguments about dating women who aren't Jewish, what it can lead to."

"So, if you know…?"

"Dad, I'm very confused. I've never had a relationship like I've had with Marie over this past week. I just don't know how to handle it. I need advice from someone who loves me."

"Well, you've come to the right person. You want my advice? Here it is: Forget about her. Maybe you've been spending too much time with Sol. Go back to Chicago and get your Ph.D. By then you'll be a couple of years older and wiser, and you'll realize that a descendant of the Vilna Gaon and Reb Meir of Rothenberg does not get involved with a Christian girl, no matter how nice she is. That's my advice."

"That's pretty much what I thought you'd say. I just needed to talk it out with someone who I know cares about me. I've got a lot of thinking to do."

"A *lot* of thinking. That's for sure!"

They walked on silently for a few minutes until Isaac said, "Here's Sturgis Street. We'd better turn and get back to the house. I know that Tamara cooked up something special for you for dinner. I told her how you like roast brisket; that's what she made." He laughed, "I think she wants your approval, Jakie."

"Well, you can tell her she's got it. You're a lucky man, and she's an even luckier woman."

When they got back to the house, Jacob told his father and Mrs. Sandler that he wanted to try to get in touch with Koppel Ganzfried while in Boston. His father didn't remember the name, and so he reminded him about the old man who had appeared at Reb Yisroel's funeral four years earlier. "I don't know whether he's still alive; he must be around seventy-five or so, but I remember his saying that he was living in the *moshav zekenim* in

Mattapan. Do you have any idea how I can call the *moshav zekenim* to find out if he's still there?"

It turned out that Mrs. Sandler had a cousin in Mattapan who was a volunteer reader at Jewish old folks' homes. She called her and had the phone number for Jacob five minutes later. When he called, the attendant on duty told him that Koppel Ganzfried was indeed a resident there and that visiting hours on Monday were from eleven to four. He asked the attendant to inform Mr. Ganzfried that he'd come by to see him around eleven, and he got directions to the facility on Blue Hill Avenue.

Jacob was amused by the way that Mrs. Sandler catered to him and to his father over what turned out to be a delicious dinner. She kept urging Jacob to stay for a few days, but he explained the urgency of his getting back to Chicago by Wednesday. When he thanked her and said goodnight, she ushered him to a beautifully decorated guest bedroom where he found two chocolates on his pillow and a selection of boutique soaps in the bathroom. He fell asleep in his empty bed dreaming about Marie.

When he left the next morning after a breakfast of waffles smothered in fresh strawberry sauce, he gave his hostess a warm hug and kiss and told her how happy he was that she and his father had found each other. His father shook his hands, embraced him, and whispered in his ear: "Remember, *zunnele*; always be a *mensch* and a good Jew. And Jacob," – he looked into his eyes – "forget about this Marie."

Jacob pulled up in front of the *moshav zekenim* at a few minutes before eleven. As he walked in, he was assaulted by an institutional smell of germicide and... and what? Old age, he guessed. He asked for Mr. Ganzfried at the reception desk and was directed to the solarium on the second floor. There he found his zeyde's old friend, seated in a wheel chair dozing, with a copy of *Der Tog Morgen Zhurnal* in his lap. Jacob tapped the old man on his shoulder. His head snapped up and he looked at Jacob, confused for the moment. But when Jacob stretched out his hand and greeted him with a warm *Sholom alaichem,* he smiled and responded, "*Alaichem sholom. Vie haist du, yunger mann?*"

Jacob responded with his name, and reminded the old man that they had met at Yisroel Forshtayn's funeral. He spoke in Yiddish, the Vilna accented Yiddish that he had first learned from his *zeyde* and then mastered on his own through his voracious appetite for the works of Peretz and Sholom Alaichem. Ganzfried was delighted to be able to converse in Yiddish, and he told Jacob that he was the first person under the age of forty with whom he had spoken in Yiddish since he arrived in America. He asked Jacob if he was indeed Yisroel Forshtayn's grandson and told him how happy he was to see him again. He examined Jacob's face carefully and then nodded. "Yes, I can see a little of my old *chaver* in your face. Are you a scholar like he was?"

Jacob told him a bit about himself, especially about his love for his zeyde and how he studied with him. He also told him about his more advanced Jewish studies and about his matriculation at Harvard and Chicago. Ganzfried had heard of Harvard, and he said with a nostalgic smile that if he and Yisroel had arrived in America together when they were young, they might have gone to Harvard. Noting that Ganzfried was wearing a *yarmulke,* Jacob told him that there was only one student that he knew of who went through Harvard with his head covered, "and he was the son of a Chassidic rebbe."

Ganzfried still had a sense of humor. He said that he and Yisroel would keep their *yarmulkes* in their pockets and slip them on when there were no professors around. "If a Chossid could get away with it, so could we. Your zeyde and me, we did a lot of things that we weren't supposed to do."

"I came to you to learn more about my zeyde. It's hard for me to think of him as a young man, someone about my age. So what kinds of things did you do?"

Ganzfried thought for a minute, and then he looked into Jacob's eyes. "You really loved your zeyde very much?"

"Of course! I wouldn't love learning and *Yiddishkeit* and even music the way I do if it were not for Zeyde. I used to love to sit and study Bible with Zeyde and to sing *zemiros* with him on Shabbes."

"You know, *bocher,* it sounds so strange to me when I hear you calling my *chaver* Yisroel Zeyde. We were boys in the gymnasium together; we were young men in the tsar's army together; we were the leaders of our Vilna self-defense together, all young men. I was there at his wedding to Bryna Rivkes, and when their beautiful little Ephraim was born.... You know about Ephraim?"

"I know that he died in some kind of accident when he was a little boy and that Zeyde loved him very much. I was with Zeyde when he died. He was confused then, and I think that he died happily because he thought that I was Ephraim and that I was calling to him, waiting for him to come. When I was a boy in the shul choir and I used to sing *Ha-ven yakir li Ephraim* as a solo, Zeyde would hug me and kiss me. Sometime I thought that he thought of me as his Ephraim."

Ganzfried didn't respond for a few minutes. Jacob thought that he might have dropped off momentarily, but then he looked deeply into Jacob's eyes and said, "I'm going to tell you something about Yisroel Forshtayn that no one ever knew, no one but me and a few of our *chaverim,* all dead thanks to the Nazis and our good Christian neighbors. Even Bryna didn't know. Maybe when I tell you this, you'll learn something else from your zeyde."

For the next ten minutes, with a quivering voice, Koppel Ganzfried told Jacob how he and Yisroel had stood side by side and shot two tsarist cavalrymen on the night that Yisroel left Vilna forever. He told Jacob about the pogroms, about their miserable years of army service, about training their self-defense group, and about the troop of cavalrymen who had trampled over the body of three-year-old Ephraim. "We would have killed all of them, if we could, but only two bodies that night we threw into the Vilejka before your zeyde took the train to Riga."

He paused, allowing Jacob time to absorb the vision of his gentle zeyde standing over two bodies with a smoking pistol in his hand, and then he said, "You think maybe it helped, killing a couple of miserable anti-Semites? *A nechtige tog!* You know, Yaakov, not one of the boys in our group survived the Nazis, not one except for me. Most of them, along with your zeyde's mother and father and all the Rivkes family, were shot down at Ponary, and some died in the concentration camps where I was for three years. Did you ever hear the song, *Shtiller, Shtiller*? It tells about how quiet it is now in Ponary, just a few miles from Vilna. We used to go to Ponary for vacations before the war. It was a nice place, a resort, in the country. The Nazis along with Lithuanians who they trained, killed over a hundred thousand Jews there. That song I mentioned; it has a line: *'Many roads lead to Ponary, but no road leads back.'* So you never heard of Ponary? Oy, you in America! How fortunate you are. I wonder if Yisroel knew about Ponary. If you ever get to Vilna, *bocher*, you go there and say *Kaddish* for your family and for all the good Jews of Vilna."

Jacob had still not recovered from the image of his zeyde standing with a pistol over the bodies of two dead cavalrymen. "And you? You were there with him? You both had pistols?" Ganzfried nodded. "How did you feel after you killed them?"

"How I felt? Look, I was trained to shoot and kill Japanese, and I had nothing against them. So why should I care about a couple of Cossack murderers? All the time in the concentration camp, the only thing that made me feel good was when I remembered shooting those two anti-Semites. But your zeyde, with him it wasn't so easy. He got sick to his stomach when he saw that the two of them were dead. He was a scholar like you, not a killer."

Jacob thought for a minute and then said: "I wonder if I could ever do a thing like that. You say that I'm like my zeyde, and I always thought I was. But I can't help wondering if I could ever kill someone, even a Nazi."

"Yaakov, if you had to live under the heels of Nazis or Lithuanian *mamzerim*, I think you would do what your zeyde and I did. There comes a time when even a Jew has to stand up and fight. I wish that I were living in Israel now so that I could fight against Nasser and all of those *mamzer* Arabs who want to wipe Israel off the map. If you take after your zeyde, Yaakov, you'll do whatever you can in your life for the survival of the Jewish people."

Just at that moment a nurse came in to tell Ganzfried and the others in the solarium that it was time for lunch. Ganzfried asked Jacob if he could stay for lunch, but Jacob explained that he had to get back on the road. He extended his hand, but Ganzfried got up on his feet shakily and put his arms around Jacob in a bear hug. "I'm hugging you like I wish I could hug my *chaver* Yisroel. I've missed him every day of my life since he left Vilna." There were tears running down his cheeks as Jacob returned his hug. When he turned to leave, Ganzfried called after him, "Yaakov ben Yisroel, *Gedenk, zei a mensch und a guter Yid.*"

Jacob stopped in his tracks – the same words from his father when they parted that morning; the same words that his zeyde said to him more times than he could remember. What they wanted most from him was to be a good Jew. As he got into his car, he realized that he would have to eat lunch somewhere before he got on the road to Chicago. He thought of stopping at the G and G, but as he drove back down Blue Hill Avenue, all he could see around him was deterioration. He decided that he deserved one last good kosher-style meal before driving to Chicago, so he steered the car toward Brookline and the favorite oasis of his college years, Jack and Marion's deli.

As he arrived at Coolidge Corner and turned right onto Harvard Street, he thought of the many times that he had had dinner or lunch there with Shelley. He was always tempted by the smell of corned beef and pastrami, but those were his kosher days, and Shelley was even more careful about *kashrut* than he. She disapproved of restaurants that advertised themselves as kosher-style, feeling that they were misleading people who thought that they were eating rabbinically supervised kosher food when, in fact, they were eating *treif.* She only agreed to come along with Jacob to Jack and Marion's because they had delicious fresh bagels and nova and Jacob's favorite combination borscht. Even she could eat those dairy dishes, though, because of the venue, with not quite the same gusto as Jacob.

Jacob sat down at the counter and ordered a corned beef sandwich and coffee. As he was eating, he thought of the good times that he had shared with Shelley. He hadn't spoken to her since a few weeks before leaving for Maine, and that conversation was strained. With all that had happened in Maine, it seemed like a year ago. All he wanted was to call Marie, to hear her voice, to tell her again that he'd be back in less than three months, to imagine her body next to his. But as soon as he approached Coolidge Corner, he began thinking about Shelley. Why?

As he was sinking his teeth into the succulent corned beef sandwich, he knew why. His father's words, Ganzfried's words, were ringing in his ears: Be a *mensch* and a good Jew. How could he be a good Jew with Marie and her Jesus? How could he be a good Jew living on Bailey Island, miles and miles away from any real community of Jews? Didn't he owe something to all those good Jews who had been eradicated at places like Ponary? He wondered if he had the time to make a stop in Philadelphia before returning to Chicago? Would he be betraying Marie after telling her that he loved her? Should he ever have told her that? Was he crazy? How could he have said such a thing to a girl whom he knew for one short week? Would a real *mensch* make love to one girl and then think about another? And what about Trudy in Chicago? Had he forgotten about her completely after sharing his bed with her more times than he could count?

Unexpectedly, he made a decision. He would call Shelley just to find out how she was. Maybe he could stop by quickly. He took a last sip of his coffee, got two dollars in quarters, and went to the phone booth at the back of the deli. A minute later he was talking to Shelley's mother, who, after determining that she was talking to "that nice fellow that Shelley often talks about," told him that Shelley was at a meeting for the counselors of the Orthodox day camp where she would be working through the summer. He looked at his watch. It was one-thirty. He could be in Philadelphia by nine. He explained where he was to Mrs. Newman and asked her if Shelley would be home at about nine and if that wouldn't be too late to visit. She was very gracious, invited him to sleep over, and told him that she could have a snack waiting for him so he wouldn't have to stop at some *treif* place on the road. When he protested that he didn't want to inconvenience them and that he could stay in a motel on the road, she insisted. "What kind of a Jewish mother would I be if I let a nice Jewish boy sleep in a motel when we have a perfectly good guest room? Would your mother do that?" He thought better of commenting on his mother and agreed, hoping that Shelley wouldn't be annoyed at her mother for inviting him to stay over.

As he drove west on Route 9 to the new Mass Pike, he was mentally kicking himself. He didn't really want to see Shelley. Why had he called? Just because he had been admonished to be a good Jew by two men whom he respected and he was feeling guilty about Marie? Was Shelley the antidote to Marie? Did he want an antidote? He thought of Marie standing naked at his bedside as he stared at her, and he felt the tingling that precedes an erection. He had heard the story several times from his uncle Sol of how he had brought Sarah to meet his parents for the first time after their elopement. They had not approved of her because she was a farm girl. But look how that had turned out. Sarah was as good a Jewish wife as anyone could want; it was Sol who was the problem. Was *he* a *mensch* and a good Jew? There was so much to think about. Thank God he had been able to put Sol off until September… and Marie too. He had a good ten weeks to think it all out, and stopping to see Shelley would just complicate things. Stupid decision! But he was committed.

He rang the Newman doorbell just a few minutes after nine, and Shelley came to the door wearing an unaccustomed beret. He didn't know whether to give her a kiss, but she solved the problem by extending her hand and saying, "Jacob Ross! What a surprise! I thought you had forgotten about me."

Before he could answer, Shelley's mother came to the door and invited him in. "So this is the young man you've been telling us about. I understand that you're working for your doctorate at the University of Chicago. Where are you coming from?"

Jacob explained that he had been visiting with his uncle and aunt in Maine and that he had gone up there for the groundbreaking of a concert hall at Borden College in memory of his grandparents. When they went into the living room, Mrs. Newman took Jacob's hand and introduced him to Shelley's father who was sitting and reading. "Honey, this young man has just come from Maine to see Shelley." The two men shook hands as Mrs. Newman went on to tell her husband about the Borden concert hall. Mr. Newman was impressed.

"A concert hall at Borden. That must have cost your family a pretty penny. Very nice! And what do you do?"

Shelley broke in. "Dad, Jacob is the Chicago grad student I told you about. He's only here until tomorrow morning. He's been on the road all day and is probably tired and hungry."

"She's right, Honey. Let's feed this young man and then let the two of them talk before we all go to bed." Mrs. Newman led Jacob to the kitchen where she had prepared a plate of *gefilte* fish and *chale* left over from Shabbat. There was a bottle of Black Cherry Wishniak on the table and a glass and ice. "Shelley, pour Jacob some soda, and then you can both sit and talk. I'll go down to the family room to watch television. I was just watching the Dinah Shore show when you rang the bell, and then comes the Loretta Young show, my favorite. I never miss it. She's such a lady."

Jacob thanked her and sat down. Shelley poured the soda and then sat down across the table without saying a word. He looked at her and, not knowing quite how to open the conversation after not seeing her for a year, he just smiled and said, "Your mother is very nice, and this is a beautiful house."

"Thanks," and silence.

He took a forkfull of fish, and as he was lifting it to his mouth, she said, "Jacob, what are you doing here? I don't hear from you for a month, not a letter, not a call; you go up to Maine for an important family event and you don't tell me about it. Do you really think we still have a relationship? Go ahead; eat if you don't want to talk. But why are you here?"

"Shelley, I'll be honest. I'm really not sure why I'm here. I stopped in Boston for a day on my way back to Chicago, and I had a long talk with my father and then with an old man who knew my zeyde in Vilna half a century ago, and then I was planning to drive straight through to Chicago. I've got to be there on Wednesday afternoon to meet my dissertation advisor. But there was something that both my father and the old man said to me about living a good Jewish life that made me think of you. We used to have such good times together in Cambridge..."

She interrupted him. "That was over three years ago! Since then I've seen you three or four times, each time for just a few hours until you're off to somewhere else, and you call me every couple of months sort of to check in with me. I don't understand you, Jacob. What do you want of me? There was a time when I thought that maybe we'd .... I don't know. But I do know that I'm getting too old for games, and a lot of things have changed for me. So what's on your mind, Jacob Ross?"

"Shelley, you're the only girl who I ever really liked who took being Jewish seriously. There was that and your love for music .... I don't know; I guess I just wanted to see you to find out if there might still something between us..."

"Like what, Jacob?" she interrupted again. "Like what? Like what you were always trying to do with me when we came back from our dates? I told you then that I don't like hands on my body. There'll be enough of that after I'm married. I feel more strongly than ever about that, so if you have any ideas..."

"Shelley, I didn't come here to make out. I came here because we once had real feelings for each other, at least *I* did."

"And I did too, Jacob; I did. But I've changed a lot since our Cambridge days. You haven't said anything about this beret that I'm wearing. Do you know why I'm wearing it?"

"I guess it's stylish or something; I don't know. Why?"

"I don't go around anymore with my head uncovered. I take *tzniyut* more seriously now, and *negiyah* too. I allowed you to shake my hand when you came in, because I didn't want an awkward scene with my mother around, but I've learned that it's wrong to let a man touch a woman before marriage. I'm studying with the wife of a Chassidic rabbi, and I often stay over in their house for Shabbat. It's up on Bustleton Avenue in the northeast. They live a beautiful life, and they've promised to find me a good husband, a student in their *kolel* with whom I'll be proud to raise good Orthodox Jewish children."

As she spoke, Jacob couldn't take his eyes off her. He could hardly believe what he was hearing. It was only then that he noticed that she was wearing heavy dark stockings and that her skirt reached almost to her ankles.

"But you're a Radcliffe graduate, Shelley! You've learned things that certainly aren't acceptable in Chassidic circles. Do you believe that the world is about fifty-seven hundred years old? And how about your lovely voice? I thought maybe you'd go on to Juilliard or Eastman after you finished Longy. You're giving all that up?"

"I don't think I'm giving up anything; what I'm doing is gaining. My singing is a good example. I don't sing anymore in public because of *kol ishah...*"

"*Kol ishah!* You can't be serious. You can't sing in public because some fanatic man might hear you and get turned on? What about singing *zemirot* at your guru's table? You just listen?"

"I hum along. And don't be insulting; he's not my guru; he's a very pious rabbi who could teach you a lot. Anyway, I'm not the innocent little Radcliffe student that I was when we were dating. And there is no more dating and having to fend off wandering hands. When they think I'm ready, the rabbi and his wife will invite some young student for Shabbes and we'll see if we like each other under proper conditions."

"Wow! Shelley, this is the twentieth century! You're an intelligent young woman. It's one thing to be a good Jew, but this? This is going back to a seventeenth-century ghetto! That's the kind of life you want?"

"Jacob, if you were really serious about living a good Jewish life, you'd give up your *goyishe* studies and become a *baal teshuvah* like me. I gave up all that materialism and hedonism that you think is so wonderful, and now I'm really happy."

"Shelley, how come you never gave me a clue about all of this during some of our telephone conversations? I'm really in a state of shock. Not a clue…"

"You want an honest answer? Okay; here it is. I thought that I loved you, Jacob Ross. I actually thought that we might get married someday. But every time I was with you, you'd start getting amorous. We'd have a lovely time at a concert or a museum or studying together, and then you'd start with your hands. It was like you were obsessed with sex. I didn't know whether it was *me* you were interested in or my body. More than once, I almost gave in, but *Ha-Shem* stopped me in time. And then when you hardly ever came to see me and you mostly stopped calling, I gave up on you. But I needed something, and that's when I met Rebbetzin Rosenberg. She sort of took me under her wing, and now I've found my place in life, and I'm happy. You made me *un*happy, Jacob, and now I'm happy. That's it."

"So this is all my fault. God, I'm sorry."

"Please don't take *Ha-Shem's* name in vain, Jacob."

"Shelley, I don't know what to say. It's very late and I've had a long day. I think I'd like to go to sleep. Can you show me my room?"

"It's the one at the top of the stairs, on the right. I won't go up with you; you'll find it."

"Thanks. I guess we don't kiss goodnight."

"No, we don't; not ever again."

He gave her a long look. She reddened as he appraised her body, and then he shrugged and followed her directions up to the guest room. As he looked around the room, he spotted a book on the bed table. He picked it up, leafed through it and smiled. It was Luzzatto's *Messilat Yesharim – The Path of the Righteous,* an eighteenth-century tome about morality and proper behavior. He had studied parts of it at Hebrew College. Shelley was never subtle.

Jacob was so tired and bewildered that he flopped on the bed in his clothes without even visiting the attached bathroom. He slept fitfully until he was awakened by the urging of his bladder.

He looked at his watch and saw that it was almost six. Slowly, he got off the bed and tiptoed to the bathroom where he peed and brushed his teeth. Then he zipped up his overnight bag, silently opened his door, made his way down the stairs, and sneaked out of the house. As he started his car and slowly rolled down the street, he didn't realize that Shelley was watching through her window. Would it have mattered if he saw that there were tears streaming down her face? Probably not. He pulled into the first service area on the Pennsylvania Turnpike and had some coffee and a couple of doughnuts, not regretting the fact that Mrs. Newman would have provided a more ample breakfast.

By the time he reached Wheeling, he knew that he was too tired to drive any further. He pulled into the first motel that had a AAA sign and slept for ten hours straight. Late Tuesday night he pulled up to the Windermere and found a slot for his car. His apartment was as he left it what seemed a lifetime ago. It was hard to realize that it had only been twelve days since he left for Maine. The thought crossed his mind to call Trudy, but he cancelled it. He knew that she'd probably be miffed if she found out that he had arrived and not called her, but he was simply not ready for her. He decided to call her after he met with Dr. Gold, his dissertation advisor.

The meeting with Gold did not go as well as he had expected. Gold thought that he had bitten off well more than he could chew. He insisted that a history of French anti-Semitism going back to pre-revolutionary days and then proceeding through the writings of the philosophes, the contrasting attitudes toward Alsatian and Sephardic Jews, the Napoleonic Sanhedrin, the rise of the House of Rothschild, the Dreyfus Trial, and the Vichy collaboration with the Nazis was far too much to be covered in one doctoral dissertation. He wanted Jacob to concentrate on at most one century, roughly 1750 to 1850 or 1850 to 1950 and to leave the rest for, as he put it, "the book that you'll have to write in your first academic position in order to secure tenure."

Jacob left Gold's office despondent, realizing that he had wasted months of reading and note taking because of his much too broad approach to the subject and, more so, because of his anger at what he considered to be the anti-Semitic gene that he saw as *enraciné* in the French. He should have realized that a good Ph.D. dissertation should have a narrower and more pointed focus. Gold had warned him about that when they first began discussing the dissertation the previous September, but the more he read, the more he wanted to get it all in. And Gold was not at all gentle in his critique; he told Jacob that if he wanted to be a scholar, he had better learn how to approach a subject dispassionately and objectively.

Jacob went back to his apartment to lick his wounds, and after a couple of hours of self-pity, he realized that he wanted to talk to somebody. No, not *somebody*; he wanted to talk to Marie. He could call Trudy and let her know that he was back in Chicago, but why inflict his problems on her? He hadn't seen much of her in the month before he left for Maine; she had seemed preoccupied and he suspected that she might be seeing someone else. The last time that he saw her before leaving, she had told him that she was going to spend the summer as a counselor at a Jewish camp in Wisconsin, and he wasn't sure whether or not she had already left. There was always Rabbi Persky at Hillel, but he might have left already for his summer vacation now that classes at the university were over for the summer. No, he wanted to talk to Marie; he wanted *desperately* to talk to Marie.

Stupid! Stupid! Jacob castigated himself. How was he going to talk to Marie? They had never thought to discuss how they might communicate during the long weeks of his absence. He couldn't call the house and ask his aunt or his cousin, either of whom was likely to pick up, to let him talk to Marie. He often called to speak to his aunt, but to speak to Marie? On what pretext? "Aunt Sarah, I'd like to talk to the woman I think I might love but forgot to tell you about." Ridiculous! And if he called at night when Sol, who knew that his nephew was involved, was likely to be home, how could Sol explain to Sarah why Jacob wanted to talk to Marie rather that to her? And if Marie were called to the phone, he could just picture her sitting in the kitchen or the living room with the phone at her ear for fifteen or twenty minutes with Sarah or Hope hovering nearby. God, why hadn't he thought of that before he left. Why hadn't they worked out some kind of plan? Stupid!

As he sat on his couch wallowing in self-pity and regrets, he thought back to his last night with Marie. When she was sure that he had finally fallen asleep after telling her that he loved her, he thought he heard her crying and whispering his name. Is it possible that she was crying because she knew that communicating over the months when they were apart would be a problem and that he had not even thought about it? Did he really want to stay in touch with her after his talks with his father and Ganzfried? Is it possible that she thought that he had just said the magic words to shush her so that he could sleep? He had to talk to her. But how? Well, maybe he could write to her, even though it would take at least two days for a letter to reach her and two or three more days for her reply, if any, to reach him. But even that was problematic. Sarah or Hope usually picked up the mail that was delivered to the box at the end of the driveway. Surely they would be curious about any mail addressed by him to Marie.

He thought for a while longer and then looked at his watch. It was almost six, almost seven in Maine. Sol would be home from the office; they were probably eating supper. He dialed the Fairstone number, and a minute later Sarah picked up the phone. She was delighted to hear from Jacob. "I knew you would call when you got to Chicago. I was worried with you on the road for two days. So how did your meeting go with your advisor? You had it already?"

He lied, telling her that it had gone well. "But I called to thank you and Uncle Sol for everything this past week. It was really great, and I can't wait to see you again in September."

"Jakie, some good news about September. Marie, bless her, convinced Hope to apply to one of the schools in Boston that might accept her, maybe Leslie or Simmons or maybe even B.U.

She really wants to go, Jakie; we're very happy. You remember, she had trouble graduating from Malden High, but she did graduate and since then she's been reading a lot. Sol thinks maybe he can get President Coles here at Borden to write a letter for her. She's right here at the table listening. She says Hi. Marie's here too; she's a darling. She says Hi too. So anyway, try to get here as early as possible in September, because, if Hope gets accepted somewhere, we'll be leaving here a little earlier than we planned for her first semester. And Jakie, don't forget; Rosh HaShanah comes early this year; I think around the fifth."

"That's really good news about Hope. Give her a kiss for me and wish her good luck. And thanks for reminding me about Rosh HaShanah. I didn't realize that it was coming so early this year. I better start thinking about finding a shul that needs a cantor for the High Holy Days. It's an easy way for me to pick up five or six hundred dollars. Anyway, Aunt Sarah, can I talk to Uncle Sol for a minute? There's something I have to ask him."

"You can ask him for anything, Jakie. He never says no to you. Here he is."

After exchanging pleasantries for a couple of minutes, Jacob said, "Uncle Sol, I have to ask you for a big favor, but I don't want Aunt Sarah or Hope to know."

"You know you can always count on me; how much do you need?"

"No, no; that's not it. No, it's something different and private."

"So tell me already?"

"Uncle Sol, you know that Marie and I… well, that we like each other very much."

"I'm not blind; I could see."

"Uncle Sol, I want to talk to her. I want to be able to write to her or call her, but I don't want Aunt Sarah or Hope to know. It's sort of a delicate situation."

"So what do you want me to do? I'm with you, *bochur*."

"Well, first, when Aunt Sarah and Hope aren't around, please tell Marie that I'm trying to find a way to keep in touch with her.

Just tell her that. But then, if I were to send her letters at your office, could you get them to her without anyone seeing?"

"Sure; that's easy. But let me think a minute." There was a brief pause, and then he said, "I've got an idea. Call me at my office tomorrow morning. I think I have a solution to your problem."

"I'll be very grateful if you can figure something out. And if the ladies are wondering what we're talking about, you can tell them that I needed some advice about my apartment or something. Tell them I'm thinking of moving, and I needed your input."

"So we'll talk tomorrow."

"Thanks again. Give my love to the women."

"You seem to be good at that," he sniggered. "You take after your uncle. We'll work well together." And they both said goodbye and hung up.

Jacob slept late the next morning and was awakened just before ten by a call from Rabbi Persky. Persky told him that he had tried to reach him earlier in the week but that there had been no answer. Then Trudy showed up on Friday night for the Shabbat dinner and service, and she told him that Jacob was in Maine for the week. Jacob filled him in on the ground-breaking at Borden and Persky was quite impressed. "Maybe you can get some of your uncle's largesse directed to our Hillel house. We could sure use some refurbishing here. But Jake, that's not why I'm calling. I'm trying to convene a *bet din* for a conversion early next week, and I thought that you could be one of the members."

"Me a member of a *bet din*? I thought you needed three rabbis."

"Not necessarily. According to the tradition, any three good and knowledgeable Jews can serve as a *bet din*. I'll be frank with you; I would have preferred two rabbis to sit with me, but the only other Reform rabbi I could find available here on the south side was Rabbi Weinberg. He's happy to participate because the convert is a professor here at the university, and he knows him. When I mentioned your name to Weinberg as a possible third member, he agreed. He said that you were the best teacher he ever had in his Hebrew school. You certainly know more than enough to serve on a *bet din*."

Jacob thought for a moment and then said, "I'd be honored to sit with you and Rabbi Weinberg. I'm one of his admirers. So who's the professor who's converting?"

"Do you know Wesley Mortensen in the near eastern department?" Jacob replied negatively, and Persky went on. "He's an archaeologist and an associate professor, and he's a friend of Trudy Friedland. She steered him to me. Mortensen teaches a course in ancient near eastern texts. He's quite a guy; he can handle Ugaritic, Akkadian, Greek and Aramaic as well as German and Hebrew, and he dabbles in archaeology too. It's a pleasure to have a convert who knows Hebrew as well as I do. He spent a couple of summers in Israel on digs, and I guess he developed a real bond with the people from Hebrew U that he was working with. Anyway, he approached me about a year ago about the possibility of converting, and we've been studying together twice a week ever since."

"Sounds good."

"Well, there's something else I should tell you. When we began studying together, he wasn't sure he wanted to convert. He was interested in Judaism, but he wanted to learn more before making his decision. By the way, he was circumcised when he was a baby, and he agreed to the symbolic *tipat dam*. You might not be too pleased when I tell you what I think was the main thing that made him finally decide, but I believe in full disclosure, so here goes. You should know everything if you're going to sit on his *bet din*."

Persky paused for a few moments and then asked, "I don't like to get personal, but how involved are you with Trudy Friedland?"

"I guess we've been pretty close friends over the past two years. You see us a lot together at Hillel, and we go to concerts and movies together. She's very nice, but that's about it."

"I'm relieved to hear that it's not more than that…" Jacob rolled his eyes realizing that he couldn't count the number of nights that he and Trudy had frolicked together in his bedroom.... "because he's really fallen for Trudy. You know that she's a near eastern major, and so she was in a few of his classes. He didn't say anything to her the first couple of years, because he thought that it was wrong for a teacher to get involved with a student, but this past year – I guess he thought it was all right because she was a senior – he began inviting her for coffee after classes, and then he invited her out for dates a few times, but she always refused. Finally a few months ago he asked her why she wouldn't go out with him, and she told him that it was because he wasn't Jewish. She had promised her father when she was in high school that she would never date a non-Jew. Anyway, since he decided to convert, they've been seeing a lot of each other. Is that a problem for you?"

"No, no," Jacob replied quickly, "we were seeing a lot of each other for a while, but I didn't see much of her in April or May. I guess that was because of this guy Mortensen."

"Anyway," Persky continued, "I think that his attraction to Trudy is at least a part of the reason for his conversion. And she told me that she's delighted that he's converting. So his conversion won't just be because of his love for Judaism; Trudy is a good part of the attraction. But that's okay with me. I believe that anyone who converts to Judaism should be attached to a Jewish family. It's pretty hard to be Jewish alone."

They agreed on Monday morning as the time for the conversion ceremony, and after Jacob set down the phone, he sat there thinking about Trudy. He couldn't believe how casually he had dismissed his relationship with her. "That's about it?" Really? All those nights, all those sex games; she had been his primary diversion through his three years at Chicago. He had never thought that he could find an intelligent girl as in love with Judaism and as in love with bawdy sex as Trudy turned out to be. But yet....

But yet he had never really taken her seriously. They had never once talked about family, about goals, about the future, and certainly not about marriage. With all her sexy playfulness and lack of inhibition, he had never felt the kind of emotions with her that he experienced with Marie. But still he was amazed to learn that she was involved with Professor Mortensen during a lot of the time that they had spent together. He knew that she was seeing, as he thought, other men, but as it turned out, it was not other *men* but one man in particular. As he was sitting and thinking, not sure whether he was happy or sad about what he had heard from Rabbi Persky, the phone rang again. It was Trudy.

"Hi, glad you're back. I missed you. I thought you'd call me as soon as you got back, but whatever. Anyway, how'd it go in Maine?"

He gave her a quick rundown of the visit with not a hint of the most essential elements. She told him that she had a lot of news and that she was leaving for camp in Wisconsin next Tuesday. "So we better get together to begin our goodbyes tonight, okay?" They agreed to meet for supper at the Windermere restaurant, and he hung up confused.

"Begin our goodbyes?" Did she mean what he thought she meant? But how about the Mortensen guy? He was converting for her? How did she feel about that? And Marie? He picked up the phone again and dialed the number of his uncle's office. As soon as his secretary put him through, Sol announced without even bothering with a Hello: "Boychik, your problem is solved. First, I caught Marie as she was going up to her room last night, and I told her that you were trying to find a way to keep in touch. She looked relieved, and she gave me a squeeze on the hand. I've got to say, you know how to pick them. She's got such *chen*. Hey, can you say about a Christian girl that she has *chen?* Anyway she has it."

"You said you solved the problem. How?"

"Easy. I'm having a phone installed in your room. Why shouldn't you have a phone up there? I told Sarah that it's a shame that you can't make calls to your parents, to your teachers in Chicago, or to whoever you want in private, without having to use our phone. And I told her that maybe Marie would like to talk to her family in private. Anyway, the phone will be installed tomorrow. So you can call Marie or she can call you without anyone knowing or picking up. They already gave me the number, but you have to wait until tomorrow, sometime after noon, they said."

Jacob carefully copied down the number and thanked his uncle profusely. His mind was more at ease when he realized that he would be able to talk to Marie whenever he wanted. He spent the rest of the day in his carrel at the Harper Library rethinking the scope of his dissertation. He decided to go with the earlier dates suggested by Professor Gold, because he wanted to include the events leading up to Napoleon's Assembly of Notables and then his Sanhedrin and the establishment of the Jewish consistories. Regretfully, he separated out his copious notes on the Dreyfus Trial, Herzl and Zola, and the Vichy collaboration. They would have to wait for the book that he might someday write. He then outlined a work schedule for the next ten weeks. His goal was to present a detailed outline and at least two chapters to Gold in September before the beginning of the next semester. All of his course work was completed, as well as his competency exams in French and German. If Gold approved his new outline and the introductory chapters, he felt certain that he could complete his dissertation by the end of the next school year. He doodled "Ph.D. 1957" on one of his file cards, tacked it onto the carrel partition in front of him along with a dozen or so other reminders, and left to meet Trudy at the Windermere.

When he walked into the restaurant, Trudy was already there seated at a table waiting for him. As soon as she spotted him, she jumped up, gave him a hug and a kiss and told him that she had great news. He anticipated her. "Would this have anything to do with a certain Professor Mortensen?"

"You spoke to Rabbi Persky already? He's the only one who knows."

"Well, Persky called me this morning and asked me to serve on the *bet din* for Mortensen's conversion. From what he told me, Mortensen sounds like a nice guy."

"Oh, he is; he is! I never spoke to you about him because he wasn't Jewish, so I didn't think that I could ever get involved with him. He began asking me out on dates last winter, and I kept saying no even though I really liked him. And then he told me that he was going to convert to Judaism, and so I began going out with him. He's a wonderful guy and really intelligent. And, believe it or not, I fell in love. Me! I never thought that any man could get to me the way he has. Anyway, he's been studying with Rabbi Persky over the past year, and ..." she squealed, "last week he asked me to marry him. Can you believe it? He asked me to marry him!"

"So quick? Wow! So what was your answer? I think I can tell already."

"I said yes, on condition of his converting, so I'm provisionally engaged. What do you think of that? Me, a married woman! But we won't be getting married until he gets back from Israel."

"Oh? He's going to Israel?"

"Yuh, he's going on a dig again, Tel Dan, and I'm going to the camp in Wisconsin for the summer. We're both leaving on Wednesday. He's really a great guy; you'll like him when you meet him. Did Rabbi Persky set the time for the conversion? It has to be soon."

"Monday morning, along with Rabbi Weinberg."

"Great. That'll give us at least two nights together before we both leave. I'll try to make it memorable for him."

"You mean you haven't ...."

"Jacob, he wasn't Jewish! I would never sleep with a *goy*. I've always felt that my vagina would reject an uncircumcised penis," she laughed.

"Well, I have it on good authority that he's circumcised. So look at all the fun you missed."

"Yuh, but he still wasn't Jewish. I'll make up for it on Monday and Tuesday, before we both leave. Depend on it!"

"You *are* dependable. I can swear to that." And they both laughed.

When dinner was over, they walked out the door of the restaurant into the lobby, and Jacob asked her if she wanted a ride back to her dorm. She looked at him in surprise. "Jacob Ross! Are you going celibate on me? You're not inviting me upstairs?"

"Trudy! I can't believe you! You just told me that you're going to get married. No, I'm not suddenly celibate, but… but you're engaged."

"Relax, Jacob, relax. I was just kidding. I wanted to see your reaction now that you know about me and Wesley. You and I have had a lot of fun together, but from now on, I'm a one-man woman. I'm going to be a one-hundred-percent loyal wife, a real *eshet chayil.* It's going to be a long summer, and who knows what kind of guys I'm going to find at camp? Oy, what they're going to be missing."

"Trudy, you really are something. But actually, well… I'm sort of relieved that you're not coming upstairs with me. I met someone up in Maine, and I'm trying to figure out that relationship. A night with you would be great, as usual, but it would leave me even more confused."

"Wow! Sounds serious."

He spent the next few minutes telling her about Marie, without mentioning her name or her religion. She was just this lovely girl whom his uncle had hired as a companion for his cousin. They were in adjoining rooms in the Fairstone attic, and they fell for each other. Simple.

"So what's the problem? You're *here,* and she's *there.* Was she a virgin and you were her first? Shame on you, Jacob Ross, deflowering an innocent maiden." And she laughed.

"No, it wasn't like that, and she wasn't a virgin. But she's very nice, and I have really strong feelings for her. I've been away from her for four days, and I really miss her."

"So you're planning to be celibate over this long hot Chicago summer? Good luck. But hey, what about that girl from Radcliffe? I thought you had a thing for her. What happened?"

He suddenly began laughing. "What's so funny?" And he told her about Shelley, her beret and dark stockings, and the copy of *Messilat Yesharim* that he found on his bed table.

"So Shelley's history? Fuck Shelley!"

"I tried to, often; but no luck." They both laughed, and then Jacob turned serious. He told Trudy about the offer from his uncle. "I've got to decide between now and September whether I'm continuing on for my Ph.D. and an academic career or I'm going to settle for being just another millionaire. If I don't work every day this summer, I won't have enough to show Gold, and that'll settle it. But I don't want to take my uncle up on his offer just because I couldn't make it here. I want to be able to choose what I really want."

"Just another millionaire! Wow! Why didn't you tell me that before I accepted Wesley's proposal? Ha, ha; just kidding. Seriously, not that you ever asked, but I couldn't marry you. You're a terrific guy, and I really love being with you, but… I'm not quite sure how to put it, and I don't want you to get offended, but you seem to be so unsure about where you're going in life. You usually say that you want to be a professor, but I remember a couple of times that you said how you'd really like to be a rabbi. And then there were other times that you said you might go in business with your uncle. You didn't mention that millionaire bit, but you were considering it. And I remember once when we were listening to that great Rosenblatt recording, you said that you'd really like to be a cantor. Jacob, one of the things that I love about Wesley is that he's so solid. He's committed to teaching, because he really enjoys it. And *he* knows and *I* know that someday he'll get tenure at a good university. Jacob, what do you *really* enjoy… aside from sex, that is."

"I'm not offended. You're right. I keep asking myself what I want to be when I grow up. Anyway, I've given myself a deadline, and it's this September, after the High Holy Days. I'm going up to Maine at the beginning of September and I'm going to make a decision. I don't know what I'm going to decide, but I *am* going to decide. I have to."

"Mazal tov! Okay, now that that's settled, do you really want to go to Harper, or would you like to climb into bed with me?"

"Very funny…. and very tempting. Hey, can I give you a brotherly kiss? A *mazal tov* kiss on your engagement?"

"Thought you'd never ask." And they held each other for a few nostalgic moments before she left.

On Friday he started the day in the Harper Library catalogue room, looking for the newspapers that he needed to trace the events leading up to the Assembly of Jewish Notables. They had the *Moniteur,* the *Journal des Debats* and the *Journal de l'Empire* on microfiche. He decided to begin his search in early 1805, hunting through all the columns of the newspapers for the words *Juif* and *Hebreu.* It would probably take a couple of weeks, but he doubted that anyone else had ever gone at it as thoroughly as he planned to do. He began with a reel of the *Moniteur,* and when he came across the name Furtado, identified as a Jewish leader from Bordeaux, he decided to broaden his search to include any Iberian names that might belong to influential Sephardim who might have been delegates to the Assembly. He made a valiant effort to focus on the work at hand, but he couldn't help thinking about the phone call to Marie that he would make that night, a week exactly from their phenomenal Shabbat *mitzvah.* He had a slip of paper with Marie's new phone number tucked into his wallet, and three or four times that afternoon, he took it out and stared at it between issues of the *Moniteur.*

A Shabbat dinner alone is no Shabbat, and all he could think about was Marie. When would be the best time to call Maine? It's an hour later there; they're probably done with dinner; she would not be going straight up to her room. He'd better wait until about nine, ten o'clock in Maine. By then she'd probably be in her room. The deli chicken was tasteless and the knish was greasy. After a few bites, he tossed them in the garbage and washed his few dishes. He sat down with his copy of Anchel's *Napoleon et les Juifs* but realized after a few minutes that he was not absorbing anything. And so he just sat there, the book on his lap, staring at the clock.

At precisely nine, he dialed the number that his uncle had given him. He let it ring nine or ten times; no answer. Too early. He turned on the radio to WFMT and sat there, his eyes closed, listening to one of the Mahler symphonies. As soon as it ended, he dialed Marie's number again. She picked up after the first ring. "Jake?"

"O God, say it again. I love to hear you say my name."

"Jake, Jake, Jake. There; I said it three times. So how are you?"

"I'm fine. I called you about twenty minutes ago, and you didn't answer. Didn't you hear the ringing?"

"No, sorry. I set the ring tone on low so that no one will hear when you call, and I was down in Hope's room for about an hour after dinner. So you can call me any time; if I'm up here, I'll hear it and nobody else will. Jake, I feel so alone up here in the attic without you. I was going to move downstairs to the guest room, but then Mr. Fairstone told me that you had called and that he was going to put a phone up here. It's in your room on the bed table. I'm sitting on your bed right now, but you're not in it…."

"I wish. You can't imagine how much I wish that I were there with you. You okay?"

"Yuh, fine. I just miss you terribly. I'm counting the weeks; the first one will be over on Sunday."

They went on for about half an hour, trading the events of the past week, without mention of Shelley or Trudy. He told her about his disappointing meeting with his advisor, and Marie told him about her progress with Hope and how she had convinced her to apply to some colleges. And then she told him that the Shabbat dinner that night had been nothing like the previous week. She described how his aunt and uncle had tried to replicate it, but everyone agreed that it wasn't the same "without Jakie."

"My Shabbat wasn't much of a Shabbat either, sitting here in my apartment alone. God, I miss you!"

He heard what sounded like a sniffle, but then, after a short pause, she said, "I guess that my work here will be done when Mrs. Fairstone and Hope move back to Malden. And that'll depend on whether she's accepted and when her semester begins. My new semester at Hudson doesn't begin until September 13, but Mr. Fairstone said that I could stay here until then even if Hope leaves earlier. He knows about us, and I think he wants us to have some time together. He's sweet."

"Oh, I know; he can be *very* sweet. He's my uncle, and I love him, but be careful of him."

"Are you kidding, Jake? Be careful about Mr. Fairstone? He's about as old as my miserable father. He's got to be at least *fifty*."

"Actually, he's forty-eight, but he has an eye for beautiful young women, so watch it."

"Well, he's been very nice to me. I know how anxious he is to have you as his partner so, as you suspected, that might be why he wants me to be here when you arrive." She laughed. "He wants me to seduce you to take his job, but he doesn't know how hard it is to seduce you."

"You can seduce me all you want. I can hardly wait."

The mutual endearments went on for another few minutes, and then Jacob realized how late it was in Maine. "Marie, I'll call you again tomorrow and whenever I can. And look, since you have the phone up there and it's private, you can call me if you want to." And he gave her his number.

"Jake, I love you. I'll be thinking of you in bed tonight."

"Me too. Kisses."

He called again the next night and the next after long days, Sunday included, in Harper. And then on Monday morning at a little after ten, he went over to Hillel House where Rabbis Persky and Weinberg, along with Wesley Mortensen and Trudy, were already waiting. Rabbi Persky ushered the three men into the chapel and asked Trudy to wait outside. "It wouldn't be proper for someone not on the *bet din* to be present for the questioning. There shouldn't be any outside influence on the *ger,* but if everything goes as I expect, we'll invite you in for his formal declaration."

Rabbi Persky opened the proceedings by introducing Mortensen to his two colleagues on the *bet din* and informing them that he had been studying with Mortensen for a year, that Mortensen was already circumcised and had submitted to the taking of a ritual drop of blood, that the two of them had gone to the Lake Michigan beach for his immersion on Friday; and that he believed that Mortensen was prepared in every way to enter the covenant of Abraham. He then invited Rabbi Weinberg and Jacob to ask any questions that were on their minds. Rabbi

Weinberg asked him if he was converting entirely of his own free will. He told Mortensen that he had heard from Rabbi Persky that he was in love with a Jewish woman, "in fact, the young lady who's waiting outside."

Mortensen answered that he had been considering conversion to Judaism ever since his first trip to Israel and that the impulse had grown stronger over the past two years. "But what brought it to a head, I readily admit, is my love for Trudy Friedland. She's delightful, a good scholar and a good Jew. I want to have a Jewish home and raise Jewish children; I think that I can do that best as the husband of a deeply committed Jew."

Rabbi Persky confirmed Mortensen's words and then asked Jacob if he had any questions. The thought flitted through Jacob's mind to ask him whether he would like the testimony of anyone who really knew how delightful a woman Trudy Friedland was, but he stifled the impulse. Instead he asked Mortensen, thinking of another Christian involved with a Jew, "What are your feelings about Jesus?"

Mortensen thought for a while and then answered, "I was brought up in the Congregationalist Church where Jesus is considered an exemplary teacher and a model of compassion and concern for the needs of humanity. My studies over the years have shown me that his message was substantially the same as many of his contemporaries in the Judean academies. I do not consider Jesus to be my savior, and I do not believe in the miracle stories that accrued over the centuries to his legend, especially the myths of virgin birth and resurrection. I do not revere Jesus, but I put him in the same category that I would put Hillel or Rabbi Akiba."

Jacob nodded and said that he was satisfied, and Rabbi Persky said: "Wesley, you have considered the declaration that I gave you. Do you feel ready to read it to the *bet din*, and to sign it in the presence of these witnesses?"

"I do."

"All right. Let's all stand in front of the ark. Rabbi Weinberg, you open the doors and, Wesley, you make your declaration." The four of them stood in front of the Torah scrolls, and Mortensen read in a determined voice:

> *Of my own free will, I choose to enter the eternal Covenant between God and the people of Israel. I accept Judaism to the exclusion of all other religions. I will always be loyal to the Jewish people under all circumstances. I promise to establish a Jewish home and to participate actively in the life of the Jewish community. I commit myself to the pursuit of Torah and Jewish knowledge. And if blessed with children, I promise to raise them as Jews.*

The four of them stood silently in front of the ark for a moment, and then Rabbi Persky said, "Jacob, would you please go out and get Trudy. I'm sure she'd like to see the conclusion of this ceremony."

Jacob went out and found Trudy pacing up and down in the foyer. He smiled at her and took her hand. "Rabbi Persky would like you to come in now."

She walked in with Jacob hesitantly and took in the scene of the three men standing in front of the open ark. Persky said, "Come on in, Trudy. Please join us on the pulpit."

As she joined them, Persky took out the center scroll and handed it to Mortensen, saying: "I place this Torah in your arms, symbolic of the fact that you have now accepted it as yours. In it is the supreme declaration of faith that has always sustained the Jewish people, in life and in death. I ask you now, in the presence of this *bet din*, to make your declaration of faith."

Mortensen clutched the Torah to his breast and declared in a loud voice: "*Shema Yisrael, Adonai Eloheinu, Adonai Ehad!*"

Rabbi Persky took the Torah from Mortensen's arms and returned it to the ark. When it was resting securely between the other two scrolls, he said: "Wesley, there is one final part of this ceremony, and that is the bestowing of a Hebrew name. We've discussed this. Would you like to tell the others what name you've chosen and why?"

Mortensen said, "I'll be happy to. You all know that my first name is Wesley. The name Wesley has very definite Christian connotations. John and Charles Wesley were prominent eighteenth-century English theologians and hymnists and the founders of the Methodist Church. I want to give up that name, not to reject the good intentions of my dear parents who gave it to me, but to affirm my membership in my new faith community. And so I've chosen a first and a second name which retain four of the letters of the name that my parents gave me. I want to be known from now on as Elisha Yisrael; Elisha because his story in the Bible is full of miracles, and I think of my joining the Jewish people as a miracle, a gift from God. And Yisrael, that's pretty obvious. I'm now a member of the people Israel. So I want to be known from now on as Elisha Yisrael Mortensen."

Jacob stood there deep in thought and hardly heard the words of Rabbi Persky as he bestowed the name *Elisha Yisrael ben Avraham ve-Sarah* on Mortensen. Yisrael! His grandfather pronounced it the old way, Yisroel, but it was his *zeyde's* name, without the disguising Isidore. Throughout the ceremony, he had been thinking of Marie and wondering if she could ever do what Elisha Yisrael Mortensen was doing. God, if only she would tell me some day that she wanted to be Yisraela or possibly Miriam instead of Marie. He had been thinking of her when he asked Mortensen about his feelings for Jesus. She had told him quite honestly that she didn't believe that she could ever give up Jesus. In fact, Mortensen had not said that he was giving up Jesus; he just said that he considered him to be a teacher, a human being like Rabbi Akiba. He and the other two members of the *bet din* had accepted that. Could Marie?

Rabbis Persky and Weinberg raised their hands over Mortensen's head and concluded the ceremony with the Priestly Benediction. They then closed the ark and Persky said jokingly, "Now, Elisha, you may kiss the bride."

Trudy didn't hesitate for a second. She leaped into Mortensen's arms and planted a resounding kiss on his lips, as the two rabbis looked on benignly. When she detached herself from him, she said to the three of them, "You're all invited to our wedding; it will take place right here a few days after Sukkot. By then Elisha will be back from Israel, and I'll be studying for my doctorate in near eastern languages under him." She reddened. "Well, not exactly *under* him but... well, you know what I mean."

They all laughed, especially Jacob who had no problem taking her *lapsus linguae* literally. Mortensen then invited the group to join him and Trudy at the Quadrangle Club for lunch, and they all accepted.

When the five of them sat down to lunch, Jacob made it a point to sit next to Rabbi Weinberg. He was curious about Weinberg. From his volunteer work with the Southeast Chicago Commission, he knew about Weinberg's involvement in efforts to maintain Hyde Park as an integrated community. Whites, and Jews in particular, were fleeing from Southside Chicago and Rabbi Weinberg had been offered a position with a new congregation in one of the posh northern suburbs where dozens of his member families had relocated. He had been tempted by the importuning of some of his wealthier members, and at first he seemed ready to go north with them, but then he had second thoughts. He delivered an impassioned sermon, equating the sins of real estate dealers who exploit blacks with the prophet Amos' sinners "*who sell the righteous for silver and the needy for a pair of shoes.*" And he announced that he would remain with his dwindling congregation in Hyde Park in order to fight the exploiters on their turf.

Jacob asked Weinberg why, as a rabbi, he would want to get involved in the nitty-gritty of urban politics and race relations. Weinberg seemed genuinely pleased with the opportunity to talk to a young man about his rabbinate. He told Jacob that he had been inspired as a rabbinic student by the prophets who preached social justice and that he had decided that he would use his pulpit to teach his people that when Isaiah and Amos and Elijah spoke truth to power, demanding justice in ancient times, they were setting an example for future generations of Jews who should do likewise.

Jacob thought for a minute and then said, "You know, I studied those prophets in Hebrew College and with my grandfather who probably should have been a rabbi, but I never thought of them as addressing the problems of contemporary society. I had teachers who forced us to memorize chapter after chapter of the prophets, and I can still recite several of them by heart, but I never pictured any of them standing on Michigan Avenue or Times Square and railing against the injustices of today."

They went on talking about the problems caused by unscrupulous real estate speculators in the Hyde Park-Kenwood area, and Weinberg told him about a meeting that he and the local Unitarian minister had had with the former president of the University of Chicago, Robert Maynard Hutchins. They wanted Hutchins to use some of the Rockefeller wealth that sustained the university for the renovation of housing in Hyde Park in order to attract faculty members to remain in the neighborhood rather than moving to northern and western suburbs and only coming to the university as commuters. "Do you know what Hutchins said to us? He said that the University of Chicago was in the education business, not the real estate business. He just couldn't understand that if the university didn't get involved in the stabilization of Hyde Park, the university itself would have to move out someday. Fortunately his successor, Kimpton, has some more enlightened ideas about the responsibilities of a great university to its neighborhood."

Jacob was fascinated by Rabbi Weinberg and was paying hardly any attention to the conversations of the other three at their table. Noticing how involved they were, Trudy waited for a lull and then broke in, "Hey, you two, we're here to celebrate with Elisha, but you're suddenly thick as thieves. What's it all about?"

Rabbi Weinberg apologized for ignoring the others and then said, "I'm very interested in this young man. I think that he'd make a good rabbi. What do you think, Shai?"

"I've been telling him that for the past three years, ever since he came to Chicago. Sometimes he leads services at Hillel; he has a nice voice too. Is that what you've been talking about?"

Jacob laughed and said, "No, we haven't been talking about me being a rabbi. I'm still aiming at an academic career, but Rabbi Weinberg has been telling me some things about his rabbinate that I find fascinating. I never thought of the rabbinate as a way to be involved in the problems of contemporary society. Something to think about."

Trudy gave Jacob a knowing look and said, "Still trying to figure out what you're going to be when you grow up? How about a fireman?" Jacob grimaced and blushed. "Whoops, sorry; I shouldn't have said that, but we've been good friends for a long time. Mad at me?"

"No, of course not," Jacob answered. "I'm the one who should apologize. I just never met a rabbi like Rabbi Weinberg here, and I got carried away. Trudy and Elisha, you have our undivided attention."

Mortensen had ordered a bottle of wine and said that he wanted to offer a toast. "First, to my bride-to-be, my most brilliant student, who taught me how good and how pleasant it can be to be a Jew; second, to Rabbi Shai Persky who encouraged me along the way and revealed new insights into Judaism for me; and third to the two other distinguished members of the *bet din* that welcomed me into the Jewish people. *L'chayim!*" They all chimed in with *L'chayim* and clinked their glasses.

After they had all taken a sip, Trudy stood up and offered a second toast. "To my dear fiancé, *Elisha Yisrael ben Avraham ve-Sarah,* who I feel certain will discover the altar of the golden calf during his excavations this summer at Tel Dan and will then be given a named chair at this august institution. *L'chayim!*" Again the group raised their glasses and drained them.

As soon as lunch was over, Jacob hurried back to the library and immersed himself in his search for evidences of Jewish activity in the pages of the early nineteenth-century French press. That search took him until the end of June by which time he had a picture of where the delegates who assembled in Paris in 1806 had come from and what their occupations were. He devoted the month of July to the proceedings of the Assembly and the formulation of their answers to the twelve questions put to them by Napoleon's emissary, Count Molé. In August he focused on the Sanhedrin of 1807 and the so-called "Infamous Decree" issued by Napoleon in 1808, restricting the commercial activities of Jews in the Rhenish provinces. These were the things that he told Marie about in their nightly telephone conversations, all of which ended with expressions of frustration at being so far apart.

In one of their first conversations, Marie asked him how he was getting along with "Miss Radcliffe" and "Miss Chicago." He was almost honest about Shelley. He told Marie that he had heard from a Harvard friend who knew Shelley that she had become a religious fanatic and that he was sure that he would never see her again. As for Trudy, he told Marie that she was engaged to a professor at the university, and he described Mortensen's conversion ceremony in detail, including his question about Jesus. Marie was eager to know how he answered, and when Jacob repeated Mortensen's statement almost verbatim, she asked him to repeat it. When he did, she sounded puzzled. "He was brought up as a Christian, and he said that he doesn't consider Jesus to be his savior?" She mused over that for a few moments and then said, "Well, you said that he was a Protestant. I don't think that a Catholic could give up Jesus that easily. I don't believe in all those miracles either, but I know that Jesus helped me." Jacob replied that they could talk about that when they were together.

He also neglected to tell Marie about the call that he received from Trudy a couple of weeks after she arrived at the camp in Oconomowoc. She was exultant about her two nights with Mortensen before his departure for Israel. "I didn't tell you, but I was worried. I had no idea of how he'd perform in the sack. You know, he's an academic; you can never tell about testosterone levels with people who spend so much time in libraries… Whoops! Excluding you, of course. Anyway, we never even got to the sack. He was all over me as soon as we stepped over his threshold that first night. It was glorious, like never before. We didn't fall asleep until it was almost light outside. He's quite a man, and" – she guffawed – "whoever circumcised him left an awful lot there!"

She went on to say that she had checked out the camp's male staff and had found no one to even tempt her over the summer. "There's one guy, an Israeli, who would have been a possibility if it weren't for Elisha. But what an ego! He served in *Tzahal* with the paratroopers, and that's about all he talks about. I'm not quite horny enough yet to see if he has the real stuff."

Toward the end of July, Trudy called again. "Jacob, I'm lonely up here. I'm surrounded by kids all day, but the nights are lonely. I'm almost tempted to give that Israeli paratrooper another chance. But I just keep dreaming of Elisha, which brings me to the main reason for my call. Did you ever hear about Maxwell Street Days?"

Jacob replied that he knew about Maxwell Street in Chicago where the Jewish pushcart peddlers used to hawk their wares back in the twenties and thirties, but that he had never heard about Maxwell Street Days.

"Well, the merchants in the town of Oconomowoc, a few miles from the camp, have these days each summer when they sell merchandise from pushcarts. And from what I've heard from some of the counselors who've been here before, some of the merchants dress up like immigrant Jews – you know, beards and *kapotes* and fake long noses – and haggle over prices. It sounds rather anti-Semitic to me. Anyway I thought that you might be interested in seeing it.... and me."

"Look, Trudy; I'm tempted. You know how I feel about you, and it's been a really lonesome summer. But... come on, Trudy. Wesley... Elisha is a really nice guy. I'm happy you found him, and I don't want to mess things up."

"I hear you, and you're right, but let me finish what I was saying. I told the camp director here about you. He's always looking for interesting people to come up for a weekend to give a couple of talks to the staff on some Jewish topic. So I told him about your background and that you could give a couple of interesting talks about French Jewry and anti-Semitism. He liked the idea, and he told me to call you and invite you up for a weekend. They have a guest house here for visitors, and there's actually a small honorarium – about fifty dollars, I think. So I thought that you could kill two birds with one stone. Maxwell Street Days are the first weekend in August, and you could give a couple of talks here on Friday and Saturday nights in the lodge. What do you say?"

It didn't take Jacob very long to agree. As an added bonus: he'd have a real Shabbat at camp. He needed a break from the drudgery of his research; a weekend at a camp with a lake and with no expenses might just be the ticket. What he told Marie when they spoke later that night was that he had been invited to a Jewish camp for the weekend to give some talks to the staff and that he might not be able to talk to her for a couple of days. She was happy for him. "The way you've been describing those long hot summer days in the library, you deserve a break. And if you manage to go swimming, remember that Saturday when we went swimming here. The water probably won't be as cold in Wisconsin."

Jacob's weekend in Oconomowoc began with a Shabbat service in a pine grove overlooking Lac LaBelle. There were a couple of talented song leaders who accompanied the service with their guitars. The campers who read the service and who added their own creative prayers were a novelty to him, and he particularly appreciated the traditional Shabbat dinner, complete with *Kiddush* and *zemirot* that followed. After the kids were put to sleep, the staff reassembled in the lodge, and Jacob gave the first of his two talks. None of the staff, aside from Trudy, had ever heard of the Napoleonic Sanhedrin, and they were fascinated with the questions that Napoleon had posed to the Jewish delegates. Jacob described the events leading up to the convening of the Sanhedrin and promised to discuss the responses of the delegates to Napoleon the next night. The evening ended with cold drinks and fruit, and the director accompanied Jacob to his room in the rustic guest house and left him with profuse thanks for a stimulating session.

Jacob was surprised that Trudy had not sat near him during the session in the lodge. In fact, she hardly said a word to him after her initial welcome and a perfunctory kiss. During the service and at dinner, she sat with her campers and only waved to him. She seemed about to say something to him when the session with the staff ended, but he was monopolized by a couple of the counselors who had comments and questions, and then the director came over to take him to his quarters. As he was preparing for bed, he half expected Trudy to barge in, and he was both relieved and, he had to admit, disappointed that she did not. Smiling inwardly he fell asleep satisfied that he would be able to give Marie a complete and honest report of the weekend when he got back to the Windermere and his phone.

After the Shabbat morning service and lunch, at both of which Trudy sat with her charges, Jacob made his way to the Lac LaBelle beach. It was a particularly hot day, and the director had announced at lunch that the counselors could take their kids to the beach for as much time as they wanted. Jacob spotted the camp raft about fifty yards out in the lake. It was empty, and so he asked one of the lifeguards who was standing on the dock whether he was allowed to swim out to it. The lifeguard asked him about his swimming proficiency, and when Jacob answered that he had Red Cross certification, he was given permission to swim wherever he wanted as long as he had an equally qualified "buddy" with him. Jacob looked around and saw Trudy walking down to the beach along with a dozen girls and her junior counselor. He went over to her to ask her if she could recommend someone who might swim out to the raft with him.

"Hey, I'd love to go with you. Wait a minute." She said a few words to her junior who nodded her assent. "Stacy said that she'd watch the kids. It's really no big deal with all the lifeguards on duty. Anyway, I wouldn't trust you with anyone else. I saw the way that a few of the female counselors were looking at you during your talk last night. Let's go.

They threaded their way through the mass of kids on the beach and swam out to the empty raft. Jacob was surprised to see that Trudy could match him stroke for stroke, considering the double-Ds that she was carrying along. As they climbed up on the raft, Jacob was laughing. "What's so funny?"

"I never knew what a good swimmer you are; you must get extra-mammary buoyancy. It's called e-m-b, and it's intended to make young men salute. Trudy, you sure do know how to fill a bathing suit. Wow!"

"Control yourself, Jacob. There are about a hundred pairs of eyes on us. Thank you for what I'll take as a compliment, but boy! Do I wish that Elisha were here to say that."

"You really miss him, huh?"

"More than I can say. I get letters from him every few days, and after each letter I just yearn to feel his arms around me. I go to bed with his letters."

"I know the feeling."

"Really? You? So tell me already. I'm all ears."

Jacob thought for a while and then said, "Okay. I need someone to talk to about that girl whom I met in Maine, Marie…"

"*Marie!!* You're dating a *Marie?* Don't tell me that she's a *shikse!* You?"

"Trudy, please don't use that obnoxious word. I hate it. Yes, she's not Jewish, just like your Wesley wasn't Jewish."

"Hey, there's a difference. I wouldn't go out on a date with Elisha until he decided to convert. And you saw how committed he is. He'll be a great Jewish husband and father. So what about this Marie? I can't believe it; *Marie?*"

"Maybe I shouldn't be talking to you about…."

"Come off it, Jacob," she interrupted. "You know you can tell me anything. I'm the last person to be judgmental. I'm just surprised that you of all people would be interested in a *shi…*, excuse me, a non-Jew."

"Well, I guess that these things just happen. Look, you know how much I like you. For a while when we got started, I actually thought that I loved you and that we might get married someday. But… look, I'll be honest; no offense. There was something missing. We had great times going to concerts and hanging out together and making out. You're always terrific in bed, you know just the right moves…."

"Something I picked up in the ninth grade from the only Jewish guy on our high school football team. Every fifteen-year-old should have a Sammy Spiller. He had great equipment below the belt, but he was sort of challenged intellectually. We had fun together, but then it got sort of tiresome."

"Trudy, I don't want to get you started on an account of your sexual history. We only have two days." She gave him a poke. "Sorry. Anyway, what I was getting at is that I really fell for this girl; my uncle hired her as a companion for my cousin Hope..."

"She's the sort of fat and dull one you've told me about."

"Yuh, my cousin Hope. Well, Marie's been working with her for just a few weeks and she's already lost a lot of weight; she's beginning to dress nicely; and, most important, she's coming out of her shell. She can actually be sociable. I never thought it would happen, and it's all Marie. By the way, I should add, she's gorgeous, movie-star gorgeous."

"Friend, you sound smitten. So where do you go from here?"

"I don't know. I just don't know. I think that I love her. It took a while before we had sex, but when we did, it was different from ever before. I don't understand how, but it was different. I can say this to you, especially now that you've found someone whom you love. You remember when you called last month, you said that those two nights that you had with your Elisha was like nothing before? Well, that's the way it was with Marie and me. You and I have had some great times in bed, and I don't want you to take this the wrong way, but I felt something special with Marie. I guess that's what love is, the x factor."

"Mmmm," she answered, and they lay there quietly for a while, thinking and soaking up the sun. They were both tired, and they dozed off briefly. When Trudy awoke, she nudged Jacob. "Time to swim back. I've got to relieve my junior, and I think we've had enough sun."

They both got up and, as they were about to dive in, Trudy laughed and said, "Hey, do you realize that about a hundred people just saw us sleeping together? We'll have to find a more private spot." She sliced into the lake with hardly a splash, and Jacob followed in her wake.

Supper that evening was followed by a *Havdalah* service around a camp fire. The teenagers in the Hebrew-speaking group led the service, explaining the significance of the twisted candle and the spice boxes that they passed around during the chanting of the blessings. The brief service ended with the entire cohort softly singing *Eliyahu Ha-navi* as the fire died down and flickered. It was a beautiful, star-studded night, and Jacob remained seated there while the counselors shepherded their charges back to their bunks for stories and sleep. He sat there thinking about Trudy's reaction to his revelation about Marie. If that's how someone like Trudy reacts, he thought, how about the Vilna *Gaon* and Meir of Rothenberg? Could he mix their genes with those of a French Catholic, not matter how lovely she was? He sat there musing for a while until he saw the counselors heading for the lodge. He sighed, got up and followed them.

That night's session was even better than the previous night. He went over the twelve questions again and asked them how they, understanding the precarious position of French Jews in 1807, would have answered. A lively discussion followed, during which Amnon, the Israeli lifeguard, insisted vigorously that the Jewish deputies should have stood up to Count Molé and demanded their rights as Frenchmen. He accused the hapless Jews who were treading on very thin ice with Napoleon, of having a ghetto mentality. "That's not the way we do things in Israel. We stand up and demand our rights as men! They should have done the same."

Jacob was pleased that he wasn't the only one who disputed Amnon's macho stance. It was a bright group of young adults, and they seemed to understand how tenuous was the security of the Jews of Alsace in particular as a consequence of the unscrupulous activities of the money-lenders among them. One of the young women shut Amnon up by reminding him that the Israeli army was not available to the Jewish delegates in early nineteenth-century Paris. They had only their wits to negotiate with, she said, adding "Where are yours, Amnon?" The group laughed, and Amnon, red-faced, shut up.

When the session was over, the attractive young woman who had challenged Amnon introduced herself to Jacob and offered to accompany him to the guest building. He thanked her but said that he was pretty sure he could find the way by himself. She smiled and replied that she wouldn't want him to lose his way and that she had a question about his lecture. He shrugged and looked over to Trudy who was sipping a cold drink; she smiled back, giving him a surreptitious thumbs up.

On the way to his quarters, the young woman introduced herself as Esther Ginsberg, a junior at Northeastern, majoring in European history. "I was fascinated by your presentation, Jacob. I've been focusing on the rise of nationalism, especially in Germany and Italy, but I think I should pay more attention to France. Could you give me some advice? When Jerry introduced you, he said that you were a Harvard grad. I'd really like to pick your brains."

He agreed, although the signal that he had received from Trudy made him a bit suspicious of her motives. As they walked along under the starry canopy, his suspicions were confirmed as she took his hand with the excuse that the path was uneven and they had no flashlight. When they reached his room, she walked in with him and asked where she should sit. He indicated the one chair in the room and cleared a space for himself on the bed. As soon as she was seated, she asked him if he knew anything about the role of the old Italian-Jewish community in the *Risorgimento.* "You said that there were some Italian Jews among the delegates to Napoleon's Sanhedrin, and so I was wondering if they went back and got involved with people like Cavour."

"That's a very good question," he said admiringly, "and I probably should have looked into that angle." He was speculating about various possible answers when she got up and walked toward him.

"Jacob," she took his hands. "you're a terrific teacher." She looked into his eyes and asked, "Would you like me to spend the night with you? My bunk is covered." And before he could answer, she lifted her polo shirt over her head, revealing an amply stuffed lacy bra.

"Wait! Wait! Hold on a minute." He looked at her and hesitated for a moment but then recovered quickly. "Look, I thought you wanted to talk. I think you've got the wrong idea about me. You're lovely and I appreciate the offer but..."

"Are you going to kick me out?"

"I wouldn't put it that way, but... well, I can't."

"You *can't*!?"

"No, what I mean is, it's not right. I'm a guest here. And... and it wouldn't be right. Please, you're very nice and pretty, but I'm just not in the mood. Okay?"

She hesitated, looking into his eyes, and then shrugged and pulled her shirt back down. "I thought that we could have some fun. Sorry, I guess I misjudged you. This never happened." And she was gone.

Jacob sat on his bed for a few minutes without stirring. He was trying to explain to himself why he had forfeited a golden opportunity with a bright and lovely young woman. Was it Marie? Then why did he feel aroused, he admitted to himself, when he was out on the raft with Trudy. He couldn't say anything to her because of Elisha, but the old desire was there. He shrugged but then smiled as a verse from *Proverbs* came to mind:

There are things that are just too wonderful for me,
Things that I don't understand:
the way of a vulture in the sky,
the way of a serpent on the rock,
the way of a ship out at sea,
and the way of a man with a maiden.

I guess I'm not the first person who doesn't understand, he thought, as he stripped down to his skivvies and climbed into bed.

He was beginning to drift off when Trudy burst into his room laughing uproariously. "Jacob, you're not going to believe this. I don't know what you told Esther, but she came back to the lodge while I was still there with a couple of the girls, and she announced that you were a homo. You! A *feygele*! She was pretty miffed."

"Trudy? Hey, I didn't expect to see you in my room tonight. What…" he laughed. "So Esther thinks I'm a fairy? Sorry I disappointed her. She seemed like a nice girl, but… I don't know. It just didn't seem right."

Trudy laughed again and then looked Jacob straight in the eye and said, "Jacob Ross, now that there's a rumor going around that you are a *feygele*. I want you to prove to me that it's not true." To Jacob's amazement, she began to slip out of her shorts, but then she stopped and looked at him. "Jacob, why didn't you *shtup* Esther? She was ready and willing. Why, Jacob?"

"I wish that I had an answer, a nice moralistic answer. I guess I just didn't want to. I… I'm not sure. It's probably Marie. I don't know. But what are you doing? What about Elisha?"

"Please don't ask any questions. Let's just say that I'm feeling super horny and, as the feller says, a fuck is just a fuck. No strings."

They were both quiet for a few minutes. Then: "Isn't it wrong, Trudy? Us screwing? Now?"

Trudy hitched up her shorts and sat down on the bed. She sat there silently for a minute and then began to cry. "Jacob, I miss him so much…. So much! I think that maybe I feel like punishing him for being so far away. He's all that I want, Jacob. I think I would die if he ever found out. But… I don't know; I feel safe with you. I'm sorry; this shouldn't be happening."

"You're right; it shouldn't. But why? Tell me why? We've always enjoyed each other in bed. You love Elisha, and I'm more and more sure that I love Marie, so why do I feel like sleeping with you now, me thinking about Marie and you thinking about Elisha. Why? I'm not saying that it's right or wrong, but why? 'The way of a man with a maiden.' I simply don't understand it. Do you?

"No, Jacob, I'm as clueless as you are. You know, I love you... not the way that I love Elisha, but in a different way, sort of like a brother. Hey, maybe we're guilty of incest." She laughed. "I don't know...."

"And I love you, too, Trudy. I do... like the sister that I never had or...." He thought for a moment. "Or like my Aunt Sarah. Ever since I was a teenager, I wondered what it would be like to make love to *her*. I *know* that would have been wrong. So when is it right, and when is it wrong? Tell me, o wise woman."

"Jacob, I'm as confused as you are. This may sound perverted, but I'd like to spend this last night with you. No right, no wrong. I don't mind if you think about your Marie; I know I'll be thinking about Elisha. We'll be surrogates."

"Just your saying that makes me hard. Enough rationalizing; we'll never figure it out. Let me get rid of my skivvies." And the four of them proceeded joyously to plumb the depths of the mystery of man and maiden.

The next morning it was raining heavily, and so they cancelled their excursion to Maxwell Street Days. "Just as well," Jacob told Trudy as they hugged and kissed goodbye; "I've lost two days out of my study schedule. I can get back in time for a few hours in Harper today. I've only got less than a month left 'til my next meeting with Gold. Give my regards to Elisha if he calls. I think he's really a nice guy."

"I'm really glad you came. You were able to forget about your dissertation for a couple of days, and you had a nice Shabbat, and.... well, let's forget the and. I was going I was going to tell you to give my regards to Marie, but you'd better not."

He put the MG in gear and drove away waving.

That night, after three hours at the library, he called Marie and reported on his weekend. He described the Shabbat services, the chapel in the pine grove, his swim in the lake, his presentations to the staff, his nice room in the guest house, and even the stupid comment by Amnon. Everything that he told her about the weekend was true....expurgated, but true.

During the next two months, Jacob allowed himself virtually no time off, with two exceptions: his nightly calls to Marie, usually a half-hour or so of yearning chit-chat before bed, and an hour's meeting that he arranged on an impulse with Rabbi Weinberg.

It was a hot mid-August day, but Jacob decided to walk over to the Drexel Boulevard Temple. The further north and west that he walked away from the university, the more run down were the blocks that he traversed. He wondered if the four Jewish congregations that still remained in Hyde Park could survive. He began his meeting with Rabbi Weinberg with that question, and the rabbi did not equivocate. He insisted that it was the moral responsibility of anyone, Jewish or Christian, who claimed to believe in justice to work for the stabilization of an integrated community. "You know, Jacob, the most repeated *mitzvah* in the Torah, over thirty times, is the *mitzvah* to treat the stranger as the home-born. For a Jew to be a bigot or for a Jew to exploit blacks is an unforgivable sin. But, sad to say, our people are not angels. They're fleeing north at a frightening rate."

Jacob asked him if he sometimes got frustrated and wanted to give up and just be the usual kind of rabbi. "You know: officiating at weddings, funerals and bar mitzvahs, and visiting the sick and conducting services. Doesn't all of that take most of your time?"

The rabbi thought for a moment and then looked at Jacob. "Tell me, young man; why are you asking me these questions? What's really on your mind? I think that you had more than community renewal on your mind when you made this appointment."

Jacob smiled. "Rabbi Persky told me that you were very perceptive; I guess he was right. Okay, here it is. Actually, there are two things that I wanted to talk over with you. I'll start with the matter of my choice of profession. My zeyde who was the best teacher I ever had never quite said it, but I know he wanted me to devote my life to Jewish studies. I remember him saying dozens of times that I would make a good rabbi, and I sort of laughed it off. During my college years I decided that I didn't really believe in a God that one could actually communicate with, like in prayers. I enjoy going to synagogue, and I love to chant the prayers, but I haven't believed that there was a big old man with a flowing beard up there listening and deciding who shall live and who shall die since I was about sixteen. And I certainly didn't want to spend my life just conducting life-cycle ceremonies and preaching to a congregation, most of whom doze off when the rabbi speaks. But when I was talking to you at the conversion a couple of months ago, I began to get a very different image of the rabbinate. You're an activist; you actually believe in prophetic Judaism. And so I've sort of been reconsidering. I'm working for my Ph.D. with Professor Gold, and I'm almost ready to present him with a final outline and two completed chapters of my dissertation. I've been aiming at an academic career ever since I entered Harvard, but now I wonder. Maybe I *should* consider the rabbinate. So that's the first thing that I wanted to talk to you about."

"And the second?"

"The second thing is very delicate and very confidential, and if you don't want to discuss a very personal matter, that's okay. I understand."

"Well, let me judge whether or not it's something we can talk about."

"It's about a girl, a girl who I think I love, but she's a Catholic."

"Mmmm. Go on."

"Well, Judaism is very important to me, as I've said. No one in my family has ever married a non-Jew, and that's going pretty far back. Most of my ancestors were rabbis, some of them pretty famous. Believe it or not, I've only been with this girl for a week. It's crazy! But I think I'm in love. And it's not that I haven't had girlfriends before; I've had quite a few, two of them sort of serious. But I've never felt about any girl the way that I feel about Marie. Her name is Marie, Marie Beaulieu, French Canadian."

Jacob went on to describe how he and Marie were thrown together in his uncle's house and what a wonderful person she was. Rabbi Weinberg let him go on for a while, occasionally punctuating his remarks with an "I see" or an encouraging "Go on." But then he stopped him and said, "You do see, Jacob, that your two problems are intimately related. You do see that, don't you?" And he then went on to suggest that Jacob might be considering the rabbinate because of his guilt about falling in love with a Catholic girl, that he might be using the possibility of the rabbinate as a way to make any further involvement with Marie difficult if not impossible. "Mixed marriage is quite acceptable in an academic community like the University of Chicago. There are quite a few Jewish faculty members here married to non-Jews of one kind or another. But that's certainly not the case in the rabbinate. So, Jacob, you've got a lot to think about, and if you do decide that you want to explore the rabbinate, come back and we'll talk some more."

As Jacob was leaving, Rabbi Weinberg had an afterthought. "I remember that Rabbi Persky told me that you have a very nice voice and that you often lead services at Hillel. Have you ever acted as cantor over the High Holy Days?"

Jacob answered that he had on a couple of occasions during his Harvard years at small congregations in Natick and Lexington and that he had been hoping to do it again. "But I've been so bogged down with my dissertation, that I didn't have time to make any calls, so I'll probably be a congregant this year."

"You might just be in luck; it's good that you came in today. You told me that you have family in Maine and that the girl that you're interested in up there. Well, I got a call from an old friend of mine, Rabbi Himmel in Portland, just yesterday. Do you know him?"

"I've met him. My uncle belongs to his congregation. We went there one Shabbat morning back in June, and I chanted the *haftarah*. What about him?"

"What he called me about – not just me but several of his colleagues around the country – was that they had hired a guest cantor for the High Holy Days a couple of months ago, and then he just got a call from the guy reneging because he got a better offer from a synagogue in New York. Not very ethical. Anyway, he's desperately looking for a cantor with Rosh HaShanah less than a month away. Are you interested?"

As soon as Jacob gave his assent, Rabbi Weinberg picked up his phone and put a call through to Portland. He asked Himmel if he was still looking for a cantor, heard his response, and said, "I think I've got just the guy for you, and you won't even have to pay for his expenses. He's a very nice young man with a good Jewish background, and he's got family in Maine. He says he met you last June when he chanted a *haftarah* in your shul. He's right here; we've been having a talk. Shall I put him on?"

Rabbi Himmel remembered Jacob and his relationship to Sol Fairstone. "You probably know that there's bad blood with our president, Berel Glick. But it was Glick who hired that no-goodnik who broke his agreement with us. He's in no position to object because, I'll be honest, we're desperate. You've done this before?"

Jacob gave him a brief resume; Himmel offered him five hundred dollars; and the deal was struck. He set down the phone and looked at Rabbi Weinberg in amazement. Weinberg laughed and said, "I think I deserve a finder's fee. This seems to be a crucial period in your life, so I want you to do some heavy thinking and come back to see me when you get back to Chicago. That's my fee, and I usually collect, young man."

They shook hands, and Jacob thanked the rabbi profusely. He walked out with his mind spinning – dissertation, Marie, Fairstone Trucking, the rabbinate, and now the Portland synagogue. He headed back to the library where he had prepared all the material that he needed for his annotated outline, introduction and chapter one. He couldn't type in his carrel, so he had to carry all his books and manuscripts and notes back to the apartment and the portable Smith-Corona that his parents had given him when he entered Harvard. He managed a few quick swims at the Point during the searing heat of late August Chicago, but the rest of his days were spent feeding sheets of paper and carbons into his typewriter and laboriously pecking away with his two index fingers. Trudy called once, urging him to drive up to Oconomowoc for the last Shabbat at camp, but he refused, not only for lack of time but also because Trudy simply added to his confusion.

He called his uncle to tell him about his arrangement with the Portland synagogue, and Sol was delighted. "Oh boy! That'll show that *mamzer* Glick. He wasn't very happy when you sang that *haftarah* so beautifully. This'll give him apoplexy; ha! Anyway, remember, *boychik*, we've got a lot to talk over when you're up here, and Marie is on *shpilkes* waiting for you."

When Jacob began saying goodbye, Sol stopped him and said, "I've got one not such good bit of news. No, I shouldn't say that. I told her it was her right; she'll be better off."

"Who are you talking about? Aunt Sarah? Marie? What happened?"

"No, no; neither of them. It's Claudette. She told me a couple of days ago that she's going to get married. She met some guy, a regular customer in her bakery, and he asked her to marry him. He's divorced, but he seems to be okay. I checked him out. I called her every few days, and I was looking forward to seeing her again in September, but then she told me about this guy. I promised her way back that she could do whatever she wanted with her life, because I was never going to leave my Sarah. So that's what she did. What can I say? I'll send them a nice wedding present. But anyway, Jakie, if I get the kind of answer that I'm expecting from you when you get here, everything will be fine."

Jacob's only happy hours during those final weeks before his meeting with Gold were his nightly conversations with Marie. Whatever doubts he had about her dissipated within seconds of hearing her voice. She was devoting her spare hours to reading books that he had suggested. She particularly enjoyed two of his favorite authors, Chekhov and Babel, and she retold their stories in ways that made his heart ache to be with her. He remembered an etching that hung in his zeyde's study where he had sat learning so many hundreds of times. It depicted a weary pioneer in Palestine coming back from the fields toward his tent where his wife was waiting, holding out her arms with their baby to him. The caption underneath was from *Ecclesiastes*, *"Helki mi-kol amalai* – My reward for all my labors." He described it to Marie and told her that she would be his reward. She responded with a laugh, "I'll be here waiting with my arms out when you arrive, but I can't provide the baby... not yet."

The meeting with Professor Gold wasn't a disaster, but it was disappointing. Jacob had left his written material with Gold's secretary two days before the meeting, and Gold had given it a careful reading. He thought that the first chapter was well written and to the point, but he disapproved of the introduction. He thought that it covered too much territory, that it promised too much, that it went far beyond the one century that was supposed to be the focus of the dissertation. He scolded Jacob, telling him that they had already decided that he was to concentrate solely on the period 1750 to 1850 and not to anticipate the Dreyfus Trial and beyond. Jacob argued that he thought it essential to indicate in the introduction that the events he would be describing in his dissertation were a prelude to the anti-Semitism of the following century, but Gold wasn't buying. "Back to the drawing boards, Mr. Ross. When I put my seal of approval on a doctoral dissertation, it has to be a worthy contribution to historical knowledge. Your first chapter indicates that you can make a contribution, but your introduction is way off."

Jacob left the meeting despondent. That introduction had taken most of the summer, a good seven or eight weeks of work. And, of course, Gold was right. He had used the introduction to circumvent the limits that Gold had imposed on him back in June. He should have realized that Gold wouldn't accept it. That meant that he would have to spend a year or more refocusing his work and then writing the eight additional chapters that he had outlined so meticulously. Gold hadn't even mentioned his outline. He was full of resentment, thinking "Who needs this?" He wanted to just forget about the whole damned dissertation and leave for Maine. The sooner he got there the better, not only because he was yearning for the comfort that Marie could provide but also because he had to meet with Rabbi Himmel at least a week before Rosh HaShanah to get his instructions for the services.

He called Marie that night and told her about his disappointing meeting. "I'm tempted to chuck the whole thing. I'm disgusted. I've been working on this damned degree for four years already."

She wanted to know whether that meant that he might accept his uncle's offer and move to Maine. He could tell from the tone of her voice that she was hoping for an affirmative answer, and he was tempted to just blurt out a yes and have done with his years of equivocation. He could have the whole package – a fantastic salary, a lovely home on the coast, *and* Marie. Who could blame him? Who indeed? His father, Koppel Ganzfried, his zeyde, the Vilna *Gaon*.... And what about the rabbinate? Was he just wasting Rabbi Weinberg's time? "We'll see," he answered. "Right now I just want to hold you in my arms. It's been so long."

"Me too. And Jake? I've got a surprise for you, a little gift that I picked up."

"Tell me."

"No; it's a surprise. No big deal, but I think you'll like it."

"I'll get there as fast as I can. Tell Aunt Sarah to expect me in three days, Sunday night, the second. I've got to stop first in Portland to meet with Rabbi Himmel. I told you about him and that I'll be his cantor for our holidays, so I made an appointment to spend Sunday afternoon with him to go over the services. I'll spend Shabbat with my father and Mrs. Sandler in Winthrop, and I'll expect to see you with outstretched arms when I drive up to the house around four."

"Do you really want me to greet you with outstretched arms, like in that picture you told me about? Really, Jake? I'd love to, but aren't you forgetting Mrs. Fairstone and Hope? Is it all right with you if they see us .... kissing? Are you ready for them to know? Oh, please say yes."

"Sorry, Marie: I sort of got carried away. I'm not quite ready yet for Aunt Sarah. She'll have all kinds of questions and .... Well, we've got to talk some more before we let everyone in on our secret. When will she and Hope be leaving for Malden? Was Hope accepted somewhere yet?"

"Yes! That's the really big news here. She was accepted provisionally at Simmons College. If she passes her first semester courses with a C+ average or better, she'll be accepted as a regular student. Mr. Fairstone made all the arrangements, and Hope is very happy. I think she'll make it. She's really come a long way"

"Thanks to you!" Jacob interjected.

"Anyway, they'll be leaving right after that holiday of yours on Wednesday. They all want to hear you singing in Portland, and then they'll go on from there to Malden, because Hope's semester begins on the tenth. So they'll just be here for just a couple of days with you. And Jake, don't forget; my semester at Hudson begins on the thirteenth. My job here is over as soon as Hope and Mrs. Fairstone leave, but Mr. Fairstone said that I can stay here until school begins. I really hate the idea of leaving. I wish I could stay."

"God, I've been so wrapped up in my work here that I didn't realize that you would be leaving so soon. We'll have to work something out. I've got to be with you for more than just a week. Anyway, this will probably be my last call. See you on Sunday night."

"I love you, Jake."

"Me too."

Marie

When Jacob drove up the long driveway to the Fairstone estate after spending three hours with Rabbi Himmel and the organist going over cues for the Rosh HaShanah services, he found Hope and Marie waiting for him at the front door. As soon as he extricated himself from the roadster, Hope ran over and hugged him. She was bubbling over with the good news about her acceptance at Simmons. "I'll probably be the oldest girl in the freshman class, but I don't care. Maybe that'll give me an advantage with some of the male professors." She turned to Marie who had remained standing on the stoop; "Marie, come on over and give Jakie a hug. I know that you want to; I'm no dummy."

Marie hesitated for just a moment, looked around to see who might be watching, and then flung herself at Jacob. They embraced for a long moment without saying a word, and then Jacob whispered, "I've been dreaming of this all summer. I've almost forgotten what it feels like to hold someone in my arms." And he kissed her behind the ear.

When they went into the house, they found Sarah in the kitchen preparing supper. She gave Jacob a warm hug and kiss and said that she was looking forward to hearing him lead the *davvening* in Portland. "Hope and I decided to stay an extra couple of days so that we could hear you. I'm just sorry that we can't stay through Yom Kippur, but Hope has to start *college*! Can you believe it? My Hope is going to college, to Simmons yet, and we owe it to Marie. I mean, it's really because Hope has been spending most of the summer since you left reading. She has a good head, but she didn't use it before. Marie set a wonderful example for her. They each spend a few hours each day reading – *good* stuff, not the trash that Hope used to read. You know, we've got that nice little library here in Brunswick; well, these two young ladies are their best customers. On the rainy days, they sit in the library reading, and when the weather is nice, they sit under a tree on the Borden campus or here on the beach. I'm so happy."

Sol was engrossed in the final innings of the Red Sox game in the living room. He jumped up when Jacob walked in and shook his hand. "Lousy Red Sox; they're losing again. Fourth place! With Williams and Jensen and Piersall, they're only in fourth place. It's the pitching. Parnell is over the hill; Brewer and Sullivan are okay; and Porterfield stinks." With that vehement analysis, he switched off the television and gave Jacob an intense look. "Nu, Jakie, you came back for the big decision. I've got everything arranged." And he went on to explain that they would spend Monday and Tuesday driving around to a few of his farms so that Jacob could see for himself where the product came from. They would take a break for Rosh HaShanah and the *Shabbat Shuvah* weekend; on Monday they would visit the truck depots in Cooks Corner and Kittery; and on Tuesday and Wednesday they would spend the days in his office meeting the personnel and going over the books. "So you'll be able to give me your answer by Yom Kippur. Right?"

"I'm impressed, Uncle Sol; that's a pretty detailed schedule. I promised you my decision by next June, but I've decided to make it during this visit. I don't want to keep you hanging, but please let me make one little revision of your schedule." He looked toward the kitchen where the three women were to make sure that no one was within earshot. "Uncle Sol, you know how it is with Marie and me. Well, she told me that she'll be going back to Hudson to start school on the thirteenth. By the way, *mazal tov* on Hope's acceptance at Simmons."

"Well, I was able to pull a few strings, but she'll do okay after this summer with Marie. That Marie's a real gem."

"She's more than a gem to me, Uncle Sol. The only problem is that she's not Jewish. Aside from that, she's perfect. Anyway, that's not your problem; it's mine, and I've got to make a decision about her too. Look, I've got to spend some good time with her this week before she goes back to school. So I'd like you to relax your schedule a bit, especially after Aunt Sarah and Hope leave. If it's all right with you..." – he paused and reddened slightly – "maybe we could move into the same room?"

"All right with *me*? Of course it's all right with me. Did you think that suddenly I became a prude? You know me better. Look, I'll be completely honest with you, *boychik*. The more you sleep with Marie, the happier I am. I was even hoping that maybe, ha ha, you'd get her pregnant. Then you'd have to stay up here, like you should."

"God forbid! Don't say such a thing, even as a joke. If I decide to accept your offer and stay here with you, it will be because that's what I want to do and not because of Marie. She's a powerful inducement, and I'll admit that she's a factor in my decision, but she's just one of several factors. I'm still considering an academic career although I had a little set-back with my advisor before I left Chicago. Anyway, what I was getting at is that, not only do I want to spend as much time as possible with Marie, but I want to drive her up to Bangor next Sunday. She has to start at Hudson next Monday."

"So? Bottom line?"

"Bottom line is that I'm going to take these High Holy Days seriously, Uncle Sol. When I sing about soul-searching and judgment day on Rosh HaShanah and Yom Kippur, that's what I'm going to be doing, looking inside myself and trying to figure out what I should do with my life. So I want you to do me a favor. I'll drive around with you tomorrow and Tuesday and I'll spend as much time with you as you want after I get back from Bangor, but I want to defer my decision until the day after Yom Kippur, two weeks from today. I've thought this all out; I made a schedule like you did. If I tell you after Yom Kippur that I accept your wonderful offer, I'll leave my car here, fly back to Chicago to close up my apartment and tell Professor Gold to shove it, and I'll fly back here and get to work with you by the twenty-fourth. What do you say?"

"What can I say? It sounds to me like you're leaning my way, so I'm encouraged, but I'm not sure I understand what you said about Yom Kippur. Do you think maybe when you're singing *Kol Nidre*, God will tell you what to do? I don't think you believe that."

"No, no. That's not what I meant. Whenever I'm in shul on Yom Kippur, and this goes all the way back to when I was a little boy standing next to Zeyde in Malden, I get to know myself better. I don't know whether it has anything to do with God or not, but Zeyde used to tell me that Yom Kippur was a good time for thinking about how to make myself into a *mensch*. So on the day after Yom Kippur, I'll give you an answer, and I hope it will be the answer of a *mensch*."

"My father was a wise man. Okay; that's what I want from you, the answer of a *mensch*. I know you'll make the right choice. It's your life.... *and mine,* don't forget. As your zeyde used to say when he made a deal, *Gemacht!* Agreed! And he would shake hands."

"*Gemacht*, Uncle Sol?"

"Gemacht!" They shook hands, and then Sol grabbed his nephew in a bear hug and whispered, "*My* Jakie; *my* Jakie."

After supper that night and about half an hour watching television with the family, Jacob announced that he was tired after his long day's drive and went up to his room. Marie remained in the living room long enough to satisfy the appearance of decency, and then excused herself and followed him up. She went first to her room to retrieve a package and then went through the bathroom to the door of Jacob's room. She knocked lightly and received a gruff response, "We don't want any; go away!" She was startled for a moment until the door was pulled open from the other side and Jacob, laughing, grabbed her in a crushing embrace. He covered her face with kisses as she murmured, "You scared me; you scared me."

He pulled her toward his bed, but she said, "Wait! Wait! I told you I had a surprise for you." And she handed him the package that had been hidden in her room for two weeks awaiting his return.

"What is it?"

"Open it and you'll see."

He ripped off the wrapping paper impatiently and found three lp records, all Bidu Sayao recordings, her *Opera Arias and Brazilian Folk Songs, The Art of Bidu Sayao,* and *Bachianas Brasilieras.* As he read each of the titles on the record sleeves, handling them reverently, he looked at Marie who was standing near him watching for his reaction.

He felt tears welling up in his eyes as he looked at her and asked, "How did you get these? There's no place around here where you can buy these. I love them. Where did you get them?"

Her answer gushed out. "You remember I told you about this guy Hank at Hudson who invites a group of us to his house on Monday nights to listen to classical music? Well, I called him on that wonderful phone that Mr. Fairstone got for us, and I asked him how I could get some Bidu Sayao records, because I remembered that you said you loved her voice. Anyway, he told me about this place in New York, Sam Goody's, where he buys his records. He gave me their phone number, and so I called them and asked them for their best Bidu Sayao records. They told me to send them a check and they would send them to me. It was lucky that I had a checking account. Mr. Fairstone told me that I should open one when he gave me my first salary check back in June; he helped me open it at his bank in Brunswick. So I sent Goody's the check, my first check ever, and about ten days later, the records arrived. End of story."

"But why a present? My birthday isn't until March."

"It's not a birthday present, dummy. It's just a present, a love present. The first record says 'I'; the second one says 'love'; and the third one says 'you'.

"I… I don't know what to say. This is such a beautiful present, and I don't have anything for you."

"Oh yes you do." And she began peeling off her clothes.

They spent the next hour getting playfully reacquainted with each other's body parts and then slept contented and spent until, awakened by the light streaming in his room, Jacob jumped out of bed to get ready for the day's excursion with Sol. Marie stretched and asked, "Where are you going? I miss you already."

He explained his arrangement with Sol for the next few days and added, "After Aunt Sarah and Hope leave on Thursday, Uncle Sol said we could move in together. No more having to hurry back to our beds in the morning so that nobody catches us where we're not supposed to be."

"You think of everything. Just give me a little cuddle before you go." They held each other for a moment, and then, as he left the room, she said, "Thanks for the present."

The two men left the house before eight in Sol's Cadillac and drove first to Bascomb's for breakfast. Sol explained that he preferred to eat his breakfast at Bascomb's most mornings rather than at home because, for one thing, he didn't want to awaken Sarah, but, more important, he met many of the town's businessmen there and got a feel for what was going on before going to his office. "And now they're getting their muffins from Claudette again. You remember I told you that she was getting married? Well, they got married about a week ago, and the guy she married delivers her muffins to about half a dozen restaurants in Brunswick and Topsham and Freeport early in the morning. So if I don't have Detty anymore," he added with a wry laugh, "at least I have her muffins."

They spent the rest of the day visiting Sol's farms in Cumberland, Androscoggin and Oxford counties, stopping for lunch in Lewiston. Sol introduced Jacob to easily a dozen farmers or farmers' wives that day, and Jacob tried to look interested as he learned about debeaking baby chicks, the ventilation of hen houses, incubators, combinations of feed, and the virtues of brown versus white eggs. In mid-afternoon they pulled into a farm near South Paris that, as Sol informed Jacob, was operated by a widow whose husband had been killed in a tractor accident the previous year. "A really nice lady. She runs the place mostly by herself with a couple of guys, Canucks, who do the heavy stuff." He then introduced Jacob to an attractive woman, Nell Graham, fortyish, who invited them in for coffee. They talked business for a while, and then Sol said, "Jakie, why don't you go and take a look around the farm. Nell here has a new feeding set-up; if you go over to that hen house there, one of the guys will explain it to you. And if you take a walk through the woods there, you'll find a very pretty pond. Take your time; look around and get to know the place."

When he returned to the house about half an hour later, having learned more than he wanted to know about the feeding of chickens, he didn't find his uncle or Mrs. Graham in the kitchen. He called out, and he heard Sol's voice from somewhere in the house calling to him to wait just a minute. He came back to the kitchen alone about a minute later looking flushed and explained that he had to use the bathroom. When they got back into the Caddy and were driving toward Grey, Jacob looked at his uncle and asked, "Is Mrs. Graham Claudette's replacement?"

"No, no. How could you say that?"

"Uncle Sol, it's me, your maybe partner. We tell each other the truth."

Sol was quiet for a minute as they continued speeding southward toward another farm in Gray, and then he said, "Jakie, I always trusted you. You know that I have certain needs. I haven't been with Detty since your aunt came up, but you know how it is. Once in a while I visit one or two ladies on the farms. The farms belong to me, and I treat the farmers very nicely. So, if I play around a little, who does it hurt? Nell lives in that nice house rent free. She's a good woman, hardworking, so I spend some time with her once in a while. I need it."

"Look, Uncle Sol; I'm not planning to be your conscience, but I love Aunt Sarah very much. She always gave me the love that your sister couldn't manage to give. I just don't want to see her hurt again, like she was when Sumner told her about Claudette. She's fragile. You know that."

Sol sighed. "I know; you're right, but dammit, I'm me, and I like women. I'm careful; there's no way that Sarah is going to find out about Nell. I never take that blabber-mouth Sumner to the farms, and South Paris is pretty far from Harpswell. I'll never touch another woman anywhere near Brunswick again, but the farms way out in Androscoggin and Oxford counties are another matter. And another thing, *boychik*; these farms will be yours someday. I know that you like women too. Please God, you'll marry a nice woman, maybe someone like Marie, and what you choose to do out on the farms, that's your business."

"Is this supposed to be a selling point for me? If I join you in the business, I can have my pick of farmers' wives and I can have Marie too? Look, maybe we shouldn't talk about this anymore; it makes me uncomfortable. I think that you're making a mistake and that there's a real danger, no matter how careful you are, that Aunt Sarah is going to find out and end up back in the Institute. And as far as I'm concerned, whether I eventually get married to Marie or someone else, I don't plan to fool around."

"Well, maybe you're stronger than I am. You're right; let's drop the subject."

They spent about half an hour walking around a farm near Gray with another of Sol's tenant farmers, and then they headed back toward home. As they turned up Route 1, Sol said, "You said something before about maybe someday marrying Marie. And when we were talking yesterday, you said something about having to make a decision about her. Look, Jakie, I'm probably the last person who should be giving advice about marriage, but are you sure you know what you're doing? It's okay to have some fun with a beautiful girl like Marie; I mean, who could resist a girl like her? Not me! But, Jakie, she's a Catholic! *You* can't marry a Catholic; not *you*. Hell, you're going to be the cantor in Portland in a few days. Those people have parents and grandparents who were killed by Catholics, and so do you. So what's this about marriage? Has she made you *meshugah*?"

"Uncle Sol, that's a problem that I'm trying to work out. Marie is the most amazing woman I've ever been with. You're right. Everything in me tells me that I can't marry her, but she's not just a Catholic. She's much more. She's sweet; she's intelligent; she's fun to be with. You have no idea how I've missed her over the past months. Who knows? Maybe she'll decide to convert. In Chicago I attended the conversion of the guy who's going to marry an old girlfriend of mine, and it was beautiful. I know that he's going to be a good Jew; in fact, he's in Israel right now." He was quiet for a minute and then went on. "I don't know. I told you that I'd be looking for some answers during Rosh HaShanah and Yom Kippur. So that's the story with me. I just don't know."

As Sol pulled into the long driveway up to the house, he patted Jacob on the thigh. "Jakie, I want the best for you. I want you to come work for me, and I want you to get married someday to a good woman, someone like my Sarah. On Rosh HaShanah you won't be the only one praying for answers. I'll be praying there too, for you, that you should make the right decisions. Nu, tomorrow we'll drive north to a few of my farms in Waldo County. One of them, you'll see, is really beautiful. It has a little lake and about thirty acres for logging. So now let's go in and see what the ladies made for us for dinner."

It was decided over dinner that Sarah would take the girls to Freeport again for shopping the next day while the men were off to the farms. Hope needed a new wardrobe for school. She was down to a pleasantly plump 130 pounds, decently distributed over her five-foot-one frame, and, as she proudly told Jacob, she had had a couple of dates with a guy whom she and Marie had met at the Arctic Museum at Borden. "His name is Nat, and he's a docent there. When Marie and I came in, he volunteered to take us around. Naturally, he asked Marie here for her number, but she told him that she had a boyfriend and suggested that he ask me for my number. And guess what. He did! And he called me the next day, and we've gone out twice already. He's going to be a junior at Borden, and when I told him that I was going to Simmons, he said that he'd like to call me if he gets to Boston. He's from somewhere in Connecticut."

"And he's Jewish," Sarah added. "He's a nice Jewish boy. We met him when he came to pick up Hope, and he was very polite. He drove up in a little coupe that must have been ten years old or more, a real rattle-trap that looked like it was falling apart. I didn't want my Hope driving around in that car, so I told them to take the convertible. At first he said he didn't think he should; he was embarrassed. But then he took it, and they had a nice time."

"We're going out again tomorrow night," Hope added. "I asked him if he'd like to join us for Rosh HaShanah services in Portland, but he's going home to Connecticut for the holiday."

"That's too bad," Sol responded with a grin. "I was going to ask Rabbi Himmel to set up a chair for your Nat on the *bimah*."

"I hope you're kidding, Daddy."

"Sure I'm kidding, honey." And then, shooting a glance in Jacob's direction, he added, "I'm very happy that you found a fellow and that he's Jewish. You look like a million bucks now; you'll have a lot of boys asking you out when you get to Simmons. Maybe you'll find a nice Harvard man like Jakie here."

Hope reddened. "Oh, I'd settle for Jakie, but I think he has other ideas."

"Whatever do you mean, Hope?" Sarah looked uncomfortable. "When the time comes, Jakie will find a nice Jewish girl and settle down. He's not ready yet; he's still playing the field. Am I right, Jakie?"

It took Jacob a bit too long to answer his aunt's question, but then he smiled and said, "Aunt Sarah, you know me too well, and I love you for it." And four of them laughed.

Two hours later he tiptoed quietly into Marie's room and was surprised to find her in her robe, sitting at her table reading a book. "Marie, are you okay? I thought you'd come into my room when you heard me come up. Are you upset by what Aunt Sarah said?"

She looked at him, and he saw that her eyes were red. "No, what she said didn't upset me so much, although it didn't make me happy. It was your answer."

"But my answer wasn't an answer; I couldn't give her a straight answer. You understand."

"I'm not sure I do. I didn't expect you to tell her that we were going to get married tomorrow, but I thought that maybe…. well, that maybe you'd tell her that you and I …. that you and I…. I don't know, Jake; that you and I are what? I really don't know. All I know is that I love you and that you've told me that you love me. Is this Jewish-Catholic thing so important? Aunt Sarah is so happy that Hope is going out with a *Jewish* boy. She should just be happy that she found someone, *anyone*. That fellow Nat whom she's going out with, first he asked for *my* number, and he didn't ask if I was Jewish. Explain it to me, Jake; why does it make such a difference?"

"Marie, I don't want to stand here with you sitting at the table with a book. I don't think that I'm really ready yet to give you a good answer, but I don't want to put you off either. Look, I'm desperate to put my arms around you, and it's chilly standing here. Can we talk in your bed, under the covers? I promise I'll be a good boy, but I want to hold you, just hold you. Okay?"

She hesitated, looking doubtful, but as she looked at him standing there uncomfortably in his shorts, she relented. She got up and let him put his arms around her. When he kissed her neck, she pulled back just a bit and looked him in the eye. "Jakie, we've got to reach some understanding. You told me that you're going to be completely involved with those services in Portland from Wednesday until it's just about time for me to go back to Hudson. I can't go back there without knowing where we stand. You know what it's like, Jacob Ross? It's as if I'm standing here in front of you naked, and you've got all your clothes on. It's not fair."

She took off her robe and climbed into her bed. "Hurry up and get your clothes off." He shucked them off quickly, climbed in beside her and took her in his arms. When he was settled, she said, "Jake, this might sound strange, but you know what I want you to do?" He nuzzled her neck and shrugged. "Jake, I want you to *fuck* me." He flinched at the word. "You heard me right. I want you to *fuck* me, not make love, but fuck me, quickly. I just don't want any sexual tension between us when we talk; it's too important." She reached down to his crotch and found him erect and ready. He mounted her without hesitation and began thrusting without a thought of foreplay. In less than a minute, he ejaculated violently and then just lay there on top of her speechless.

"Satisfied?"

"No," he answered reaching for her breast. "I don't think that you enjoyed that."

"You're right; I didn't. It reminded me of an unpleasant incident with a guy I thought I liked at Hudson. And please don't," she scolded, removing his hand from her breast. "Now we can talk."

She nudged Jacob off of her, and they lay side by side for a while in silence until Jacob looked at her and said softly, "Marie, I love you. I really truly love you. But I don't know if love is enough."

"Tell me what you mean, Jake; please explain it to me. We're two young and healthy people in love. You're always telling me how beautiful I am, and you're one of the most handsome men I've ever met. We enjoy music together; we enjoy books; we enjoy swimming and boating; we're concerned about things like justice; we both hate our mothers; and I don't have to remind you how much we both enjoy making love, not fucking like we just did but making real love, soul-meeting love. Am I right?"

"Yes."

"So what's missing? Why can't you do something as simple as saying to Aunt Sarah, 'I think I love Marie.' *Mr.* Fairstone certainly knows, and Hope is pretty sure that we do more than talk up here. Boy, is she curious! Anyway, what's holding you back. Please tell me. And remember our agreement; honest."

"Maybe I can explain it by beginning with something that flitted through my mind when you just asked me if you were right about all the things we enjoy together. I answered with a simple yes, but I was about to say 'Yes, *dodati kallah*."

"What's that?"

"That, my beloved Marie, is my problem. My immediate inclination was to answer with Hebrew words of love. I wanted to call you *dodati kallah* – my beloved bride, but I realized, of course, that you wouldn't understand those words. Marie, what I'm trying to tell you as honestly as I can is that being Jewish is very *very* important to me. I couldn't lead High Holy Day services sincerely if Judaism weren't so important for me. There's three thousand years of Jewish history that I bring to bed with me. That's who I am. And you, my lovely sweet darling, are a Catholic. No, you told me that you're not a church-going Catholic, but you do love Jesus, the same Jesus whose message was distorted into hatred of Jews. What can I say? Those Lithuanians who massacred my grandparents' families in Vilna were Catholics. You don't know how much it hurts me to say that to you. You're so good; you're so innocent; you're so lovely. But can you understand that I just can't announce to the world that I'm in love with a Catholic? Maybe we can work it out somehow. I hope so. I *pray* so, but I'm not ready. Not yet."

"Wow! I wasn't ready for that. Let me catch my breath." She shifted a few inches away from Jacob and lay there without speaking. And then she laughed wryly and said, "So Jesus the Jew is the problem. He's lying here between us, keeping us apart. Strange."

Jacob had not wanted to pressure Marie in any way, but he decided to tell her a bit more about Wesley Mortensen's metamorphosis into Elisha Yisrael. He described it in detail, omitting only his relationship to Trudy. "It was a beautiful ceremony, and I think that he's going to be a really good Jew. He didn't reject Jesus entirely; he said that he considers Jesus like any of the other great Jewish sages of antiquity." He let that sink in for a few moments, and then he said, "Marie, I can't ask you to reject Jesus and become a Jew. I respect you too much to even suggest that you abandon your religion for mine. If Catholicism is as precious to you as Judaism is to me, that would be wrong."

Again there was a long silence with neither of them stirring. And then Marie turned to Jacob and asked, "And if I were to convert like that Mortensen fellow, then everything would be okay between us?"

"I can't ask you to do that."

"But if I wanted to, theoretically? I'm not saying that I would do it; I never even thought about it before tonight. I just didn't realize how important it is to you. You should have warned this innocent little Catholic girl before you introduced her to your circumcision."

"Seriously, Judaism does accept converts, but Judaism is not a conversionary religion. We don't go out looking for converts, because we believe that all good people, whatever their religion, find salvation, whatever that means. So I would never ask you to convert, but yes, conversion is a possibility."

"So tell me, Jake. What are your plans with me?"

"Honestly, I don't know. I know that I love you, and I know that I let that carry me away. Maybe I should have told you from the very beginning that I doubt that I could ever marry a non-Jew, but I didn't think it would ever come to this point. I… I just wasn't thinking."

"So I'll ask you again," she bit off the words. "What are your plans with me?"

"I want to spend the rest of the week with you, and I don't want ever to fuck you again. I want to make love with you, because I love you. On Sunday I'll drive you back to Bangor, and then we'll spend a week without seeing each other, a week for some serious thinking on both our parts. Then after Yom Kippur, if you agree, I'll drive up to Hudson on Sunday, and we can spend some time together before I leave to go back to Chicago. I have to be there by the nineteenth because I've agreed to be Professor Gold's teaching assistant in his course on Zionism and Nationalism this semester. That's about all I can say right now." Silence. "Are you okay?"

She didn't answer immediately, and so he asked, "Do you want me to go to my room?"

"N… no, Jake, I don't. I'd feel terrible lying here alone now, and I know I wouldn't be able to sleep. Could we…. you remember the last night you were here back in June? We just slept together without any sex… well, at least at first. Do you think we could do that again?"

"I'd love it, my darling." He kissed her lips, and then they arranged themselves spoon-fashion, his right arm around her waist. Within minutes they were asleep.

Tuesday on the road with Sol was pretty much a repeat of the previous day, without a coital break. When they stopped, though, for lunch at Moody's between visits to farms in Union and Warren, Jacob noticed that one of the waitresses seemed to know Sol well enough to call him by his first name and take him by the hand when she led them to one of her tables. He also took note of the fact that Sol left a five dollar bill on the table before paying their four-dollar check at the cash register. Back in the car Jacob asked, "Friend of yours?" Sol was noncommittal, saying only that she was a very nice lady who worked hard and deserved a nice tip.

On the way back to Harpswell, Jacob reminded Sol that he would not be able to resume his introduction to the many facets of Fairstone Trucking until the following Monday. "But what you've seen so far, Jakie; what do you think?"

"I think that I've learned more about raising poultry than I ever thought I'd want to know. Some of those farms are really beautiful, especially that one in Union with the lake. Do you know what I was thinking as we walked around that farm? I was thinking that it would make a great summer camp for kids." He went on to describe the camp at Oconomowoc and how the program there was aimed at making the kids into better Jews while having a lot of fun. "When we were walking around that farm, I saw that there was plenty of flat ground for a baseball field and cabins, and the lake was really beautiful, not as big as Lac LaBelle in Wisconsin, but big enough for about two hundred campers and staff."

"So that's what you were thinking about there? You were supposed to be thinking about hauling poultry and you were thinking about a summer camp for kids? Oy, *boychik*, you've got a lot to think about over the next week."

That night Sarah and Hope began packing for the trip back to Malden. They wanted to have it over with by the time they all drove down to Portland for the first Rosh HaShanah service on Wednesday evening. Sarah was also busy preparing a special Rosh HaShanah eve dinner for the family, including Sumner who would be joining them. Marie alternated between helping Hope pack in her room and helping Sarah in the kitchen, while Jacob sat in his room at his table going over the Rosh HaShanah liturgy. Wednesday evening would be easy, the service was only slightly different from a regular Shabbat eve service, except for the *nusach* – the special chant mode of the holy day. Depending on the length of Rabbi Himmel's sermon, he figured that the service would take no more than an hour and a half. But the Thursday morning service was far more elaborate, with the awesome *Un'taneh Tokef* prayer, the reading of the Torah, and the blowing of the *shofar*.

Jacob had asked Rabbi Himmel about the second day of Rosh HaShanah, and he was relieved to learn that the Portland congregation, comprised mainly of Reform and Conservative Jews, rarely attracted enough people on the second day to warrant a formal service with cantor. Himmel conducted a brief study service on the second day for those few who insisted that they had to hear the *shofar* blown on both days, but he did want Jacob to assist him at the *Shabbat Shuvah* services, and he assigned him the chanting of the special *haftarah* from Hosea about repentance.

When Marie came up to the attic, Jacob was so immersed in his preparations that he didn't hear her. He had finished with the liturgy and was practicing his chant of the Hosea verses when he looked up and saw Marie watching him from the bathroom doorway. "It's so late I thought that I'd find you asleep already. What is it that you're singing? It sounds sort of strange."

He explained about the *haftarah* and then had an idea. "Look, Marie, why don't you come to the services with us? You don't want to stay in this big house all by yourself while we're all in Portland. And you'd be able to see me in action. I won't be able to sit with you, because I'll be up on the pulpit with the rabbi, but you can sit with the family, and Sarah or Sol will explain whatever's going on. How about it?"

"Do you really think it would be okay? Don't you do things like communion that are just for Jews? I'd be embarrassed if everybody went up to the altar and I was left sitting alone."

"Don't worry. We don't have anything like communion. The people sit through the entire service following the service in their prayer books. At the morning service on Thursday a few people are called up to the Torah reading, but just a few, usually men. And half the people just sit there like sticks without even opening their mouths. Why don't you come along?"

"So I could just sit there like a stick? I'm not sure I like the image."

"You, Marie Beaulieu, are anything but a stick, but you know what I mean. What do you say?"

"Well, I remember the sisters telling us that we should never go into a Protestant church, but they never said anything about a synagogue."

"They probably couldn't imagine anyone going into a synagogue. Have you ever seen a synagogue?"

"No, I don't think so. There certainly isn't one in Presque Isle, and I never saw one in Bangor. What's it like?"

"Well, the one in Portland is a modest building, sort of Moorish in style. The people sit in pews facing the ark where the Torah scrolls are kept, and the rabbi and cantor lead the service from what's called the *bimah* in front. The service is about fifty-fifty, Hebrew and English, so you'll be able to follow most of it. There are no statues and no pictures. At the morning service, the men wear prayer shawls and skull caps but the women don't have to wear anything special. Please come … if not for me just for your general education."

"You're sure I won't be embarrassed?"

"I promise."

She thought for a moment and then agreed. "I'm a little frightened, but I'm glad you invited me. I want to share things with you, and I know how important this is to you. But do you think people will notice me and ask questions? Won't the rabbi want to know who I am, sitting with the Fairstones?"

"If anyone asks, we'll tell them that you're cousin Miriam from Brooklyn. Can you fake a Brooklyn accent?"

"Sure; I'll tell them that I flew up foist class. That'll convince them. Anyway now that we've decided that, it's late." She hesitated a moment but then, "Do you want to sleep together tonight?"

"What a question! Ever since I was a little kid I've wanted to sleep with my cousin Miriam." He closed his book, got up and gave her a kiss.

"We don't have to have sex every night, so if you just want to just sleep with me, I mean *sleep*, that's okay."

"However the spirit moves us. You go get into bed; I'll be in soon."

A few minutes later, he crawled in beside her. They settled themselves in the spoon position for a while, but then Marie turned to him and the spirit moved them.

Sol and Sarah were delighted that Marie wanted to accompany them to the synagogue on the eve of Rosh HaShanah. Jacob drove down to Portland by himself an hour before the service, so that he could go over the service again with Rabbi Himmel and the organist. The synagogue owned a squeaky little Hammond that the organist referred to as his calliope, but it had been donated by one of the members, and attached to it were the names of his deceased parents. Both Jacob and the organist would have preferred the baby grand piano that was in the social hall, but *force majeure*.

When Jacob stepped out onto the *bimah* with Rabbi Himmel at seven-thirty, wearing a white robe and a *tallit*, they found a crowd of almost two hundred people waiting for them. Jacob quickly scanned the crowd and spotted the Fairstones and Marie taking up five of the eight seats in the fifth row left. Marie was seated between Sarah and Hope, and when Jacob looked occasionally in their direction, curious as to how Marie was taking it, he saw Sarah pointing out passages and whispering explanations. He wondered whether Sarah had any idea of his relationship to Marie. If she did, she certainly did not give any indication of it. As the service progressed, he felt sorry that he had not confided in his aunt. She had always been so supportive in matters of the heart. He would trust her instincts far more readily than Sol's, but she would be leaving after the service the next day, and he did not want to have a last minute heart-to-heart that night.

The service went very smoothly. Jacob was in good voice, and the organist missed only one cue. Rabbi Himmel was his usual affable self, congratulating people in the congregation from time to time for their contributions or their volunteer work over the past year. Among others, he thanked Sol for a generous gift, and he informed the congregation that their "handsome young cantor with the beautiful voice" was the Fairstone's nephew. Berel Glick grimaced visibly at the mention of Sol Fairstone, but that was his only reaction. And, in fact, as soon as Jacob concluded the service, leading the congregation in *Adon Olam*, Glick, who had been sitting next to the rabbi, came across the *bimah* and thanked Jacob for his participation. Himmel's sermon was mercifully brief. It was about the dire situation faced by Israel with Nasser massing troops along the Suez Canal and buying large quantities of armaments from the Soviet Union and Czechoslovakia. The gist of the sermon was that it would be a *mitzvah* for everyone in the congregation to buy at least one new Israel bond in the new year – timely but not very spiritual.

Marie drove back with Jacob in the MG. She seemed at first a little in awe of him. "When I saw you walk out onto the stage in a white cassock and a.... what do you call it?" – He explained the *tallit* – "I could hardly believe it. You didn't tell me you'd be wearing a cassock. You looked like a priest. I sat there for a minute wondering whether I was guilty of a venial sin or a mortal sin for sleeping with a priest."

Jacob laughed and reached over to give her a quick hug. "Don't worry. I'm far from being a priest. A rabbi is nothing like a priest; he's just a layman with a lot of Jewish learning. And he can get married and have kids like anyone else. Sometimes I think about becoming a rabbi; it's a possibility." He said this last rather lightly but he wondered how she would react. It didn't take long.

"Do you really mean what you just said? That you might become a rabbi? Do rabbis often get involved with Catholic girls or did you just say that to shock me?"

"Hey, forget what I just said. There's a pretty small chance that I would ever become a rabbi, but I do think about it occasionally. Right now I'm trying to decide whether I want to be a millionaire or not."

"And you're trying to decide about me too; right?"

"I don't like the way that sounds. You and I love each other; we *both* have to decide what's best for us."

"But if you take the job with your uncle, I could sort of be part of the deal. And if you don't...."

"Marie, please. Don't put me on the spot. I've got a big service tomorrow, and I said last night that we both had a lot of thinking to do over the next week. Can we leave it at that for now? Please?"

"Okay, Father Ross; I'll be a good girl and stop pestering you."

They drove on quietly for a while and, more to change the subject than anything else, Jacob asked, "Can you drive?"

"No, why do you ask?"

"I was just wondering. I'll probably be pretty worn out after the service tomorrow morning; it's a long one with a lot of singing. So I thought maybe you'd drive us home. How come you don't drive?"

"How could I ever drive? My parents had a broken down old truck for the farm, but we never had a car. I took driver's ed in high school, but I never went for a license because we didn't have a car. I'm one of the few kids at Hudson who doesn't know how to drive."

"Gee, I wish that we had enough time together for me to teach you and take you for your license. You really should have one."

"I know. Maybe I'll figure out a way to get one in Bangor this year. When it comes time for me to find a job, I'll probably need a license."

When they pulled into the Fairstone driveway, they saw that Sol's Caddy was already parked in front of the house. As Jacob helped Marie out of the car, he said, "If you do get a license, make sure you don't drive like Uncle Sol. He's a very fast driver, and he takes too many chances. I've been driving around with him for two days, and it hasn't been fun."

She nodded and said, "I noticed that when we drove down from Bangor back in June, but I wouldn't say anything."

"Not many people say anything to Uncle Sol; he's pretty set in his ways."

When they walked into the house, everyone greeted them with *Le-Shanah Tovah*, and Jacob explained that they were wishing them a good year, the traditional greeting over the High Holy Day period. Sarah had, as usual, prepared a deiicious festival dinner, beginning with the traditional apples dipped in honey and a round *challah*. Jacob led them in the special Rosh HaShanah *Kiddush*, and Marie watched him very carefully as he poured the wine from his beaker into six small cups. As he handed one of them to her, she smiled and said, "Thank you, Father." He looked at her to make sure that she was smiling and answered, "You're welcome, Daughter," to the amusement of all the Fairstones.

As soon as dinner was over, Sumner got up to go back his apartment. Sarah wanted him to stay longer and to sit with the family for a while, but he simply wasn't comfortable in the midst of an animated group enjoying the holiday atmosphere. She accompanied her morose son to the door, but before he walked out, she wanted to say something conciliatory to him in the spirit of the new year. "Sumner, I wish you would come to visit with us more often. You know this house is yours too. You have a key, and you can come and go whenever you want. There's the boat and the beach and the tennis court; it's all yours too. I wish you would come more often and enjoy it with us."

"Yea, M…Mom. I know, b…but I'm n…not happy here with D…Dad. You want the k… k… key back? I don't need it."

"No, Sumner; I don't want the key back. I just want you to come around more often." He gave her a quick kiss and told her that he would not be joining the family at the Rosh HaShanah services the next morning. Sol overheard it all and, with a futile shrug, went into the living room to watch the news on television.

Marie and Hope went into the kitchen to help Sarah; and Jacob went up to his room to review the next day's liturgy. He was particularly concerned about the *U'netaneh Tokef* prayer, the most profound of all the Rosh HaShanah prayers, with its chanted refrain reminding the congregation that the verdict for the year to come is written down on Rosh HaShanah and sealed on Yom Kippur. "*Mi yamut u-mi yihyeh,*" he chanted softly; "Who shall live and who shall die…." He remembered the melody that the cantor in the Nightingale Street synagogue in Dorchester had chanted when he sang in his choir. It was a particularly poignant melody, especially the lyrical passage describing God as the benign shepherd who causes the sheep to pass under his staff. He decided that that particular melody plus the standard Janowski *Avinu Malkeinu* would be the centerpieces of his performance the next morning, and it was after midnight when he closed his books to prepare for bed.

He hadn't heard Marie come up, and so he knocked lightly on her door after he finished in the bathroom. When she didn't answer, he quietly opened her door and looked in. He could see her lying in her bed, but he couldn't tell with the faint light from the bathroom whether she was asleep or not. He tiptoed over to her and listened to her regular breathing. He leaned down to kiss her on the forehead, and she stirred. "Jake?"

"It's okay," he whispered. "Sleep. I'll go to my room."

"Wait, wait a minute." She leaned up on one elbow. "I looked in and saw that you were preparing for tomorrow. You were singing, and I didn't want to disturb you."

"It's okay," he whispered again. "It's probably better if I save my energy for tomorrow morning. Sleep; I'm sorry I woke you."

He gave her a lingering kiss on the lips and pulled up the light blanket around her shoulders."

"Goodnight, Father Ross."

"Goodnight, my lovely daughter."

It was decided at their hasty final breakfast together that Jacob and Sol would drive down to Portland in Sol's car while Marie helped Sarah and Hope pack up the convertible for their trip back to Malden following the service. The three women arrived at the synagogue as Jacob was singing the opening *Mah Tovu* prayer, and they joined Sol who had been saving the same seats for them that they had occupied the night before. Marie was surprised to see that Sol, along with all of the other men in the synagogue, was wrapped in a *tallit.* Another question for Jacob when they got home.

Jacob was in particularly good voice that morning, and when, about an hour into the service, he began chanting *U'netaneh Tokef,* Marie couldn't help but notice that several of the women in the congregation, Sarah among them, were weeping quietly and that several of the men had wrapped their prayer shawls around their heads. Curious, she began reading the English introduction to the prayer, attempting to understand what had so moved the congregation and especially what it was that was moving Jacob to chant so poignantly. In her prayer book, she found the story of Rabbi Amnon of Mayence who was tortured and murdered by a bishop back in the eleventh century because of his refusal to give up his faith. The introduction went on to explain that he uttered this prayer with his dying breath and that his words were recorded by a student. She followed along the translation as Jacob sang:

V'chol baei olam yaavrun l'fanecha....
All who live pass before You like a flock of sheep.
As a shepherd gathers the sheep and causes them to pass beneath his staff,
so do You pass and record and count every living soul,

appointing the measure of every creature's life
and decreeing its destiny....

There was something about the image of the shepherd that struck a chord with Marie. As she sat listening to Jacob, verses that she had learned from the sisters came flooding into her mind: "*I am the good shepherd; the good shepherd lays down his life for the sheep.*" But wasn't that Jesus? *"Our Lord Jesus, the great shepherd of the sheep..."*. She could suddenly see, as clearly as she saw Jacob on the stage in front of her, a picture that hung in the church of her childhood, a picture of a bearded Jesus in a long brown robe with a staff in his hand, looking out at a flock of sheep grazing in the meadow. And she too began to weep. Rabbi Amnon was martyred, but so was Jesus. She looked back into her prayer book, trying to follow Jacob's chanting.

Who shall live and who shall die?...
Who by fire and who by water?...

Does he want me to give up Jesus? Why? He has his shepherd; why can't I have mine? Jesus has been my shepherd ever since I was a little girl. He was with me when my brother tried to rape me; he was with me when I found the strength to leave my parents; and he brought me here, to Jacob. She didn't realize how copiously she was weeping until she felt Sarah's arm around her. She looked at Sarah whose eyes were also wet, and she saw concern. She whispered, "Sorry, Aunt Sarah; I don't know what came over me. Sorry."

Sarah whispered back, "You're not alone. That prayer always gets to me." Marie nodded and looked back up at Jacob who was resoundingly singing out the final words of the hymn: "*Repentance and prayer and charity avert the severe decree,*" and she wondered if she needed to repent, to repent for thinking that she could give up Jesus. And was Jacob, who sounded so sincere, so caught up in the majesty of the words he was singing, was he repenting? For what? For saying that he loved her, knowing that she was a Catholic? But he *did* love her; she was sure of it.

As she was wrapped in her own thoughts, she realized that the congregation was rising and that a congregant had gone up onto the stage and opened the ark. It seemed to be a special prayer, and she looked at Sarah for help. Sarah pointed out the page and whispered, "This is a very beautiful prayer, *Avinu Malkeinu.* We ask God for a lot of different things in the new year. I always add a few personal requests at the end." Again Jacob was chanting beautifully, accompanied by many in the congregation who seemed to recognize the musical setting. She listened to Jacob's emotive repetition of all the *Avinu Malkeinu* verses, and as he approached the final verse, she closed her moist eyes and whispered words that had never before been uttered in a synagogue: "*Avinu Malkeinu,* please, O God, please let me have my Jesus and my Jacob." And she kept repeating the words silently as a mantra through the rabbi's sermon and the series of *shofar* blasts that concluded the service.

It took a good half hour for the congregants to file out. Rabbi Himmel and Jacob stood at the door greeting the people with *Shanah Tovah* and good wishes for the new year, and the people were enthusiastic in their praise for Jacob's participation. The Fairstones and Marie waited until everyone had filed out, and then they had their chance. Sol was ecstatic. After hugging Jacob and telling how beautifully he had done, he whispered in his ear, "And that *mamzer* Glick actually came over to me and wished me a *Shanah Tovah.* You really impressed him."

Hope gave her cousin a big kiss and then said to Marie, "It's all right now. Everybody's gone. You can give him a kiss too." She reddened and gave Jacob a peck on his cheek, but the adoring look that she gave him before the kiss made the kiss itself superfluous. As they began walking with Sarah and Hope to Sarah's convertible to say goodbye, Sarah took Jacob's hand and said, "You all go on; I have something that I want to tell Jacob… in private."

When they were out of earshot, Sarah took Jacob's hands in hers and said, "Jakie, you know I love you very much, and so what I'm going to say now comes from my heart. I'm not blind; I know that you and Marie are… well, how can I say it? I know that you and Marie have been very cozy up in our attic. I could see it on both of your faces, how you look at each other. And I know that she loves you. What young girl wouldn't? I sat with her through the service, and she was crying some of the time. I think that she was crying over you, Jakie. What can I say? She's a lovely girl; over this summer I've come to love her myself. What she's done for Hope is a miracle. But, Jakie, listen to me; she's not for you. I listened to the way that you *davvened* this morning. Every bone in your body is Jewish. You love everything Jewish. Jakie, she's a Catholic! You understand that? Really understand? She's a wonderful young lady, but she's a *Catholic,* and you're Reb Yisroel's *einikl,* his favorite. What would he say if he knew? I wish I could say you should just drop her, quick, like a hot coal. But I don't want you to hurt her either. She doesn't deserve that. So Jakie, find some way. Be gentle with her, but she's not for you. That's all I have to say. Now give your auntie a kiss."

They embraced warmly, and he handed her into her car where Hope was already seated waiting. He walked around the car to Hope and leaned in to give her a kiss. "Good luck at Simmons. You can do it. Keep in touch and let me know how it's going. And take good care of your mother. Bye."

On the drive back to Harpswell, Sol suggested that they stop at the marina in Falmouth for lunch, but Marie told them that Sarah had given her strict instructions about their holiday lunch. "She told me that Jake – I can call you Jake now that Mrs. Fairstone and Hope are gone? – anyway, she told me that the cantor here wouldn't want to go to a restaurant after praying all morning, so she left a delicious holiday lunch for us. She showed me everything and asked me to serve it. It'll just take me a few minutes after we get home to put it all together; okay?"

Jacob was relieved. He was still feeling a kind of elation in the aftermath of the service, and the last place that he wanted to be on Rosh HaShanah was in a seafood restaurant sitting among *goyim.* Rabbi Himmel had invited him to lunch at his home in Cape Elizabeth, but, not wanting to abandon Marie, he had demurred. Sarah had left a dish with apples and honey along with roast chicken and sweet *tsimmes* in the refrigerator. There was another special round Rosh HaShanah *challah* and for dessert a delicious peach and pear compote, all served by Marie.

As they were enjoying a final cup of coffee, Marie's personal addition to the meal, Sol said, "You know, Jakie, this young lady would make a good *balaboste.* Don't let her go!" Marie, of course, wanted to know what a *balaboste* was, and Jacob explained that it meant a good traditional Jewish housewife. As he explained, he couldn't help but contrast Sol's half serious remark with Sarah's parting admonition. When they got up from the table, Sol said that since it was such a nice day, he thought he would take a ride out to a couple of his farms. "You mind if I leave the two of you here alone?" he asked with a laugh. "No; I didn't think so."

Five minutes later, he was barreling down the driveway, and they heard the squeal of wheels as he swerved just missing a car driving down Route 24. Jacob had a good idea of where his uncle was headed now that Sarah was gone and no excuses were needed. What he did not realize was that throughout their lunch Sol had been imagining what these two handsome young people would be doing without the constraints of Sarah and without Marie's obligations to Hope. He thought of himself lying in his big bed alone while the kids were doing whatever in their room upstairs and, appraising Marie as he did more often than he would admit even to himself, he chose to leave.

Jacob joined Marie in the kitchen as she was washing the dishes and cleaning up. When he put his arms around her, she turned to him and asked, "Is it a *mitzvah* on Rosh HaShanah too?" It took him a moment to realize what she was asking, but two minutes later they were reveling in each other's bodies in what was now *their* room. But there was an unwonted reserve to their coupling, a disquieting reserve that both of them were uneasily aware of. They were also aware of the fact that Marie would be leaving in just three days and that a week later they would once again be separated by half a continent. There was so much to talk about.... later.... later ....

When later came, as the sun was beginning to set across Merriconeag Sound, Marie shifted in Jacob's arms. He was still asleep. She nudged him, and he replied with a "hmmm?".

"Wake up, lazy bones. It's not as if you did anything today."

"Yuh," he said stretching. "Just another dull day in Maine."

"Okay, you awake?"

"Awake and willing."

"No, Jake, not right now." She held him off and continued, "Jake, you know that we've got a lot to talk about. I was so proud of you this morning, I could hardly keep myself from running up on the stage and kissing you in front of the whole congregation. So now you know that I've got self-control. But when you were singing that beautiful prayer about the shepherd and his sheep, I had some thoughts that I've got to share with you, but… well, but not today and maybe not tomorrow either. I'm leaving on Sunday, and I want the next two days to be perfect. But there's one thing I need to hear from you if we're going to get through these next two days without a serious conversation."

"What is it, *Dodati*?"

"God! When you call me that, I just want to melt in your arms."

"What would you like me to say?"

"Without any commitment and without any baggage, I want you, the cantor who sings so elegantly to God, to *our* God, Jake; I want you to look me in the eye and say what I'm about to say to you." With that, she took his hands and put them on her breasts and whispered, "I love you, Jacob Ross, with all my heart."

He took his hands from her breasts and laid them on his heart, looked into her eyes, and said in a firm voice, "I love you, Miriam Beaulieu, *Dodati*, with all my heart and soul."

"What did you call me?"

"I called you Miriam. Marie comes from the Hebrew Miriam. I just sort of wish that that was your name. Things would be so much simpler."

She sat there pensively for a few moments and then said, "But my name isn't Miriam, Jake, it's Marie. I don't know what's going to happen to us after I go back to Hudson, Jake, but from right now until you drop me at the door of my dorm, I want us to act like we're … well, like we're betrothed. I don't want to sound corny, but you know that Eddie Fisher song? *"Heart and soul, I am yours."* Well, at least for the next few days, that's my motto."

They lay down again, just holding hands and looking at the ceiling, until they heard a voice calling from the bottom of the steps. "Hey, you kids, it's time to come up for air. I'm taking you out for dinner tonight. Ingrid's okay?"

"Fine," they both yelled, laughing together, and a half hour later, with Sol driving at his usual break-neck speed, they arrived at the Bath restaurant and were sharing a bottle of Vouvray. Sol was in a particularly good mood, and after his second glass of wine, he said, "I want you both to know how happy it makes me to see you having such a good time together. Marie, I want you to keep Jakie happy so he'll stay here. And Jakie, I know that you're a very smart fellow, but I hope you're smart enough not to let this beautiful girl get away." And then with a chuckle and a leer, "I know *I* wouldn't let her get away."

When they were preparing for bed later that night, Jacob said, "I've got an idea for tomorrow. I have to be in Portland on Saturday for the Shabbat service; there's a special reading from the prophets on the Sabbath between Rosh HaShanah and Yom Kippur, and I promised Rabbi Himmel that I would chant it and do the rest of the service with him. So we won't have much time on Saturday, and you'll have to pack too. So we've got tomorrow. It looks like it's going to be a nice day; the TV forecast said sunny, clear and crisp, low sixties. I thought it would be a great day to go back up to Camden and to climb Mount Megunticook. It's the mountain near Mount Battie where we climbed with Hope, but Megunticook is a little higher and tougher; Hope wouldn't have been able to do it."

"Sounds like a challenge. If that's what you'd like to do, I'm all for it. And with the leaves beginning to change, there should be some nice scenery. Agreed! See? I'm easy to get along with."

"I know you're easy to get along *with*; I just wonder if I could ever get along *without* you."

"Shhh," she put her finger on his lips. "Not time yet to talk about that."

Their love-making that night was gentle and unhurried, each wanting their intimacy to go on and on and on without the rush to a climax. On the floor below, Sol lay alone in his king-sized bed, listening for a hint of what was going on above. He envisioned Marie nude, lying next to him in Sarah's place, and he climaxed well before the youngsters. As he tried to fall asleep, having wiped away the sticky pool from his thigh, he thought, "So now I've got something else to atone for on Yom Kippur. She is one gorgeous *shikse*! If Jakie gives her up, maybe… maybe…" And with just the thought of her naked body next to his, he felt the blood again coursing to his pendular brain.

Friday was, as promised, a beautiful day. They thought that they would have breakfast with Sol, but he was already gone, and so Jacob decided to introduce Marie to the wonders of Claudette's muffins since they had to drive through Bath anyway on their way northward. As soon as they walked in to Claudette's Kennebec Kitchen, Claudette recognized Jacob and gave him a warm welcome. He introduced Marie, and they were both surprised to learn that Claudette knew who she was. "Sol told me a few months ago that he had hired a really beautiful young woman from Bangor as a companion for his daughter. I took one look at you, and I knew that you must be the one. He was right about you. Good for you, Jacob. You still going to school in Chicago?"

They exchanged information for a few minutes, and then when Jacob and Marie were seated and far enough away from Claudette at the cash register, Marie asked, "Who is she, and how does she know you and Mr. Fairstone so well?"

Jacob thought for a minute and decided to tell her about Sol's affair with Claudette. As he began to share the details, he realized that he actually wanted her to know about his uncle's peccadilloes. He felt miffed at Sol's remarking the previous evening that *he* wouldn't let Marie get away, and so he told her the whole story while they were enjoying their the hot coffee and muffins.

"But is he still carrying on with her? He seems so loving when he's with Aunt Sarah."

"This affair is over because Claudette got married a couple of months ago, but, well, my dear uncle has appetites. And he's rich enough that he can satisfy those appetites. But enough about him; what do you think of these muffins?"

"Delicious! I've already had too much. Let's get out of here so that we can work them off mountain climbing."

A half hour later they passed the entrance to Camden Hills State Park, and Marie didn't have to ask why he didn't turn right in. "You're going to pay homage to Bidu Sayao again?"

"I always do when I'm up this way. Someday she's going to be out in the driveway or looking out the window, and she'll wave to me. And then I'll drive in and tell her about that lovely gift that you gave me."

"Can I honk this time?"

"Sure."

Marie reached over and made five short beeps on the horn as soon as they spotted the red and white name plate, but they didn't see anyone, and Jacob turned the car around.

It was a perfect day for climbing Mount Magintocook. At first the rise was gradual, but as they trekked higher and higher the trail became steeper. They stopped for a ten-minute breather and a few sips of water at Ocean Lookout, and then they proceeded another half mile up the increasingly rocky trail, broke through the trees and emerged to a bright and sunny peak and a light breeze. It was well worth the effort. There was a great view of neighboring Mount Battie, the ocean, the Camden Harbor and the dozens of boats bobbing there. As they were sitting on a boulder holding hands and enjoying the view, Marie said, "It's funny that we climbed a mountain together today."

"Why funny?"

"Well, when the rabbi was reading from the Torah yesterday morning, I was reading the translation that Aunt Sarah showed me, and it was about Abraham and Isaac climbing Mount Moriah for the sacrifice. I should have checked you out for a knife before we climbed up here. After all, you know: Abraham, Isaac and *Jacob.* You don't believe in sacrificing innocent young virgins, do you?"

"You'll never know, but it's a lucky thing for you that you're not a virgin."

"Lucky thing for *you*, you mean." And she turned and kissed him.

They sat there quietly for another few minutes, and them Marie said, "Seriously, Jake; I was thinking about that Torah reading. The sisters in my high school taught us that story, and they said that Mount Moriah was Calvary, where Jesus was crucified. They said that just like Abraham was prepared to sacrifice his only son, God was willing to sacrifice *His* only son on the same mountaintop for the sake of humanity." She looked at him. "I guess you don't believe that."

"No, I don't. I believe that that story about Abraham and Isaac was written by some prophet in the days when people were sacrificing their first-born sons to the Babylonian god Moloch. The prophets were disgusted by that horrible practice, and so they invented that story to indicate that God did not want human sacrifice. They made Abraham the main character in the story to show that the very first Jew was told by God, just in the nick of time, not to sacrifice his son, so that Jews would never do such a thing in the future. And I don't believe that there's any connection between the Abraham story and Jesus."

"But don't you believe that Jesus died for the sake of humanity?"

"No, I'm sorry; I don't believe that. To begin with, the way I believe in God, God could never have a son. For me, God is entirely spiritual, the guiding force of the universe. I don't believe that God ever interacts directly with human beings."

"But the way you were praying yesterday; it was as if you were talking to God. Was it just an act? You were singing so beautifully about God being the shepherd, and I couldn't help it. I was thinking about Jesus."

"I hope it's not an act. I love the prayers that I chant, not because I think that God is listening – who knows, maybe God *is* listening, but that's not the reason I pray. I pray because those prayers are the expressions of the ideals and the hopes of my people."

"The *Jewish* people. No Jesus; right?"

"Marie, what can I say? I don't believe in Jesus as anything more than an inspired teacher. But there's no way that I want to get in the way of what you believe. But hey, we didn't come up here to talk theology."

"I know. Sorry I brought it up, but I'm just not sure what I believe. I know that I love being with you, and I worry about whether two people like us, coming from such different backgrounds, could ever be happy spending the rest of their lives together. I really didn't want to start talking about this, not with just this day before I have to leave. I don't know; climbing this mountain with you right after reading about Abraham and Isaac on Mount Moriah, it just came out. Jake, do you really love me?"

"More than I can say, no matter how different our backgrounds. And do you know why I wanted us to climb up here today, with all this beauty spread out below us?"

"Why?"

"Because I wanted to give you something here, a gift of love like the gift that you gave me on Sunday night. I didn't have any time to buy you anything, but there's something that I have that's precious to me, and I want you to have it. And I wanted to give it to you while we're here in this beautiful spot."

"Jake, you don't have to give me any gifts."

"But I want to." He reached into his pocket and he took out a heavy gold ring with a crimson stone set in the center. "This is my Harvard ring. I've had it with me since my graduation. Can I slip it on your finger?"

She looked at it and then looked at him, and then very slowly she said, "Jake, are you sure?"

"No, *Dodati,* I'm not sure about anything right now except that I love you. I don't know if we'll ever get married, and I don't even know if we'll be alive tomorrow. All I *do* know is that I love you and that I want you to have something that reminds you of me whenever we're not together."

He slipped it on her finger, and they both started laughing uproariously when they realized that it was much too wide for any of her slender fingers. "Not a problem," Jacob said as their laughter subsided. "We're going to be driving back through Bath, and I know a jewelry store on Front Street. We can stop there and buy a chain so that you can wear it around your neck."

Marie's laughter had turned to tears of joy. She put her arms around Jake and whispered in his ear, "I'll wear it always. I love you so much. Thank you for making me so happy."

They stopped for a late lunch in Wiscasset and then headed for Bath. When Jacob pulled up in front of Springer's Jewelry, Marie said, "I don't want you to spend much on the chain, but I want it to be long enough so that your ring can nuzzle right between my breasts like you like to do. Okay?"

He looked at her with awe. "You are something! You always know what to say to turn me on. Now we'll have to wait a minute before I can get out of the car and stand up straight." And again they started laughing. She reached her hand over to his lap and said, "Umm. I have a feeling that we're going to do another Shabbat *mitzvah* tonight. Can you save it?"

"If you'll take your hand away and let me sit here for a minute, I promise my friend will revive in time for the *mitzvah*."

"Promise?"

"Promise."

They were able to find a reasonably priced gold-plated chain of the requisite length, and when they got home twenty minutes later, Jacob slipped the chain through his ring and placed it around Marie's neck. The ring seemed to fall in the right place, but Jacob said, "Why don't you take off your blouse so that we can see if it nuzzles where it should."

She laughed. "If I do that, we're going to end up on the living room floor, and Mr. Fairstone will walk right in on us. Anyway, I want to make us a nice Shabbat dinner, and it's already after five. Aunt Sarah told me that she left some breaded chicken breasts in the freezer for us, and there's other stuff that I want to prepare. Can you control yourself until tonight?"

They settled for a long embrace, and then Marie went to the kitchen while Jacob went up to their room to do a little reading. Less than an hour later Sol walked in and yelled. "Hello, kids. Tonight I'm taking you out to dinner at Jameson Tavern in Freeport, so get ready."

Marie came out of the kitchen and asked him if it would be all right if they ate in that night. "Aunt Sarah left us most of the makings for a nice Shabbat dinner, and I'm preparing the rest. I think that Jake would like us to eat at home. Is that all right with you?"

Sol looked at her in her apron over her Bermudas. "What a *balaboste*! If I had a *balaboste* like you to come home to every night, I'd come home earlier. Of course, it's all right. If our cantor wants a Shabbes dinner, we'll have a Shabbes dinner. We can go out tomorrow night."

"Well, tomorrow night might be a problem too. It's going to be my last night here, and… well, no offense, but I thought that maybe Jake and I would go out alone somewhere. Would that be all right?"

"Look, I'm used to eating alone. You two enjoy yourselves tomorrow. And thanks for reminding me that it will be your last day here. I'll give you a check tomorrow. It'll be for the whole month and a nice gift added on. You deserve it. And I want you to stay in touch."

"I will; I will. Can I give you a thank-you kiss?"

"Any time." She came over to him to plant a kiss on his cheek, but he put his arms around her and kissed her back on the lips. She was flustered and not sure what to do, but after a few seconds he relaxed his grip and allowed her to extricate herself. When he saw how red her face was, he laughed and said, "Marie, we're family. You're like Hope, like a daughter. That's all it was."

"That's okay; I was just surprised for a minute." She decided to put a good face on it. "You're right. We're family." And she walked quickly back to the kitchen deciding not to mention it to Jacob.

Their Shabbat dinner was pleasant, although they all missed Sarah and Hope. Jacob performed the rituals and even sang two *zemirot* that he thought Sol would remember. He then reminded them of the *L'cha Dodi* that he had taught them at their last family Shabbat and was delighted at how much of it Marie remembered and how lovely her voice was. After dinner Marie insisted on taking care of cleaning up alone, shooing the men into the living room for the Red Sox telecast. She joined them for the last inning, and they were delighted when the game ended with a walk-off home run by Mickey Vernon. Sol remained in the living room to watch the news but was not surprised when Jacob and Marie left, hand in hand, to go upstairs.

Jacob, though, did get a surprise that night. Marie took a bit longer than usual in the bathroom, but when she came out to join him in their room, he was delighted to see that she was wearing nothing but his ring nestled precisely between her elfin breasts. Jacob could see that something was bothering Marie, but he surmised that it was because of their imminent separation, and he didn't say anything. He initiated their love making eagerly, but when he realized that he was about to climax before she was ready, he slowly withdrew so that he could stimulate her with his finger and bring her to the point where he was. But as he slipped his finger between her labia, he felt something strange and sticky. He looked at his finger and saw that there was blood on it. Instinctively, he recoiled and gasped, "Marie, what's this?"

She answered, "It's okay. Don't worry. It's just the beginning of my period; I thought that my diaphragm would keep it from oozing out, because it just started. It's probably because of all that climbing today. It wasn't supposed to come for another couple of days. But it's okay. Don't stop."

"Marie! I can't! You should have told me. I can't make love to you like this. It's not right."

"Why? What's wrong? I didn't want to say no to you after our lovely day and your ring. And why are you looking at me like that?"

He climbed out of their bed and looked down at her. "Marie, it's just wrong and disgusting. I'm surprised at you."

She looked at him in shock. "Jake, Jake, I'm sorry if what I did was wrong. I just wanted to make you happy. But how could you use that word disgusting? Jake, do I really disgust you? How could you say that?" And she began to cry as Jacob stumbled to the washstand, wet a washcloth and cleaned himself. When he was satisfied that no vestiges of blood remained on his penis or his hand, he went back to their bed and stood over her as she curled into a ball and wept.

"Marie, I'm sorry I used that word. I didn't mean it. Of course, you're not disgusting. It's just that I've been taught ever since I was old enough to understand about periods that men and women should stay apart during those days. It's called *niddah*, and there's a whole tractate of Jewish law forbidding sex or even contact during *niddah*."

"But Jake," her crying had turned into gasping heaves. "I ... I didn't know. How could I know about your Jewish law? Jake... Jake... I'm not disgusting."

He reached down awkwardly and touched her head. "No, you're not disgusting. I was just shocked. I'm sorry for how I reacted. It's not your fault, but I can't make love to you while you're bleeding."

Her crying subsided gradually as he caressed her hair. "Jake, can you come back into bed? Please?"

He thought for a minute and then lay down beside her, maintaining a small distance between them but holding her hand. After several minutes of silence, she stirred and told him that she had to go to the bathroom to clean herself up. She carefully climbed over him and ran to their bathroom. He could hear her weeping softly as she took care of herself. When she came out, she was wearing the terrycloth robe. "Can I get back in bed with you?"

He nodded, and she slid in beside him. "Do you have to keep away from me, or can we hold hands?"

He took her hand, kissed her on the cheek, and said, "I'm sorry. I shouldn't have said what I said."

She squeezed his hand. "Goodnight, Jake; I love you." They lay there awake without saying anything for a long while, with Marie fingering the ring that was hanging from her neck. Then she whispered, "Are you awake?"

"Yes."

"Will you do me a favor?"

"Sure; what is it?"

"Just call me *dodati*, and I promise, I'll fall asleep."

He turned to her and kissed her again, this time on the mouth and whispered into her ear, *"Dodati kallah, dodati kallah."* And they fell asleep.

On the floor below, again alone in his bed, Sol listened for sounds from above. He heard some hurried steps and the sound of running water, and he let his imagination fill in the details. "Lucky bastard!" he groaned and decided that Saturday would be a good day for a visit to one or two of his farms.

Marie was fast asleep when Jacob went down for breakfast, and he decided not to disturb her. He found Sol just about to leave, and when Sol asked him if Marie would be going to Portland with him, he answered, "No, not today. She's not feeling too well this morning, and she's got a lot of packing to do. When I get back, I'll help her. When will you be home?"

"Probably not until late. I'll tell you what. I have to give Marie a check; I'm going to give her double what she earned last month. I wanted to invite you both to dinner tonight, but Marie told me that she wanted to be alone with you her last night. So let's plan to have breakfast tomorrow morning at Bascomb's. You can sleep late and we'll have a brunch there at about ten-thirty, and I'll say goodbye to her, and you'll be able to get on the road to Bangor before noon."

"Good plan. See you tonight or tomorrow morning. Good Shabbes."

Jacob arrived at the Portland shul about twenty minutes before the service and had a brief conversation with Rabbi Himmel about a time for them to meet to plan out the Yom Kippur services. There were less than thirty people in attendance when they walked out onto the *bimah* and Himmel voiced his disappointment. "I guess it wasn't necessary for you to come all the way down for just a handful of people. You'd think after the beautiful Rosh HaShanah services there'd be more people here today. Nu, what can you do? My twice-a-year Jews will all be here again on Yom Kippur."

Jacob's mind was somewhere else as he chanted the *Shacharit.* He knew he had handled the situation with Marie badly. But how could she have thought that he would want to make love to her while she was menstruating? Hadn't someone ever taught her? Her mother? Fat chance! The nuns? Instruct their nice little Catholic girls in the etiquette of intercourse? No way. If they taught them anything at all about the menstrual cycle, it would be that the only legitimate form of birth control was to desist from sex in the *middle* of the cycle, not at the beginning. How was she to know how he would react to her bleeding?

But wasn't that just a symptom of their much bigger problem, sort of a warning to him? He hoped that the congregation couldn't tell how distracted he was during the service, but Himmel noticed. Twice he had to repeat his announcements of the correct page before Jacob picked up the cue and resumed his chanting. During Himmel's reading of the Torah portion, Jacob was able to sit and collect himself, and then came the special *haftarah* for *Shabbat Shuvah* which Jacob was to chant. He knew the text by heart, but as soon as he heard himself chanting the ancient words, he felt for the first time that they were directed squarely at him:

Shuvah Yisrael…
Return, O Israel, to Adonai your God,
For you have stumbled in your iniquity.

Take words and return to Adonai;
Say to Him, Forgive my iniquities….
Those who are wise will understand these things….
But sinners will stumble….

Driving back to Bailey Island, he couldn't get the words out of his mind. Had he stumbled in iniquity with Marie? He was supposed to be wise, but did he understand? Really understand? How could he have so completely fallen for a non-Jewish woman? Worse; how could he have told her that he loved her? How could he have given her his ring and made her believe that they had a future together? But she was so lovely, so irresistible, so delightful to be with. She was like no one he had ever met before. He thought of his father; he thought of Koppel Ganzfried; he thought of his zeyde: Be a *guter Yid,* a good Jew, a *mensch* and a good Jew. Does a good Jew fall in love with a *shik…*(Dammit, Jacob) a non-Jewish girl? Does he lead her astray, making her believe that they might marry some day? But how could she have thought that he would want to make love to her while she was bleeding? Where did she come from? He knew the answer. She came from a Neanderthal farm family; she was forbidden fruit from twisted vines…..

But…. They would have the house to themselves for the rest of the day. They could do whatever they wanted. She was so beautiful, so desirable. Maybe they could…. No! What the hell was he thinking. With all of this racing through his mind, he pulled up the long driveway, parked, and walked into the house, not knowing what to expect of her or of himself.

He found Marie in their room packing. She was still in her robe and said that she was feeling sort of punk, but she wanted to know how the morning had gone. He described the small crowd and admitted to her that he had been distracted through the service. Why? she wanted to know. At first he equivocated, but she was looking him squarely in the eye. It was the same look that he recalled from the night after he had met her, the look that said, "I want you to be completely honest with me."

"Marie, I don't know what to do about you. Last night was more my fault than yours. I shouldn't have reacted as badly as I did. You just wanted to please me. You had no way of knowing how I would react to your bleeding. But you see, that's just it. We come here from such different places. You are the most lovely person whom I have ever had the good fortune of meeting. When I told you that I loved you, and when I called you *dodati,* I was telling the truth, but .... I just don't know, Marie; I don't know. I feel almost bewitched, like I'm not in control of myself when I'm with you. In the Bible portion that I chanted this morning, it says that the wise should understand. Well, I guess that I'm just not as wise as I thought I was. I'm just an ordinary guy who can't help giving in to his passions. I guess I'm sort of like my Uncle Sol that way. Maybe I should just chuck my idea of being a scholar and admit that I just want to stay up here with you. Marie, I don't know. I just don't know." He looked up at her, and when he saw tears in her eyes, he began crying too.

She sat down on their unmade bed and looked up at him, a handsome young man in his Sabbath suit, standing in front of her and crying. She held out her hand, and he took it. She patted the place next to her, and he sat down. She opened her arms, and he fell into them. They sat there rocking in each other's arms for what seemed an eternity until she reached for a corner of the sheet and used it to dry his eyes.

When she felt sure that he was in control of himself, she said, "You must be hungry. You worked this morning. Did you have anything after the service?" He shook his head negatively. "Come on downstairs. I'll fix something for you. Aunt Sarah left us with enough to get us through the winter."

When they both stood up, he started laughing. She looked at him and asked, "What brought that on?"

"Suddenly you're Aunt Sarah. Whenever I used to go to her house in Malden and pour out my heart about some girl who wouldn't let me get to first base, the first thing she would say is 'You must be hungry,' and she would feed me. Marie, you have the makings of a Jewish mother."

Down in the kitchen, Marie put on a pot of coffee and took out a plastic dish filled with sliced chicken from the refrigerator. As she was making a sandwich for Jacob, she said softly, "You didn't say goodbye before you left this morning. You just sort of sneaked out."

"I didn't want to wake you up."

"I thought maybe you didn't want to talk to me after last night. Jake, I was so worried. I don't want you to be mad at me....ever. I thought that we'd be able to spend this whole day making love with no one else around, but I guess that's out now."

"That's what I thought too. But anyway, you've got packing to do. I'll help you."

"And then you'll be rid of me."

"Marie, please don't say that. I don't want to be rid of you. Let's not make a big thing about what happened last night. You've got to get back to Hudson, and I'm going to drive up there with you. You've got your first week of school, and I've got to prepare for Yom Kippur. And I also promised Uncle Sol that I'd spend some time with him looking over his operations so I can make that big decision. We'll have a whole week apart to think about things, and then I'll drive up to spend Sunday with you before I drive back to Chicago."

"I don't know whether to look forward to next Sunday or to dread it. Decision time...." Marie sat looking at Jacob as he chewed on his sandwich, and then she said, "Jake, I was thinking about us all morning while you were away. Would it make a difference to you..." she paused for a moment and then blurted, ... "if I became Jewish? You said that people can become Jewish like that friend of yours in Chicago. Could I become Jewish?"

"Marie, you would do that for me? You'd give up being a Catholic? I don't know what to say." He put down his sandwich, thought for a long minute, and then said slowly, "But a person shouldn't convert just for another person, no matter how much in love they might be. You've got to be sure that you really want to be Jewish, even without me. You'd have to study for about a year and then be able to say sincerely that you accept Judaism and want to be a part of the Jewish people. Right now, I don't think that you know all that that means. And how could you learn about Judaism in Bangor?"

She smiled and said, "Jake, when you left me this morning without giving me a kiss or even saying goodbye, I really felt terrible. I was even thinking of doing something stupid. Sometimes I get some weird ideas when I have my period. But then, as I was lying in bed pitying myself, I prayed, Jake; I prayed, like you were praying in Portland. I'm always completely honest with you, Jake, like I hope you are with me, so I'll say it. I prayed to Jesus to tell me what to do. And then I got an idea. I called information on the telephone, and I asked if they had a listing for a synagogue in Bangor. Well, it seems that there *is* one; it's called Beth El. I tried to call them, but they didn't answer, probably because of Shabbat. Anyway, Jake, there is a synagogue in Bangor, and I could probably study there while I'm at Hudson. What do you think?"

"*Jesus* gave you this idea?"

"Don't make fun of me, Jake. No, Jesus didn't give me the idea, but when I pray to Jesus, I… I don't know how to put it, but I sort of get inspired to do something, to solve my problems. So what do you think?"

"Do you realize that if you do become Jewish, you'll have to give up Jesus?"

"But you said that your friend in Chicago didn't give up Jesus completely."

"Yes, but he gave him up as anything more than a teacher. He doesn't *pray* to him."

"Well, when I get back to school, I'm going to find Beth El and see if I can study there. Then we'll see what happens."

As they were drinking their coffee, Marie said, "I guess we won't be making love today; I was hoping that we'd have at least one last time."

"Me too. Look, I've got an idea. I was planning to drive up to Bangor to see you next Sunday, but what if I drive up right after the Yom Kippur service is over, on Saturday night. Then we could spend the night together in a motel and all day Sunday together.

I'll be fasting on Saturday and the services won't end until about six-thirty. I can grab a bite and then drive up. I could probably get there before ten. What do you say?"

"O Jake, I'd love it. And by then I'll be clean enough for you; promise."

That night they slept together as they had the night before, holding hands but with a good bit of space between them. Instinctively, Jacob reached for her several times in his sleep, but each time he recovered in time and moved back to his side of the bed. Marie didn't get much sleep, hoping that he would indeed embrace her, and she wasn't of much help when morning came and Jacob was trying to pack all of her belongings into his little MG. Sol didn't make an appearance, and when Jacob checked his bedroom, he saw that the bed had not been slept in. When he reported the fact to Marie, she said, "I guess he had a better night than we had."

They met Sol, as planned, at Bascomb's and shared a delicious brunch, during which Sol handed Marie her check. She looked at it and whistled. "You don't owe me anywhere near this much, Mr. Fairstone. Thank you! Thank you!"

She leaned over and gave him a kiss on the cheek, to which he responded with "That made it worthwhile. I'll really miss you. Maybe next summer you'll come down and visit with Hope. And if everything goes the way it should, Jakie will be here too. We'll be one big happy family again."

After Jacob promised his uncle that he'd be ready to meet with him bright and early the next day, the couple took off northward, driving along Route 1. They avoided any talk of the future during the drive, confining themselves to small talk about the scenery, the courses that Marie would be taking during her junior year, and the parietal regulations of the Hudson dorms which they agreed were from a different generation. As they passed through Camden, Marie asked if she could make the beeps for Jacob when they passed Casa Bidu. He was delighted that she wanted to participate in his ritual, and he thanked her again for the lovely gift that she had given him on his return from Chicago. As they approached, they both looked around for any sign of life, but there was no one to be seen. Marie reached over and hit the horn five times in rapid succession and then planted a kiss on Jacob's neck and said, "I think that if Miss Sayao saw us, she'd approve." And then she leaned back and dropped off to sleep until they reached Bangor.

When they finished unpacking the car, checking in with the dorm supervisor, and carrying the suitcases and cartons up to the third floor room assigned to Marie, it was almost five. Cramps and her lack of sleep the previous night had Marie feeling a bit testy and less than desirable, and Jacob was eager to get back on the road for the long drive back. She managed to accompany him down to the ground floor, and their farewell, in the midst of a dozen other coeds saying goodbye to family and friends, was just a bit warmer than perfunctory.

There was no telephone in Marie's room, but she did manage to find a nearby pay phone twice that week to call Jacob. She apologized for the way she had been feeling on Sunday and asked him if he had decided yet about the job with his uncle. He answered cryptically that he was leaving all major decisions until Yom Kippur. She called a third time at lunchtime on Friday to wish Jacob success with the Yom Kippur services and to let him know that there was a nice motel just south of town on the Penobscot River and that she had informed the dorm supervisor that her 'brother' would be picking her up on Saturday night for a Sunday with her family. He thanked her for her initiative and told her that he could hardly wait. "I love you, Jake." "And I love you, Marie." And they hung up.

Jacob also made a couple of calls before leaving for Portland. He called his father to wish him and Tamara a *G'mar chatimah tov*, and he called Trudy in Chicago with the same pre-Yom Kippur wish. Trudy was delighted to hear from him and told him how eagerly she was anticipating Elisha's return from Israel. "He writes to me at least twice a week! He's been having a ball at Tel Dan, brilliant colleagues and terrific students. The students all left before Rosh HaShanah, but he and the other archaeologists came back to cover over the site and leave it in good shape for next summer's crew. God, I love him so much. I never thought I could become this mushy over a man"

"So he's not back yet? Doesn't he have to start teaching next week?"

"That was his plan originally, but he was invited to spend the week after Yom Kippur at a dig that they're doing at Ramat Rachel outside of Jerusalem. It's supposed to be a very important site, so he changed his plane reservation to the 24th. He made arrangements for his assistant to cover his classes the first week. And we've set the date for our wedding; we're getting married at Hillel House as soon as *Simchat Torah* is over, that night. You'll be here?"

"I wouldn't miss it for the world. I have to kiss the bride."

"I don't know if I can allow you that liberty."

"I'll be sure to make it look platonic."

"So how's *your* love life, dear friend? How you doing with that girl you told me about in Maine, your little Catholic fluff?"

"That little Catholic fluff, as you call her, is the main thing on my mind right now. You have no idea how lovely she is! But I just can't make up my mind, about her or about the job that my uncle offered me. I'm hoping that the Yom Kippur services will give me some insight. I've resolved to make my decisions by tomorrow night."

"Wow! Heavy! Well, I wish you good luck, dear friend. Call me when you get back here. I'm sitting on *shpilkes* until Elisha gets back. Ten days."

"I should be back in time for Sukkot. Maybe we can share some meals in the Hillel *sukkah*."

They offered each other the traditional pre-Yom Kippur greeting, and Jacob began to get dressed for the sacred day. He packed a small bag, because Rabbi Himmel had invited him to spend the night in his house just a block from the synagogue rather than commuting from Harpswell while fasting. As he was driving southward, he thought back over his conversation with Trudy. Tel Dan, Ramat Rachel, *Simchat Torah*, sitting on *shpilkes*,

G'mar chatimah tov; all of this would have been incomprehensible to Marie. Was he crazy to think of her as a life partner? Yea, crazy; crazy in love....

When he emerged from the vestry onto the *bimah* with Rabbi Himmel, both of them in their white robes and *tallitot,* he spotted Sol sitting a few rows back, wrapped in his *tallit.* He wondered what kind of an affect Yom Kippur had on a reprobate like his uncle. He has the sweetest woman in the world for a wife, and yet he fools around. What do women see in him? Well, he's good looking for a guy near fifty; he's got oodles of money, and he's generous. Was he like his uncle? Was he fooling around with Marie or was he ready to make a commitment? She got her answers from Jesus; would anyone answer him?

A few minutes later, he began the awesome chant of *Kol Nidre* that introduces the long day of fasting and introspection. He pictured his zeyde standing in a front corner of the Winthrop shul with his *tallit* wrapped around his head, and he prayed, *"Zeyde, tayere, ich bet dir; gib mir an eitzeh* – Dear Zeyde, I beg you; give me an answer." He repeated that prayer in his heart as an accompaniment to the traditional prayers of that evening.

The next afternoon, when one of the congregants came up to the *bimah* to read the story of Jonah, he thought of himself as the reluctant prophet, unable to understand the will of God, and when the gates of heaven were closing toward the end of the day, he pleaded, "Wait! Just another minute. Please; give me an answer." And then he heard the final long *shofar* blast, and, with Rabbi Himmel, closed the ark, feeling as spent as he had that amazing first night with Marie.

When he had taken off his robe and hung it in the vestry closet and said goodbye to Rabbi Himmel, he went back into the synagogue where he found his uncle waiting. "Jakie, you were magnificent! You must be starved and exhausted. Let's go somewhere for a good meal now, and when we get home, if you can stay awake, we'll talk. I know a restaurant just down the block. Come on; I'll drive and then we can come back for your car at Himmel's."

"Uncle Sol, I can't. I promised Marie that I'd drive up tonight to see her, and I'll stay over in Bangor. I'll just grab a quick bite, some orange juice and eggs and coffee, at the diner on Route 1."

"Jakie, You're going to drive almost a hundred and fifty miles?! As tired as you must be? And you said that you'd give me your answer right after Yom Kippur. I've been praying all day that you'd make the right decision. So when?"

"I can't help it; I've got to go. I'll be back sometime on Sunday afternoon or evening, and we'll talk then. I've got to run. I love you, Uncle Sol." And he gave him a kiss.

He spent no more than twenty minutes in the diner and ran out wiping his lips. The bag that he had packed for his night with the Himmels was in the trunk with the change of clothes that he would need for the next day. He drove northward at a speed like his uncle's, but he didn't fail to pay homage to Miss Sayao as he sped past her darkened house. When he pulled up in front of Marie's dorm, she was waiting just inside the door with a little overnight bag. As soon as she got into the car, they wrapped their arms around each other and hugged tightly. She told him where to go, and fifteen minutes later they were registered at the sparsely occupied Penobscot Shores Motel as Mr. and Mrs. Jacob Ross, no questions asked.

When the door closed behind them and they had dropped their bags on the floor, they stood looking at each other. Then Jacob took her in his arms and they stood glued together for a few minutes without saying a word. Marie broke the silence with a chuckle and said, "Mr. Ross, Mrs. Ross thinks that the first thing that you did after your day of atonement was to tell a little white lie. But Jake, I loved seeing you write Mr. and Mrs. Jacob Ross. I loved it; if only it were true. If only..."

He kissed away her last words and said, "I would have carried you over the threshold, Mrs. Ross, but you have no idea how tired I am. I was on my feet almost the whole day singing my heart out. I might not be any good to you tonight. I just feel like sleeping. Sorry, it was a long drive from Portland."

"You poor thing. Sit down and I'll help you take off your clothes. Old married couples like us don't have to make love every night."

Jacob sat down on the edge of the bed, and Marie knelt beside him and took off his shoes. He managed to get out of his jacket himself and drop it on the floor, and then he fell back to the pillows. Marie picked up his jacket and hung it over the back of the chair. She looked at him not quite sure what to do next as Jacob muttered, "Sorry, sorry," with a helpless grin.

"Some honeymoon," she giggled, and she put herself to the task of undressing the dormant body that was sprawled across the bed. She unbuckled his belt and pulled off his trousers and then his necktie. His shirt, damp with the day's sweat, was more difficult, involving her lifting first his left shoulder and then the right. She then struggled to pull down the bedspread and the linens from under him and was relieved that he still had enough energy to shift his body so that she could get the job done. She decided that leaving him in his underwear and socks would not affect his sleeping comfort, and she went to the bathroom to get herself ready for bed. She came out, took a long look at his inert body, and then arranged her body, naked except for the pendant ring, as close as possible to his without awakening him.

It wasn't until almost five in the morning that Jacob awoke from his deep sleep. At first, he didn't know where he was. It was pitch dark, but when he shifted slightly, he realized that there was a body next to his. It took him a moment to remember what he was doing in a strange bed, and when his head cleared a bit more, he remembered the purpose of his trip. He had to reach some kind of an understanding with Marie that very day, before leaving for Chicago. Two conflicting things had become crystal clear to him during the long day of prayer in Portland: he was deeply in love with Marie and he was just as deeply aware that they had no future together. He could never marry a non-Jew; there was simply too much that was precious to him that they did not share. And there was her devotion to Jesus which he found distressing. She had asked him about the possibility of becoming

Jewish; Jewish but… Jewish with Jesus. And the other but….but I love her.

All of this was churning through his brain as he lay there. But as he stretched and came in contact with the warm flesh beside him, he felt an insistant stirring. Hardly moving, he furtively slipped his shorts down past his stockinged feet and eased them off. He then inched closer to Marie and let his erection touch her. Still asleep, she moved her hand down to her thigh, felt the intruder and whispered, "Welcome back from the dead." Not another word passed between them until Marie, ecstatic minutes later, lifted herself off her lover and said, "I guess you had some energy in reserve. I've been dreaming of this all week." He whispered, "*Dodati,*" as they drifted back into euphoric sleep and didn't wake up until the mid-morning sun came streaming through the window.

They awoke hungry but didn't deny themselves the time that it took for a languorously erotic shower before walking hand-in-hand across the parking lot to the motel coffee shop. They were welcomed with hot coffee and both ordered stacks of buttermilk pancakes. Once the edge was off their hunger, Jacob decided that it was time for some serious talk. Marie could see from the way that he looked at her that he was about to address the subject that was foremost on both of their minds, but before he could say anything, she put her hand on his lips and said, "Shhh, let me talk first."

He nodded, and she began. "Jake, I love you more than I can say. I can't say that I love you more than I've ever loved anybody else, because I never really loved anyone else, not my mother, not my father, nobody. And that has me worried, because I'm going to be twenty in a couple of weeks and I don't know much about love. I don't know if I could ever love anyone else the way I love you now. Do you know what I did yesterday? I wasn't going to tell you, but I went to that little synagogue that I told you about here in Bangor because I wanted to sort of feel what you were going through in Portland. I went in and sat in the back. Some man gave me a prayer book and I tried to follow the service, but I couldn't. I didn't have Aunt Sarah sitting next to me and explaining. I sat there for over an hour trying to figure out what was going on so that I could sort of become a part of the congregation, but I couldn't, and so I walked out, frustrated.

"Jake, what's to become of us? I want to spend the rest of my life with you. If you ask me to quit Hudson and go to Chicago with you, I will in a minute. I will! But I have to bring who I am with me, and that includes Jesus. Jake, I can see what's on your face when I even mention Jesus. But Jake, that's a part of me. I don't know. Maybe if I studied Judaism long enough, I could get rid of my feelings about Jesus. Maybe… I just don't know. All I know is that I love you and I want to spend my life with you. Jake, you're smart; tell me what we're going to do, but…." She seemed afraid to utter her next words.

"But what, Marie?"

"But, Jake, remember what we promised each other. Honest. You've got to be honest with me."

Jacob reached across the table and took her hands. "Okay, Marie; honest." He looked into her eyes, searching for the right words. "You said that I'm smart; well, I'm not that smart. I've been wrestling with my feelings about you ever since our first night together last June. You were uppermost on my mind all through the Yom Kippur services Friday night and yesterday. There's only one thing that I know for certain, and that's that I love you. Nobody has ever affected me the way that you do. Could I take you with me to Chicago? Sure I could, but I don't think that you'd be happy there. I'm up to my ears in Jewish stuff there – my friends, Hillel, the synagogue where I teach, even the work that I'm doing for my Ph.D. Jewish, Jewish, Jewish; all Jewish. That's who I am. You feel that Jesus talks to you somehow when you have a problem; well, my zeyde was talking to me yesterday the same way. And he kept telling me to be a good Jew.

"Marie, I was wrestling with *two* problems yesterday. First you, and second, that offer that Uncle Sol made to me. I haven't told him yet – that'll be tonight – but I'm not going to accept his offer. I'm not cut out to be a businessman. I spent about twenty hours with him this past week, at his farms and his depots and his offices, and I was bored silly. It's not for me, even with the hundred thousand dollars that he kept dangling in front of me, and even with all the hints that he made about being able to live up here with you. But I'm not going to live up here; I can't."

"Let's get back to your *first* problem, me. Do you love me? Really? Do you really love me?"

He could see that she was beginning to look distressed, but he went on. "I *do* love you, but ..." He paused and looked into her moist eyes. "Let's say.... okay, let's say we had a kid. Would you want him or her to be baptized?"

"I... I guess so. Every child *has* to be baptized. Of course." She saw Jacob flinch. "But... but... but then we could bring it up Jewish. That would be okay, wouldn't it?"

"No, Marie; it wouldn't be okay. I could never *never* allow a child of mine to be baptized. And it's not only about some theoretical child that we might have. There are so many other things that are working against us."

As he spoke, he saw that her eyes were filling with tears. "Marie, Marie. I might be making the biggest mistake of my life, because I love you so much, but I.... I .... Look, I want us to keep in touch. I can keep calling you from Chicago. Who knows? Maybe what I feel for you will be strong enough to bring me back here, but...."

"But you're Jewish, and I'm Catholic. You're rich, and I'm poor. You're Harvard and I'm Hudson. And I'm Marie, God dammit, *I'm Marie not Miriam*! I get it."

She began weeping quietly, not wanting to make a scene in the restaurant, and then abruptly she stood up and said, "I want to get out of here," and she walked quickly toward the door. Jacob didn't wait for the check; he just threw a few dollars on the table and went after her. She walked past their motel room and toward the river. There were some benches belonging to the motel on the river bank and she sat down on one, her shoulders heaving. Jacob sat down next to her and tried to put his arm around her, but she shook him off. "No, Jacob Ross; no more touching. Last week you said I was disgusting, and I saw the same look on your face when I said that a child has to be baptized. I think I knew when I heard you say that word disgusting that we were done."

"Marie, please; I didn't mean that, and I don't want it to end this way."

"Oh? How would you like it to end? We have about another half hour before check-out time. You want to go in to the room for a quick *fuck*? Is that what you want? Jesus, you're no better than your uncle. No, you're worse; at least he's rich and he pays well."

"Marie, please don't talk that way." He was trying to find some words, but the best that he could come up with was, "We can still be friends."

The cliche infuriated her. She stood up, wrenched the golden chain and ring from around her neck and heaved them into the Penobscot. "Now take me back to my dorm. I've got some studying to do for tomorrow." She refused to utter one more word, despite his futile attempts to appease her, until he dropped her off at her dorm. She ran in without looking back.

Jacob felt bereft on the ride back to Bailey Island. Twice during the long ride, once at a traffic snarl in Belfast and a second time driving through Rockland, he almost turned the car around to head back to Bangor to try to salvage .... what? He had handled it ineptly, and it was over. He was so distracted that he forgot to make the accustomed five beeps when he passed Casa Bidu. But as the realization grew in his mind that Marie would never be more than a yearning memory, he felt ready to confront his uncle.

He walked into the Fairstone house at about three, and he found his uncle watching the afternoon game in the living room. He stood there watching with him for a few minutes, and then he said, "Uncle Sol, there's no reason to draw this out. I can't ever repay you for how kind you've been to me all my life, but I'm not going to join you in the business. I've made up my mind."

Sol stared at him and then shut off the television. "Do you know what you're saying? Do you know what you're giving up? Jakie, please; think it over again; you're making a terrible mistake."

"Uncle Sol, this is the second thing that I've given up today. I broke it off with Marie this morning, and that was an even harder decision. I love her, and I gave her up, and I love you, and I'm giving up your job. I want to leave tomorrow morning and get back to Chicago in time for Sukkot."

"Your mind is made up?" Jacob slowly nodded.

"No way I can change it?" Again Jacob nodded. "And you gave up that gorgeous girl? You let her get away?"

"Yes, dammit!"

"Oy, *bochur,* you're a fool. Forget the job; any man who would give up a girl like Marie is a fool. Maybe it's a good thing you're not coming into the business. Nu, what's done is done. I'll start looking for the right man tomorrow, but it won't be blood; it'll be some smart *goy*. You won't reconsider?"

"No, Uncle Sol; no."

"So what can I say? You'll never have an opportunity like this again. Anyway, you're still my favorite nephew." He gave Jacob a hug and then said, "What do you say, for your last night here we'll go have a nice meal at Ingrid's."

Trio Lachrymoso

Jacob arrived back in Chicago on the eve of Sukkot and, after dropping his things in his apartment, he went directly to the Hillel House so that he could visit the *sukkah* that Rabbi Persky and some students had erected behind the building. He found Trudy there among a group of about twenty students and she gave him a big hug as he walked in. She was bubbling over with good news and couldn't wait to share. "Elisha's going to be back in just six days! He's at Ramat Rachel right now, looking over a dig there with a group of Hebrew U and U of Rome archaeologists. He called me right after Yom Kippur to tell me that he'd arrive in Chicago next Tuesday. It's amazing! Right now he's knee-deep in the tenth-century BCE, and he'll be taking off from Tel Aviv on a jet on Monday and be here less than twenty hours later! He'll be here in time for the *Simchat Torah* celebration. Boy, is that going to be a *simchah*! And Jacob, he told me that he'd like you to be the best man at our wedding. Don't worry; you won't need a tux. It's going to be a small wedding, very informal, right here that night."

Jacob answered that he'd be honored, but she could tell by the lack of enthusiasm in his response that something was wrong. She took his hand and said, "I've been babbling on, and I haven't asked you how it went in Maine. How is it with that Marie that you told me about and your uncle's job?"

"I said goodbye to both of them. Trudy, Marie was the loveliest woman I've ever been with. Hey, don't get me wrong. We've had a lot of good times together, and I love you. You're great, but.... well, I don't know how to explain it, but there was something special about Marie, even aside from the fact that she's gorgeous. I think I was truly in love with her. But if I didn't know it before, I realized while I was *davvening* on Yom Kippur; I could never be happy married to someone who wasn't Jewish. I should have realized that before I got so deeply involved with her. Anyway, I ended it, and it wasn't pretty."

"Poor Jake." She took his hand. "I can see that you're hurting. I wish I could do something for you. If this were a couple of months ago, I'd suggest that we go up to your apartment so that I could help you forget about Marie, but with all those letters and calls that I've been getting from Elisha, I made a vow right after you left camp. No more recreational sex, not even with you. I'm saving it all up for him, and I can hardly wait. Just six more days!"

"I'm really happy for you, and I approve of your vow. Right now the best thing that I could offer you in my apartment is a good game of Scrabble. I'm not ready for another woman just yet."

"Well, I predict that you'll recover. There's a good woman out there somewhere waiting for you, a good Jewish woman. But hey, what about that fantastic job that your uncle was dangling in front of you. You gave that up too?"

"Yuh, and that was a lot easier than giving up Marie. I spent about a week going over every aspect of the poultry trucking business with him, and I was bored silly. I realized that I enjoyed poring over old French newspapers looking for the names of Jews more than I enjoyed going over reports on the health of trucks in my uncle's depots. *Yech*! But I've got to say this for him; he took it well. We parted friends."

The next few days passed uneventfully. Professor Gold sat in the back of his classroom on the first day that Jacob took over teaching his introductory course on nationalism and Zionism, and he actually complimented Jacob on his choice of material and his ability to hold the attention of the class. The rest of his time was spent in the library without access to a radio or television, and so it wasn't until he came back to his apartment on Sunday night, the 23rd – the date would remain indelibly impressed on his memory – to prepare his supper that he heard the news report out of Israel. That morning some renegade soldiers from the Jordan Legion, stationed on the outskirts of Jerusalem, had opened fire on nearby Kibbutz Ramat Rachel where a group of archaeologists were working. Several of the archaeologists were killed, one of them an as yet unidentified American, and some of the kibbutz people were wounded.

Jacob stood transfixed with a can of salmon in his hand. Ramat Rachel – wasn't that the place that Trudy said was where Elisha would be spending his final days in Israel at some dig? He dropped the can on the table and ran to his phone to call Trudy, but there was no answer. He turned on his television to see if he could get any more news, but it was already seven and the network news programs were over. He tried Trudy's phone again and let it ring a dozen times; no answer. A few minutes later he was in his car zipping over to her dorm on 59th Street. He identified himself at the desk and was allowed to go up to her room on the third floor. He knocked on the door, but there was no response. He put his ear to the door and thought that he heard faint sounds inside, and so he knocked more vigorously. Still no response. He felt certain that Trudy was inside, and so he ran down the stairs again to the desk and explained the situation to the grad student on duty who agreed to accompany him up to Trudy's room with the master key. When they opened the door, they saw Trudy huddled on her couch in a bathrobe and sobbing into a pillow. The student didn't know what to do but had to get back to his post, and so, after some reassurance from Jacob, he agreed to let him handle the situation.

Jacob closed the door behind him, went over to Trudy and gently called her name. She didn't answer but buried her head deeper into the pillow as if attempting to smother herself. When she took a breath, it was to let out a moan that tore at Jacob's heart. He reached down to touch her head, but she slapped his hand away and wouldn't even look up at him. He decided that the best thing to do would be to let her cry it out, and so he pulled up a chair and sat next to her without saying anything. An hour or more must have passed before she reached out her hand. He took it and held it, squeezing every few minutes just to let her know that he was there for her. At about nine, he said, "Trudy, I'm going to make us some tea, okay?" She nodded and he gently released her hand and went to the corner of the room where she had a miniature refrigerator, a sink and a hot plate.

He found a tin of tea bags on a shelf above the sink. As he filled the kettle and set it on the hot plate, she called his name. "Jake, Jake, please don't leave me alone. I'm afraid I'm going to be sick." He went back to her, and this time she didn't object as he stroked her head. Her weeping became softer as Jacob soothed her with murmured reassurances. When the kettle began whistling, he scooped Trudy up, carried her over the table, and sat her down. When he noticed that she was shaking and wrapping her arms around herself, he went over to her bed, removed an afghan and draped it around her. He poured tea for both of them, waited until she had taken a few sips, and then said quietly, "Trudy, tell me what happened."

It took her a few minutes of starts and pauses, punctuated by anguished sobs, for her to tell the story. She had received a call early in the morning from Elisha's parents in Bemidji, Minnesota, telling her that they had received a call from the State Department informing them of a tragic incident in Ramat Rachel and that a passport had been found on one of the bodies with the name Wesley Mortensen and with them listed as next of kin. The State Department caller asked them if that might be their son. They confirmed that he was visiting Ramat Rachel, and then they called Trudy to let her know. She told Jacob that the Mortensens had been crying through the call, and that it was difficult to understand what they were telling her. They gave her the name and phone number that the State Department man had given them, and she immediately called, certain that there must be some mistake. By the time she was connected to the agent, at about ten, he had more information, and there was no doubt that Elisha was one of five archaeologists killed by Jordanian snipers. "Five killed and sixteen wounded, he told me. He sounded so cool and professional. I guess he has to make a lot of calls like that, but I hate him." She began moaning again and then ran to the bathroom and began heaving into the toilet.

There was no way that Jacob could leave Trudy in her condition, but there was no room for him to settle into her cramped quarters. When she returned from the bathroom and finished her tea, he said, "Trudy, will you let me take you to my apartment? I don't want you to be alone tonight, and there's no room for me here."

"You go, Jake; I'll be okay."

"No, Trudy; you may be okay tomorrow or the next day, but you're not okay now. Please let me take you to my place."

She looked at him, tears still streaming down her face, and managed a smile. "No fooling around?"

"No fooling around. Promise."

He asked her what he should take along with them, and she pointed to the closet and drawers where he could find the things she needed. Twenty minutes later, he carried her into his bedroom and lay her carefully on his bed. It struck him as ironic that just a week earlier, Marie had undressed him and put him to sleep. He didn't have to undress Trudy because she was still wearing the bathrobe and pajamas that she had been wearing when the call came from the Mortensens early that morning. But he took off her slippers, pulled up the blanket around her, kissed her on the forehead and quietly slipped out to the living room. He had lost his appetite, and so he put the unopened can of salmon back in the kitchen closet, helped himself to a few crackers and water, and then tip-toed back into the bedroom to gather a pillow, blanket and a bathrobe. He took care of his personal needs in the bathroom and then made up the sofa as a bed. Three times that night, he got up and very quietly went in to check on Trudy who, to his relief, slept soundly until morning.

When Jacob woke up at seven, he peeked in again and saw that she was still asleep. He put on the coffee and, as he began preparing breakfast, Trudy came out, still wearing her bathrobe. "Smells good. That's what I need, a good strong cup of coffee."

"You feeling okay?"

"No, not really; but I've got a lot to do today. The State Department guy told me that the Mortensen's told him that I should be the one in charge of arrangements about Elisha. He'll probably try to call me at my place, so the first thing I have to do, as soon as it's nine o'clock in Washington, is to call him and let him know that I'm here at your number. Maybe he's heard something already. You know how it is in Israel. They don't let bodies lie around." As she said the word bodies, she began to cry again, and Jacob took her hand.

She shook her head and said, "I've got to get ahold of myself. Right now I feel like going into a corner and just crying for the rest of my life, but I'm not going to do that. I'm not going to indulge myself when there are things that I have to do for Elisha.... today! And look, Jake, I know that you have work to do, so after I get cleaned up and make the calls that I have to, I'll get out of your hair."

"No way! Look, Trudy, I want you to stay here for at least the next couple of days. I'll help in whatever arrangements you have to make. I just don't want you to be alone. If I went back to the library today, I'd be sitting there worrying about you. No, it'll be much better for both of us if you stay here and I stay with you. I was supposed to be Elisha's best man, so let me be his best man and help."

She smiled at him and said, "Okay, pal; you brought it on yourself. Now let me get to your bathroom to shower off yesterday. I must stink." She began to walk toward the bathroom and then turned back to Jacob and said, "I feel closer to you now than I ever did when we were in bed together."

Nine o'clock came as they were finishing their coffee and the eggs that Jacob had fried up. Trudy reached the State Department agent at the direct line that he had given her without any trouble. There was a message from Jerusalem waiting for him when he came into his office, and he was about to call her. The Israelis wanted to know what they should do with Wesley's body. They gave her two choices: they could ship the body to wherever she indicated at government expense or – and this is what they indicated would be preferable – they could bury the body in the Ramat Rachel cemetery, on a hillside overlooking Jerusalem. The kibbutz board had met a few hours after the tragedy and offered to have the victims buried with honors in their cemetery. Two of the other victims were being buried there, and the kibbutz members planned to attend the funeral along with representatives of the government and Hebrew University on Tuesday morning. Trudy listened carefully to all the details and then asked if he could give her a little time to talk it over with Wesley's family. He agreed, reminding her that it was almost Monday evening in Israel and that the decision would have to be made quickly if he were to be buried there the next morning.

Jacob was standing at her side during the call, and after she relayed all the information to him, she asked, "What do you think, best man? I want your advice before I call Elisha's parents. They're pretty old, and I don't want to burden them with possibilities. I'd like to tell them what I think is preferable and then hope that they'll agree."

They sat down at the table again and began to discuss the pros and cons of the two possibilities. But then Jacob asked, "What was the name of that town where Elisha's parents live?"

"Bemidji, Minnesota."

"I never heard of it. Do you think that there's any way that he'd have a Jewish burial there? Would he be buried as Wesley or as Elisha Yisrael in Bemidji? And what are the chances that you'd ever visit his grave in a small town in Minnesota?"

"You're right. I've always hoped to go to Israel someday. There are a lot more chances that I'd go there than to Bemidji. And in

Israel, he'd be buried as a Jew, resting near Jerusalem. Jake, that has to be it. Let me call them."

Trudy spent almost half an hour on the phone with the elder Mortensen's. There was no argument; they agreed immediately with her suggestion. The rest of the time was spent tearfully talking about Wesley/Elisha; Trudy learned more about her fiancé's early years from his parents than he had ever shared with her. And she brought them some comfort describing his reputation as an inspiring and devoted professor at Chicago.

By noon all the arrangements had been made. Within fifteen minutes after the State Department man had transmitted her reply to Jerusalem, she received a call from the chairman of the Department of Archaeology at Hebrew University. After expressing his profound sympathy, he informed her that the university, in cooperation with the government and the kibbutz, would be planning a *Sheloshim* memorial for Elisha and the other victims in Ramat Rachel toward the end of October. He told her that he would get back to her when the plans were finalized, "... but we would like very much for you and his parents to be here." He went on to explain that there was a guest house at the kibbutz, and that the kibbutz board has offered to host the families of the victims for as long as a week. Trudy thanked him and said that she would try.

She then called the Mortensens again to convey the invitation to them, but they said that they were not strong enough to undertake the long trip to Israel. They hoped, though, that she would go so that there would be someone there who loved their Wesley. By the time she hung up on the Mortensens it was already after one, and Jacob asked Trudy if she was feeling well enough to go down to the Windermere dining room for lunch. She thought about it for a minute, but decided against it. "Jake, I would feel very uncomfortable going anywhere this week. Elisha is going to be buried in about twelve hours, and I want to observe *shiva* for him. He studied for a year to become a Jew; the least I can do is to stay home for a week to think about him and ... and..." she began crying again and then continued in a manic rush, "and pray for him. So Jake, I think that you'd better take me back to my place now. I'm not going to burden you for a week with my *mishugas.* I've decided that I'm going to take this week off from my classes; maybe I'll spend it writing an article about Elisha for the *Maroon* and maybe for the *Trib* too. And when the *shiva* week is over, I'll go to his office and start putting together his papers. I worked with him on a lot of his stuff over the past year; I don't think that anyone else can do it. So I've got a lot to do. Will you drive me back to my dorm?"

It didn't take much perception to recognize that Trudy was talking compulsively, almost hysterically. He walked over to her, took her hands and said, "Trudy, you're not going anywhere. You're not yourself, and I'm not going to dump you in your room. I can take some time off. I want you to stay here. I'll talk to Rabbi Persky, and we'll arrange to have *shiva minyans* here where there's more room. Look, if I go out and get something for us to eat, will you be okay? I'll just run over to the deli on Cornell and get us a couple of sandwiches. And while I'm gone, you make us some more coffee, okay?"

She nodded, "Okay, mother. Don't worry; I'll be good."

When he returned a half hour later, she was lying on the sofa with her hands over her eyes. He bent down and smoothed her hair. "Hungry?"

"I guess so." And he led her to her chair in the kitchen.

During lunch, he asked about her family, realizing that she had always avoided talking about them. He thought that they might be of some help. At first she was evasive, but then she said, "What the hell? If I can't talk to you, who can I talk to? You asked for it, so here goes."

She described an idyllic childhood in Portland, Oregon, where her father was a professor of ancient history and Bible at Reed College. She was an only child, and her parents doted on her. Everything was wonderful until she was twelve years old, and then, as she put it, "the shit hit the fan." Two women students accused her father of having affairs with them, and he was summarily dismissed from the college. The scandal was so bad that no college would consider hiring him after that, and her mother simply upped and left both of them. She wandered around with her father through a series of jobs in the northwest, including a stint on a fishing boat out of Vancouver, until he began drinking heavily.

"But through it all, he kept insisting that I read. Every night before he would let me go to bed, he would make me discuss what I had read that day, and he would always expand on whatever it was, especially if it had anything to do with Jewish history. Then when I was sixteen, he got stinking drunk one night and was hit by a car and killed. That was in Seattle where we were living in a kosher boarding house run by a nice old woman, Mrs. Schloss, bless her. She let me stay there for the rest of the year until I graduated from high school. Luckily I did well enough in high school to get a full scholarship to Chicago. That was five years ago that my father died. He was all I had, and now Elisha's gone too. Story of my life. Sorry you asked?"

"No, not at all. I was just wondering if I could call any family for you. I guess not."

"Family? When I was a kid I heard about some relatives living in the east, but I never met any of them, and I have no idea now who or where they are. Anyway, what difference would it make? I guess when it comes to family, you're it. You asked for it."

"My honor. You called me mother before, so let me be your mother for the next week, okay?"

She managed a little laugh. "Okay, you're on. Hey Jake, did anybody ever tell you that you're a *mensch*?"

"No, but my zeyde always told me that I should *be* a *mensch*. And just last June, my father and an old man who was a childhood friend of my zeyde said the same thing to me. I wish that Marie thought that I was a *mensch*, but I doubt it. She was awfully mad when we ended it. I'm still having trouble getting over her."

"I guess in a way you're in mourning too. We'll have to support each other."

Jacob called Rabbi Persky to tell him that Trudy would be observing *shiva* for Elisha at his apartment beginning on Tuesday evening and to ask him to let Trudy's friends at Hillel know about it. He then called the secretary of the near eastern department and asked her to inform as many of Professor Mortensen's colleagues and students as she could reach about the *shiva.* That evening Trudy wanted to switch places with Jacob and sleep on the sofa, but Jacob insisted that she stay in the bedroom. She didn't have the strength to argue, but before she fell into bed, exhausted by the emotions of the day, unbeknown to Jacob, she set Jacob's bedside radio alarm for four, carefully setting the volume on low.

Jacob didn't hear the radio when it went on, but at about five, he heard the faint sounds of a voice coming from his bedroom. He tip-toed to the door and opened it wide enough to see Trudy sitting on a stool with one of his Bibles in her hands. When he came closer, he saw that she was dressed and that she had ripped her blouse from the neck down a few inches and that she was softly chanting from the book of Psalms. He didn't have to ask and realized immediately that it was about the time that Elisha was being buried half a world away. Without saying a word, he went out to the living room, found another Bible and a footstool, and sat down next to Trudy. He listened for a moment and heard her chanting the familiar words of Psalm 90. He joined in, and for the next hour they sat together, occasionally reaching for each other's hands, chanting a succession of funeral psalms.

When Trudy saw light coming through the bedroom window, she asked Jacob if he would chant the *El Malei* memorial prayer to conclude their private service. He agreed, they both stood up, and he began chanting the traditional threnody in a gentle voice. "Louder, Jake." She implored sobbing, "I want Elisha to hear it." He raised his voice a bit, and when he came to Elisha's name, Trudy crumbled at his feet. He knelt next to her on the floor and held her tightly, swaying back and forth, until she finally stopped crying. A few moments later she stood up, smoothed her skirt and said, "I feel like Jeremiah. I remember he said something like 'If my head were made of water. I would weep day and night.' That's how I feel, Jake; that's how I feel."

He stood there looking at her and asked, "Do you want to go back to sleep? You should; you're not rested."

She shook her head. "Maybe I'll sleep a little before the people come for the *minyan* tonight. I just want to spend the day thinking about Elisha. Jake, could you do me a big favor? Could you drive over to my place and bring me some more clothes? And also on my desk you'll find a pile of notebooks from courses that I took with Elisha, and in the top drawer of the desk, there's a packet of letters in a ribbon from Elisha. Could you bring that all back? I want to spend the day reading his words. And while you're gone, I'll make us a nice breakfast. Okay?"

"It's a deal. You okay?"

"Okay."

As it turned out, there was only one *shiva minyan* at Jacob's apartment because of the *Simchat Torah* holiday that began that Wednesday night. But that one *minyan* brought almost fifty people, including Rabbi Persky, Rabbi Weinberg and Professor Gold, to Jacob's apartment. Somehow they managed to squeeze into his living room, and after the service and the recitation of *Kaddish*, about twenty of those assembled shared memories of Elisha. Jacob could see from the look on Trudy's face as she heard all of the spontaneous encomia, that they brought her some comfort. He prevailed on her to go with him to the *Simchat Torah* service at Hillel on Wednesday evening so that they could say *Kaddish* again there, but they left right after the service, foregoing the revelry that usually follows a *Simchat Torah* service.

At breakfast on Thursday morning, she reminded Jacob that she and Elisha were to have been married that night. She insisted that Jacob go to the library to catch up on his work, assuring him that she would be all right. "I just want to sit here for a few hours reading more of Elisha's stuff, and then you know what I'm going to do? I'm going to clean up this place for you. You men! Do you realize what a mess it is?"

Jacob smiled guiltily, but inwardly he was gratified to hear her taking charge, almost like the Trudy of old. "Okay, I'll go, and I'll do a little shopping too, so that we'll have enough food for the next couple of days."

"Jake, I'm only going to stay here through Shabbat, and then I'm going back to my place. You've spent enough time on your sofa, and I love you for it, but I've got to get back to work too. And I've got to find someone to be my doctoral sponsor. Elisha was going to take care of that, but...." When her voice wavered, Jacob offered to stay with her a bit longer, but she insisted that he go, and so he did.

In his carrel that afternoon, he remembered the suggestion from the fellow at Hebrew University that Trudy come to the memorial ceremony at Ramat Rachel in October. He sat there wondering if there were some way that she could go. She was a fellowship student with a small stipend from the university, and she taught Hebrew at the same synagogue where he taught in order to make ends meet, but he was pretty sure that she didn't have enough put aside for an air ticket to Israel. He had a few hundred in the bank, but if she agreed to let him buy her the ticket, that would more than clean him out. He wanted her to go, and he was pretty sure that she wanted to. But how? They would have to talk it over that night. That night... the night when she was supposed to marry Elisha.

When Jacob returned to his apartment at about five carrying a couple of bags of groceries, he found Trudy sitting at his desk reading. She was happy to see him and helped him put away his purchases. Seeing that he had bought a steak filet, a crisp baguette and some fresh vegetables, she insisted on making dinner for them. "You just sit down in your nice clean living room and enjoy the lack of dust and cobwebs while I make us a nice dinner in honor of the wedding that was to be. I'm glad you bought steak. Elisha planned to take us all to Morton's for dinner after the ceremony, and we probably would have ordered steaks there. So it'll be a memorial dinner. I'll make us a nice salad too, and is it all right if we open that bottle of Valpolicella that I saw hiding in your cupboard?"

"Great, and you're looking much better. Okay, I'll sit down and read my mail, and then there's something I want to talk about over dinner."

It was as if their minds were operating on the same wave length. Before he could broach the subject of her trip to Israel, she said that she had been thinking about what the Hebrew University man had said. "I would love to go, just to see where Elisha is buried and to walk around the place where he spent his last hours. And I'd be able to talk to some of the people that he worked with, but it's impossible. Flights to Israel from Chicago are expensive, and the Israelis didn't offer air fare, just a week in the Ramat Rachel guest house. I'll have to wait until I get my degree and I'm earning some money. If I'm lucky, that'll be in about four or five years."

"Trudy, I want you to go, *now*, not in five years. If I had the money, I'd give it to you, but maybe I can work something out. I've got an idea."

While Trudy was cleaning up, Jacob put in a call to his uncle. Sol had heard about the Ramat Rachel massacre on the TV news. "It even made the Portland newspaper. It was terrible; those fucking Arabs. And now it looks like there might be a war with Egypt. They don't let us live. So what's new with you? I miss you. It's almost two weeks since you left. And Jakie, I guess you should know that Marie's pretty broken up."

"How do you know what's going on with Marie? Have you spoken to her."

"Yes, I spoke to her. Why not? I had to drive up to Bangor on business, and so I took her out to lunch. We talked, and she told me that she was very angry with you, that you misled her. Anyway, she's as beautiful as always, and I told her that she was like a member of the family and she could depend on me. And you know what?"

"What?" Jacob said apprehensively.

"Do you know that she can't drive? A smart modern young woman, and she doesn't know how to drive. So I promised her that I'd teach her."

"Uncle Sol, I'm getting an unpleasant feeling. Please, please, I'm begging you. Please don't mess around with Marie. You've got enough women. It would be wrong, very wrong. She's much too young; you're old enough to be her father."

"So what does it matter to you? You gave her up, right? Look, Jakie, if you're still interested in her, let me know. You know, you can always reconsider and come back here. The job is still open, and considering how broken up she is about you, you could probably get her back. But from what you told me before you left, I'm taking it for granted that you don't want the job and you don't want Marie. Right?"

"Look, Uncle Sol, that's not what I called about, but before I tell you why I called, I'll just ask you again, please don't start anything with Marie. It's just not right for a whole lot of reasons that you know very well."

"All right already; I hear you. So what are you calling about?"

"Weii, back to the subject of that terror attack on Ramat Rachel…." Jacob went on to explain about Mortensen and Trudy and the call from the Hebrew University."

"You knew the American archaeologist who was killed? You knew him well?"

"Yes, he was supposed to be married, actually married *tonight* to a very nice grad student of his who is a good friend of mine. He asked me to be his best man. So anyway, here's what I thought. She can't afford to fly to Israel; she has no family, and all she has is what she makes teaching Hebrew. I could arrange it so that if you gave a contribution to Hillel, say about a thousand dollars, Hillel would give her a grant to go to Israel for the memorial. The Hillel rabbi here was Mortensen's teacher, so it would all be kosher. What do you say?"

"What do I say? Kosher, shmosher; forget about any fancy arrangements. Her fellow was killed by Arabs, and she needs a ticket to Israel? I'll be happy to help her. In the mail in two or three days, you'll find a check for two thousand dollars made out to you. You cash it and do whatever you think is right for her."

"Uncle Sol, you always come through. I can't tell you how much I appreciate it. Thank you; thank you." They talked for a few more minutes, but before hanging up, Jacob said, "And Uncle Sol, you know I love you, but I'm asking you, man to man, please leave Marie alone."

"Oy, Jakele, that was *your* mistake, leaving her alone." And he hung up.

Jacob stared at the phone after he had hung up, shrugged futilely, and then ran into the kitchen to tell Trudy the good news. She was so overwhelmed that she burst into tears again, but this time it was tears of relief. "I wanted so much to go, but I didn't think it was possible. Jacob, I don't know how to thank you. I'll write a letter to your uncle telling him how much I appreciate what he's doing. I'll never forget this, as long as I live." And she gave him a salty kiss.

Later that night, when Trudy had retired to the bedroom and Jacob was making himself as comfortable as possible on the sofa, Trudy came out in her bathrobe, went over to the sofa and stood there for a moment looking down at Jacob. He could see that she had something to say, but seemed to be hesitant. "What is it, Trudy?" She stood there silently with tears running down her cheeks. "Hey, come on, Trudy. You were doing so much better, and you've got the trip to Israel to look forward to now. What's the matter?"

"Jake, this was supposed to be my wedding night. I got into bed and I felt so alone, so terribly alone. Everything was going to be wonderful for me after tonight and for the rest of my life, and now I'm alone."

He sat up and took her hands. "Jake, I don't know how to say this, but… but here it is. I don't want to sleep alone tonight, but I don't want sex. To make love to anyone else tonight except for Elisha would be like spitting on his grave. But I don't want to be alone. Could you…?" She turned red and couldn't bring herself to say the words.

"Hey, it's okay. I understand. You want your mother. You want your mother to hold you and make you feel better tonight.

Remember when you called me mother, I said that I'd be your mother this week? Well, I wasn't kidding. I think I can control myself, even though you are sort of cute. Come on, *tochterel*." He took her by the hand, and they walked into the bedroom together.

Jacob waited until she was comfortably settled on the far side of the bed, and then he crawled in beside her and took her in his arms. She nestled into him, and he began crooning a series of Yiddish lullabies that he had learned from his bobbe on those many nights when his mother left him with her parents. Trudy was weeping softly while he sang and caressed her head. By the time he reached the *lu lu lu lu lu* of *Rozhenkes mit Mandlen,* he was relieved to find that she had fallen asleep. It took him a bit longer.

Trudy moved back to her dorm room after Shabbat and began making preparations for her trip to Israel. She had to speak to the professor who would be her new sponsor about the classes that she would miss, both as a student and as a t.a., and she had to arrange for someone to cover her Hebrew classes at the synagogue. Jacob bought her airline tickets – Chicago to New York to London to Tel Aviv and return – and had enough money from Sol to make the London/Tel Aviv segment first class. The memorial service was scheduled for Wednesday, October 24, and Trudy arrived at Ramat Rachel two days earlier. She spent most of Tuesday sitting by Elisha's grave on a hillside overlooking Jerusalem. The staff of the guest house were extremely solicitous, and Trudy's near fluency in Hebrew made her instant friends.

There was a certain amount of apprehension in the air during the memorial ceremony. Trudy was seated in a place of honor among the families of the other victims. David Ben Gurion was supposed to have spoken, but tensions along the Sinai border prevented him from attending, and so he was represented by his deputy, Levi Eshkol. Yigal Yadin represented the archaeological community and paid homage to his fallen colleagues, making special mention of the "young American whose middle name was Israel and who now rests in the land whose every rock he loved." After the ceremony, there was a luncheon in the kibbutz dining hall, but after helping herself to a cup of coffee and a sweet roll, Trudy went back to the grave site and sat there weeping quietly and looking at the panorama below her. As the sun began to set, she was joined by the guest house manager who had gone out to look for her. They sat together for a while, not saying anything, and then the woman took her hand, gave her a hug, and led her back to her room.

When Trudy arrived back at O'Hare, Jacob was there waiting and greeted her with the news that war had just broken out between Israel and Egypt and that the Israeli army, in cooperation with England and France, was at that very moment sweeping toward the Suez Canal. She described the memorial to Jacob and especially the tension that pervaded the ceremony because of the looming hostilities to the south and the presence of Jordanian Legionnaires less than a mile away. Jacob was relieved to hear her speaking with her former animation, and when he dropped her at her dorm, she assured him that she was feeling fine and that she as ready to resume her normal life. "I'm so grateful that I was there, thanks to your uncle. I sat with Elisha for most of two days, said my goodbyes, and somehow I feel a lot lighter now. I guess that I'll still have some rough days when I'm reminded of him, but I've got a whole life ahead of me, and I'm not going to allow myself to become like one of those Greek or Italian widows who go around in black for the rest of their lives. Jacob, I thank God for the wonderful brief time that we had. It really hurts, it hurts bad when I think of what might have been, but I've got to get back to living."

That night he called Sol to convey Trudy's thanks and to report on her trip, but before he hung up, he asked, "Have you heard anything from Marie?"

"Heard anything? Sure, you remember I told you I was going to teach her to drive? You know, so she can drive around with Hope next summer? Well, that's what I'm doing. I'm giving her driving lessons. I drive up to Bangor on Sunday mornings, twice already, and we spend the afternoon driving around. She's real smart. She's good company, and she's doing pretty good with the driving."

"Uncle Sol, do you know what you're doing? Marie's not some farmer's widow; she's just a kid. She should be spending her Sundays with guys her age, not with a married fifty-year-old."

"Hey, *boychik,* I'm only forty-eight, and there's plenty of life left in me. And anyway, what do you care? You gave her up, and she's still pretty mad at you."

"Uncle Sol, I gave her up because I had to. I couldn't keep up my relationship with her without marrying her, and that was impossible. But I still have strong feelings for her, and I don't want her to be hurt."

"Jakie, I'm not going to hurt her. As tempting as it is when I'm with her, I haven't touched her. But she's so nice. You know what I'm going to do? When she gets her license in a couple of weeks, I'm going to buy her a little car so she can get around by herself. After the way you dropped her, she deserves a nice present."

"Uncle Sol, please, please. Please leave Marie alone."

"Nu, we'll see. You know I love you, Jakie, but Marie isn't your business anymore."

That was the way they left it, and Jacob didn't have an occasion to speak to his uncle again until the Thanksgiving recess. Some of his happiest childhood memories were of the Thanksgiving dinners that the family celebrated together, usually at the home of the elder Forshtayns in Malden, and so on the morning of the holiday, before he left for his dinner invitation at the home of Rabbi and Mrs. Weinberg, he called his father and then his Aunt Sarah to find out how the family was celebrating the holiday. Sarah was delighted to hear from him, and after they had reminisced for a few minutes, he asked to speak to Sol.

"Jakie, it's the usual with Sol. He's too busy even to spend Thanksgiving with his family. He never takes a break from that business. When I spoke to him yesterday, he said that there was some trouble at the depot in Kittery. So he's got to be down there for a few days, even on the holiday. So what can I do? My friend

Rose Levine here in Maplewood invited Hope and me to her house for the dinner. I'm bringing the turkey. So that's where we'll be."

Jacob was distressed by the sound of disappointment in his aunt's voice, and it haunted him through what was otherwise a very pleasant dinner at the Weinbergs. The Perskys were there also along with two faculty couples, and both the food and the conversation were *gemutlich*. When he got back to his apartment that evening, there was something nagging at him, and he decided to call his uncle to find out how he had celebrated the holiday, if at all. It took a few rings, but when Sol finally answered, he didn't seem eager to talk to his favorite nephew.

"I tried to call you in Malden this morning; I thought I'd find you there celebrating with the family, but Aunt Sarah said that you had some emergency in Kittery. I was surprised to hear that you had to go down to the depot on the holiday; it must have been pretty bad. What happened?"

"What happened in Kittery? Well, you know how it is; there were uh... there were problems.... too complicated to explain, but thanks for the call."

"Uncle Sol, don't hang up. It's me, your confidant. Tell me the truth. Why didn't you go home for Thanksgiving?"

There was a long silence, but then he said, "You remember I told you I might get a car for Marie when she got her license? Well, she got it last week, and I gave her a beautiful Chevy Corvette. It's a nice sporty car, a convertible. So, since she has off this weekend, I drove up to Bangor to tell her that I had the car here at the house, and she said that she wanted to come right down to see it. So I drove her down here, and she loves the car. She likes to drive fast, like me, not like you. She drove us down to Cook's in her new car, and we had Thanksgiving dinner there. Jakie, she's such a lovely girl. I don't know how you could give her up."

Jacob took a deep breath and said very slowly, "Uncle Sol, where is Marie now, right now?"

"She's somewhere around the house, maybe downstairs; I'm not sure."

"Uncle Sol, Where is she? The truth!"

For a moment there was no response, but then, "All right! All right! You want the truth? I'll tell you the truth," he yelled. "The most beautiful girl in the state of Maine is lying right next to me here in my bed. And you know what? She's laughing now, and she says that I should wish you a happy Thanksgiving."

Jacob couldn't answer. He just stood there with the receiver in his hand, mute. After a moment, he slammed down the phone, vowing never to speak to his uncle again. He kept that vow until the night in late December when his uncle called him and, through blubbering gasps and sobs, told him the sordid story that ended with the snuffing out of a precious soul. After trying to make sense out of the bits and pieces that Sol blurted through the phone, augmented by what Essie told him when she called, Jacob was able to reconstruct what had happened.

Marie drove down to Harpswell in her Corvette to spend her Christmas vacation with her besotted benefactor. The day after Christmas, in the middle of a snow storm, Sumner drove over to the house because he needed some money to pay off one of the mechanics in the depot who was his source for drugs. When he was halfway up the long driveway, he spotted the Corvette in the driveway, and he figured that his father had company, most likely female. He reasoned that if he caught his father *in flagrante*, he would have a better chance of touching him for the couple of hundred dollars that he needed. And so, instead of ringing the bell, he used his key and, finding no one on the first floor, he sneaked up the carpeted stairs and tiptoed toward his parents' room. The door was open, and he stood there for a few minutes, gaping at his father who was grunting and thrusting over a female figure. He stood there transfixed until he heard his father ecstatically gasping her name before rolling off exhausted.

Sumner stormed into the room, calling his father and Marie all the filthy names that he had picked up over the years in the depot and demanding five hundred dollars or he would tell his mother. While the two men were yelling at each other, Marie jumped out of the bed, grabbed her clothes, pulled them on in a frenzy, dashed out to her car, zipped out of the driveway, and headed north.

Sol didn't know what to do, standing in his room naked and confronted by his frothing son. Finally after long minutes of screaming at each other, he gave him the three hundred dollars that he had in his wallet and promised him two hundred more when he got to the bank the next day, all on the condition that he not tell anybody what he had seen. Sumner left triumphantly with a grin on his face, envisioning Marie jumping naked out of the bed, and muttering, "The old f…f…fuck!"

Jacob learned most of the details about Sumner from his subsequent conversation with Essie, who called him from the Institute for Life where she had just deposited her hysterical sister. But that was far from the worst. Sol concluded his account in pitiful tears. "She drove fast to get back to Bangor, I guess, and right after she drove through Camden, she skidded on some black ice. The police called me because they found the registration with my name in the wreck. They told me that the car crashed into a big tree at a high speed. I gave her that car so that she could have some fun, and it killed her. How could such a thing happen? Just five weeks I had with her, just five weeks and I loved her!" By then he was crying so uncontrollably that Jacob, his stomach churning, hung up and ran to the bathroom where he sat crouched on the floor next to the toilet. When he was feeling strong enough to stand up, the phone rang again. It was Essie.

She told him that Sumner had called Sarah when his father didn't show up at the depot the next morning with his money. He blurted out the whole story to Sarah, referring repeatedly to Marie as "that money-grubbing whore," and Sarah collapsed on the spot. Luckily, Hope was home at the time, and she called for an ambulance. They took Sarah to the Malden Hospital, and Essie flew in that same day. When Sarah regained consciousness, she arranged for a limousine to take them back to New York and the Institute.

"Jake, she's not doing well. This might not be a valid medical diagnosis, but I think that she's suffering from a broken heart, not only because of that bastard, your dear uncle, but because of Marie too. She really liked that girl. I don't know what could have driven such a beautiful young girl to screw around with that miserable lecher. I thought she had more sense. In fact, I thought that *you* had your eyes on her. She must have been desperate if she settled for Sol. I guess money talks. Who would believe it?"

Abruptly, Jacob excused himself, hung up and ran to the bathroom again. This time he heaved his guts out as Trudy had done in that same toilet two months earlier.

Sitting in his library carrel trying to work over the next few days, he couldn't get his mind off Marie. If only.... If only.... regrets and recriminations. It ate at him that she crashed, as Sol had informed him, after driving through Camden. They had enjoyed themselves so much in that neighborhood. He could picture her when he gave her his ring on the top of Mount Megunticook. She asked him if he was sure, and he had answered by calling her *Dodati.* He wanted to know more about the crash. Where, exactly, had it happened and why? He went to the reference room and found what he was looking for, the name and phone number of the Bangor newspaper. As soon as he got back to his apartment, he put in a call and asked to talk to the city editor. When he was connected, he asked whether they had printed an article about the Hudson student who was killed in an automobile crash near Camden on December 28.

"Sure; we wrote about it. It was really tragic. So what can I do for you?"

"Well, I was a good friend of hers, and I was wondering if you could send me a copy of the article."

"Sure, happy to do it. But say, if you were a friend of hers, maybe you could clear up something we were wondering about. Her family didn't claim her body for a funeral; it was like they didn't even care. So the police contacted the guy that the car was registered to. Turned out he's the owner of Fairstone Trucking. Anyway, since there was no one else, he claimed the body and I guess he buried her. You know anything about that?"

"Yes, he's my uncle. She was the companion of his daughter. She worked for him. I guess he felt responsible. Anyway, here's my address."

A complete copy of the Bangor Daily News for December 29 arrived a few days later, and Jacob found the article on page three under the caption: HUDSON COED KILLED IN CRASH. He read the article over and over again, with tears streaming down his face:

> *On Friday evening a Hudson student, Marie Beaulieu, was killed in a one-car crash on Route 1 in Lincolnville, just north of Camden. The police reported that Miss Beaulieu, aged 20, was traveling north at high speed, when she skidded on ice and crashed into an oak tree in front of an estate belonging to retired opera diva, Bidu Sayao.*
>
> *Miss Sayao witnessed the crash and told the police that she had heard a few blasts from an auto horn while in her living room and that when she looked out her window, she saw the car skid and crash into one of the big oaks that border her property.*
>
> *Authorities at Hudson College reported that Miss Beaulieu was an honor student in the junior class and that she had once been urged by the student body to compete in the Miss Maine beauty pageant but had refused. There will be a memorial to Miss Beaulieu at Hudson at a date to be announced.*

Jacob pictured Marie upset, speeding up the highway and then recognizing that she was in front of Casa Bidu. Distracted for the moment as she beeped her horn and glanced at the mansion to see if there was any reaction from within, she failed to notice the black ice and lost control. God, he thought, it's my fault. Why did I ever have to tell her about that stupid habit? Why did I give her up and let her fall into Uncle Sol's clutches? Why? Why? Why? And then he thought of Sol's other victim, Aunt Sarah, who also loved Marie, and he determined to go to New York to visit her at the Institute at his first opportunity.

Jacob found a way to get to New York three times that winter and spring. He stayed overnight each time with Essie and Rob in their Morningside Heights apartment and spent those days visiting with Sarah. She was a mere shadow of herself, barely a hundred pounds, and had difficulty focusing during their conversations, but from the way that she held his hands and kissed them every few minutes, he knew that she appreciated his visits. In April, just after Passover, he received a call from Essie informing him, through tears, that Sarah was failing fast and that if he wanted to see her again, he had better hurry back to New York. He told her that he would leave as soon as he could arrange coverage for his classes, but he received a second call the next morning as he was about to leave, letting him know that Sarah had passed away during the night.

During his flight to New York on the 'red-eye' for her funeral, he slipped out a little card from his wallet that had Sarah's name on one side and his own name, hastily written, on the other side, and he thought back to his bar mitzvah and how his aunt had salvaged the day for him. He thought back over the scores of times that he had sat with Sarah in her Malden kitchen unburdening himself about his mother, about classes, about his grandiose plans for the future and especially about his girlfriends. When his parents wouldn't pay for driving lessons, Sarah had taught him and accompanied him to the motor vehicles bureau for his test. He remembered Sarah's admonishment to him on Rosh HaShanah morning about not hurting Marie, but he *had* hurt her, and that hurt had led not only to Marie's death but also, it pained him to admit, to Sarah's.

When he arrived at the Riverside Funeral Chapel just before ten, he found Essie and Rob sitting on one side of the family room and Sol and Hope on the other. Sumner, he found out later, had been banned by Sol from attending, even if he had wanted to. Jacob sat down next to Essie, and when their rabbi came in to cut the black mourning ribbon, he asked if he might wear one also. And so the four mourners – Essie, Sol, Hope and Jacob – stood together and, as the rabbi cut their ribbons, they joined hands and tearfully recited the ritual acceptance, *Baruch dayan ha-emet. Emet,* truth, Jacob thought ruefully; that was what Marie had demanded from him, truth. And when that moment of truth had come, the result was disaster.

As the family followed the rabbi out to the chapel, Jacob asked him if he might chant the *El Malei* at the conclusion of the service. The rabbi looked doubtful, but Essie assured him that Jacob was qualified. There were only a handful of people in the chapel, some associates of Essie's, a close colleague of Rob's, and a couple of non-Jewish men whom Sol had coopted to accompany him from Fairstone Trucking. The rabbi had never met Sarah, but Essie had briefed him when he visited their apartment the previous evening, and he delivered a short but sensitive eulogy, appropriate for a woman who lived for her family and died in the prime of life. He concluded with a quotation from a poem by Bialik:

Before her time her life was ended
and the song of her life was broken.
She had so many more songs to sing,
and now those songs are lost forever,
lost forever.

The rabbi then nodded to Jacob who walked up to the podium slowly and, fighting back his tears, sang the ancient dirge like a lullaby for the lovely woman who had so often crooned lullabies to him while his mother was engaged elsewhere. When the time came in the prayer for her name to be uttered, he sang *Sarah Leah bat Arieh Leib* in a loud voice while adding silently, in his heart, *Miriam bat Adam.*

It had been agreed beforehand that Sarah would be buried next to her parents and the Forshtayns in the Malden section of the old Jewish cemetery in Everett. Sol had made those arrangements with Stanetsky's, and there was a limousine waiting for Sol, Hope and Jacob at the front door of the Riverside Chapel when the service concluded. Essie apologized to Jacob for not accompanying them to the cemetery, but she could not bear the sight of Sol for another minute, let alone for a five hour trip. Hardly a word passed between Jacob and Sol during the drive, though Hope made a few abortive attempts to initiate some communication.

They arrived at the Everett cemetery just before five, and they found Stanetsky's men waiting at the gate along with the *shammes* and five elders from *Litvishe* shul whom Sol had arranged would be there to complete the *minyan* needed for the recitation of *Kaddish.* Jacob, Sol and Hope followed the cemetery workers as they carried the coffin to the freshly dug grave, but before they could lower the coffin, Jacob took the little card with Sarah's name on one side and his on the other out of his pocket and slipped it beneath the lid. Then he watched as the coffin was eased to the bottom of the grave. When it was settled gently on the earth below them, Jacob and Sol and Jacob picked up shovels and began covering the coffin. A moment later Hope picked up a third shovel and, watching her father and her cousin, joined in the sacred task. When they had covered the coffin adequately, they stepped back and the three of them joined in the *Kaddish* with the others adding their Amens at the appropriate times.

When Stanetsky's men resumed the task of filling in the grave, the three mourners stood silently watching. When they had finished, Jacob looked at his uncle for a moment and then turned toward the gate. But before he could take a second step, Sol grabbed his hand and pulled him over to the grave diagonally across the path. There was a double stone there identifying the entombed as Yisroel and Bryna Forshtayn. They stood there for a moment in silence, and then Sol put out his arms to Jacob and cried with abject remorse, "Jakie, Jakie, please don't hate me. I'm a weak man. I did wrong, terribly wrong. I admit it here in front of my father and mother and my daughter. I admit it. Jakie, you've got to forgive me. I need you. All I have now is you and Hope. Please, Jakie, please."

Jacob looked at the double gravestone and then at his disconsolate uncle, unsure of how to react to the heart-rending plea. He stared at Sol, standing with his arms outstretched, and without moving, asked, "Uncle Sol, tell me; where did you bury Marie. I found out that you claimed her body. So where is she?"

"You ask me that now? Here? Right after I buried my Sarah?"

"Yes, I want to know, now."

"All right. I'll tell you; I guess you should know. Jakie, she was so sweet and so ... vulnerable. When I was with her, I just wanted to take care of her. I knew that she didn't love me; maybe she wanted to get back at you. I don't know. But I loved her, and so I buried her near me, in that beautiful little cemetery on Bailey Island, looking out over Casco Bay. You can walk there from the house in ten minutes."

Jacob looked at the graves of his grandparents and his heart spoke: *Zei a mensch, Yaakov.* For a moment, he didn't move, but then slowly he succumbed to Sol's embrace, reminding himself that an earlier Jacob who had submitted to the embrace of his alienated brother, Esau, and the text goes on to say, "*and they wept.*" And so it was, late on an April afternoon in the Malden cemetery.

About a week after Jacob returned to Chicago, he received a call from a certain Irving Gould, a lawyer in Malden, informing him about the details of Sarah Fairstone's estate. Jacob had not realized that his aunt had either a lawyer or an estate; he took it for granted that everything belonged to his uncle. But, as Gould explained, Sol Fairstone had, for tax purposes, put a lot of his holdings in the name of his wife. After what Gould was informed was some problem between Mrs. Fairstone and her husband back about five years earlier, her sister from New York had advised her to prepare a will, and so she had come to him. The details: she left the bulk of her estate to her two children, but she left the house on Bailey Island, along with a generous endowment for its maintenance, to her nephew, Jacob Ross.

"The house belonged to my aunt?" Jacob asked incredulously.

"Yes; Mr. Fairstone put it in her name shortly after he bought it. This is what she had me write in the will about the house: "I bequeath the Fairstone estate on Bailey Island, Maine, to my dear nephew, Jacob Ross, because he loved it and always enjoyed himself there. I trust that he will always welcome my children, Sumner and Hope, to the estate and that they will often enjoy it together."

"I can't believe it! It's legally mine? Along with some money to maintain it?"

"Yes, quite a bit of money. It certainly should be adequate."

Gould proceeded to ask Jacob a few questions to enable him to make the transfer, and Jacob, who had never had a lawyer, agreed to retain Gould as his lawyer in matters dealing with the estate.

The next Friday night Jacob met Trudy at Hillel, and he told her about the Maine estate. They hadn't seen much of each other since Trudy left Jacob's apartment, but they made it a point to sit together at the Shabbat dinners, and Jacob always stood next to Trudy when she rose for *Kaddish.* For a month after Marie's death, he joined her in the *Kaddish,* and then again, after his aunt's death. They were usually the only two mourners in the congregation of collegians, and they appreciated the empathetic amens of their younger co-worshippers. Neither of them had attended a concert or a movie since their losses, both of them finding refuge, however inadequate, in their reading, their classes and their teaching jobs. Jacob had been tempted on a few occasions back in December to ask Trudy out to dinner, but then, after Marie's death, he, like Trudy, preferred to lick his wounds in private. It was as if they had each touched a hot stove and were afraid to risk being burned again.

In mid-May, Jacob received a call from Sol informing him that the construction of the Fairstone Concert Hall at Borden was almost complete and that President Coles had asked him when he would like to have the dedication ceremony. "Jakie, to tell you the truth, I don't feel like having any celebration after these terrible months, but President Coles said that it wouldn't be right to just start using the place without some kind of a ceremony. So what do you think? And oh, by the way, I decided to change the name of the building to just the Fairstone Concert Hall instead of the Isidore and Bryna Fairstone Concert Hall, because I want to add Sarah's name. And anyway my mother and father were not really Fairstones. So what we decided was that inside the door there would be a big plaque which would explain that the hall is named after Isidore and Bryna Forshtayn and Sarah Fairstone. But Jakie, I don't want to do this without you. You have to be there with me, especially now that Sarah left you the house."

"Uncle Sol, I want you to know that I had nothing to do with that. I was completely surprised, and I want you to know that you can stay there as much as you want. I'll probably only use the house during the summer."

"Jakie, don't worry about it. I'll tell you, I was glad when I found out that she left it to you. For me the place is full of memories that haunt me now. Really, I was glad. Nobody loves the place like you do, certainly not that shmuck of a son of mine, and I'm sure that you'll always welcome Hope there. As for me, I just completed a deal on a nice place in town, on Federal Street. So don't worry about it; it's yours. But that's not what I called you about. The dedication, what should we do about it? What do you think?"

"I think that we should go ahead with it. And I'm glad that you added Aunt Sarah's name. As far as I'm concerned, any time after the first week in June would be good for me. I finally got the okay from Professor Gold, so I'll be getting my Ph.D. at the commencement, and I could use some time in Maine to unwind. It's been a rough year. The second week in June will be around Zeyde's *yahrzeit*, so that's probably a good time."

"Okay, so I'll set the date with Coles. How about the program for the ceremony? What do you think?"

"Well, it's going to be a concert hall, so maybe there should be some music. I haven't been going to any concerts since Marie and then Aunt Sarah died, but I guess that I might start listening to music again by June."

"So what kind of music? You know about those things. What do you think?"

Jacob thought for a minute, and then he chuckled. "You know what would really be great .... But no, it would be impossible?"

"Nu?"

"I was thinking that Jascha Heifetz was born in Vilna, the same as Zeyde and Bobbe. But no way are you going to get Heifetz. Wow! Wouldn't that be something? Jascha Heifetz doing a recital in Maine in honor of Zeyde and Bobbe and Aunt Sarah. *That* would impress President Coles and everybody else in the State of Maine."

"So how do I reach Heifetz?"

"Are you kidding? He would never come. He lives in Los Angeles, and he tours all over the world."

"I could try. Who should I call?"

"Well, the impresario who handles most of the great musicians is Sol Hurok. Maybe if you call his office in New York, he can tell you who might be available. You can never tell."

Jacob left it at that and thought nothing more about it until he received an engraved invitation from the office of the president of Borden inviting him to the dedication of the Fairstone Concert Hall on Monday, June 12. The ceremony, it went on to say, would feature a recital by the Budapest String Quartet. He immediately called Sol and asked him how he managed to get the Budapest.

"Jakie, you wouldn't believe it. At first I had trouble getting through to Hurok, but when I made it clear what I was willing to spend, he called me back. We had a nice talk, and it turns out that he's a Russian Jew, not a Litvak like us, but a Jew. So when I told him that I wanted Heifetz because he's from Vilna, first he told me that Heifetz is impossible, but then he told me that there was another great violinist, Alexander Schneider, and his brother

Mischa, a cellist, who were both born in Vilna, and that they're part of this wonderful quartet. You heard of them?"

"Heard of them! Uncle Sol, the Budapest String Quartet is world famous. They're the best! I'm surprised that they're available."

"Well, they weren't so available. That's why we chose June 12; it's the one day they had free between two tours. And when I told Hurok what I was willing to pay, he got them."

Jacob debated about whether he should invite Sol to his commencement ceremonies but decided against it. The pain was still there. He didn't even consider extending an invitation to his mother, and that made it possible for his father to attend along with his new wife, Tamara. This was Isaac's first visit to Chicago, but Tamara was familiar with the city from previous visits to dental conventions with her first husband. She arranged for them to stay at the Ambassador East and hosted a post-commencement dinner in honor of the new doctor in the Pump Room.

Jacob invited Trudy to join them for the festive dinner, but she said that she wasn't ready yet to participate in a *simchah.* She had put in a lot of work to catch up after returning to her studies about a month after her return from Israel, and Jacob was worried about her. She was so different from the devil-may-care Trudy of the past. It was as if the starch and sparkle had been knocked out of her, and he wanted to do something to help her recapture her old self. The invitation from Borden gave him an idea which he broached to her as they were sitting together at Shabbat dinner the week before commencement.

"Look, Trudy; I know that you're still in mourning, but it has to end sometime. You were one of the most up-beat people I've ever known, but the tragedy with Elisha and all the work you've been doing since then, well, it's like you're burying yourself. I hate to see you like this. I understand you not wanting to come to that family dinner at the Pump Room, but, well, I've got an idea. Are you willing to listen?"

"I'll listen, Jake, but I won't promise you anything."

"Okay, agreed. Here's my idea. I think you need a change of scenery. I know that you're planning to start working on your dissertation this summer, but I think that you should take a break for at least a week at the end of the semester."

He went on to explain the situation in Maine and the dedication of the memorial concert hall. "And Trudy, this wouldn't be a *simchah* like that party for me in the Pump Room. There'll be some music, but the whole ceremony is in memory of three wonderful people whom I've told you about. How about coming along with me? The house is mine now, so I can invite anyone I want. You could have your own room and private bath there, and you could spend a week just relaxing and breathing that wonderful Maine sea air. What do you say? It's over eight months since Elisha was killed. It's time to begin getting back to yourself."

"No, Jake; thanks. I really appreciate the offer, but I'm just not ready yet. Don't worry so much about me; I'll snap out of this one of these days."

"Trudy, listen to me. You remember how you felt when you got the terrible news? We spent the next few days together, and you let me take care of you. Why don't you let me take care of you now? A week in Maine would do wonders for you."

"Jake, Jake, I know that you mean well, but please don't push me. I don't think I'm ready yet. I'll tell you what. Give me a night to think it over, okay?"

The next day, Trudy called Jacob. "Jake, I've thought it over and I think maybe you were right. I'm a little worried about imposing on you and your family, but I would like to come along with you. A week in Maine sounds great. I could really use it, but... well, I'm not sure how to say this, because I don't want to sound ungrateful or prissy."

"What is it?"

She hesitated but then forced herself to say it. "Jake, we know each other very well,... uh, in every way, if you know what I'm saying. Well, I'm not ready for that yet. If I go along with you, I don't want you to get the idea that we'll be sleeping together. Are you okay with that?"

"Trudy, I told you that you'll have your own room and bath. I have my favorite room in that house, and it's on the floor above where you'll be sleeping. That's always been my room. And hey, Trudy, listen. I've gone through a loss too. Maybe it wasn't as tragic as yours; we weren't about to get married. But I loved Marie, and she was killed too, not by Arab soldiers but by a lousy piece of ice." He paused for a moment and then added what he had not said to anyone: "And that may have been my fault. So I'm not looking to jump in the sack with anyone just yet. You said you weren't ready for another emotional involvement yet; well, I sort of feel the same way, not ready."

As he said those last words, he laughed. "You know what just crossed my weird mind? I was reminded of an ancient Anglo-Saxon king who was known as Ethelred the Unready. You're Trudy the Unready and I'm Jacob the Unready. We're quite a pair. Anyway Trudy, I don't want to compare wounds. I would never say to you that I know what you're feeling, but we've both had a rough year, and we could both use some R and R."

"Okay, Jake, you've convinced me. You're on, and I'm glad we settled that. I'll be happy to go with you. When do we leave?"

He told her what she should pack and that he would pick her up on the morning of the ninth. "And bring along a real dowdy bathrobe, because if it's all right with you, we'll share a motel room somewhere in Pennsylvania the first night. The second night we'll spend with my father and his wife; she's got a big house, so you'll have a room of your own. And then the third night we'll be in *my*.... Can you believe it? *My* cottage by the sea."

They spent a pleasant night with the newly-wed Rosses in Winthrop, and Jacob invited them to stay in the house on Bailey Island for a few nights after the dedication. Tamara had prepared a lovely dinner for the four of them, during which Isaac kept asking Trudy about her doctoral work. He was impressed by her fluency in Hebrew, and when he managed to get Jacob alone for a minute, he nudged him and said, "*That's* what I call a nice Jewish girl, and a scholar too. So maybe...?"

"Dad, I'm glad you like her, but she's just a friend, a good friend who needs some healing right now." And he went on to tell his father about Elisha. "So don't get any ideas. And please don't say anything that could make her feel uncomfortable. She's coming up to Maine just to relax and unwind. And please tell Tamara; no suggestive remarks while we're together."

As they drove up the long driveway to the house on Sunday afternoon, Trudy was bug-eyed. "This fabulous house is yours?"

"I guess so. I'm not used to the idea yet. Maybe you can give me some ideas about what to do with it. But in the meantime, enjoy." He found the key in the planter next to the front door where Sol had told him he had put it. The house was in perfect order, and Jacob found a note from Sol on the foyer table informing him that he had arranged for a housekeeper to come in twice a week, that he had moved into his new house on Federal Street on Friday, and that Hope would be staying with him.

After reading the note, he laughed and said, "It's a darn good thing you came along. Otherwise I'd be rattling around in this huge place all by myself after my dad and Tamara leave. We could have invited the whole near eastern faculty to come along. Come on; let me show you around."

Trudy followed him around in awe – through the living room, the dining room, the kitchen with its restaurant stove and refrigerator, the wrap-around veranda, and then out to the massive lawn and the tennis court and down to the dock where the boat was berthed.

"My God, Jacob! Is that boat yours too? You didn't tell me about any of this. You just said that you had been left a *cottage.* I had no idea."

"That's what they call these mansions by the sea in Maine – cottages. Actually, the boat isn't mine. It doesn't come with the house. It belongs to my uncle, but it will probably stay here, and I guess we can use it."

As they walked back up to the house, Jacob said, "I want you just to relax and enjoy yourself here. You have no obligations.

We didn't open the refrigerator, but I'm pretty sure that it's well stocked with stuff for breakfast and lunch. It always was when my aunt was in charge. Anyway, what I recommend now is that you take a rest until about six. Then we'll go out to a nearby restaurant, Cook's, for supper, and then we can turn in early. The dedication begins at ten tomorrow morning, and I have to say a few words about my grandparents and my aunt. I'll have to prepare something tonight. And then there's going to be a recital by the Budapest String Quartet…."

"The Budapest String Quartet! You've got to be kidding. Here in Brunswick? The Budapest String Quartet? And is Eisenhower going to be here too? You didn't tell me any of this, Jake."

"Well, I wasn't sure how you'd feel about attending a concert yet. Neither of us has been to a concert since … well, you know since. Let's not talk about our sinces this week, okay? Anyway the concert is part of the memorial dedication. Okay? Will you attend?"

"Well, I'm certainly not going to walk out. Of course, Jake, I'll attend. I'm just a bit overwhelmed right now. All this," she swept her hand around, "and the Budapest String Quartet too. Wow and double wow!"

When they got back into the house, they carried their bags up to the second floor where Jacob said, "Choose a room, any room, or if you want you can have two. The master down at the end has a private bathroom and there are two bathrooms between the other three rooms. And that room at the other end is sort of a library-TV room. I'll be up in the attic, my old room, and I have my own bathroom up there. So you choose whichever room you want."

She went through the master bedroom and the room next to it and came out shaking her head. "Jake, the closet in that big room is as big as my dorm room, and so is the bathroom. And that bed! My God! It's like a football field! So this is how the rich live. And this is yours now? I can't believe it."

"Neither can I. I never thought I'd own a place like this, and I doubt if I'll be using it for more than a few weeks or maybe a month each year. I haven't had time to think this all out yet. Maybe if we talk about it, I'll get some ideas. Anyway, for now, let's just enjoy. So, which room?"

"Can I see yours?"

"Sure, but it's nothing like these. It was probably a maid's room before my uncle bought the place. Let's go up."

He led her up to the attic and dropped his bag on the floor of the room to the left. Trudy looked around and went through the bathroom to the second room, just a bit larger than her dorm room. "Maybe I'll stay up here; would that be okay? I'm a bit intimidated by those beautiful rooms downstairs."

"Trudy, I don't want to explain right now, but I'd rather you not sleep in that room. You'll be much more comfortable down on the second floor, and you'll have your own bathroom. And look, if you're downstairs there won't be any midnight temptations. Okay?"

She smiled. "Okay; I understand."

"Look, one other thing. You get settled. If you want, you can take a nice relaxing bath and then a nap or whatever, and there are plenty of books around. I want to go out for no more than a half hour. There's something just down the road that I want to see. Okay to leave you alone for a while?"

"Fine; I'll be okay, if I don't get lost in this place. If you can't find me when you get back, call in the bloodhounds."

Trudy chose the room next to the master bedroom, and after Jacob put her suitcase on the chest at the foot of the bed, he left the house, walked down the driveway and turned right. A few minutes later he arrived at the small Bailey Island cemetery, situated on a grassy ridge overlooking the sea. He had no idea where Marie's grave was, but he walked around among the weathered stones, some dating back to the eighteen hundreds, searching for a new gravestone. Within a few minutes, he found it. Engraved on the smooth granite was a small angel and below it on three lines, the name Marie Beaulieu, Born October 22, 1936, Died December 28, 1956. At the bottom of the stone four words were engraved, words that Sol must have recalled from his sister's words when she first met Marie, now in the past tense: "She walked in beauty." Jacob stood there for a while, his eyes moving back and forth from the image of the little angel on the stone to a sailboat scudding along no more than a quarter of a mile away. He felt a tremor passing through his body as a tear trickled down his cheek, and he simply muttered over and over again, "I'm sorry. I am so so sorry." And then, his head down, he walked slowly back to the place where she had brought him more joy than he had ever imagined.

When he got back, he didn't hear anything, so he went up to Trudy's room. The door was open and he peeked in and saw her sound asleep on her bed. She had opened the window, and a light breeze was wafting in. He couldn't help staring at her for a minute and, although he didn't want to, comparing. Marie's beauty was ethereal, almost unreal, a slim and flawless body and a delicate face framed by soft golden tresses. Trudy was the pretty girl next door. He looked at her curly brown hair, splayed on the pillow, and the outline of her pleasantly *zaftig* body beneath the afghan that she had thrown over herself, and he thought, "I don't know; I just don't know." And he went up to his room and began composing his tribute for the next day.

Over a delicious dinner of fresh broiled haddock at Cook's, Jacob described his zeyde and bobbe and his aunt to Trudy. He hadn't intended to share the information about his zeyde's early life that he had gleaned from Koppel Ganzfried a year earlier, but Trudy seemed so interested in everything that he told her about him that he told her the story of that night in Vilna after the murder of three-year-old Ephraim.

"But you described your zeyde as such a gentle man and a scholar. And somehow for one night he became a killer. God, people are so complex! So your zeyde and bobbe lived with that tragedy, the senseless killing of their baby son; they uprooted themselves and built a new life in America out of nothing; and they had enough inner strength to raise a family and to give you all the love that you told me about. I guess I could take a lesson from them."

"Look, Trudy. I'm learning that we each have to find our own ways back to normal life. They say that time heals all wounds, but how much time? I guess it's different for each of us; there's no standard timetable. Just take your time; no one is pushing you.... or me, for that matter. We'll know when we're ready. But in the meantime, I like having a good friend nearby."

"Me too." And she reached across the table and gave his hand a squeeze.

When Jacob, after dressing himself in the dark suit that he had brought along for the occasion, came downstairs at about eight the next morning, he was attracted to the kitchen by the aroma of coffee. He found Trudy in the kitchen, dressed in a grey suit, reading and sipping a cup of coffee.

"Good morning. Hey, you look like you're ready to go. I see you found the coffee. I'm glad that you're making yourself at home."

"Jake, this kitchen is fantastic! It has everything. I found the eggs and a frying pan, and there's cereal...."

"Hold it. I was going to take you out to breakfast; there's a great place in town with muffins that you wouldn't believe."

"Maybe tomorrow, but I'm feeling domestic today. So how would you like your eggs, sir?"

"I didn't know that you were such a *balaboste*."

"Jake, I have talents you can't even imagine."

"Well, I know about some of them...."

"Let's not go into that right now."

"No, no; I meant your piano playing and the way you zip through those *Times* crossword puzzles. Honest."

"Right, 'nuf said. Hey, how did you do with your memorial remarks?"

"I'm not sure. I think it will be okay. We'll see."

A half hour later, they were driving up Route 24 toward Brunswick. As they passed the Bailey Island cemetery, Jacob pointed and said, "That's where Marie is buried."

"Is that where you went yesterday when you left me in the house?"

"Yes; I just couldn't settle in without seeing where she was buried. It still hurts."

"You know, friend, we have a lot to talk about, but this morning we're going to put on happy faces, right?"

"Right, although I'm expecting to run into my mother at the dedication. I've told you all about her. That might not be pretty. She doesn't react well to seeing me with women, and then with my father there with his new wife.... I'm not so sure about happy faces."

Jacob parked his MG in front of Moulton Union, and they walked toward the building across from the college chapel. There was still scaffolding around the building, and there was a makeshift banner over the entranceway indicating that this was the Fairstone Concert Hall. Waiting for them in the foyer, among about thirty early arrivals, were Sol and Hope, and a few minutes after they walked in, Isaac and Tamara showed up. Jacob looked around, expecting and dreading an encounter with his mother, but she wasn't anywhere in sight. He walked over to his uncle to ask him about it, but he was engaged in conversation with President Coles.

Coles shook Jacob's hand and told him how happy he was to see him back at Borden. "Your uncle told me that you just received your doctorate from Chicago. Congratulations. Are you planning an academic career? If you are, I'd be happy to discuss it with you. Who knows? There may even be a place for you here at Borden."

"Well, my field is modern Jewish history, and I don't think that you have a Jewish studies department here. I think that I'd like a position at some university, but I haven't quite made up my mind. I'd certainly appreciate discussing it with you. My uncle has a lot of respect for you, and I'd value your opinion."

Coles told him to call his office for an appointment and then went on to discuss the morning's program. "We were delighted that your uncle was able to procure the services of the Budapest String Quartet for the dedication. We couldn't do any better than that. They're inside right now getting ready. I thought that I would open the ceremony by welcoming everyone here in the foyer where the dedicatory plaque is located. We'll unveil the plaque, and then we'll all go in and be seated. I'll say a few words about our future plans for the hall, and then I'll introduce the Quartet. They told me that they're planning to open with the *Adagio* movement from Barber's first string quartet; they thought that that would be an appropriate way to memorialize the three family members after whom the building was named. Then I'd like you to tell us about them, so that we can understand what prompted your uncle's munificent gift. And then the quartet will play two more compositions. It should all be over by noon, and then everybody is invited to our home for a real downeast lunch. Does that sound right to you?"

"Fine; and thank you for everything."

They shook hands again, and Coles went off to greet the board members and faculty from Bates and Colby as well as Borden who were slowly filing in.

As soon as Coles was out of ear-shot, Jacob introduced Sol to Trudy. Sol looked her over appreciatively and said, "So this is the young lady who sent me such a beautiful letter after coming back from Israel. I could tell from what you wrote that you were in a lot of pain, but you took the time to write anyway to tell me about the memorial in Ramat Rachel. I cried over that letter, and I kept it."

"And I'll never forget what you did for me." And she gave Sol a hug.

Jacob had been looking around as they spoke, but not finding the object of his search, he asked his uncle, "Where's my mother? I don't see her around anywhere. I've been dreading her reaction to my father and Tamara and to Trudy here. Where do you have her hidden?"

Sol smiled broadly and winked. "Your mother is having the time of her life right now. I knew that she'd be trouble if she was here this morning, so I didn't tell her about it. But I was afraid that she might hear, so I told her that she needed a change of scenery, and I sent her tickets and vouchers for a round-trip from New York to France on the *United States* with a week in Paris and a week in Venice. She was so excited that she'd be able to visit her poets in Pere Lachaise and San Michele that she didn't ask any questions. Anyway, she left last week, and she won't be back home for about three weeks. Okay? You happy? I know that Isaac is."

"Uncle Sol, you're amazing! I was really worried that she'd find some way to ruin this morning. Trudy, you can relax now. We can all relax now."

"Nu, it's time we should go in. There's quite a crowd, but President Coles has reserved seats for us up front."

The quartet played the passionately emotive Barber *Adagio* with their usual brilliance, and it set the mood for Jacob's tribute to three people whom he loved deeply. He walked up onto the stage and began by thanking the members of the quartet individually for their participation, and then he went on to explain the appropriateness of this particular ensemble for the people to whom the concert hall has dedicated. He explained that Isidore Yisroel Forshtayn and his wife Bryna were born in Vilna, Lithuania, and that two members of the quartet, Alexander and Mischa Shneider, were also born in Vilna shortly after the departure of Isidore and Bryna for America. He went on to say that, while they had never met physically, they were meeting now through their love of music. "My grandfather Yisroel taught me the chants and the cantillations and the Sabbath hymns that add such richness to the observance of Judaism. And my grandmother Bryna enriched my childhood with the Yiddish lullabies that she had, no doubt, learned from her mother back in Vilna, possibly those same lullabies that the Schneider brothers first heard in that storied city in Lithuania." As he said those last words, he looked at the violinist and the cellist, and they nodded their assent.

Jacob continued: "I don't want this dedication to become maudlin, but I must say a few words also about my aunt-mother, Sarah Fairstone, the recently departed wife of our benefactor, Sol Fairstone. She was the *eshet hayil*—the woman of valor – who was celebrated so beautifully by the author of *Proverbs.* She saw well to the needs of her husband and children, and her words were full of wisdom and kindness. Her children, myself included, rise up and call her blessed, her husband also, and he praises her.

"But I want to return for just a moment to my grandfather, whom I called Zeyde, because he was the solid rock from which our family was hewn. It is because of his strength, his wisdom, his kindness, and the example of his life that we will enjoy this concert hall for generations to come. Among other things, he was a student of the Talmud, that ancient repository of Jewish law and lore. I can find no better way to describe him than with words spoken by the Talmudic sage Abbaye in fourth century Babylonia. He taught us: *Let the love of God permeate your acts. If a person studies well and encourages others to do so, if one is decent and trustworthy in business, what will people say? 'Have you observed the actions of this man who lives by the Torah? How beautiful! What a fine person!'* Such was the legacy of Yisroel Forshtayn whose spirit, along with the spirits of his wife, Bryna, and his daughter-in-law Sarah, will always permeate this Fairstone Concert Hall."

When Jacob finished, he went down to his seat accompanied by the appreciative applause of the audience. Sol got up and hugged his nephew and, as he took his seat, Trudy reached over and took his hand. As soon as there was silence again in the hall, Alexander Schneider got up to announce the remainder of the program. He apologized for the fact that there was no printed program but explained that the quartet was between tours and had not had time to inform the college office of their choices for the day. "We are going to conclude with the great Beethoven Quartet #13 in B flat major, opus 130, but first, in keeping with the memorial aspect of this day, we will play Franz Schubert's Quartet, number 14, in D minor, *Death and the Maiden.*" The audience applauded the choices, Schneider returned to his place, and the music began.

Jacob maintained his composure through the *Allegro* movement of the Schubert, but as soon as the quartet began the exquisitely poignant *Andante,* his emotions took control. He sat there weeping silently and was grateful when his co-mourners, Sol to his left and Trudy to his right, both of them weeping along with him, took his hands and held them through the final chord. His father, sitting directly behind him with Tamara and Hope, leaned forward and lightly squeezed his shoulder. Unbeknownst to the quartet or to the audience, Elisha and Marie were joined during the *Andante* with Yisroel, Bryna and Sarah by the profundity of Schubert's genius.

The audience gave the Budapest players a standing ovation after a brilliant performance of the Beethoven, and about two dozen specially invited guests joined the quartet and the Fairstone family at the president's house for lunch. Jacob made it a point to thank each of the members of the quartet, but he was especially eager to talk to the Schneiders about any memories that they might have about their childhoods in Vilna. Jacob told them that he hoped to travel to Vilna someday so that he might visit the grave of his ancestor, the *Gaon,* and, if it could be found, the grave of his baby uncle, Ephraim. They did not encourage him. They had been back for a concert two years before, and they said that every vestige of Jewish life in Vilna had been erased by the Nazis with the enthusiastic collaboration of the Lithuanians. "And whatever was left, the Russians destroyed." They both had fond memories of the richness of Jewish life in Vilna during their early teen years, and it seemed likely from what they told Jacob, that they had attended the same Jewish gymnasium as Reb Yisroel.

Lunch consisted, as President Coles had indicated before the dedication, of downeast specialties: New England clam chowder, steamed mussels, lobster salad and berry pie. Trudy, Isaac and Tamara found very little that they could eat, but they said nothing and made do with pie and coffee. Jacob decided that he too would also forego the downeast fare, if for no other reason than the lack of sensitivity that had inspired the menu. And it was then and there also that he decided that he would not be calling President Coles and that he still had a lot of thinking to do about what he might do with his Ph.D. He gathered up his trio of house guests, Trudy, his father and Tamara, and said, "Let's get away from all of this high *treif*, food and people. We can have a nice lunch at Bascomb's in town." They all thanked President Coles for making the day so meaningful for them and then walked out to the campus, giggling like naughty children.

Isaac and Tamara got to know Trudy even better over lunch, and Jacob could see from their animated conversation that they liked her. Their feelings were confirmed when Trudy asked Jacob to stop at a fish market where she might be able to buy some fresh salmon for their dinner that evening. Jacob demurred; "I thought that I'd take you all out tonight to a nice restaurant in Bath. Dad, it's your first night here with Tamara. Let's make it an occasion."

Tamara, though, intervened. "Jacob, this lovely young lady wants to make us a nice salmon dinner. I can't think of anything that Isaac and I would like more. So take us to a market, like she said, and I'll go in with her and buy some vegetables for a salad and maybe a little pasta. When we get back, you men can sit out in the sun, and we'll make a dinner fit for our two kings."

"What can I say? You win. Dad, you found a gem."

"And so did you, I think."

"Dad, don't jump to any conclusions. Trudy and I are just friends."

"All right, all right. I'll keep my big mouth shut." And they all laughed.

When they got back home, Jacob set the elder couple's bags down in the master bedroom and proceeded to show them around the rest of the house. Isaac had stayed there a couple of times with Rowena several years earlier, but it was all new to Tamara. As Jacob was about to leave them to freshen up in what had been Sol and Sarah's capacious room, Isaac said, "Look, Jake, we appreciate your giving up your room for us, but there are plenty of other rooms. We don't want to kick you and Trudy out of your room. We'll be perfectly comfortable in one of the smaller rooms."

"Dad, I told you before. Trudy and I are just good friends; that's all. You know that she suffered a terrible loss last October. She's not over it yet, and I still haven't quite recovered from Marie's death. You saw the effect that that Schubert piece had on both of us. We came up here to decompress and not for anything else. I'm sleeping in my old room, up in the attic, and Trudy's sleeping in the room next to yours. Understood?"

"Yes, of course, all right. I just thought.... Well, she seems like such a nice girl. You know, *chenefdik*, a lovely Jewish girl,... and so intelligent...."

"Dad!"

"All right, all right. Not my business. I hope the week up here in *gan eden* will do you both a lot of good."

Later that afternoon, while the ladies were puttering around the largest kitchen that either of them had ever seen and getting ready to prepare dinner, Jacob took his father out on the boat. Isaac, who was used to renting ten-foot dories from the concessionaire on Winthrop beach and rowing out a half-mile or so beyond the breakwater for an afternoon of bottom fishing, was thrilled with Sol's yacht. As they were cruising out toward Halfway Rock at about twenty knots, Isaac asked about the horsepower. "This boat has something like an automobile engine, more than 300 horsepower."

"You remember, Jakie, when you were a little boy and I used to take you out fishing? No horsepower, just one manpower, but we caught a lot of flounder and cod, enough for us and some of the neighbors on Neptune Avenue. Ay, the good old days. I would row, and we'd sing songs from the shul. And," he laughed, "you didn't want to touch the bloodworms."

"I remember. You were very gentle with me. You baited my hooks for me at least half a dozen times before I got the courage to pick up one of those squirmy things myself. And I remember when I caught my first flounder. I was so thrilled, I almost upset the boat. And you said, 'You hooked a fish, but the fish hooked you.' I didn't know what you meant back then, but you were right. When I caught that first fish, I was hooked by the fishing fever. There's still nothing that I enjoy more than cruising out here and fishing. Except now I usually troll for blues and stripers. There are no more flounder out here; I guess it's the pollution."

"So tell me, Jakie, now that we're alone. What are you thinking? What are you going to do with your Ph.D.? Teaching? Some university?"

"Dad, I'm really not sure. I was surprised when Dr. Gold offered to keep me on as his teaching assistant at Chicago; I didn't think that I had impressed him over these past few years, but he said that if I stayed with him for a couple of years and did some post-doc work, he'd make sure that I found a good position somewhere. But…. well, I'm not sure that that's what I want to do with my life. That was always my ambition, to be a professor somewhere. But now that I have my Ph.D., I'm not so sure."

"You don't mean you're reconsidering Sol's offer, to take over Fairstone Trucking some day!"

"No, no! Never! I'm very grateful to Uncle Sol for a lot of things, but there's no way I could work with him, not for a million dollars. I'm afraid that if I *worked* with him, I would *become* him. No thanks. That's not the kind of life that I think Zeyde would be proud of."

"Speaking of your zeyde, you did a very nice job this morning. You described him perfectly. So where did you find that quotation from Abbaye?"

"Well, I've been studying Talmud a couple of mornings a week with Rabbi Persky at Hillel, along with a couple of other grad students. I really enjoy it. We were studying Tractate *Yoma* this past month; it's there toward the end. And I've also been meeting with this other rabbi, a wonderful man. His name is Weinberg and his temple isn't far from the university. A lot of the Chicago faculty belong to his temple, even some of the outspoken atheists, because they admire him. He's a real social action man; he tells it like it is. I like him a lot."

"So are you saying what I think you're saying? You're thinking of becoming a rabbi?"

"Dad, I'm just not sure yet. I made two big decisions last September, right after Yom Kippur, and one of them led to a tragedy. It was probably the right decision for me, but it destroyed a very lovely person. I've got to be sure."

"Jakie, take it from me; you can never be one hundred percent sure. You're a man now, so I can talk to you like a man. I made a big mistake when I married your mother. I should have known better. She was a good looking woman; she had wonderful parents; she was super intelligent; but she was *meshugah* even back then. I needed a wife; she needed a husband; and so we got married. Big mistake, *but!* … The but is *you.* If we had not gotten married, there would be no Jacob Ross, Ph.D., a fine young man with a good head. So even from a mistake can come good. Who can ever be certain? You're young, Jakie. You've got time to correct your mistakes. It took me too long."

Jacob didn't respond for a while, threading his way through the bobbing lobster buoys and heading eastward toward Seguin. But then he said, "Dad, you know, I really love you and I appreciate what you said. I'm happy that you're staying with us for a few days. I think that Trudy and Tamara like each other. Hey, I've never been on a double date with my father. I like it."

They got back to the house as the sun was beginning to set and found the ladies engaged in conversation on the veranda. As they walked up the steps, Tamara said, "We've got just what you need, a pitcher of iced tea. So where are the fish?"

Isaac replied, "You know what I discovered out there on Sol's ship with Jakie? You can go out on a boat just for fun, without fishing. Can you believe it? I never did that before. You don't need to fish on a boat; you can just enjoy cruising around with someone you love, like I love my Jakie. We had a good talk, and now we'll have an even better talk with two beautiful ladies."

Tamara laughed and responded, "You sailors always know what to say to innocent young maidens. *Two* beautiful ladies, I'm not sure, but *that* beautiful lady over there prepared a lovely dinner for us. Wait 'til you see."

"She's kidding; I only helped. Mr. Ross, you married a real *balaboste*; I'll take lessons from her anytime."

"*She* take lessons from *me*?" Tamara laughed. "I'll make you a deal, Trudy. You cut me in for a piece of that Ph.D. that you'll be getting, and I'll cut you in for a piece of my *balaboste* degree. So I'll be a p-h, and you'll be a b-a-laboste. How's that?"

They sat laughing as the sun gently set over Merriconeag Sound, and Jacob, sitting with his iced tea next to Trudy and across from his father and Tamara, felt a weight lifting from his shoulders. He was about to say something, but he stopped for fear of bawling, as a still small voice within prompted, "I love these people; I truly love these people."

Sol called on Wednesday to invite the foursome to join him and Hope and a friend of hers for dinner at his new home. "I called Ingrid's in Bath, and she's sending over a couple with all the food, fresh sole almandine and all of the trimmings. They'll prepare it, serve it and clean up. So what do you say? I want to show off my new home, and I want to toast your new Ph.D. We finally have a doctor in the family!"

The evening turned out to be a very pleasant affair. Sol had bought a *mezuzah* in Portland so that it could be put up in his new home by his brother-in-law and his nephew. They began the evening with a brief ceremony in the foyer, with Jacob affixing the Israeli cylinder to the front doorpost as Isaac led the group in the *berachah.* Hope introduced her friend, Nat, who had just completed his junior year at Borden, and Jacob was pleased to see that he was familiar with the *mezuzah* ritual.

During dinner Hope reminded Jacob that she had met Nat when she and Marie visited the Arctic Museum at Borden the previous summer. During the school year, whenever Nat, whom she referred to as her boyfriend, passed through Boston on his way to visit his family in Connecticut, he would stop by Simmons to see Hope. He had a summer job again at the museum, and Hope was planning to spend the summer with her father so that she and Nat could see a lot more of each other. Jacob was particularly pleased to learn about this new relationship, because he was afraid that there might have been some awkwardness between him and Hope now that Marie was gone. Having a boyfriend on hand gave Hope a confidence that she had never had before, and, as a result, she assumed the role of Sol's hostess with grace and was particularly solicitous to Trudy whose story she had heard from her father.

When the fish was served, Sol uncorked a couple of bottles of chilled Sancerre and offered a toast. "To my favorite nephew Jakie who is now a full-fledged Phudnik. He could have been a rich man if he decided to stay up here with me, but nu, what can you do? Anyway, this I can promise him: he'll never be poor, even if he does become a professor. Jakie, do you remember what Aunt Sarah and I gave you for your Harvard graduation?"

"Of course; that great MG that I'm still driving. I love it."

"Well, Jakie, you know what goes with a car? A boat! In honor of your doctorate, you are now the proud owner of that boat that I know you love. I love it too, but I know that my Sarah would want you to have it. So this is a gift from Aunt Sarah and me."

Issac and Tamara applauded, and Jacob was for the moment at a loss for words. He simply got up from his place at the table and gave his uncle a hug. Then he said, "I know how much you love that boat from all those times when you took me out fishing. Look, I'm probably not going to spend more than a few weeks each summer here, depending on where I end up, and so want you to know that you can use it whenever you want. You too, Hope. I guess that Sumner is out of the picture, but let's consider it the family house and the family boat."

"Spoken like a *mensch*. And oh, another thing; you know what they say about boats, Jakie. A boat is a hole in the water that you have to keep filling with money. So I made an arrangement with the boatyard at Reed Cove on Orrs Island. They'll store the boat over the winter, and anything you need for the boat, just go in and ask. I have an open account there. So now, *l'chayim!*"

They all responded *l'chayim* and clinked glasses. The Sancerre proved to be a delicious complement both to the sole and the boat, and Jacob couldn't help but think back to the day that he had become a man on the boat that was now his. When dinner was over and the four guests were leaving to head back to Bailey Island, Sol drew Jacob aside and said in a low voice, "I think I remember that you once took Marie out on the boat. She had a good time?"

"Yes, she loved it. It was her first time out on Casco Bay. Why do you ask?"

"I don't know. I'm just trying to remember the happy times that she had with us. Maybe if I can remember how happy she was with us, I'll feel less guilty." His voice quivered as he reached for Jacob's hand. "I can't forget her…never…. Nu, Goodnight."

When the foursome got home, Jacob tried to convince his father and Tamara to stay for a few more days, but Isaac insisted that he had to get back for Shabbat. "This is the last Shabbat of the season for the junior congregation, my kids. Next week, they mostly go off to camp or to the Cape with their families. I've got to be there. Anyway, it'll be good. You and Trudy will have the house all to yourselves, and you won't have to worry about entertaining the old folks."

"Dad, I want you to know that you and Tamara are welcome here any time, even if I'm not here. I said that the boat is the family boat, and this is now the family house. Just give me a call in Chicago, and I'll tell you where the keys are. I'll probably be coming back here myself after I take Trudy back to Chicago to clear up a few things. It would be great if we could spend some more time together. We haven't gone fishing yet, and there are plenty of them out there. Okay?"

"Thanks. I'll talk it over with Tamara. Maybe; we'll see."

When the elder Rosses and Jacob came down the next morning, they found the dining room table already set, a glass of orange juice at each place and coffee on the sideboard. Trudy was wearing an apron and a chef's toque that she had somehow found in a pantry closet, and she stood in the kitchen doorway with a spatula in her hand. "I'm taking orders for eggs or waffles. It may not be Ingrid's, but it's good enough for us peasants. So name your poison."

Tamara, of course, announced that it was the most delicious breakfast she had ever had, and, after Trudy insisted that she could handle the dishes by herself, they all kissed and said their goodbyes. Jacob and Trudy stood at the front door waving as his father and step-mother rolled slowly down the long driveway and out onto Route 24. As soon as they were out of sight, Trudy and Jacob walked into the empty house and headed for the kitchen to clean up from breakfast. But as they were picking up dishes from the dining room table, Trudy stopped, stood still for a moment, and then looked at Jacob with tears running down her face and said, "You are so darned lucky, Jake; I hope you realize it."

"I know I am, but what suddenly brought that on?"

"Jake, you've got a family, and they all love you. You had those grandparents whom you talked about and your Aunt Sarah, and you've got your father and Tamara and your Uncle Sol and Hope. Forget about this great house and the boat; they're not important. But you have what I never had, a family. I guess that's what Elisha meant to me. I was finally going to have a family of my own in place of a mother who abandoned me and a father who loved me but died a penniless drunk. If I sound jealous, well, maybe it's because I am. Oh Jake, I don't think that this is what you want to hear this morning, me kvetching, but sometimes I just can't help it. Last September I was so happy, so very very happy. I was going to marry a man who loved me, who was even willing to convert for me. We were going to start a family; we had even agreed on three children. I don't know if it was Elisha whom I loved so much or the idea of having a prominent husband and a family and love and security, finally. And it's all gone, all gone." And she stood leaning against the sideboard, her hands full of dishes, crying.

Jacob carefully set down the dishes that he was carrying and went over to Trudy and took the dishes from her hands. He then took her in his arms as he had on the day that they heard the terrible news about Elisha, and he whispered in her ear, "Shh, shh, Trudele, maybe you want me to be your mother again? I could sing you some lullabies." And they both began laughing, crying and laughing, as they remembered that night in the Windermere not so long ago.

"Okay, I've had my cry. You too. I'm sorry. It's just that something comes over me once in a while. I'll be all right. I guess that these beautiful days with your family just got to me. I'll be okay."

"If you're really okay, I'd like to drive you around and show you some of my favorite places, but if you prefer, we can stay home and read or play Scrabble or play tennis or whatever you'd like."

"What I'd really like, I'm not ready for yet. So okay, let's get out of here and do some sightseeing after I clean up my face and we do the dishes."

An hour later they were driving up Route 1 in the MG with the top down. Jacob tried to think of some place where he had not been with Marie, but it was precisely those places that he wanted to show Trudy – Wiscasset, Boothbay Harbor, Ocean Point, Pemaquid Point, and in each place, even while holding Trudy's hand, he thought of Marie. He tried to obliterate his images of Marie staring in innocent wonder at the wild sea pounding on the rocks by imagining her in bed with Sol, but it didn't help. More than once, Trudy asked him why he occasionally seemed so distracted, but he just shrugged and answered that it was nothing.

On the way home, they stopped for supper at a nondescript diner near the Bath Iron Works, and they returned to Bailey Island, tired and windblown, at about nine. Trudy thanked Jacob for a lovely day; they wished each other a good night; and they both went to lonely beds where they could only dream of the lovers who had been on their minds all through the day.

When they woke up on Friday morning, Jacob suggested that they go to Bascomb's for breakfast, promising Trudy the most delicious muffins she had ever eaten. She agreed to go on condition that they stop at a grocery store afterwards where she could buy a fresh chicken for Shabbat dinner. She had found two challahs in the freezer, a jar of Rokeach *gefilte* fish, and a half-full bottle of Manishewitz wine, and she wanted them to have as much of a Shabbat as they could have alone on Bailey Island. Jacob agreed and suggested over breakfast that they plan to go to Portland the next morning where they could go to shul and say *Kaddish.*

"I was hoping that you would say that, Jake. I didn't want this to be the first Shabbat that I didn't say *Kaddish* for Elisha, but I didn't want to make you go. Will that be the shul where you were cantor on the high holy days?"

"Yes, and you're certainly not making me go. It won't be like at Hillel or Rabbi Weinberg's temple, but it's a nice little shul, and the rabbi's a decent guy. We'll say *Kaddish* together like in Chicago."

"You know, Mr. Ross, I could learn to love you."

"Back at you, Miss Friedland."

The next morning, they arrived at the Portland shul just as Rabbi Himmel came out onto the *bimah.* As soon as he spotted Jacob, he walked down and greeted him. Jacob introduced Trudy, and Himmel asked Jacob if he would be willing to chant the *haftarah.* Jacob thought for a moment and then said, "I'll make you a deal. You call Trudy here up for the *aliyah* blessings, and I'll chant the *haftarah.*"

"No problem. We've been offering *aliyahs* to women for two years already. You know the *haftarah* blessings, young lady?"

Jacob answered for her. "She's been teaching bar mitzvahs for your friend, Rabbi Weinberg, for a few years already, and she's on her way to a Ph.D. in near eastern studies. I think she can handle it."

"Wonderful! Beauty and brains! Where do you find them?"

"They grow like weeds in Chicago;" eliciting a sharp poke from Trudy, as the three of them laughed.

About an hour later, Rabbi Himmel called up Trudy for the final *aliyah,* and Jacob accompanied her for the chanting of the week's *haftarah* from the book of Joshua, the story of Rahab and the two Israelite spies sent by Joshua to Jericho. After Trudy chanted the introductory blessing, Jacob took over and chanted the *haftarah,* during which he couldn't resist the urge to place special emphasis on the word that the text uses to describe Rahab's profession: *zonah,* prostitute. When he finished, Trudy chanted the concluding blessings, and when they got back to their seats in the congregation, she gave him another poke and whispered, "You have a filthy mind, Jacob Ross. I heard the way you trilled that word *zonah.* Who were you thinking about?"

He whispered back, "You may not believe me, but I was actually thinking of my zeyde who first taught me the book of Joshua. I was around eleven or twelve, and he didn't want to teach me the real meaning of that word, and so he translated it as innkeeper, which is actually a possibility but not likely. I always wondered whether when those two spies got back to the Israelite camp, they told Joshua how they had spent their first night away."

"We'd better stop whispering. Later I'll tell you what I thought of while you were chanting."

When the two of them stood up at the conclusion of the service to join three other mourners in the recitation of *Kaddish,* Rabbi Himmel was surprised and concerned. He caught up to them as they were leaving and asked who they were saying *Kaddish* for. Before Jacob could answer, Trudy said that it was for her father. "He died about ten months ago."

"So sorry to hear it. Please accept my sympathy. And you, Jacob? Was it for your grandfather? If I remember correctly, his *yahrzeit* is around now. I think we sent a reminder to your uncle, but he didn't show up. Maybe he's away. He's always so busy."

"Yes, it was for my zeyde, and I think that Uncle Sol must be away on business."

They shook hands and left. As soon as they got into the car, Jacob looked at her. "Your father? But didn't he die....?"

"My father died about eight years ago, and this isn't his *yahrzeit.* I just didn't want to start explaining again about Elisha. Enough already; I've gotten enough sympathy. No reason to ruin someone else's Shabbat. And you, Jake? Your uncle is away? So we're a couple of liars."

They stopped for lunch on the way home at a seaside marina in Yarmouth, and Jacob asked her what it was that she was thinking about while he was chanting the story about Rahab and the spies. "Actually, I was thinking about *you.*"

"About me? What made you think about me?"

"Well, you know I have a weird mind. When you were chanting that part about how she took the two spies up to the roof and hid them there overnight, I was thinking of you sleeping up in your attic room. She probably had some lovely rooms for entertaining, like in your house, but they slept up on the roof like you. I know. I'm weird, but that's what I was thinking."

"Maybe one of these days I'll be ready to come down."

"And maybe one of these days I'll be ready to come up." She laughed; "Like you said, Trudy the Unready and Jacob the Unready."

"You know the Hebrew saying, *Gam zeh yaavor* – this too shall pass? Someday."

"Someday."

As they were driving down Route 24 toward home, Jacob slowed down for the Cribstone Bridge onto Bailey Island. He was doing about 25 miles an hour as they approached the old cemetery, and he slowed down even more for the left turn that they would soon be making into the estate. But as they passed the cemetery, Jacob spotted a car pulled onto the left shoulder, a large black Cadillac. For a moment he didn't know what to do, but then he pulled over about twenty yards ahead of the Cadillac and cut the engine. Trudy asked him why he was stopping, and he explained that it was Sol's car that they had just passed.

"Isn't this where you told me that Marie was buried?"

"Yes; you stay here. I've got to get out and see what he's doing. I thought that we might see him at shul for my zeyde's *yahrzeit*, but he's here."

Jacob got out of the car, taking care not to slam the door, and walked back to the entrance gate of the cemetery. He walked toward Marie's grave and was puzzled at first, because he could not see his uncle. A moment later he realized why. Sol was on his knees at the side of the grave, rocking back and forth, sort of *shokeling*, swaying as his father used to do when praying in the synagogue. He was completely wrapped up in what he was doing and was oblivious of Jacob approaching him from the rear. As Jacob drew nearer, he heard snatches of what Sol was repeating – "thy will be done…. our trespasses…. forgive… forgive our trespasses …." He was pleading, repeating the words over and over again like a mantra. Jacob watched as he saw Sol run his hands over the mound of earth covering the grave, as if caressing a body. "Thy will be done…. forgive us our trespasses…. forgive us….," over and over again. After watching for a few minutes, Jacob backed away slowly, out of Sol's sight, and climbed over the low fence by the road. When he got back to the car, he just sat there in shock, saying nothing. Trudy decided not to intrude on whatever was going on in his mind, and a few minutes later, he started up the car and drove the short distance to his driveway.

As they pulled the car up to the front door, Jacob looked at Trudy and said, "You know what I'd like to do? I'd like to go out in the boat for a while. I need some fresh salt air. Is that all right with you? We can talk about what I saw in the cemetery later."

"Sure, I've got plenty here to read. You go ahead. But are you okay?"

"Yes, I think so." He turned away to go up to his room and change his clothes, but when he reached the stairs, he turned back to Trudy and asked, "Would you like to come along? I'd really like you to. Please?"

"I'd love to, but I didn't ask because I thought you wanted to be alone. Sure; I'll come along. Just give me a few minutes to change."

Twenty minutes later, he handed her into the boat, showed her how to cast off, and started up the engine. They didn't try to speak over the roar of the engine until they were in sight of Seguin Light, and then Jacob cut the engine and allowed the boat to drift.

"Jacob, it's beautiful out here. I'm so glad you took me along. But something's troubling you. Can you tell me?"

He thought for a while, and then he described the scene at Marie's grave. "He was repeating snatches of the Christian 'Lord's Prayer,' and he was actually caressing the earth on Marie's grave as if it was her, alive. It was grotesque. Think about it. This is the week of his father's *yahrzeit*; he could have gone to a shul to say *Kaddish,* but he went instead to Marie's grave and recited a Christian prayer, or the bits that he knew of it, especially the 'forgive us our trespasses' part, and it was as if he was trying to feel her. That's probably why he was trying to recite a Christian prayer. God, I wish I hadn't seen that."

Trudy didn't say anything for a few minutes as a light breeze carried them toward Cape Small, and then she spoke very softly, "Maybe it wasn't so grotesque. It may be hard for you to believe, because of what you've told me about your uncle's history of lechery, but maybe he truly loved Marie...."

"I don't believe that. He's had so many women; why did he need Marie? Another notch in his belt without considering what it might do to Aunt Sarah? I can't accept that."

"Jake, don't forget, even during all that time that you were in love with her, *he* was in the house with you. Don't forget that it was *he* who hired her as Hope's companion, and you told me that he probably chose her because she was so beautiful. I'm only guessing now, but maybe he controlled himself while you were with Marie, because he hoped that she would entice you to stay up here and join him in the business. When you broke it off with Marie after Yom Kippur and then told him that you were not going to accept his job, well, he was probably pretty disappointed, but..."

He finished her sentence. "But that cleared the way for him to go after Marie whom he wanted all along. I guess you could be right. I've been feeling terribly guilty about Marie's death, but was there anything that I could have done to avoid what happened? I would never have believed that she could allow him to make love to her. How…?"

"She must have been very angry at you and wanted to hurt you. I think that was probably her reason. Who knows what a person who's in love might do when that love is snatched away; who knows?" she asked wistfully, gazing out to the horizon.

"Now you're thinking of Elisha, right?"

"Yes. You know, when you told me how your uncle was feeling the mound of earth over the grave, it reminded of how I felt when I was in Ramat Rachel sitting next to Elisha's grave for two days. This might sound crazy to you, but I actually wanted to crawl into that mound to be with him. I actually had that feeling."

They sat next to each other in the two seats at the helm, not saying a word, each wrapped in private thought and letting the wind and the current carry them where it might. And then suddenly, Trudy perked up and said, "Jake, how deep do you think it is here?"

"You're not thinking of …."

"No, no; I'm not crazy, but I had a thought. How deep is it?"

"I don't know what you have in mind, but I'll check the chart."

He went down into the cabin, brought out a chart of the waters from Cape Elizabeth to Sheepscot Bay, and unrolled it for Trudy to see. She looked at it and asked, "You can read this thing?"

"That's something else that I owe my uncle. He taught me to read nautical charts when I was a teenager. Anyway, here's where we are, about half way between Seguin Island and Fuller Rock. The water here is somewhere between seventy and eighty feet deep, okay?"

"Is there any really deep water nearby?"

"I wish you would tell me what's on your mind, but let me look." He scanned the chart for a minute and then looked up and said, "Well, I don't think that we want to go way out where it's over two hundred feet, but the water around Lumbo Ledge to the west and the New Meadows River is mostly about one hundred and forty feet deep. Is that deep enough for whatever you have on your mind?"

"Yes, take us there and I'll explain."

"Ay, ay;" he saluted and pushed the throttle forward. About fifteen minutes later, he yelled over the noise of the engine, "We should be in about a hundred and forty feet here. Okay?"

"Fine; now cut the engine and I'll tell you what I've been thinking." He complied and looked at her quizzically. "You know how on Rosh HaShanah afternoon we go through that symbolic ritual of casting our sins into the sea? And there's a verse that we recite when we're doing it?"

"Yes, it's from Micah."

"Do you remember the words?"

"Sure; I used to go to Winthrop Beach with my father, and we'd stand there looking out toward Graves Light and we'd say, *"Cast all our sins into the depths of the sea."*"

"Jacob," there were tears running down her face. "Do you think that it's deep enough here for us to throw away all the sadness and mistakes of this past year? I'll never forget Elisha, and maybe you'll never forget Marie, but that's a lot of baggage for us to carry around with us for the rest of our lives. I don't know about sins; maybe we could have done better. But I do know about grief, and I think that we've had enough, both of us. It's so beautiful out here, too beautiful not to be grateful and happy for what we have. Jacob, what I want us to do is to throw our grief away, along with our sins, into the depths of the sea. Do you understand?"

He took her hand. "Trudy, you are a very wise woman. Yes, I understand, and I think that a hundred and forty feet of water is just about right. So what should we do?"

She got up from her seat and went to the gunnel. "Let's just stand here and think about what we want to cast away. Okay?"

"Okay." He stood at her side, neither of them touching, but just looking at the sun's rays dancing along the ripples around them for several silent minutes. And then Jacob recited three words from the penultimate verse of the prophecy of Micah: "*Tashlich bim'tzulot yam* – Cast them into the depths of the sea."

And Trudy whispered "Amen."

They continued standing by the gunnel for a few more minutes without speaking, and then Jacob said, "Time to get back; okay?"

"Okay;" and she joined him at the helm.

A half hour later, they pulled up to the dock. It was almost six, and after they had tied up, Trudy said, "You know what? I'm hungry. And do you know what I'd like? A pizza! That's what I'm in the mood for, a big veggie pizza with anchovies. Okay with you?"

"Sure; you come up with greatest ideas!"

"Okay; here's what we do. Tamara bought a mountain of vegetables for that dinner that we made last Monday, so I'll make us a nice salad while you zip up to that pizza place that I spotted at Cook's Corner."

"Sounds like a plan. I'll be off as soon as I call them with the order and change my shoes."

During the half hour that Jacob was gone, Trudy searched the house for a piece of paper appropriate for what she had in mind. She found lovely pieces of vellum in the center drawer of what must have been Sarah's desk in the master bedroom, and she took one sheet and sat down to write. When she was done, she tucked it into the flowered envelope that she found, sealed it, and ran up the stairs to Jacob's room where she laid it carefully in the center of his pillow. Then she ran down to the kitchen to start on the salad.

They agreed that the pizza that Jacob brought back couldn't match Chicago's Pizzeria Uno, but it served the purpose, and the salad was delicious. After they had washed up, Jacob suggested that they play a couple of games of Scrabble. After the first one, a tight battle that Trudy won, she got up and said. "It's been a long day. I'm pooped, and we have to leave for Chicago tomorrow. All right if I go to bed?"

"Good idea. I'll be going up pretty soon myself."

"Goodnight, Jake. See you in the morning."

Jacob watched her go up the stairs and was tempted to follow, but the last thing that he wanted was to approach her before she was ready. He had promised her privacy during their week in Maine, and he was not going to make her uncomfortable on their last night. Somehow, though, she had become more desirable to him during their sexless week together than she had ever been during the years when they had no compunctions about jumping into bed on the merest impulse. Well, all of that was tossed into the sea along with the griefs and guilts of the past year. He turned his mind to Chicago and what he hoped to accomplish there during the new academic year. The prospect of working with Professor Gold was becoming less and less attractive. He'd have to have another long talk with Rabbi Weinberg. Did he really....? It was getting late. Trudy was probably asleep already. He tiptoed up to the second floor, paused there for a moment but didn't hear anything, and then continued up to the attic.

As soon as he turned on the light, he saw the flowered envelope on his pillow. What...? When...? Inside the envelope, he found a single sheet of creamy vellum, inscribed –

You are cordially invited to come down
from your lonely resting place in the attic
to my luxurious suite below
for a night of sensuous nepenthe.
Dress optional.

Rahab (formerly Trudy the Unready)

Epilogue

Vilnius, 1978

As his plane circled over Vilnius, Jacob looked out the window and saw the Vilejka River snaking its way through the heart of the city. He could see two bridges spanning the river and wondered if one of them might possibly be the bridge from which, as Koppel Ganzfried had told him twenty or more years earlier, four young Jewish militants, his *zeyde* among them, had thrown the weighted bodies of two tsarist cavalrymen. No, not likely. As Ganzfried had described it, the bridge from which the bodies were thrown was in a wooded area some distance from the city center. The bridges that Jacob could see from the plane were near the heart of the city, but the river was the same Vilejka into which hundreds of thousands of Jews had cast their petty sins over three centuries of Rosh HaShanah afternoons.

Jacob looked around at his fellow passengers and saw that some of them were having difficulty fastening their seat belts preparatory to landing due to their bulky clothing. While they were all waiting to board the Aeroflot plane to Vilnius in Moscow's Sheremetvo Airport, he had asked one of his fellow passengers from Chicago why he and several of the others in his group were wearing so many layers of clothing. It was spring, just a week after Passover, and not so cold as to justify the multiple sweaters and shirts that the members of this Catholic church group from the Bridgeport neighborhood were wearing. He explained that they all had relatives in Vilnius and that most of them were living in poverty under the Russians. And so each year his church organized a ten-day tour to Vilnius to bring as many articles of clothing and other gifts as they could possibly carry in their two suitcases each and on their bodies.

During the two and a half hour flight, Jacob thought about the differences between their mission to Vilnius and his. They were going to visit the living, albeit poor, and he was going to visit, for the most part, the dead who, during their lifetimes, had contributed so abundantly to the religious and intellectual splendor of Judaism. Actually, his mission in Vilnius, as in Moscow, was to meet with a handful of clandestine Hebrew teachers, to bring them books and, more importantly, encouragement. But his personal agenda included looking for the graves of his great-great-great-great-grandfather, the renowned *Gaon*, and any Forshtayn or Rivkes ancestors whose graves might have survived the Nazi and Communist occupations.

He also intended to visit the killing fields at Ponary, outside of Vilnius, and to recite a *Kaddish* there for the scores of relatives whose last gasp of air was of the salubrious breezes of what had once been their carefree summer retreat. He wondered what proportion of the clothing that the church group was carrying would end up warming the bodies of aging members of the Iron Wolf or the Lithuanian Sonderkommando or any of the other nativist fascist organizations who did not wait for invitations to participate in the extermination of over ninety percent of the Jews in the city that had once proudly referred to itself as "the Jerusalem of Lithuania."

Jacob had wanted to visit the birthplace of his zeyde and bobbe ever since he was a child. Bobbe Bryna had so often put him to sleep with the lullabies that she had learned from her mother in Vilna. (He had to remind himself to refer to the city as Vilnius, not as Vilna, its Jewish name.) And Zeyde Yisroel had taught him how to live as a Jew out of the storehouse of learning that he had acquired in that storied city. Someday, someday, he had thought since his teen years, he would find the time to visit the city that had produced not only his grandparents and their grandparents but some of the greatest Jewish poets and scholars of modernity. Someday….

And then *someday* came. It was about a month after the Yom Kippur War that Rabbi Jacob Ross, while attending an emergency fund-raising meeting of the Jewish Federation of Chicago, was approached by the president of the city's Soviet Jewry Council, Esther Steckler. She asked if he would join her for a cup of coffee to discuss an urgent matter. He agreed and, after listening to her description of the heroism of Soviet Jews who were risking imprisonment and worse for teaching Hebrew to fellow Soviet subjects who yearned, especially since the Yom Kippur War, to make *aliyah* to Israel, she put it to him. Would he be willing to travel to two cities in the USSR to meet with Hebrew teachers, speak to their classes, encourage them, assure them that American Jewry was with them and was putting pressure on Washington to, in turn, put pressure on the Soviets to allow increased emigration to Israel, and, finally, to deliver a small quantity of educational materials to the teachers? He asked what cities she had in mind, and she mentioned four – Moscow, Leningrad, Kiev and Vilnius – the principal cities assigned to the Chicago Soviet Jewry Council for visitation. As soon as she mentioned Vilnius, he said yes, even though he had not yet consulted with his synagogue officers or his wife. It was only a matter of how much time he could take from his duties as senior rabbi of Lakeshore Temple and from his responsibilities as a husband and father. When would they like him to leave? As soon after Passover as possible.

When he got back to his study, he had his secretary call the congregation's president and three vice-presidents, to ask them to meet him for breakfast the next morning. And when he got home for dinner, he took Trudy to their room and told her about the request. "My God, Jake, I know that it's important, but isn't it dangerous? You're not a kid anymore. From everything that I've read, the Russians are ruthless. I know it's a lot better than in Stalin's time, but Brezhnev is no friend of the

Jews. Can't they send someone else, maybe one of the younger rabbis?"

"Well, Mrs. Steckler said that they want me in particular for a few good reasons – first, because of my fluency in Hebrew and Yiddish; second, because I have a big audience here in Chicago; and third, because it seems that a few of the pamphlets that I've published about Zionism and Jewish practices have been circulated as *samizdat* by dissidents. I had no idea about that. Anyway, that's why they want me. And the thing that has me really enthused about this is that one of the cities that I can visit is Vilna. I don't have to tell you how long I've wanted to visit Vilna. So what do you think?"

"Any chance of me going along?"

"I wish. I suggested that to Mrs. Steckler, but she said that it wasn't advisable, that I'd be more flexible alone. And how about the kids and your job? Elisha's old enough to take care of himself for nine or ten days, but Sarah and Miriam need one of us around, especially Miriam. And do you think it would be wise for you to take off ten days in the middle of the semester, especially this year?"

"Yuh, this is *the* year. Either I get promoted to full professor or I go looking somewhere else. Last I heard, it looked pretty good, but you're right; taking off in mid-semester might not be the wisest move right now. And you're right about Miriam too. She is so whacky, whacky and loveable. You never know what she's going to do next. Anyway, back to your mission. I think we should bring the kids in on this. What do you think?"

"Family council after dinner?"

"Right. Prepare to be grilled."

Jacob smiled as he remembered how the kids reacted to his news about the projected mission. Elisha was a hundred percent in favor. A few months before his bar mitzvah, the dramatic news about the failed attempt of two Jewish dissidents, Eduard Kuznetsov and Mark Dymshits, to hijack a plane in Leningrad and fly it to freedom in Sweden, had monopolized the Jewish press. In his bar mitzvah speech, Elisha had asked the congregation to write letters to their representatives, as he had, demanding that the death sentences meted out to his two heroes by the Soviet court be rescinded. And he asked the congregation to send donations to the Soviet Jewry Council in place of gifts to him. And so, as soon as his father broached the subject of his proposed mission, he voiced his enthusiastic approval.

Sarah was more thoughtful in her approval. She asked if he would be visiting the city where the zeyde that he spoke about so often was born. She had read about Ponary and had sung Kacherginski's *Shtiller, Shtiller*, his tribute to those walking to their deaths, at her bat mitzvah. Would he go to Ponary? If he did, would he say a prayer there for all the innocent victims? He assured her that he would.

Miriam, as soon as she heard that her father would be flying to Moscow, could hardly contain herself. "Will you bring me some matryoshka dolls, please?" Jacob looked to Trudy for help and was informed that matryoshkas were those painted wooden nesting dolls that were typically Russian. He explained that he probably wouldn't have time for shopping and how important it was for him to spend as much time as possible with the Hebrew teachers. "Please, Abba, please?" bouncing up and down in her seat. "I want some matryoshkas; Emily has some. Please?"

Buying those dolls for Miriam actually proved to be of help during his three days in Moscow. He was met as he emerged from customs at Sheremetvo by an Intourist guide who accompanied him to his hotel. She was very curious about what he planned to do in Moscow and was clearly not satisfied when he told her that he was just a tourist who just wanted to wander around the city. And so he told her that one of the things that he wanted to do was to buy some matryoshkas for his daughter. She said that she would take him to one of the hard currency stores for tourists, but he said that he preferred to shop where ordinary Muscovites shopped, so she took him to the gigantic GUM store near Red Square. He spotted a public phone while they were walking around the endless galleries, and when they finally found a store with a selection of matryoshkas, he insisted that he had to examine all of them to find the right one for his very particular daughter.

After about twenty minutes of opening doll after doll, she asked him what he intended to do after his shopping. He answered that he would go back to the Intourist Hotel for lunch and a nap. "Do you know the way back?" He assured her that he did. "Good; I'll come to get you tomorrow morning at nine for a tour of the Kremlin." He agreed, and finally she left. He quickly picked up the last set of dolls that he had examined, paid the proprietor with some of the currency that he had purchased at the airport, and headed for the phone. He had memorized the number of his first contact in Moscow, Semyon Edelshtayn, and had written several others in his pocket diary, substituting Hebrew latters for numbers. Within two minutes he was informed of the corner where he would meet Edelshtayn at eight-thirty that night.

Jacob's first meeting with a dozen Hebrew students at the tiny Edelshtayn apartment was considerably more emotional than he was prepared for. When he walked in, he saw that the door was splintered and off its hinges. The simple unemotional explanation: "The KGB visited me last week." Edelshtayn opened the meeting by introducing him as the author of *Aliyah and Mitzvah*, and to his amazement, they had all read it, which was more than he could say for his congregation. When he asked that they introduce themselves, he was again amazed. They all understood English, some more, some less, but they insisted in answering in labored Hebrew. They – engineers, musicians, a chemist, a taxi driver, and a nurse – all had applied for exit visas to Israel and all had been refused and had been branded by the police as agitators.

He began teaching the lesson that he had prepared, but as he looked at the faces of the eager students who were risking so much by attending this clandestine meeting, he had to pause as his eyes welled up with tears. He thought of how he had to cajole, sugar coat and do everything short of bribery to get his Chicago congregants to attend adult classes, and here these young people whose very freedom was in jeopardy, came voluntarily to study

Hebrew. After he had regained control sufficiently, he decided to talk about the Maccabees and about the Jewish partisans in Warsaw and Vilna during the Nazi occupation who had offered their lives for the survival of the Jewish people. He concluded the lesson a little after ten by asking if he could have the honor of shaking the hands of these Muscovite Maccabees. When Edelshtayn brought him back to within a block of his hotel, he told Jacob where and when he could meet his next contact and they embraced.

Jacob was thinking back to the heroic teachers and students whom he had met in Moscow during his five days there as he was driven by another Intourist guide to his Vilnius hotel. He would be spending only three and a half days in Vilnius before flying back to Sheremetvo to catch his return flight to Chicago, and he had only one name and phone number in Vilnius, a woman by the name of Alla Feldman. His Intourist guide, taking it for granted that he was just another Lithuanian from Chicago with needy relatives in Vilnius, after checking him in at his hotel, told him that she would pick him up on Sunday at five to take him back to the airport.

As soon as he had settled himself in his room, he walked out of the hotel which faced toward a broad square across from the train station. It struck him immediately that the train station, in the heart of the city, must be the one from which his zeyde, almost seven decades earlier, had taken the night train to Riga. He walked around the square looking for an alley that might correspond to the one where Yisroel, Koppel and two other young men had murdered the two cavalrymen. But there had been so much new construction in the years since the war that it was impossible even to guess at the location of the ambush. He walked into the station, an imposing barn-like edifice, and immediately found the phone booth that he needed to call Miss Feldman. She could not speak any English, but her Hebrew was good enough so that they could arrange to meet in an hour in the café opposite Track 4. How would he recognize her? She had long brown hair and would be wearing a brown leather jacket. Would she join him for lunch in the café? Yes, thank you.

Jacob spent the hour walking around the square and several of the streets that ran off it looking for some sign of Jewish life. He knew the numbers: 200,000 Jews before the war, ninety percent of them murdered, but as he walked around what looked like the old part of the city, he thought he might find some indication of that lost civilization. Nothing. Maybe he didn't know where to look.

He was pleasantly surprised when he spotted an attractive young woman in a leather jacket standing in the doorway to the café and looking around. She appeared to be in her mid-thirties, attractive, slim, glasses, hair falling to her shoulders, no makeup. He waved and she smiled and walked over to his table. They exchanged *Shaloms*, shook hands, and she sat down opposite him. During the course of their lunch, Jacob learned that Alla was an instructor in the civil engineering department of the Soviet-sponsored Kapsukas University and that she had taught herself Hebrew from pre-war grammar texts and dusty volumes of Bialik, Tchernikovsky and Berdichevsky that she had ferreted out of the university library stacks. Her parents and an older brother were among the thousands herded to the killing fields of Ponary, after they had entrusted their baby daughter to a Lithuanian woman who had been a devoted maid in their home. She told him that she now lived in a faculty apartment with her grandmother who had survived the war serving with a small band of Jewish partisans in the forests near Kaunas.

Alla had arranged for two meetings with her class of six Hebrew students, that night and Saturday night, and they were all looking forward to learning from someone who had been to Israel and who actually spoke modern Hebrew, not the stilted classical Hebrew that she had gleaned from the library texts. She explained that her grandmother did not understand Hebrew. She spoke only Yiddish, Polish and a bit of Lithuanian, but she loved to listen in on Alla's Hebrew classes, and she considered it an honor to be able to serve tea and cookies to the students.

What were the chances that Alla and her students would someday be able to emigrate to Israel? "Who knows? We hear that some Jews from Moscow and Leningrad are getting out, but the authorities here will not even allow us to make appointments to apply. But we believe – *maaminyim,* she said with a Russian accent – that someday we will get out. And so we study Hebrew in order to be ready."

The Hebrew level of the class that Jacob met with that evening was not nearly as advanced as the classes that he had led in Moscow, but, if anything, they were even more eager. He discovered the reason as he sat with the group over tea after the class. The four men and two women in addition to Alla were all single and in their twenties and thirties. They all wanted to marry, but there were virtually no eligible young Jews, certainly none with aspirations for *aliyah,* in Vilnius. Of the approximately twenty thousand surviving Jews, most were old Yiddish speakers like Alla's grandmother, Kayle; some were Communist apparatchiks or informers, and others were scraping out a meager livelihood and avoiding any activities that might move the authorities to take note of them.

Kayle was absolutely thrilled with Jacob. As he was about to leave for his hotel, he thanked her for the tea and cookies in the Yiddish that he had learned from his zeyde. She stared at him in surprise and asked him how he, a young American, could speak such splendid – meaning *Litvak*-accented – Yiddish. He told her about his zeyde and bobbe who had left Vilna almost seventy years earlier and had been his teachers. She asked what their names were, and he told her – Yisroel and Bryna Forshtayn. No, she did not know them personally, but she remembered hearing when she was about ten years old about the tragic death of their baby son. The whole city knew about it; her parents had attended the funeral. But, as she remembered it, they left for America a few months later.

"Wasn't his father a *shochet*? And wasn't his wife, I think I remember, descended from the holy *Gaon*?"

By this time, Jacob had come back into the apartment and was sitting with Alla's grandmother at the kitchen table. Alla stood by, barely comprehending the rapid Yiddish conversation but delighted that her grandmother had someone to talk to. He asked whether she knew of any Forshtayns or Rivkeses who might have survived the war. No, she was sure that they had all been killed in one or another of the *aktions* by the Iron Wolf or the Security Police or in the mass slaughter at Ponary, where her own parents had perished. But, she told him, when the Russians cleared the old Jewish cemetery in Shnipishok for apartment houses, they moved the remains of some of the most prominent people who were buried there to a new cemetery, the Saltonishkiu, and they had erected a small pantheon-like structure over the new grave of the *Gaon* in order to mollify the small surviving Jewish community and to encourage tourism. Jacob asked whether she and Alla would take him to Saltonishkiu, and they agreed to go there together on Sunday morning. And would he join them for Shabbat dinner on Friday night? He would be delighted.

Jacob had plans for Friday. He wanted to visit Ponary, but when he asked the hotel concierge how to get there, he was told that only an Intourist guide could take him there. When the guide showed up an hour later, she tried to discourage him from making the trip, assuring him that there was nothing to see there. "It is a terrible place where the Germans killed thousands of Lithuanians and Poles. Why do you want to go there?"

"Because I think that some of my relatives are buried there." He said nothing about Jews, and after dickering for a few minutes – she wanted a hundred dollars but settled for sixty – they set out in her Intourist Zil.

The roads were pretty rough, but they arrived at the memorial in just under an hour. He asked the guide to translate the inscription on the memorial monument, and she complied. As he expected, the monument memorialized "Soviet citizens" who were killed there by the Nazis – no mention of Jews, no mention of the complicit Lithuanian Sonderkommando or Security Police. The guide was more than willing to let him walk around the site by himself, and when he was far enough away from her, on a knoll overlooking the killing field, he sat down, put his face in his hands, and wept. He wondered how many of the people buried below him were relatives. Stupid question, he answered himself; *all* of them. What would I have done, he asked himself, if I were Zeyde or Koppel? Would I have tried to kill at least a few of the murderers? Would I have had the guts? He looked over to the guide who was leaning against a tree and smoking a cigarette. Was her father or her grandfather a member of the Iron Wolf? Was he, perhaps, one of those machine gunners who sat with a cigarette dangling from his lips and coldly mowed down the day's quota of Jews and Poles? Why was she alive and all of these – innocents, lovers, mothers, scholars, doctors, rabbis – dead? Slowly, he got up, softly chanted *Shtiller, Shtiller,* with tears running down his face, and then recited the *Kaddish.*

That evening, as they were about to sit down to dinner, Kayle asked Jacob if he knew the prayers for the Shabbat table. She had set out candles and knew the prayer for kindling them, but she had not heard any of the other prayers for almost forty years. He answered that he always observed the Shabbat rituals and that he would be happy to chant the *Kiddush* over the wine that Alla had put on the table. There was no *challah,* but he recited the *motzi* over the coarse bread. Kayle could not get over the fact that a young man – he told her that he was in his forties – actually observed Shabbat. In the Soviet Union most of the young people were Communists and atheists. If anyone suspected that they were religious, they could lose their jobs or their places in the university. Only the old people like her remembered the rich Jewish life of pre-Soviet, pre-Nazi Vilna, and there were not many of those left. "Ah, if only my Alla could find a man like you. She wants so much to be married and have children, but there is no one here for her."

Before Jacob left, he asked Alla where he could find a synagogue the next morning. She answered that there was only one left, the Choral Synagogue, and that that one was just a short walk from his hotel. She drew him a map on a scrap of paper, and she agreed to meet him at the gate of the synagogue at about twelve so that she could take him on a walk around the former Jewish quarter of the old city.

Jacob had no idea what time the Shabbat morning service would begin in the synagogue, and so he made it a point to be there by eight. There was no one there yet, and the doors to the main prayer hall were locked. He carefully read the inscription to the right of the doors and saw that the synagogue had been dedicated in 1903. Although there were over a hundred synagogues in Vilna when the Choral was built, he had no doubt that his zeyde had prayed there at some time or other, even if this was not his regular shul. He walked around to the side of the building and found a door open, leading into the study hall. There were seven old men, clearly in their seventies and eighties, sitting around a table, chanting psalms and waiting for at least three more men so that they could begin the Shabbat service. They all looked up when he walked in, and he was surprised to see that they just continued with their chanting. No one got up to greet him or even to acknowledge his presence with a nod.

At first he didn't know how to respond to their lack of interest, but he decided to take the first step. He sat down at the end of the table and, recognizing that they were chanting the psalms that introduce the Shabbat morning service, he joined in without a text in hand. The chanting stopped abruptly, and they stared at him. He looked at them and then, since they had just concluded Psalm 148, he began chanting Psalm 149 by himself. With his zeyde's *Litvishe* accent, he intoned *Halleluyoh, shiru l'adonoy shir chodosh t'hilosoy....* They stared at him, and then, one by one, they picked up his cadence, and joined in with him.

As they were chanting Psalm 150, two more old men drifted in and joined the group at the table, their eyes riveted on the stranger. They all continued chanting through the Song of the Sea, and when that was done, there were a total of thirteen men sitting around the table. They all rose for the *Half Kaddish,* several of them slowly and with difficulty, but then, before proceeding with the next prayer, the man sitting at the far end of the table addressed Jacob in Yiddish. "*Sholom aleichem,* welcome.

We thought that you were a government spy, but we can see that you're not. So who are you?"

Jacob explained that he was a visitor from America. He thought it best not to describe his mission, having been warned back in Chicago that there were often government informers planted in synagogues, but he explained that he had come to Vilna from America to visit the grave of the *Gaon* from whom he was descended. He told them also that his zeyde and bobbe had been born in Vilna, and that he wanted to visit the places where they had lived. He mentioned the names Forshtayn and Rivkes – no one seemed to recognize them – but one of the men said that he thought that there was a Rivkes buried near the *Gaon* in the Saltonishkiu cemetery.

"So you're a descendant of the holy *Gaon*? Truly?"

"Through my bobbe, six generations back."

"Then will you do us the honor of leading the prayers?"

Jacob demurred, explaining that he wanted to *davven with* them, not *lead* them, but he would be happy to chant the Torah portion and the *haftarah* if they wanted. When he came down from the *bimah* after chanting the *haftarah,* the old men crowded around him, all eager to shake his hand, offer a *yasher koach,* and ask how a *yunger mann* from America knew how to read Torah. Although he tried to explain that there were thousands of observant young Jews in America and that he was not unique, they decided that it was because he was a descendant of the *Gaon,* one of them insisting that it was a *nes* – a miracle – that he had come to their shul that *Shabbes.*

The service had almost ended when Jacob looked at his watch and saw that it was already a quarter past twelve. He joined the men in the final *Kaddish,* thinking of his zeyde and bobbe who might have recited *Kaddish* for their grandparents on that very spot in better times, and when the men were seated, he slipped out without a word.

As soon as he emerged into the sunlight, he saw Alla waiting for him across the street. He wished her a *Shabbat Shalom* but then told her how sad he felt at finding barely a *minyan* of hopeless old derelicts observing Shabbat in a place where thousands of Jews of all ages used to celebrate in joy. “That is Vilnius today,” she answered with a shrug. “That’s why we have to get out of this city of death. There is no hope here. Come, I’ll show you.”

She led him through the streets of the former Jewish quarter, pointing out shops and buildings that once belonged to Jews. “When I walk here with my grandmother, she tells me about this Jewish shop and that Jewish shop. On a few of the doorposts, you can still see that there were once *mezuzahs* there. I don’t think there is even one *mezuzah* in the city today. No one wants to call attention to himself.”

As they walked along, they came to a square dominated by a huge Soviet-style building. “That’s the Ministry of Culture, built right over the heart of the old Jewish quarter. Let’s walk up the stairs, and you tell me what you see. Look down.”

Jacob looked at the smooth stone stairs and didn’t see anything unusual until they reached the fourth level. He stopped abruptly and asked, “Is that what I think it is?”

“Try to read it.”

He looked more carefully and could barely make out Hebrew lettering. “It looks like a gravestone!”

“When the Russians decided to build apartment houses over the old cemetery in Shnipishok, they removed all the gravestones, tried to polish off the inscriptions, and used them for their building projects, for roads, for sidewalks and for steps like these. If you look carefully, you can find them all over the city, wherever there is new building. Sometimes you can make out the names, a Moshe, a Leah, a David…. There! Come over there with me. I remember a Yaakov.” And sure enough, on a stone that was part of a low wall to the right of the steps, he could make out a barely visible *yod-ayin-koph* and what must have been a *bet*.

They stood there quietly for a moment, and then he shook his head. “I wouldn’t have believed it if I hadn’t seen it with my own eyes. All these traces of Jewish life, rubbed out, abandoned, like Ponary, like those old Jews in the synagogue this morning.”

"So you understand now why we have to get out of here, why our Hebrew classes are so important."

Over their second lunch together, in a café that they passed in the course of their wandering around the old city and the university, she asked him if he was married. For a brief moment he thought of his uncle Sol and how he might have answered the question of an attractive woman who was unashamedly looking for a husband – five thousand miles from home, a hotel room, no one who recognized him….

"Yes, Alla, I'm married to a lovely woman, a college professor like you, and I have three wonderful children."

"I'm happy for you…. and sad for myself. There are no men like you here. And if I do not get approval to leave for Israel within the next year or two, I will probably never have children. Every night when I go to sleep, I imagine myself on a kibbutz in Israel with a strong Israeli for a husband and two *sabra* children."

"Alla, I don't know if there is anything that I can do, but I promise you that I will tell our Soviet Jewry Council about you, and I'll write to some people in Washington. Do you remember what Herzl said? *Im tirzu, ain…*"

She finished it for him. "…*ain zu aggadah;* If you want it strongly enough, it will happen."

He took her hand and looked into her eyes. "I promise you; I will do whatever I can when I get back."

That night he met again with Alla and her students, with Kayle sitting in the doorway listening. They wanted to know all about the Yom Kippur War, and Jacob, who had been to Israel in the aftermath of the war on a UJA mission, described all that he had seen, including a walk across the Suez Canal on a pontoon bridge secretly constructed by Israeli Army engineers. They were eager listeners, and what one didn't understand, another explained, with Alla constructing little lessons out of all the difficult words.

As he left the apartment, after having set a time for the next day's pilgrimage to the tomb of the *Gaon*, Kayle took his hand

and said in Yiddish, "Alla told me that you are married. I hope that she is a good wife, but Alla would have been perfect for you."

"She is a wonderful woman, and I am sure that she will find a good husband in Israel. We can pray for that tomorrow at the grave of the *Gaon.*"

Jacob woke up to the sound of pealing church bells at about eight. He had invited Alla and her grandmother to join him for breakfast in the hotel coffee shop at nine, and so, after he dressed for the day and for the flight later that afternoon, he packed his suitcase, gave it to the concierge for safe-keeping, and checked out. Alla and Kayle arrived promptly, and he could see from their reaction to the lavish buffet that they were not used to the kind of breakfast that was offered in a tourist hotel. There were platters of pickled meats and cheeses, sausages, dumplings, hard-boiled eggs, and a variety of bakery products. Jacob would have been happier with his usual Sunday bagel and lox, a good cup of coffee and the Sunday *New York Times*, but he enjoyed seeing how pleased his guests were with the selection.

They took a tram to the end of Suderves Road and the entrance to the Saltonishkiu Cemetery, and Kayle led them through a long row of graves to the structure that housed the grave of the *Gaon*, Rabbi Eliyahu ben Shelomo Zalman. There were a few dozen other people visiting family graves that morning, and Jacob noticed that there were also a few non-Jews near the mini-pantheon, a couple of them on their knees. Kayle explained that when the government destroyed the previous resting place of the *Gaon* and reinterred his and a handful of other remains, word had spread that a 'holy man' was being buried in Saltonishkiu. That notion was confirmed when the Russians erected the domed structure over the grave, and since then Lithuanian Christians, as well as Jews, had been making pilgrimages to the site.

Jacob looked around at the nearby graves, and was able to make out the name of Moshe Rivkes on one of them – Rivkes, his zeyde's mother's name. And then he spotted a smaller grave, not nearly as old and weather-beaten as most of the others near the

Gaon's grave. He could hardly believe his eyes as he took in the engraving on the stone. At the top was a little cherub, under it the name Ephraim Eliyahu ben Yisrael, under that the Hebrew date of death, and at the bottom: *Ha-ven yakir li Ephraim.* He explained to Kayle and Alla that this was the grave of his baby uncle, the one who had been killed by the cavalrymen, the one whose funeral, as Kayle had told him on Shabbat, her parents had attended.

He had come to the cemetery to pay homage to one of the greatest sages of European Jewry, a distant ancestor, but it was at baby Ephraim's grave that he recited the *Eil Malei* threnody and then uttered an emotion-laden prayer – joy, sorrow, gratitude, longing – for Trudy and Elisha and Sarah and Miriam and Isaac and Tamara and, yes, for Ephraim's sister and brother, Raizel and Sol too, and for Kayle and Alla and ... and ... and ... and ....

Glossary

This Glossary, primarily of Yiddish and Hebrew words and phrases, is not intended to be authoritative. The definitions offered are meant to convey how the characters in the book would have used and understood them.

Adon Olam – Lord of the Universe. Hymn sung at the conclusion of a prayer service.

Aliyah – Ascension. The honor of going up to the Torah; also emigrating to Israel.

A nechtige tog – A nightlike day. Impossible, no way.

Avel – A mourner.

Avinu Malkeinu – Our Father, our King. A prayer for the High Holy Days.

Baal ha-bayit – Master of the house; head of the family.

Baal teshuvah – Master of repentance. One who has returned to Jewish observance.

Balaboste – A traditional housewife.

Balagolah – A wagon driver, a crude or unlettered person.

Babke – A cinnamon, nut and raisin cake.

Bapkes – Nothing, crumbs.

Baruch – Blessed. The opening word of many Hebrew prayers.

Baruch dayan ha-emet – Blessed is the true judge. Affirmation on hearing of a death.

Bet Din – A Jewish religious court.

B'haalotecha – The name of a Torah portion from the book of Numbers, usually read in June.

Bimah – The pulpit area in the front of the synagogue.

Bobbe – Grandmother.

Bochur – Young man, kid.

Brocha, Broches – Blessing, blessings.

Chai – Life; often featured on a pendant.

Challah – A twisted loaf of bread, especially for the Sabbath.

Chaval – Too bad, sorry.

Chaver – Comrade, friend, buddy.

Chen – Gracefulness.

Chenefdik – Attractive, genteel, homey, gracious.

Cholent – A stew of potatoes and other ingredients, kept heated through the Sabbath.

Chossid – A pietist A follower of one of the pietistic, mostly Polish, folk rabbis.

Chrain – Horseradish, often served with *gefilte* fish.

Chuppah – The wedding canopy.

Davven – Pray.

Dodati – My beloved.

D'var Torah – A homily based on a text from the weekly Torah portion.

Einekl – Grandchild.

Ein Yaakov – A tractate of legendary texts from the Talmud.

Eliyahu Ha-Navi – Elijah the Prophet: a hymn often sung at the conclusion of the Sabbath.

El Malei – A threnody chanted at funerals and memorial services.

Eshet Hayil – Woman of Valor. An appreciation of ones wife, from Proverbs, chapter 31.

Farkakte – Shitty.

Feygele – A little bird. A derogatory epithet for a gay man.

Freylich – Happy.

Gan Eden – Garden of Eden. Paradise.

Gaon – Excellency. A title reserved for a preeminent Torah scholar.

Gedenk – Remember.

Gefilte – Filled. *Gefilte* fish: a chopped fish delicacy, especially for the Sabbath.

Ger – Stranger. A convert to Judaism.

G'mar Chatimah Tov – Traditional Yom Kippur greeting; "May you be sealed for good."

Goldene Medinah – Golden land. The way that East European Jews referred to the U.S.A.

Gott tzu danken – Thank God!

Goy, goyim – Nations. A non-Jew(s)

Habonim – The builders. A left-leaning Zionist youth movement.

Haftarah – The prophetic passage read on Sabbaths following the Torah reading.

Haggadah – The telling. The popular text used by the family at the Passover *seder.*

Haimish – Familiar, homey.

Ha-Shem – The name. A euphemism used to avoid the pronunciation of the name of God.

Havdalah – Separation. The brief service that marks the end of the Sabbath.

Hazkore – Remembrance. A prayer recited in the synagogue in memory of a family member.

Ich bin doh – I am here.

Kaddish – A doxology recited in memory of a family member.

Kallah – Bride.

Kapote – A frock coat worn by east European pietists.

Kartofel – Potatoes.

Kashrut – The dietary laws of Judaism.

Ketubah – A marriage contract.

Kichel – Sweet cookie-cracker usually served at festive meals with wine.

Kiddush – Prayer chanted over the wine on Sabbaths and festivals.

Kinnahora – May no evil eye (harm one). Superstitious utterance to ward off calamity.

Kishke – Stuffed derma.

Klugger – A wise person, often used to describe a smart aleck.

Knaidlach – Soup dumplings.
Kolel – A Talmudic school for adult men.
Kol ishah – The voice of a woman. Orthodox men are forbidden to listen to female singing.
Kol Nidre – All vows. The very solemn prayer that introduces Yom Kippur.
Kreplach – Dough pockets, usually filled with ground meat.
Kugel – A pudding, usually of noodles or potatoes.
Kunnyleml – The Yiddish equivalent of Casper Milquetoast.
Kvelling – Deriving great pleasure, usually from the accomplishments of a child.
Kvetch – Constantly complain.
L'cha Dodi – Come, my beloved. One of the favorite synagogue hymns for Sabbath eve.
Le-chayim – To life. The traditional toast before drinking intoxicants.
Litvak – A Jew from Lithuania.
Litvishe – Lithuanian.
Mah Tovu – How goodly (are your tents). Prayer recited on entering the synagogue.
Mamzer – Bastard.
Mazel Tov – Good luck. The traditional blessing on happy occasions.
Menorah – Candelabrum, usually seven-branched.
Mensch – Man. Referring to a person of noble qualities.
Meshugah – Crazy.
Mezonos – Foods. The prayer recited before eating bakery products other than bread.
Mezuzah – Doorpost. The container affixed to Jewish homes containing a sacred text.
Minchah – The afternoon prayer service.
Minyan – A prayer quorum of ten.
Mirtzeshem – God willing.
Mishugas – Craziness.
Mishpocha – Family.

Mitzvah – Commandment. An act in fulfillment of a religious obligation.

Moshav zekenim – Old folks home.

Motsi – Who brings forth. Prayer over bread before a meal.

Nachas – Joy, pride.

Nafkeh – Prostitute.

Neder – Vow.

Negiyah – Thouching. A man touching a woman in any way.

Niddah – Menstruation. The Talmudic tractate dealing with rules about a menstruating woman.

Nusach – The traditional musical mode for prayer.

Oneg – Pleasure. Particularly the enjoyment of the Sabbath.

Paskunyak – A boor, cad, lout.

Penkes – The pinfeathers on a fowl.

Rosenblatt – Yosele Rosenblatt, one of the greatest 20th century cantors.

Rov – A rabbi of the old school.

Rozhenkes mit Mandlen – lit. Raisins with almonds. A popular Yiddish lullaby.

Schach – The foliage covering a *sukkah.*

Schlachthoiz – Slaughterhouse.

Seder – The ritual family dinner on Passover eve.

Selichot – Penitential prayer service held on the Saturday night before Rosh HaShanah.

Shabbat Shuvah – The Sabbath of Penitence, between Rosh HaShanah and Yom Kippur.

Shacharit – The morning service.

Shabbes – The Yiddish pronunciation of Shabbat.

Shammes – The sexton of the synagogue.

Shandeh – Scandal, catastrophe.

Shayles – Questions about Jewish religious practices.

Sheloshim – Thirty. A memorial gathering about a month after a death.

Shema – Hear. The first word of "Hear, O Israel: the Eternal our God is one."

Shikse – Derogatory name for a non-Jewish woman.
Shishi – The sixth of seven *aliyot.*
Shiva – Seven. The traditional seven-day period of mourning after burial.
Shlemazel – An unlucky person, often the butt of humor.
Shlemiel – Dope, ninny.
Sh'lom bayit – Serenity of the home. Ideal family life.
Shochein Ad – A prayer recited early in the Sabbath service.
Shochet – Kosher slaughterer.
Shofar – The ram's horn blown at Rosh HaShanah services.
Sholom Aleichem – Peace be with you. Traditional greeting; also a pen name.
Shomrim – Guardians. Jewish self-defense groups.
Shpilkes – Sitting on *shpilkes*, i.e. champing at the bit; over-eager.
Shtetl – Town or village in eastern Europe.
Shtarke – A strong, brawny person.
Shtiller – Silently. A Yiddish song written in memory of Holocaust victims.
Shtup – Shove in. A vulgar term for copulation.
Shul – School. A synagogue.
Simchah – A joyous occasion.
Simchat Torah – Joy of the Torah. The joyous final holiday of the fall festival cycle.
Smetine – Sour cream.
Sukkah – The harvest booth erected in observance of Sukkot, the harvest festival.
Tallit – Prayer shawl.
Tipat dam – Drop of blood. Part of the conversion ritual for a man previously circumcised.
Toches – Buttocks.
Toches af'n tisch – Buttocks on the table. Straight talk; the bottom line.
Tochterel – Little daughter.
Treif – Non-kosher food.
Tzahal – The Israel Defense Forces.
Tzimmes – A sweet mixture of cooked vegetables.

Tzniyut – Modesty; avoidance of lascivious acts or appearance.

Tzur Mishelo – A popular Sabbath table song thanking God for the festive meal.

UJA – The United Jewish Appeal. A prominent philanthropic agency.

Un'taneh Tokef – One of the central prayers of the High Holy Day services.

Yah Ribon – A popular Sabbath table song celebrating the majesty of God.

Yahrzeit – The anniversary of a death.

Yam Suf – The Sea of Reeds crossed by Moses and the Israelites.

Yarmulke – Traditional Jewish head covering.

Yasher koach – May you be strengthened. Traditional blessing for one having an *aliyah.*

Yeshiva – Talmudic academy.

Yiches – A distinguished lineage.

Yidden – Jews.

Yiddishkeit – Jewish culture and practice.

Yomtov – A Jewish holiday.

Yoshke – Derogatory Yiddish reference to Jesus.

Zaftig – Attractively plump.

Zemirot – Festive table songs.

Zeyde – Grandfather.

Zissinke – Sweet one; a term of endearment.

Zunnele – Sonny boy.